W9-COL-478

A World
Away

NANCY GROSSMAN

SCHOLASTIC INC.

No part of this publication may be reproduced, stored in a retrieval
system, or transmitted in any form or by any means, electronic, mechanical,
photocopying, recording, or otherwise, without written permission of the publisher.
For information regarding permission, write to Hyperion Books for Children, an
imprint of Disney Book Group, LLC, 114 Fifth Avenue, New York, NY 10011.

ISBN 978-0-545-63950-7

Copyright © 2012 by Nancy Grossman.
All rights reserved. Published by Scholastic Inc.,
557 Broadway, New York, NY 10012,
by arrangement with Hyperion Books for Children,
an imprint of Disney Book Group, LLC.
SCHOLASTIC and associated logos are trademarks
and/or registered trademarks of Scholastic Inc.

12 11 10 9 8 7 6 5 4 3 2 1   13 14 15 16 17 18/0

Printed in the U.S.A.   40

First Scholastic printing, September 2013

This book is set in Lapidary 333 BT.
Designed by Abby Kuperstock

To my parents, who read to me
To Kevin and Maggie, who let me read to them
To Shari, who reads with me
And to Kenny, who reads me

CHAPTER

 1

The strangers were coming, as they did every Thursday night, to bring a burst of color into our plain home. I circled the dining room, checking each lantern to be sure there was enough fuel inside. June sunlight streamed through the windows, but by the end of dinner we'd need the lanterns to brighten the room and help the guests find their way back to their cars, parked in a crooked row on the lawn behind our buggy.

"How many strangers are coming tonight?" I called to my mother, in the kitchen.

"Visitors, Eliza, not strangers," my mother said. "We'll be having eight guests tonight."

I tried to settle my jittery limbs as I folded a napkin beside each plate. My head was filled with thoughts about what the strangers would look like and how many holes would be in their earlobes and how many colors would streak through their hair. My mother always scolded me that these guests were coming to dine on a simple Amish meal and take a peek at our lives. She didn't want me to be peeking at theirs. *They live in their world and we live in ours,* she would say, as though that would satisfy my curiosity.

My mother and I had been busy in the kitchen all afternoon, preparing roasted chicken and mashed potatoes, and the air in the house was thick with cooking smells. I walked around the table setting the silverware neatly on each folded napkin. Then, pitcher in hand, I stepped through the arched doorway that connected the dining room and the kitchen.

"Is everything ready?" my mother asked, plunging the masher in and out of the fluffy white potatoes. "The English will be here in five minutes."

"The table's set," I said, carrying the pitcher to the small pump mounted on the side of the sink. I pushed the handle up and down a few times until the cold water gushed from the spout, then pumped the handle more slowly until the pitcher grew heavy in my hand. Back in the dining room I filled the glasses before my mother and I made two trips to carry the piping-hot food to the sideboard.

I watched my mother as she arranged the serving dishes. She's never said so, but I had the feeling that she liked these Stranger Nights. While she lit the two candles that stood in the center of the table, I tried to see her the way the visitors would. Her brown hair was twisted into a severe bun that pulled the skin taut around her gleaming silvery eyes. A white bonnet, called a kapp, sat on top of her head, the two strings untied and draped over her shoulders. Her dress was a dark gray, contrasting with the crisp white apron tied around her waist.

Looking down, I smoothed my own apron and fingered my bonnet strings. My dress was blue and slightly rumpled, but otherwise my clothing was identical to my mother's. Sometimes visitors would ask about our clothes, and my mother would explain how our dresses are sewn in a uniform style—a square neckline, three-quarter sleeves, the skirt settling just below the knees. The dress is fastened with snaps because buttons are considered fancy and are forbidden. Our clothes are plain, and so are we.

A car door slammed, and the murmur of voices reached me from outside. My mother nodded to me in her serious way, and I went to my usual spot beside the table while she greeted the visitors at the front door. They came into our living room as they always did, eyes round, heads down-turned a bit, as though trying not to stare. I saw a woman with short choppy hair scanning the books on the wooden shelf. Another woman brushed her fingertips along the back of the rocking chair, her red dress swaying as she walked. Then Mr. Allen, who owns the inn where the guests were staying, led the group to the dining room table. Mr. Allen isn't Amish, but he knows our ways. He brought the idea of these dinners to my parents a year ago, and since then he has been a weekly guest at our table, along with the visitors.

The guests filed to the table in a quiet, orderly way, their eyes taking in the cherrywood furniture that my father had made with his own hands. I knew from other dinners that their conversations would start up again during the meal, but for now they were hushed and alert. As I watched them settle into their chairs, their eyes roaming around the dining room and the adjoining kitchen, I knew they weren't noting what was in our house, but rather what was absent. A computer, electric lights, a telephone.

Five women and three men were gathered around the table. When I looked closer, I realized that two of those women were actually girls about my age. They sat between a man in a navy sweater and a woman with hair as orange as the carrots in the garden. I assumed they were a family. This was the first time there had ever been English teenagers in our house, and a nervous excitement rose in me. One of the girls was wearing black pants that looked more like heavy stockings than trousers, and a black shirt that hung in a billowy way just past her hips. Her hair was the color of strong coffee, and the black lines drawn around her eyes contrasted sharply with her pale skin. The other girl wore tight blue jeans and a V-neck T-shirt with bursts of pink and purple, as though a tin of paint had tipped over onto her clothing. Her dark hair was feathered with uneven streaks of deep red.

I wondered how the girls' hair hung so straight and silky, as though it had been draped across an ironing board and pressed flat. Maybe they had used one of those gun-shaped hair dryers I'd seen at the inn. My fingers flitted to the thick brown hair trailing down my back. It was pulled back with an elastic band, but curly wisps had already come loose, and fluttered around my face. I thought fleetingly that maybe a hair dryer could help me.

The girl with the paint-spattered shirt was looking at me. Our eyes met for a moment, and I saw that her eyelids were tinted the color of lavender. The dark-haired girl stared down at her lap while the colorful girl spoke. "Hey, I'm Jess," she said, as though it was perfectly natural to have a boy's name. "This is my sister, Caroline." The other girl didn't look up.

"I'm Eliza," I said. Then my mother stepped beside me and cleared her throat. The faces around the table turned to us, open and expectant. My mother stood serenely, one hand folded over the other, and I watched the "stranger smile" sweep across her face. I've come to know this expression that brings her lips outward but not up. It's a polite smile, but not a friendly one. I glanced back at Jess and let my smile lift up in a way I hoped she would consider friendly. She grinned back, and I felt a tiny thrill.

"Thank you all for coming," my mother said. "My daughter Eliza and I are happy to have you here. Now, let us all bow our heads in prayer."

Before my chin dropped down to my chest, I raised my eyes and caught a quick glimpse of the strangers. Their heads were lowered, but a few kept their eyes on my mother as though waiting for the command to be lifted. Jess and Caroline looked at each other, their eyebrows raised. Their mother nudged Caroline, and she lowered her head inch by inch. The dinner prayer raced through my mind, and I felt my lips move silently along with the familiar words my mother spoke. "We thank you, our heavenly Father, for the gifts which we are about to receive. May we be truly grateful for the bounty you have bestowed. Amen."

The guests began to raise their heads as soon as my mother and

I did. Some glanced at each other, slightly embarrassed. The two girls exchanged a look as if they had just been part of a joke.

I turned to see if my mother had noticed, but she looked the way she always did after devotions: peaceful and refreshed, the lines around her mouth and between her eyebrows lightened. After prayers, my mother actually looks pretty. I've noticed this every time, but it's always a revelation.

"Eliza and I will be serving you," my mother announced. "After your meal, I'll be happy to answer your questions."

At her cue, I picked up the tray of chicken and balanced it on my left arm. "Do you prefer white or dark meat?" I asked one of the women. She wore a simple dress the color of cherries, with no adornments of any kind. Her brown hair swam around her shoulders, and her eyes were pretty in their plainness, with none of the painted-on colors that I'd grown accustomed to seeing on the faces of English women. She looked too boring to be English. "White meat, please," she said. She was watching me closely as I served her. "Thank you, Eliza," she said, as though she already knew me. "So, are you fifteen, sixteen?"

"Sixteen," I said.

She nodded and smiled. Not knowing what else to say, I kept moving.

I reached the orange-haired woman, whose silver bracelets sang like sleigh bells when she pointed to the piece of chicken she wanted. When I got to Jess and Caroline, I gripped the tray carefully. Jess pointed to a breast, and I set it on her plate. Her sister was looking down, a sour expression on her face. "Do you prefer dark or white meat?" I asked her.

She shook her head. "Are you serving anything that doesn't have flesh?"

"Caroline!" Her mother looked at me with an apology on her face. "I'm sorry. She's a vegetarian."

"We'll also be serving potatoes and some mixed vegetables from our garden," I said.

Caroline nodded, her arms folded over her chest. I wondered if her parents had forced her to come to our house for dinner, the way my parents require us to go to church and to fellowship meetings. Setting the platter of chicken on the sideboard, I picked up the vegetable bowl. My mother followed me with the basket of bread until all of our guests were served.

While they ate, my mother disappeared into the kitchen to prepare the dessert. I stood by the sideboard, ready to serve second helpings or refill water glasses. Usually I liked this arrangement because it let me quietly watch the English and hear their stories. But that night my hands dangled uselessly at my sides. My dress and apron felt baggy and unbecoming next to Jess's and Caroline's sleek outfits.

I'd often thought about what it would be like to meet English teenagers. In my imaginings I would strike up clever conversations with them, and they'd tell me about music and movies and dancing. But now they were here, and I was awkward and tongue-tied.

Occasionally, one of the girls would take a small black object out of her pocket and rest it in the palm of her hand. She would glance down at it, tap it a few times with her thumb, and slide it back into her pocket. I wondered if these were cell phones, but the girls weren't putting them to their ears or talking into them. At least they had something to stare at besides me.

I picked up the water pitcher and walked around the table, refilling the glasses. When I reached the woman in the cherry-colored dress, she said, "You work at the inn, don't you?"

"Yes," I said. "I started there last week."

"I thought I saw you there," she said. "How do you like your job?"

"I like it fine," I said, aware that Mr. Allen was sitting nearby. Then the orange-haired woman spoke up, asking Mr. Allen where she could buy a quilt.

"Right here," Mr. Allen said. "Mrs. Miller makes quilts to order. I can bring you back tomorrow if you'd like."

I stepped over to the girls and refilled their glasses. "Would you like more of anything?" I asked. Caroline gripped her phone in both hands, her thumbs moving wildly. "No thanks," said Jess. "But could you show me where the bathroom is?"

I set the pitcher down and led her through the hallway. When I pointed to the bathroom door, she turned to face me with a smile. "I have to admit," she said, her voice lowered, "I was worried it might be outside."

I felt a wave of embarrassment when I realized this girl thought we did our business in an outhouse. But her smile was open and warm, and she seemed ready to admit her mistake. "We do have plumbing," I said, grinning. "But don't look for a hair dryer. There's no place to plug it in." Jess laughed, and I tingled with an odd sense of pride.

Later, as the guests exclaimed over my mother's apple pie, and I poured rich black coffee into everyone's mug, I waited for my favorite part of Stranger Night, when my mother would ask, "Does anyone have questions that I might answer?" It was amazing to me that these fancy people wanted to learn about our world. "How do you dry clothes in the winter when you can't hang the wash outside?" asked a man in a red tie.

"We run the clothesline through the living room, and on wash day we all have to dodge around it when we come in and out of the house," said my mother.

"Is Eliza in school?" asked the woman with the short haircut.

"Our children go to school through eighth grade," said my mother. "So Eliza's been out of school for two years now." I looked down, not wanting the strangers to see that I was still a little sad to have left school behind.

When a man asked about television, my mother answered the way she always did. "I have been in English homes when the television is on, so I have seen what it is." The teenage girls looked at each other. "No MTV?" asked Caroline. I didn't know what she meant, so I just shook my head.

The man said, "You just mentioned the 'English.'" He paused for a moment with a small laugh. "Is that us?"

My mother gave him a polite smile. "Yes," she said. "It's a term that we Amish use to refer to anyone who is not Amish."

As always, my mother's answers were quick and blunt. *Never give too much information,* she has told me. *We have invited them into our home, but not into our lives.*

The orange-haired woman mentioned that she has heard about "courting carriages" and she wanted to know if any children in the family were courting.

"Our son James has a courting carriage," my mother said. "But, like some of you with your teenagers, I'm not always sure where he goes in it."

There were soft chuckles around the table. "Are there any other questions?" my mother asked.

"Yeah," said Caroline. "What do you do for fun?"

My mother turned to me. "Would you like to answer that, Eliza?"

Everyone looked at me, waiting. "Well, we get together with our friends," I said. "There are parties. We go into town." My words felt weak. The sisters exchanged one of their looks.

Now I wished that I could be the one asking the questions. I would ask these girls what they did for fun, and how they painted their eyes, and what it felt like to pick out different clothes to wear every day. I would ask them what it was like not to be plain.

I took a breath as though to speak again. My mother glanced at me, and I held my tongue.

The woman in the cherry-colored dress cleared her throat, and when I heard her words, I froze. "Has Eliza reached the age for rumspringa?"

My eyes opened wide. Rumspringa is a time when Amish teenagers are allowed to run wild. To step out of the plain world. It was not a subject that ever came up at Stranger Night, and for once I didn't know how my mother would answer.

My sister Margaret passed rumspringa by going right to baptism and marriage. Margaret is what the elders call "Good Amish." My brother James had left home to apprentice at a woodworking shop and had written us letters about computers and video games. After he returned to work with our father, I would sometimes catch him staring out the window, and I wondered if he was thinking about that other world, where buttons aren't sinful and where cars speed by, leaving the buggies behind.

Now it was my turn. Since my sixteenth birthday, three weeks ago, I'd been waiting to see what rumspringa would bring me. My head was filled with thoughts of leaving my home in Iowa and seeing how they live in the fancy world. But so far my parents had told me nothing about their plans.

Taking in a breath, I watched my mother's hands clasp together a bit too tightly in front of her apron, and I waited to hear what she would tell these visitors. When she spoke, her voice was smooth and polite, the way it always is when she talks to the English.

"I suppose there are some of you here who don't know what *rumspringa* means."

The strangers shook their heads, and my mother continued.

"The Amish lifestyle is one that we choose, not one that we are born into. In order to choose properly, we Amish feel that our children must be given the chance to see what the outside world is like. So, our teenagers have a period of independence before they take up our ways."

"What do they do?" asked Jess.

"They probably do a lot of the same things you do," my mother answered. "They ride in cars and go to movies. They wear blue jeans. They have parties." She paused with a smile. "I don't think I want to know what goes on at the parties."

The adults around the table smiled in a knowing way—except for the woman who had asked the question. She was watching my mother intently. I wondered how this English woman knew about rumspringa.

I set down the coffeepot and turned back to my mother. She nodded to me before speaking again. I was beginning to think that her answer was for me, and not for the people gathered at our table.

"So, we parents turn our heads and let our teenagers run a bit wild. And we hope that soon they will come back to us."

"What about Eliza?" Jess asked. "What's she doing for her rum . . . for her running-wild time?"

I waited, holding my breath, hoping that my mother's answer would give me a clue about what was ahead for me.

"Eliza has a job at the inn. Some of you might have seen her there serving breakfast and tidying up the rooms. Her father and I wanted her to see a little more of the world than we can show her here, so we talked to Mr. Allen about finding some work for her." My mother and Mr. Allen nodded to each other.

I let out the breath I had been holding. Now I had the answer I'd been waiting for these past weeks. Rumspringa wasn't going to take me into the fancy world. It was taking me to an inn, where I'd watch English tourists watching us. I felt myself sinking, and there was only one thing I knew for certain.

I needed to run wild.

CHAPTER

2

At the inn the next morning, Jenny, the cook, greeted me and gave me instructions as she pulled a tray of muffins out of the oven, filling the room with a warm, fruity scent. Her kapp was a bit askew, as though she had put it on in a hurry. "We're serving breakfast in a half hour," she said, handing me the small silver bell. I hated this part of the job. In the hallway, outside the guest rooms I rang the bell and called out, "Breakfast will be served at nine o'clock." I heard a man grumble from behind one of the doors, "What is this, Amish boot camp?" I didn't understand what that meant, but it didn't sound pleasant. Back in the kitchen I could hear people assembling in the dining room and helping themselves to coffee from the big urn. The murmurs of their conversations floated into the kitchen.

Jenny was suddenly in a hurry, and I rushed to keep up with her instructions. She showed me how to plate each breakfast with a scoop of egg soufflé, a spoonful of cut fruit, and a muffin. She would carry out two plates at a time, and I had to be ready with the next ones when she returned. I would rather have been serving the guests than standing in the kitchen getting the food ready, but Jenny was in charge, so I had to do as she told me.

Cleaning up at the inn was easier than at home, because a machine did most of the work. On impulse, I placed the palms of my hands on the front of big dishwashing machine and felt a warm vibration against my fingertips. Jenny seemed unimpressed by the wonders of this invention, and sat at the counter, hunched over her grocery list. "I'll be gone for about an hour," she said. "You can dust the parlor while I'm out."

Pulling my hands away from the machine, I looked at my fingers, which didn't appear to be any different after the close contact with electricity. I was turning toward the closet to find the dusting supplies when the kitchen door swung open. There stood the woman from Stranger Night, the one in the red dress who had asked about rumspringa. She wore black jeans and a T-shirt with the words "University of Illinois" across the chest. Her hair was pulled back in a silver barrette. I watched as recognition lit the woman's face.

"Well, hi, Eliza. I'm Rachel. Rachel Aster." The woman held her hand out, and I felt the unusual softness of her skin. "I was wondering if I could trouble you for a pot of tea to bring up to my room. I didn't make it down in time for breakfast."

Mrs. Aster perched on a stool while I filled the teakettle and set it on the stove. "I enjoyed my dinner at your house last night," she said. "Your mom's a great cook." I turned the knob on the stove until the circular coils under the teapot turned a bright orange.

"Thanks, I'll tell her you said so."

"I have to admit something," Mrs. Aster said, her voice low, as if letting me in on a secret. "I was disappointed to hear that you had a job."

"I beg your pardon?" I asked.

"Last night when I asked you about your job here, I had an ulterior motive."

Setting the basket of tea on the counter beside a small china teapot, I turned to her. "I'm afraid I don't understand what that means."

Mrs. Aster smiled and rested her elbows on the counter. "An 'ulterior motive' is when someone hopes to gain something by their actions. So I was hoping to gain something by asking you that question."

"What were you hoping to gain?"

She let out a little laugh. "You."

The teakettle whistled, and I twisted the knob to shut off the burner. I turned back to her. "Me?"

"My nanny is leaving after this week, and I'm about to hire a new one. The way you helped your mother last night made me think you could help me the same way. Then I realized that you looked familiar, so I asked you about your job. And that ended my hopes."

Breath that I didn't realize I'd been holding pushed through my lips. "You want to hire a babysitter?"

She nodded. "You see, I'm working on my master's degree, and I need some help with the children so I can get my thesis finished. That's the big paper I have to write. As a matter of fact, the reason I'm here right now is to get some work done away from my family. It was a gift from my husband. A week away from home to write."

I tried to keep my hands from trembling as I poured the hot water into the teapot and set the kettle back on the stove. But, I reminded myself, my parents would never approve of my leaving home and working for someone they didn't know. I took a tea bag and let it bounce in the hot water.

I set the teapot and cup on a small tray, along with some packets of sugar. Mrs. Aster's eyes were searching mine. They were a golden color, like honey.

"How many children do you have?" I asked.

"Two," she answered. "Ben is eight and Janie is five."

I tried to think of what to say to this woman, but I knew that I couldn't discuss the possibility of working for her until I'd talked to my parents. Too quickly, the conversation ended and Mrs. Aster carried the tray upstairs. While I dusted, I listened again to her words in my mind. I didn't know where she lived, but it was far enough away that she was sleeping at the inn each night instead of at her own home. This could be my chance to step away from here.

Throughout the morning I watched the comings and goings of the guests, hoping to see Mrs. Aster again. Later, when I was cleaning the guest rooms, a familiar voice answered my knock. Mrs. Aster was propped up on a four-poster bed, a small machine with typewriter keys on her lap. Several open books were scattered on the bed, and she pushed them aside when I came in.

"Excuse me," I said. "I can come back later."

She gathered up the books and stuffed them into a canvas bag at the side of her bed and closed the lid on her typewriting machine. "You can do what you need to in here," she said. "I'm going to go out for a while." Watching Mrs. Aster sling the canvas bag over her shoulder, I tried to gather courage for what I wanted to say.

I cleared my throat and took a shaky breath. "If you have a moment, I'd like to talk to you about what you said earlier. About my working for you as a nanny."

Mrs. Aster sat down on the edge of the bed, her bag clutched in her arms. "Are you looking for a new job?"

"I've been thinking about it."

"I live near Chicago. It's about three hours away from here by car. How would your parents feel about your living away from home?"

"We'd have to talk about it," I said, groping for the right words. Then I remembered what my mother had told the guests last night. "They do want me to see more of the world."

"Well, should I go over to your house to talk with them?"

My heart pounded. "Things are a little busy at home right now.

Sunday is my sister's barn raising. But I'll talk to them over the weekend, if that's all right."

"I'll be here until Tuesday," she said.

I nodded as Mrs. Aster stood up and shouldered her bag. "I'll let you know what my parents say."

"Wonderful!" she said. "I hope this works out. I could really use your help."

And I could really use yours, I thought, as I watched her go.

CHAPTER

Calling good-bye to Jenny, I headed toward home, the conversations with Mrs. Aster filling my head. I would have to find a way to bring up the idea of leaving. If my parents seemed open to it, then I could let them know about the job that Mrs. Aster had offered me.

Back home, after the initial flurry of questions about my day at work, I perched myself on the stool in the kitchen and helped my mother slice vegetables for dinner.

"I saw that English woman again, the one who knew about rumspringa," I said. "Her name is Rachel Aster."

"That's nice," said my mother, her eyebrows lowered.

"She'll be at the inn until Tuesday," I said. "She's working on a writing project, and her husband is home taking care of the children while she works here. Can you imagine that?"

"No, I can't," said my mother. "But they live in their world—"

"I know," I interrupted. "And we live in ours."

My mother looked up, startled. "That's right."

"They're fancy and we're plain," I added. "They're peeking at our world, we're not to be peeking at theirs."

She set down her knife. "What's this about, Eliza?"

I took a breath and looked right into my mother's silvery eyes. "I'd like to live away from home for a while. And I have an idea of how I might be able to do that."

She picked up her knife and sliced through a zucchini with quick chopping motions, throwing the round disks into the bowl. "Leaving home is not an option."

I tried to keep my voice calm. "I've always loved hearing stories about your rumspringa, when you worked for the tailor and listened to music with his daughter and went to movies. I'd like to live that way for a while."

My mother wiped her hands on a dish towel. "You're going to get to do some of those things. Soon you'll be going to movies with your friends. And I know there's music at your parties." I watched as she searched for words. "And I think you glorify those stories I've told you. I had to go away from home because my family needed the money. It was very hard for me to be on my own in a strange place. I don't want that for you."

"I want it for me."

"Eliza," she said, exasperation in her voice. "You don't know what you want."

Anger rushed up in me. "That's just it. You said yourself that we make a choice after rumspringa. How can I make a choice if I'll always be wondering what I'm missing?"

My mother turned away and picked up the spoon to mix the vegetables we'd been cutting. I knew from the set of her chin that the conversation was over. That's the way things were with her. She always got to decide when we were finished talking.

"Please set the table," she said, her voice quiet and tense.

I was happy to leave the kitchen. As I entered the dining room I almost collided with James, who was standing near the kitchen door. He put his finger to his lips, then took hold of my arm and led me out of the room.

"What is it, James?" I asked. "I have to set the table."

He led me out the front door to the porch. Curious, I sat on the porch swing, and he sat beside me. "Listen," he said. "I heard part of your conversation with Mom."

I looked down and sighed. "It's like talking to that tree," I said, pointing to an oak spreading shade in the yard. "But I think the tree might actually be listening to me."

James laughed. "You're talking to the wrong tree."

I turned to look at him. He had a teasing smile on his face. His straw hat cast a shadow across his brown eyes. "Go to Dad," he said. "You're never going to convince Mom to let you leave home, but Dad might help. He talked her into letting me go away."

"You're a boy," I said. "It was different for you."

"Not so different. She didn't want me to leave either. She thought it wouldn't look good. And I'd be too tempted out there."

"Were you?"

"Jah," he said with a smile. "I was tempted."

"But you came home."

He nodded. "I did."

I waited to hear if he would say more. Since he'd come back from his apprenticeship I'd been eager to hear more about his time away, but he'd kept pretty much to himself. "I came home because Dad needs me in the shop. It's where I've always known I'll be. But I'm glad I had the time away." He paused and turned, looking out at the yard and the dusty path leading to the carpentry shop. He spoke without looking at me, his words quiet but insistent. "You need to see it for yourself," he said. "So get Dad on your side." He turned, and our eyes met.

"I understand," I whispered. "Thank you."

I set the table, thinking about what James had told me. It hadn't occurred to me that my father might be the one to approach. My father sat at the head of the table for meals, and tugged my ponytail when he kissed me good night. He held the reins when we rode together in the buggy, and set out the benches when it was our turn to host Sunday services. But whenever I asked him questions, he would say, "Go ask your mother. She'll know." So I fell out of the habit of going to him. But if he had helped James get permission to leave home, maybe he could do the same for me.

When the table was set, I checked the kitchen. My mother looked up from the stove and said, "You can tell your father that supper will be ready soon." It was just the excuse I needed to have a bit of time with him in his carpentry shop. Hurrying along the path,

I hoped that James was right. I hoped my father would understand.

The air was dusty when I entered the shop, and I waited to let my eyes adjust, breathing in the damp smell of sawdust. The floor was cluttered with half-finished projects and piles of wood pieces in assorted sizes. In one corner, my father kept some completed pieces that he showed to customers—a bookcase with adjustable shelves, a desk with tiny cubbyholes, and a rocking chair like the one in our living room.

My father was bent over the planing table, feeding two-by-fours into the machine. When they came out the other side, the surface of the wood was smooth and even. He looked up when he saw me and pulled the lever to stop the machine. The roaring sound of the planer died down, leaving only the drone of the hydraulic engine that powered it.

"Is dinner ready?"

"Just about," I said. "Do you need any help finishing up?" When I was younger, my father used to let me stand on the other side of the planer to collect the boards as they came out, and stack them according to size.

"No," he said. "I'm ready to stop for the day." He turned a switch on the wall panel, quieting the noise of the engine, and the shop fell into a comforting silence. I perched on a stool and watched as he hung up his tools and brushed the sawdust off the table with a short-handled broom. When he finished, I filled my lungs with the musty air and prepared to speak.

"Can I talk to you for a minute?"

My father nodded and leaned back against the planing table, his arms crossed over his broad chest.

"Ever since my birthday, I've been thinking about what I want to do during my rumspringa. And I've decided that I'd like to get a job away from home. Maybe live at an English home and work as a babysitter." I waited, holding my breath.

My father took off his hat and rumpled his dark hair, sending more sawdust into the air. I wasn't sure, but it looked like he was trying hard not to smile.

"Your birthday was three weeks ago, Eliza. Have you only been thinking about this for three weeks?"

I couldn't tell if he was being agreeable or accusatory. "No," I said. "I've actually been thinking about it for a while. I've always wanted to see more of the world, and this seems like the time to do it."

"And have you spoken to your mother about this?" he asked, one eyebrow raised.

I nodded. "She isn't happy about the idea."

"I didn't think she would be," he said, turning his hat in his hands. "Your mother has very definite ideas about teenagers leaving home. It was hard for me to convince her to let James go away."

"That's why I came to you," I said. "I was hoping you could talk to her for me, like you did for James. Maybe you can persuade her to let me go."

My father settled his hat back on his head. "That's a tall order, Eliza. You know that when your mother has her mind set, it's hard to change it."

"I know," I said, my hopes plunging. "But you've changed her mind before."

My father laughed. "I did persuade her to marry me," he said, shaking his head. "That took a lot of work." He smiled at me, and I felt more hopeful. "I can't promise you anything, Eliza, but I'll talk to her tonight."

"Thanks, Papa." I threw my arms around his shoulders, swallowing back a warm feeling.

He patted my back with his sturdy hands. "Don't thank me yet."

At dinner I was awkward around my mother after our harsh words earlier, and I felt an unfamiliar kinship with my father, who I knew would be speaking on my behalf later in the night. And every time I looked at James, I could sense his connection with me; I could feel him urging me forward. Only my younger sister, Ruthie, seemed unchanged, chattering about her list of arithmetic problems and the homework that Miss Abigail was piling on her without mercy in this last week of school. I thought about how hard it would be for Ruthie if I left home, and I looked away from her.

After dinner I stood beside my mother at the kitchen sink, but our movements were jerky and poorly timed. When I finished drying a plate I reached for the next one, only to find that my mother was still scrubbing it, leaving my hands frozen in the air. When I finally received the plate to dry, the next one was soon waiting for me, and my mother waved it impatiently.

"You have to be faster with the drying," she said, breaking the silence.

"I know," I said. Then I paused and turned to her. "And I hope you're not angry about our conversation. It's just that I so want to have my rumspringa at an English home. Like you did."

My mother sighed and dried her hands on her apron before turning to me. "Ever since you were little, you've always been so curious," she said. "Margaret could play for hours arranging quilt swatches, but you always followed me around with questions." She put her warm damp hand under my chin, raising my face until our eyes met. "As your mother, I want you to be safe. To me that means keeping you in our world."

Sadness spread through my throat and trickled down to my chest. When my mother took her hand away, I could still feel the dampness on my skin. "I know you're disappointed," she said. "And I'm sorry to be the one to disappoint you."

My eyes burned, and I blinked hard to hold back the tears. I hung on to the hope that maybe later, after she talked to my father, she'd change her mind. She rinsed a plate and handed it to me to dry. I set it on the rack and waited as she washed the next one. Our rhythm was still off.

CHAPTER

4

That night, while Ruthie slept, I sat in bed with my ear pressed to the wall, listening to the low murmur of my parents' voices. I could hear some gentle arguments back and forth, mostly what I expected. Would I be safe? What if something happened to me when I was far from home? My mother's voice was more insistent than my father's. She spoke of her sister, and I wondered what my Aunt Miriam had to do with this. My father's voice was steady. A couple of times he mentioned that I was hardworking and they could trust me. My mother said, "Other parents have felt the same way about their children and they were wrong."

Then their voices got lower, and I strained to hear them. My mother sounded fierce. What if I liked it there and didn't want to come home? Then came my father's voice. What if they forced me to stay home and I was unhappy? My mother answered firmly, "I'd rather have her unhappy at home than happy there." Those words rattled inside of me, and my hopes seeped away. I went to sleep bathed in disappointment.

In the morning, we all joined hands and lowered our heads to say grace before passing the bowl of scrambled eggs and biscuits around the table. After breakfast, when I helped my mother with the dishes, her words came back to me. She didn't care if I was unhappy, as long as I was home. I reached for the dishes with my head turned to the side. I couldn't look at her.

Later, as I got ready to leave for the inn, my father stopped me at the door. "After dinner tonight we'll have a talk." His voice sounded a bit gruff, but he reached around and tugged on my ponytail in his playful way, and I let myself feel a tiny bit of hope.

At the inn I cut the fruit and rang the breakfast bell and readied the plates, feeling the monotony settle inside me. It was only my second week at the job and I was already bored and restless. After the breakfast dishes were cleaned, I stood outside of Mrs. Aster's room, carrying the cleaning supplies in a bucket, and knocked quietly at the door. "Come in," she called. When I opened the door, Mrs. Aster turned from the desk at the window. She smiled in a cautious way when she saw me, and I felt a wash of nervousness. "Have you had a chance to talk to your parents about my job offer?"

I hesitated. "Things have been busy at home, so we haven't been able to discuss the specifics. I had hoped to give you an answer today, but my parents and I have a few more things to work out." This was almost truthful, I told myself.

"I'm leaving on Tuesday, but if your parents decide that this is an arrangement they want for you, I'll be happy to come back to get you."

I smiled at the idea of stepping into this woman's car and speeding away from here. But it didn't seem like it could happen.

That night after dinner, my mother and father settled on the couch, and I sat facing them in the big armchair. "So, Eliza," my father began, "I understand that you want to see what's out there in that fancy world." His wide-brimmed hat hung on the wall hook, and his dark hair was disheveled. Bits of sawdust had collected in his beard, and I knew that later he would lean over the washstand and comb them out.

"I do," I said, searching their faces, trying to see a hint that they would have good news for me.

My parents were glancing at each other and having one of those conversations without words, speaking with the movements of their eyes, a tip of the head. My father spoke. "As I'm sure you know, we aren't comfortable with the idea of your living away from us." He paused before adding, "I know that James spent some time away, but I think you understand that his situation was different than yours. He was in an apprenticeship to prepare for his trade. Your mother also spent some time away when she was young, but that was a financial necessity for her family."

My chest felt like a balloon with its air rushing out. He had anticipated my arguments and left me with nothing.

"And we can't send you away to help another family when your family at home needs you," he added. "I think we'll have to find a way for you to have your 'running wild' time without running too far." He smiled as though his play on words had pleased him. He looked at me, and I thought I saw an apology in his smile.

My mother spoke without a hint of the regret my father had shown. "I know you're disappointed, but you're going to have to trust us. We know more of the world than you do."

I forced myself to look directly at her. "So you've decided to keep me from it?"

My father and mother exchanged another glance, and my father looked away. "Every sixteen-year-old gets to have some freedom," said my mother. "But the parents are the ones who measure out that freedom. We'll find ways to give you independence, but it has to be under our roof."

I turned to my father. Our eyes met briefly, and then he looked down, unable to hold my gaze.

It was final now. No last shred of hope to hang on to. I was wild with disappointment, and it was because of my mother. This was her doing.

My father got up and reached for his hat. "I'm going to get a little more work done," he said.

My mother nodded and picked up her quilting. I looked at her, wondering how she could be so satisfied with her little routines. She pulled the needle through the fabric in quick, even motions, occasionally glancing at a piece of paper with the customer's specifications scribbled over it. She looked up and saw me watching her.

"I don't want to be your enemy, Eliza," she said. "Will you try to understand this from my perspective?"

I struggled not to show my anger. Instead I tried another approach. "What was it like there?"

My mother set her quilt square aside. "You've heard it so many times," she said. "My father found me a job at a tailor shop, and I lived with the tailor's family." I drifted into the rhythm of her words, hearing again about her teenage life, how she'd shared a bedroom with Debbie, the tailor's daughter, who went off to school each day with an armload of books while she went off to the shop each day with her sewing basket. My mother spent her days handling clothing the likes of which she had never seen before. Sparkling gowns, trousers for women, and skirts that her customers wanted so short she would blush while pinning them.

In the evenings she listened to music from a CD player with the tailor's daughter, who was almost like a friend. She watched television and saw movies. She had especially liked a movie called *The Sound of Music*, about some children who learned how to sing and whose father lost his sad strictness when music came into his home.

It was the story I'd heard my whole life, but now it was different. Now it was the story of the experience my mother had had that she wasn't allowing me to have myself.

"And I was homesick," she continued. "I couldn't wait to earn enough money so I could come back to this world that I knew. And when I did, your father was waiting for me." Her words sounded rehearsed.

I didn't know how it was possible to miss something when it had never been mine in the first place. But as I listened to what my mother described, I suddenly understood the hollow feeling in my chest. I was homesick for a world I had never seen.

CHAPTER

 5

Sitting in the back of the buggy between Ruthie and James, I listened to the comforting clip-clop of the horse's hooves and tried to push away my disappointment from last night. We were on our way to Margaret and Jacob's barn raising. My sister had married Jacob six months ago, at the end of the wedding season, and now all of the Plain people from the district would be there to raise the walls and build the roof of their barn in one day. Barn raisings are joyous occasions, but after my conversation with my parents it was hard to feel happy. I tried to focus on seeing my friends. Annie and Kate would be there, Mary and Sally, too. They always looked forward to my stories about the English who came to our dinners, and today I'd have so much to tell them.

I hopped off the buggy and went in search of Kate and Annie, finding them at Margaret's kitchen table, tossing lettuce and vegetables into a big wooden salad bowl. They looked up with matching smiles when they saw me. Kate's blond braids hung down her back like pieces of rope. She looked at me with eyes the color of a summer night. Annie gave me an easy nod before turning her attention to the window, where she had a clear view of the men working on the barn. I knew she had an eye out for one boy in particular, as she always did these days. I picked up a head of lettuce and began tearing pieces and tossing the shreds into the bowl.

"There were English teenagers at my house last week," I said.

"What were they wearing?" asked Kate. She set down her knife and listened intently.

I told my friends about the darkness of Caroline's clothing and the chaotic colors Jess was wearing. "And they had these little phones that they didn't talk into," I added. "They just pressed some buttons and stared down at them."

"They were texting," said Kate. I looked at her in surprise. Kate was always surprising me. She had a quiet way about her, but in that quiet she was as alert as a guard dog. "They type messages," she continued. "And the person they send the message to reads the words on a little screen on their phone." I tried to imagine being able to send messages to Kate or Annie during Sunday services or at home on a quiet afternoon. I tried to picture this world where I could communicate with my friends any time I had the notion, instead of waiting for these moments when we were together, face-to-face. I glanced over my shoulder at the women working at the stove. I was anxious to talk to my friends about Mrs. Aster's job offer and my parents' refusal to let me leave home, but I'd have to wait until my mother was out of earshot.

My thoughts were interrupted by Annie, who burst out, "Do you think Marc will be here today?"

"I don't know," said Kate, and she and I exchanged a smile. Annie had been sweet on Marc for a while now, but they hadn't quite made it to the courting stage, and she was losing her tiny store of patience waiting for it to happen.

She turned to me. "Has Daniel said anything to you? Does Marc ever ask about me?" She flicked at a stray clump of hair that didn't fit into her chestnut-colored ponytail.

"He hasn't said anything lately," I said, disappointed that the subject had changed. I wanted to know where Kate had learned about texting. "Do you want me to ask him?" Daniel was beginning to come around in his carriage at night, shining his lantern in my window to call me out and keep company. Sometimes my friends asked if Daniel was my beau, but I couldn't think about him that way. My head was so filled with leaving, I didn't want to focus on anything that would make me stay.

Annie shook her head, another clump of hair falling loose. "No, I don't want him to think I'm pining for him. Let him come to me on his own."

I threw the last shreds of lettuce into the bowl and started chopping carrots. I listened to Kate's announcement that she had sold her first quilt, and Annie's story about how she'd spotted Sally in Peter's courting carriage.

"There you are," said Margaret, standing beside my friends in her tentative way. I gave my sister a kiss and listened as Kate and Annie asked her about married life. She looked down as though she was undeserving of all this attention, her thin fingers patting at her tidy bun.

"I should go help Mother," she said. "I just wanted to say hi to you and your friends."

Margaret started to walk away, and I reached for her hand. She turned to me. After checking to see that my mother's back was to us, I lowered my voice. "Did Mom tell you that we're arguing?"

"Are you and Mom mad at each other?" Margaret asked gently. "Or are you mad at Mom?"

I looked at my sister's quiet features, her pale hair and sand-colored eyes. She was waiting for my answer, and I knew that if it took me an hour to respond, she'd still be standing there, calm and attentive. "Mostly I'm mad at her," I said. "And with good reason."

She put her hand on my shoulder. Her touch was so subtle, I could hardly feel its weight. "You think Mother's against you, but really she's not."

I sighed and shook my head. I started to turn back toward the table, where my friends were talking about next Friday's party. Margaret's hand was still on my shoulder, but now there was more pressure to her touch. I turned back to her.

"Trust me," she said. Then she left as quietly as she had come, my Good Amish sister who had been so certain of her life plans. I watched as she took her position beside the other women bustling about with the lunch preparations. Even though I didn't understand her willingness to pass up the freedom of rumspringa, I was glad she had found Jacob. Whenever they were together he always put his arm across her shoulders in a careful way, and she leaned in to him as though his closeness filled her up.

Kate pointed out the window. "Daniel's here." I nodded at the familiar sight of him, his rust-colored hair bristling from beneath his straw hat. Like all the boys, Daniel wore a white shirt and black trousers held up with black suspenders. He was holding a plank of wood steady while another boy hammered. I swallowed back a warm feeling. Daniel always understood me. He listened to my stories about the English and didn't change the subject or wonder at my curiosity. Suddenly I wanted to talk to him. I wanted him to know about my wish to leave home, and my job offer from Mrs. Aster, and the feeling of restlessness that I couldn't shake off.

When we finished making the salad, Annie went over to the table where dishes and serving pieces were stacked for lunch. She came back, her eyes glinting, balancing three pitchers and a stack of plastic glasses. "Let's bring water to the boys," she said. Kate and I smiled as Annie led us out to the pump in the front yard.

I held my pitcher under the flow while Kate pumped. When all the pitchers were filled we divided up the stack of glasses and each went off to bring water to the various clusters of men hammering and sawing, turning wood planks into walls. I found Daniel and handed him a glass, which he took gratefully, his green eyes squinting in the June sun. "Would you like to take a walk later?" he asked.

I nodded happily and moved on with the water pitcher. The day was turning out just fine.

At noon we carried our lunch plates to the long tables laid out in Margaret's yard, and all bowed our heads together to say grace. Sally and Mary joined us at the girls' table. We glanced furtively at the boys as we ate, and talked about the upcoming parties and the rumors about who was courting whom. Sally blushed when Annie told her that she'd been spotted in Peter's carriage, and laughter flowed around the table.

Lunch was a short break in the day. The men couldn't waste precious daylight if they were going to get the barn finished by sundown. The women gathered in Margaret's living room and kitchen. Some busied themselves washing and drying the lunch dishes, leaving them in stacks for the dinner that would be served after the barn was raised. My mother oversaw Margaret and a group of older women who were preparing the evening meal.

In the living room, the rest of us gathered around different quilt projects. Ruthie and the young girls sat with a pile of colorful cut shapes, piecing them together to form squares. In another part of the room, a group of Margaret's friends sat in a loose circle, stitching together the squares Margaret had completed for her wedding quilt. I sat with Kate, Annie, Sally, and Mary, a nearly finished baby quilt that Kate had brought stretched over our crossed legs. Working together, our knees bumping, we sewed the quilt top to the batting and the back, adding decorative stitches to the color-ful quilt squares.

Kate was the most advanced quilter of my friends. Her stitches were fine and even, her patterns intricate. She'd tried to teach me some of the more complicated squares, but I was always too impa-tient to learn the complex placement of the shapes, the delicate distinctions of color values. Kate loved her job in the quilt shop and was anxious to sell more of her own work.

The tip of my finger felt sticky inside the thimble, and boredom stirred in me as I pulled the thread up through the three layers of fabric, only to pull it down again. It was monotonous work, up and down, in and out, all of our hands rising and falling in unison. We sat stiffly because too much movement could throw off someone else's stitches.

These girls, my closest friends, bowed their capped heads over their work. My gaze slipped down to the five pairs of hands working over the same quilt. I knew my friends so well that I could identify each of them by their hands alone. Annie's nails were bitten, and Mary's were long and curved. Kate's slim hands worked quickly, placing the stitches with certainty. Sally's short fingers tugged cau-tiously at the thread.

Pulled into the tightness of our work together, I suddenly wanted my friends to know about these past few days and the rise and fall of my hopes. I set down my needle, and the four bowed heads lifted up. I glanced at the kitchen to be sure my mother was out of earshot. "So, I've been trying to figure out how to live with the English. I want to go away for a while and see what it's like there."

The needles dropped, settling in steely slivers against the quilt. "Do your parents know?" asked Mary.

"I talked to them about it last night. It didn't go well."

"Did you think it would?" asked Kate.

I shook my head. "You know my mom."

"Where would you live if you went away?" asked Sally.

I took a breath. "Maybe I'll find a babysitting job and live with the family." I waited for their response.

When Kate spoke again, her voice was low and wistful. "What if your parents change their minds?"

"That would be incredible."

"Not for me," said Kate.

"Don't worry, Katie," I said. "My mother has no plans to let me out of her sight." Kate picked up her needle, and everyone else did the same. Her steady fingers seemed to be faltering a bit as the quiet rhythm of the stitching resumed.

Annie spoke next, the words rushing out. "Marc wanted to know if I'm going to Susie's party next Friday. I told him I was thinking about it."

I smiled and shook my head. We were back to Annie, but that was all right.

"Thinking about it?" said Sally. "You've been talking about that party for a month!"

"I know," said Annie, "but he doesn't have to know that."

We all exchanged glances, and Mary swallowed back a giggle. We had returned to the world we knew. Annie wondering if Marc wanted to court her. Sally sneaking into Peter's carriage—hoping we wouldn't notice, but happy that we did. Friday night parties. Sunday services. Barn raisings. In a few years there would be baptisms and weddings, then babies.

All at once I needed to get up from my crouched position, to stretch and breathe in some fresh air. "I've got to see if Margaret needs me in the kitchen," I said. My friends shifted to fill the space I'd left behind. I slipped away quietly, hoping they wouldn't notice that I wasn't going to the kitchen, but outside. The air was warm and new, and I inhaled deeply, stretching my cramped limbs. I searched around until I saw Daniel, sawing a piece of wood, his elbow moving up and down in a sure rhythm. He looked up at me and continued to saw until the severed piece dropped at his feet. Then he set the saw down and unhooked his tool belt. "I'm taking a break," he told the boy beside him.

Side by side, we followed the path from Margaret's house that led to a forested area. As we walked, Daniel reached for my hand and I let him hold it. "You first," he said. "I can tell you want to say something, and so do I. So you start."

We stopped walking and he reached for my other hand. We stood there a little awkwardly, like children about to play London Bridge.

"I want to go away. During my rumspringa. I want to live somewhere else and try out the English life." I waited to hear what he thought of my idea. My hands, nestled in his, felt warm and comfortable.

"I don't think the English life is something you can try out," he said after a moment. "It's not like a pair of shoes."

"You know what I mean. This is the time when we're supposed to have some freedom. I don't want to just talk about that life. I want to live the way they do."

"How do they live?"

"That's the point," I said, hearing the exasperation in my voice. "I don't know how they live. That's what I want to find out."

"Is there something here that you don't like?"

Daniel's face was so familiar. I knew the tiny indentations above his cheekbones, and the way the edges of his eyes tilted up when he grinned. His voice was even and steady, like a straight road. I knew I could stay here and be drawn into the comfort of him. Then I'd never know what I was missing in that world away from here.

"This is all I've known," I said. "So I can't like it or not like it. I have nothing to compare it to."

Daniel nodded, still listening, waiting for more. But I couldn't find any words to describe the restless feeling that had filled me in these past months. He squeezed my hands. "Then you should go," he said. "You should find a way to make it happen."

I took a breath, encouraged by his words. "I thought I had," I said. "I met someone at the inn who offered me a nanny job in Chicago."

"That's far," he said.

"I know."

"It's what you want?" he asked. I nodded. "Then what's stopping you?"

"My parents," I said. "They need some convincing."

A grin slid up his face. "So convince them. You're good at that."

Stepping forward, I felt the solid warmth of him. We stood together for a few minutes wrapped in a gentle hug, before Daniel reminded me that we had to get back. Together we started down the path toward Margaret's house.

Suddenly I remembered something. "What did you want to tell me?"

"Never mind," he answered. "It's not important."

Ahead, the men were in a row, preparing to hoist up a framed wall that would soon be part of Margaret and Jacob's barn. The women were in the house, quilting and cooking. I let go of Daniel's hand, and we both hurried off to return to the men's work and women's work that was ahead for us. We hurried off toward the world we both knew.

CHAPTER

6

The next day, Monday, was my day off from the inn. My mother and I were together in the kitchen, canning strawberry preserves. While my mother stirred the boiling mixture of strawberries, sugar, and lemon juice, I sterilized the jars. Holding a pair of tongs, I watched the water roiling around the jars and lids and rings, checking the clock to be sure it boiled for a full ten minutes. On the counter I laid out a clean towel, ready to arrange the items when they came out of the pot. I was still angry with my mother, but I thought in this quiet work we were sharing, there might be a way to bring up the conversation again.

In the afternoon I would be picking up Ruthie from school. I planned to leave a little early so I could stop at the inn and speak to Mrs. Aster. I would tell her that my parents had had a change of heart and didn't feel that it was a good time for me to leave home. But if my mother gave me any indication today that she might be softening to the idea, I would tell Mrs. Aster that I would be in touch with her again when it was a better time for my family.

As I prepared to lift the first jar out of the boiling water, I heard a knock at the front door. My mother went to answer, and I heard her greet a quilt customer in her cordial way. I imagined her at the door, her face settled into the lines of the stranger smile. But there was something about my mother's voice, confused and cautious, that made me set the tongs down on the towel. I heard her say, "I don't understand. Surely there must be some mistake." I turned off the gas burner and moved toward the front door, to see my mother standing face-to-face with Mrs. Aster.

Both women turned to me with confused expressions, and I swallowed back a wave of dread. "Eliza," said my mother, "Mrs. Aster tells me that you've discussed a position with her. Do you have something to say about this?"

I turned to Mrs. Aster, who seemed to take stock of the situation quickly. "It's my fault, Mrs. Miller. I was so eager to hire a new nanny for my children that I jumped ahead before checking with you. I should never have mentioned the job to Eliza without talking to you first."

I shook my head. "No," I said to my mother. "This is my fault. I thought that if I had a job offer, you might agree to it. But when you were so firm about not letting me leave home, I didn't even have a chance to tell you about the job." I turned to face Mrs. Aster. "I was going to come to the inn today to explain that I couldn't accept the position. I'm so sorry."

We were all standing in the front hallway, facing each other in an awkward circle. Mrs. Aster's expression held concern and discomfort. My mother's was unreadable.

She turned to Mrs. Aster. "When your children are teenagers, you will learn that they don't always like to follow your rules." I looked down, heat pumping to my face, as my mother continued, her voice polite and even. "I'm sure that you had the best of intentions, but I hope you understand our decision that Eliza will not be leaving home."

"Of course," said Mrs. Aster. "And please know that I meant no disrespect."

"I understand," said my mother.

As Mrs. Aster turned to step onto the front porch, our eyes met. I tried in that flash of an instant to show her how sorry I was for putting her in this situation. And how sorry I was that I couldn't go with her.

When the door closed, my mother faced me. I expected anger, but instead I saw tired resignation. "Will there be any more surprises for me on my front porch, Eliza? Will any other strangers be stopping by to ask me if you'll be living with them?"

"No," I said miserably.

"Good," she said.

I started to go back to the kitchen to pull the jars out of the boiling water. My mother reached for my arm, and I turned around to face her. When she spoke, her voice was urgent.

"One day you'll understand, Eliza."

I nodded, even though I knew it wasn't true.

I left early to pick up Ruthie, giving my mother the excuse that I had an errand to run in town. I hurried to the inn, hoping that Mrs. Aster would be there. I wasn't sure what I wanted to say to her, but I knew that I didn't want to leave things this way. When she answered my knock, I stepped into the room, feeling shivery even in the June heat. She looked up from the papers spread across the bed, and sat up quickly.

"Eliza, I thought you weren't working today."

"I'm not," I said. "I just wanted to explain things before you left."

She got up and pointed to the two wing chairs in the corner of the room. We sat down, and she turned to me. "I hope I didn't cause any trouble for you today," she said. "When I met you at your mother's dinner, I dreamed of having that kind of help around my house. I realize now that I shouldn't have talked to you about the job without first checking with your parents."

"I gave you every reason to think they'd be agreeable. I'm afraid I wasn't completely truthful with you."

Rachel spoke quietly. "Do you want to be truthful now?"

I nodded. "I've always wanted to leave home during my rumspringa and see what the English life is like."

"I take it from your mother's response today that your parents feel strongly about keeping you at home."

"My mother does. My father was more open-minded about

it, but he couldn't get her to change her mind." I glanced at the clock. "I have to go now. It's time to pick my sister up from school. But I wanted to tell you how much I appreciated your offer—even though I can't accept it."

"I'm sorry it didn't work out," she said. "If anything changes, Mr. Allen knows how to get in touch with me. He's a friend of mine, and he knows how to get in touch with me." I smiled my thanks and hurried off to pick up Ruthie, knowing that I would never have the need to contact Mrs. Aster. It was time for me to put that hope aside and move on. I just wished I knew where I was going.

That night after dinner I tried to feel more positive about being at home during my rumspringa. Some of my friends were starting to wear blue jeans at the parties, and we were all planning for the movies we were going to see together once our parents agreed. And now that I'd be staying home, I could consider the idea of having Daniel as my beau. I had a feeling that was what he wanted, too. It was only my wish to leave home that kept me from feeling the same way.

Before James went out for the evening, he came over to the table, where I was helping Ruthie with her arithmetic problems. He looked at me in a cheerless way and said, "I'm sorry it didn't work out."

"Me too," I said. "But thanks for your help."

While Ruthie was bent over the paper, I noticed my parents

standing together in the kitchen. Their voices were so low I couldn't make out any of the words, but I knew my mother was telling my father of Rachel's visit this afternoon. My father looked up for a moment, and our eyes met. Instead of disapproval, I saw sadness in his expression, and I knew that I had disappointed him.

I checked Ruthie's division problem and reminded her to carry the remainder over to the next column. She rubbed her eraser so roughly over her mistake that it ripped the paper and she pushed it away in frustration.

"Here," I said, blowing the eraser dust away and smoothing out the tear in the paper. "Let's start this one over again. I had a hard time with long division, too, but I learned it eventually." I brushed a strand of golden hair off her damp face. "And so will you."

As I reached for a new piece of paper, I heard my father at the front door. "I'm going out for a little fresh air," he said. I waved to him over my shoulder and went back to Ruthie's homework. "See?" I said, when she corrected her mistake. "I knew you could do it."

She looked up at me, a combination of boredom and gratitude in her round eyes, and we went on to the next problem.

CHAPTER

 7

On Friday night, James pulled the buggy up in front of Susie's barn, and I climbed out. "Will Daniel be taking you home?" he asked.

"I don't think he'll be here," I said. "He didn't send word to me that he'd be picking me up."

"Okay, then. I'll come to get you at eleven," he said. I nodded and waved as he pulled on the reins to guide the horse back to the road.

I stepped into the barn, ready to return to the life I hadn't had the chance to leave. Lanterns hanging from the hayloft lit the barn in a soft way, and I spotted Kate, Annie, and Mary sitting together on a pallet, sipping from cans of soda pop. They waved me over, and I settled in next to them, pulling my skirt over my knees.

Mary pointed, and we all looked in the direction of the door, where Sally and Peter were slipping out, hand in hand. My group of friends had just started going to parties, most of us having turned sixteen in the past months. We had spent the last year waiting to be old enough for these gatherings, but now we were still figuring out what to do at them. Some of the kids in the wilder groups were already finding ways to get alcohol, but our get-togethers had been pretty tame so far.

On this night, a group of boys, some wearing blue jeans, were crouched together gambling with playing cards. A few couples were off in distant corners, sitting close together and sneaking kisses, which they would tell their friends about later. At the last party, Daniel and I were one of those couples, hiding behind a hay bale, reaching for each other in a cautious way.

I took a sip of the soda pop that someone had handed me, swallowing down its fizzy sweetness. I turned to Kate, remembering something she had said at the barn raising. "I've been meaning to ask how you knew about texting."

"I was in line to check out at the dollar store," she said, "and I heard these little beeps from behind me. I turned around and the girl showed me the words on her phone."

I smiled. "So I guess I'm not the only expert on the English."

"No, you're not," said Kate. "I'm as taken with them as you are."

I had always thought Kate didn't share my curiosity, but it was clear now that she did.

"But you seem so content," I said. "You never talk about leaving home."

Kate fingered the hem of her apron. "That's because I know it will never happen."

"It turns out it's not going to be a possibility for me either," I said.

"What happened?" asked Mary, leaning in, pulling her dark silky ponytail over her shoulder so it cascaded down her chest. Annie was glancing at the door, no doubt waiting for Marc to arrive. But she looked back at me when I started my story.

I took a breath and told my friends about my encounters with Mrs. Aster, about James and my dad trying to help me, about my mother's resolve. I saw their surprised expressions when I told them about Mrs. Aster coming to our house and my mother's reaction. When I was done I waited for the sympathy I knew would be coming.

"I'm sorry," said Mary, shaking her head. "But I really couldn't imagine why you wanted to leave us in the first place."

"It's not that I wanted to leave you," I said, stung. "I was just looking to have some different experiences for a while."

"I could never leave," said Mary, her voice firm.

"Really?" I asked. "You aren't even a little bit curious?"

"Oh, I'm curious. But I like knowing what's expected of me. I feel safe here."

I tried to understand Mary's feelings, but I couldn't imagine that safety could be someone's burning desire. I turned to Annie. "What about you? Don't you ever feel curious about the English?"

"I hear that Yankee boys are cute," she said with a grin.

"Can we change the subject?" said Kate. "You're not leaving, so why are we still talking about it?" Her voice had a harshness I felt under my skin.

"We can talk about whatever you want," I said. "I didn't know this would bother you."

Kate looked away. I waited to hear what her response would be. The room was filling up with people. Near the door, two boys were smoking cigarettes, the acrid smell drifting into the barn. A borrowed machine that Susie called a boom box sent out weak blasts of music, which settled into the background of our conversations. Music was new in our lives, available to us only at these parties. We didn't know anything about what we were listening to, but it was forbidden, which made it desirable.

"It does bother me," said Kate, turning back to face me. "And I guess now I'm sorry for you that you're stuck with us."

Before I could answer, she got up and walked to the table where the refreshments were. I turned back to Mary. "What's the matter with her?"

Mary shrugged. "Maybe she wasn't happy about the idea of you leaving."

"But I'm not leaving."

"I know," said Mary. "And maybe she wishes that you weren't so disappointed about it."

I shook my head, a nameless anger trickling through me. Kate was my best friend. Surely I could be truthful around her. "But I *am* disappointed," I said. "Does she want me to lie about it?"

"No," said Mary. "But maybe you can at least pretend that you would miss us."

I looked at Mary, her hands folded in her lap as though she were at her school desk. Mary was keeping company with Nicholas, a boy who would be happy to stay close to home. They were perfect for each other. "I would have missed you very much," I said. And I meant it.

Annie was staring at the door, waiting for Marc. I smiled watching her. She wore her feelings for everyone to see. Suddenly her expression changed, and I followed her gaze to the door in time to see Daniel walking in. At first I was surprised to see him, since he hadn't offered me a ride to the party. Then I saw why. Beside him was Hannah, tall and slim, her pale hair in one long braid that fell over her shoulder. Her lips were thick, like two puffy hearts, and they turned up in a smirk when she saw us.

Hannah was on the edge of our group of friends. She and I were forever arguing and then making up. I found her exhausting. And here she was on Daniel's arm. The room suddenly grew too hot and too noisy. Hannah detached herself from Daniel and waved, walking toward me with her arms swinging casually. "Hi," she said to all of us. Mary and Annie moved slightly to let her sit down. "Have I missed anything?"

"No," said Annie, with a grim smile. "I think the party is just starting now."

"Good," Hannah said, flinging her braid back and stretching out her long legs. "I was running late, and poor Daniel had to wait for me."

I mumbled something about wanting another drink, and stood up on shaky legs before making my way to the refreshment table.

Kate was there, talking to our friend Robert. "What's wrong?" she asked.

I nodded toward the pallet where we'd been sitting. Annie and Mary were there, looking uncomfortable as Hannah chattered to them, a beaming smile on her face. "She came with Daniel."

"You're kidding," said Kate. "Where is he?"

I looked around the room and saw him standing with a group of boys. He had a can of soda pop in each hand, and was probably about to bring one to Hannah. Kate turned to me, her eyes sympathetic.

"When Daniel and I took a walk at the barn raising, he was planning to say something. Then he changed his mind," I said. "Do you think he was going to tell me that he's courting Hannah?"

"This is news to me," said Kate. "Are you going to be okay?"

"I guess so," I said, trying to hide the quaver in my voice. I took a breath. "But I really want to be sure that everything is all right with you and me. You were pretty angry before."

Kate looked down. "Not angry. Jealous."

I waited for more.

"I know that I can never leave my mother. She hasn't been the same since my brother left home."

"Oh, Katie," I said, putting an arm across her shoulders. She slipped her arm around my waist, and we stood together quietly, feeling the nearness of each other. I breathed in Kate's smell, like warm milk, and thought of how we used to hold hands at recess, and how in our plans for growing up, we always lived next door to each other.

Kate's older brother, William, had refused baptism and left

the district a year ago, when he was nineteen. At first his family received occasional mail from him, but after a few months the letters stopped coming. I wondered if my mother had been thinking of William when she fought against James leaving, and when she made her decision to keep me at home.

"I wasn't thinking about William," I said, shaking my head.

"That's all right," said Kate. "He's been gone so long, I understand that people don't think about him all the time, like I do."

"I'm sorry I was one of those people."

"And I guess I was upset that it was going to be so easy for you to leave me," Kate said. "I know that's selfish, but it's how I felt."

"Leaving you would have been the hardest part." We turned to face each other. I looked into her blue-gray eyes and I knew she believed me.

We let go of each other, but still stood close. I turned to the table, scanning the baskets of chips and popcorn and trays of cheese and crackers. I didn't want any of it. My stomach was tight, the air thin. Then I felt a warmth beside me, and I looked up into Daniel's green eyes. "Hi, Eliza," he said, his voice smooth and easy. "I didn't see you when I came in."

Out of the corner of my eye I saw Kate slip away and join another group of girls. I took a breath. "You mean when you and Hannah came in."

Daniel's eyebrows rose. "Is something wrong with that?"

"I just didn't expect to see you with another girl," I said, swallowing back my nervousness. "At Margaret's barn raising, you didn't seem like you were interested in any other girl."

"Hannah's not my girl," he said. "She asked me for a ride and I gave her one." I nodded, feeling a little better. "And last weekend you told me you were planning to leave home."

"Well, I'm not," I said. "My parents won't let me go."

"I'm sorry, Eliza," he said. I had to admit that he did sound sorry. "You must be disappointed."

"Jah, disappointed," I said. "That's one of the things I'm feeling." I looked into Daniel's face and saw concern there. But I couldn't be comforted by his kindness right now, because he was here with another girl.

"There you are, Daniel," came Hannah's voice. It sounded high-pitched and pouty, like she was imitating a stubborn child. She stood beside him, facing me. Her hand slipped through his arm. "I thought we were going to take a walk."

I looked at Daniel, who seemed just a little bit uncomfortable. "Go ahead," I said, making my voice sound bright. "I was just going to join Kate." I turned away and walked toward the group of girls sitting at a round table. Daniel and Hannah left together, and I sat down next to Kate, feeling a rush of emotions clattering inside of me. I didn't want to be here right now. I wanted to be away from these teenagers trying to act like their little rebellions meant something. We'd all end up like our parents one day, working hard, going to services, teaching our children how to be plain.

As I tried to force a smile on my lips, I wondered if anyone else felt as trapped in this place as I did.

CHAPTER

It was the Yoder family's turn to host services that Sunday morning, and I was glad we had arrived early, so I could see Kate. I jumped down from the buggy and went off in search of my friend, finding her in the front yard, getting the table ready for the lunch that would follow services. I helped her spread out the tablecloth and stack the plates and napkins. We worked together in silence until Kate's eyes met mine. "How have you been since the party?"

"Not great. I don't know if I'm more disappointed about not being able to leave home or about seeing Daniel with Hannah."

Kate nodded solemnly. The bell on the porch rang, summoning everyone inside. "You know, we all would have missed you—me, Annie, all of your friends. Daniel, too."

I shook my head, setting my kapp wobbling. "It's not worth talking about something that isn't going to happen," I said. Then I followed Kate's gaze to the front porch. Daniel was leaning against the railing. He nodded to us and tipped his hat.

I watched him step down from the porch and walk toward me.

"Good luck," whispered Kate. After a brief nod to Daniel, she hurried past us and up the steps.

Daniel stood before me now, and I looked up into his face. The edgy anger I'd had since the party was sifting through me. But Daniel looked as calm as ever. Only a few people still lingered on the porch. Most had gone inside to find a seat. I started walking toward the house, and Daniel fell into step beside me. He looked like he wanted to say something, so I turned to him.

"Is everything all right? You didn't even say good-bye when you left the party Friday."

The bell rang again. "We should go inside," I said. "We can talk later." I paused for a moment, seeing again the bulk of his shoulders under his suit jacket. Then I ran up the porch steps and slipped through the open door, hurrying over to the women's section. I saw Daniel glance at me before finding a seat among the men.

The German prayers I knew by heart swirled around me. A warm energy usually pumped through me when the service began, and then drifted into boredom by the time it ended, three hours later. But today I felt restless right from the start, my fingers and toes twitching.

I looked around the room. My mother was sitting beside her sister. Aunt Miriam was plump and dour, her eyebrows always lowered in judgment. My sister Margaret was on my mother's other side, prim and dutiful and content. Ruthie was next to Margaret, holding the hymnal tightly, trying to look grown-up. I would have sat with them, but I had gotten in late, so I took the nearest open seat, next to my cousin Clara. Around us were the other women of the district, my friends and their mothers and sisters, all in white kapps and aprons, dresses covering their knees. On the other side of the room, my father sat with the men, between James and my uncle Ike. Daniel was there, and Robert and Marc, each wearing a black hat and a formal black suit coat over their white shirts and black trousers.

I clutched the Ausbund that someone had handed me when I came in. The well-worn book held all the hymns that had been used in Amish services since the 1500s. The first preacher was standing in the middle of the room, and he called out a hymn, which everyone around me chanted back. The voices followed the familiar cadence, with the preacher leading. We all knew to pace ourselves along with the preacher, holding our notes as long as he did, pausing when he paused. I wondered if it was always this slow. I concentrated on holding the note with everyone around me, but I didn't have enough breath, and I cut it off too soon. I gulped in another breath and tried again. Clara turned her page, so I turned mine. I had a feeling like motion sickness, when I had to get off the buggy because the rocking sensation filled me with nausea.

I rose from the hard bench and quietly edged toward the door. My heart clattering, I stepped onto the porch, breathing in the fresh air of early summer. I would just stand out here for a few minutes, and then slip back in later in the service. If anyone asked, I would say that I had a headache.

I looked out at the road leading away from this place, and in that moment, I knew I had to leave. I stepped cautiously down the stairs and walked toward the street. Then I was running. The wind caught at my hair, and I clasped a hand over my kapp to keep it from flying off. When I got to the path along the highway, I slowed to a walk. Breathing in the calming June air, I felt relieved to be out of that stifling room, and away from the people who all looked the same. Cars whizzed past me, and I wished I could feel what it was like to be in one, to speed away from everything I knew.

Home was two miles away. I walked with resolve, trying not to think about the consequences of this action. Attending services on alternate Sundays was expected of all Amish. It wasn't something that was discussed or debated. It was the strictest of our rules, and I was breaking it.

I kept walking, past the farms and small enclaves of Amish shops that the tourists frequented to buy quilts and handicrafts. Dampness spread down my back. My breath came out in quick pants as I doggedly marched toward home and the eventual recriminations of my parents.

A carriage was coming behind me, with the distinctive clip-clop of horse's hooves, and I wondered who else had skipped services. I stepped farther to the side to be sure it had ample room. When the buggy passed in front of me, it pulled off the highway onto the side of the road. I started to go around it when I heard a familiar voice. "Eliza, get in," called Daniel. I walked to the side of the buggy and turned to face him. He held the horse's reins in one hand, and reached the other toward me to help me up into the carriage.

I shook my head. "I don't need a ride," I said. "I can walk home."

"I'd like to drive you home," he said. "Please let me."

I waited a moment before reaching up and allowing him to guide me onto the seat beside him. He nodded to me in a cordial way, then looked out at the road and pulled on the reins. The horse started trotting, and the clopping sounds of his hooves filled the space around us.

"Are you going to be in trouble for leaving?" I asked.

"I don't think so. Your father looked relieved when he saw that I was going after you."

I sighed. "I guess I'll hear it from them when they get home."

"What was wrong?" he asked, his voice kind. "Aren't you feeling well?"

"I just couldn't sit there anymore. I felt like I was climbing out of my skin."

"I know that feeling," he said. "When the service gets to the two-hour mark, I'm never sure I can make it through that last hour."

I grunted a laugh. "I didn't even make it to the one-hour mark."

"Actually, I'm glad this happened," he said, his voice more serious. "I wanted to talk to you about Friday night."

"You don't have to," I said. "You have the right to take another girl to a party. It's not like we're courting."

"That's what I wanted to talk to you about," he said. "At Margaret's barn raising, after you told me you wanted to leave home, I decided not to tell you what I had planned to say." I turned to him, waiting. "I was going to ask you to be my girl."

"But you changed your mind?"

"You had just told me you wanted to live with the English," he said. "If I'd asked you then, you might have thought I was trying to get you to stay here. And that didn't seem right."

My chest warmed, and I looked up at Daniel, seeing him in a different way. He glanced at me before returning his gaze to the road ahead. His eyes looked hopeful.

"Thank you," I said, "for wanting to be my beau. And for knowing that it wouldn't have been a good time to ask me then."

"Is it a good time now?"

"I'm not sure," I said. "You really threw me off when you came to the party with Hannah."

Daniel shook his head. "It was a mistake to give her a ride."

We pulled in front of my house and he stopped the horse, holding the reins lightly across his lap. He turned to me. "Do you want to think about it?"

"Yes," I said. Then I added, "First I have to deal with what my parents are going to say when they get home. I may not be allowed out of the house for a while." I stepped down from the buggy and waved. Daniel nodded and tipped his hat before pulling away.

At home, I tried to fill the time with useful activities to keep my mind off of what was ahead. I pumped white gasoline into the lanterns and put fresh sheets on the beds and set the table for Sunday dinner. I wanted to show my parents that I was still helpful, though not always obedient. Finally I settled down with a square for a quilt that my mother was behind on. I hoped that even in her anger she would appreciate the smooth stitches in the zigzag pattern.

When I heard the buggy pull up, I put aside the quilt square and mentally rehearsed the excuses I'd prepared. Ruthie and James came in first, and James gave me what I thought was a sympathetic look. I realized that they had probably heard the discussion of my punishment on the ride home. My gaze went from James to Ruthie, and I saw that she was crying. Hot dread filled me as I watched James lead her upstairs. What could they be planning for me that would make Ruthie cry?

When my parents came in, my father took off his hat and jacket, and my mother hung up her shawl. They walked quietly into the living room and sat on the couch, facing me.

My mother was the first to speak. "First tell us that you're all right, that you didn't leave services because you're ill."

"I'm not sick," I said in a small voice. "I just didn't want to be there. I felt like a prisoner."

They looked at each other for a moment, then turned back to me. "Eliza," my father said quietly, "I think you know that your behavior today was not acceptable."

"I know. And I'm sorry."

"I don't have to tell you that it doesn't look good in front of the elders for one of our children to be running away from services," said my mother.

"I know," I said again. It seemed to be taking them a long time to let me know my punishment. I expected that I wouldn't be able to attend the next month of parties. Maybe worse. I wished they would just tell me.

My father cleared his throat, and I prepared to receive my penance. "As you know, we Amish hope our young people will take up our ways after they have their bit of wildness." I sighed, realizing this was going to take longer than I thought. My father's voice was formal, as though he were delivering a speech. "But sometimes, when we don't allow our children some freedom, they choose to leave our ways behind to see what they're missing. I believe that's what happened with Kate's brother William." I nodded, unsure of where my father was going with this.

"Do you understand what we're telling you?" asked my mother.

"No," I said. "And why was Ruthie crying?"

My mother glanced at my father before turning back to me. "Ruthie was crying because she's going to miss you."

I straightened, my heart hammering. "Miss me?" I asked. The words came out in a hoarse whisper.

"Last Monday, after Mrs. Aster's visit, your father went to the inn to meet her and to talk to Mr. Allen. Apparently she is a good friend of Mr. Allen's, and he gave her an excellent reference as an employer for you." My hand covered my mouth. I wasn't sure this was really happening.

My father continued. "Your mother and I have been talking a lot, and we don't always agree." He turned to her with a smile. She nodded and looked down. "But we both want to do what will be best for you. I am comfortable that Mrs. Aster will provide you with a safe home while you're away from us. We discussed your wages and agreed that you will work for her through the summer. Mr. Allen will send word for her to come for you once we've finalized our plans."

I let my hand drop from my mouth. "Even after the way I behaved today, you're still going to let me go?"

"Maybe because of it," my father said. "I think you need some time away to learn the value of what we've been trying to teach you. To answer some of the questions you have about the life outside of here. We're afraid that if we don't let you leave, you might go away on your own. And that would be worse, for all of us."

On wobbly legs, I made my way over to the couch, beside my father. I buried my face in his shoulder, feeling the comforting roughness of his beard against my cheek, his hand cupping the back of my head. I shook with sobs. When we let go of each other I dried my eyes with the edge of my apron.

I looked past my father to my mother, who suddenly seemed small, her hands upturned in her lap, her expression sad. My father got up and left us together. My mother placed her hand over mine. "Thank you," I said. She reached her arm around my shoulders and pulled me into a stiff hug. I was bursting with feelings I couldn't name, and I wanted to hold on to the excitement of this moment. Then my mother's voice murmured in my ear, "We're sending you to keep you."

I didn't want to think about those words. Even in my

excitement I couldn't forget how she had said she'd rather I be unhappy at home than happy far away. When I pulled away to look at her, her silver-gray eyes were fixed somewhere else.

The rest of the day had an unnatural feeling, like I was running through water. James came and lifted me into a big hug. "It's your turn now," he whispered. He sounded just a little bit wistful.

Ruthie fell into my arms, her face sticky with tears. "It's just for the summer," I said. "I'll be back before you know it."

While I helped my mother prepare the stew for Sunday dinner, I felt her looking over at me. I turned to her. "This week I'll take you to Walmart," she said. "To buy you some new clothes to take with you." A smile stretched across my face. Then her voice returned to its usual sternness. "You'll pay us back from your wages." I nodded happily.

After dinner, my father went out to meet with Mr. Allen at the inn, and returned home with a cautious smile on his face. "Things happen quickly in that world," he said. "Mr. Allen picked up the telephone, and the next thing I knew, Mrs. Aster's voice was in my ear telling me she'll pick you up on Sunday at ten in the morning." He winked at me before adding, "You won't be required to go to Fellowship that day."

I caught my breath. In just one week I would be getting into Mrs. Aster's car and riding away from here. In one week I would be a world away.

CHAPTER

9

As she promised, my mother took me shopping, and I ran to my room afterward and emptied the clothes into a colorful mound on the bed. I reached for the blue jeans first, thinking of the way my friends and I used to point when we saw English girls in town wearing what we had thought of as boys' clothes. In the fitting room I had found that the jeans didn't slip on easily; I had to maneuver my way into them. I enjoyed the way the jeans hugged my legs, but I was surprised at the stiffness of the material. When my mother noticed me tugging at the waistband, she smiled. "Blue jeans feel more comfortable after they've been washed a few times," she said. Looking in the mirror, I saw myself in trousers for the first time.

Now in my room, I felt the richness of this new wardrobe. In addition to the jeans, there were cottony soft shirts, each in a different color or pattern, blouses that buttoned from the collar to the hem, a pair of khaki pants, and two pairs of shorts. There were also new shoes—a pair of sandals and a pair of blue sneakers. Seeing all of the new clothes laid out on the bed, I thought of the day in town when Kate and I had secretly bought a copy of *Seventeen* magazine and paged through the pictures of long, thin girls painted delicately so that their eyelashes glittered and their cheeks glowed. I remembered trying, with Kate, to pose like the girls in the pictures, with a hand on a hip, a haughty head-toss, a pouty expression.

I spent some time arranging the clothes into different outfits— the lacy pink shirt with the khaki pants, the blue striped T-shirt with the jeans. The clothes on my bed didn't quite look like what we had seen in the magazine, but they were my clothes. And when I wore them I would look like a new version of me, not like every other girl in the district.

It was a busy week. On Thursday I helped my mother prepare for Stranger Night, realizing it would be a long while before I would be doing this work again. As I served the visitors I was almost giddy with the thought that in just three days I would be living in their world. I worked at the inn each day, saying good-bye to Jenny and Mr. Allen after my Saturday shift.

That night, our family and friends gathered at the house to say good-bye and to wish me luck on my journey. My mother and Margaret were in the kitchen slicing cake and pouring coffee, but I didn't have to help. I was the guest of honor.

When Mary and Sally arrived, I brought them up to my room, where I had displayed all of my new English clothes on the bed. They squealed and giggled, fingering the fabrics and holding the shorts in front of them to see how much bare leg they would reveal.

We all marveled at the buttons that fastened the pants and that marched down the front of the blouses in neat rows. We had always spoken of buttons in hushed whispers, as we did telephones and dancing and other mysteries of the English world. Now I would be wearing them every day.

Back downstairs with the rest of the guests, I received hugs and stories and words of advice about living among the English. Uncle Ike warned me to keep my money in a safe place, and Aunt Miriam, her face bitter, said, "Remember that even in the fancy world, you're still plain."

I nodded politely. It was just like Uncle Ike to be thinking about money and Aunt Miriam to give me a stern send-off. Thankfully, a hand slipped into mine, and I looked up to see Kate. "So, I guess I'll be missing you after all," she said. I squeezed her hand. Annie appeared at Kate's side, and the three of us threaded our way through the crowd to the back porch and settled ourselves on the porch swing, with me in the middle. I pushed my foot against the floorboards, and the swing swayed gently in response.

"I'll write to you both and tell you all about it."

"Be sure and write about all those Yankee boys," Annie said, her brown eyes widening.

I breathed in the sweetness of the summer night and the warmth of my friends on either side of me. "I don't think I'll be meeting any boys," I said. "There are only small children at the house where I'll be staying."

"You never know," said Annie. "I have a cousin who met a

Yankee boy and fell in love with him. She came back home and asked for permission to marry him."

"What happened?" I asked. "Did she get permission?"

"No," said Annie, her voice hushed. "She was shunned."

The swing stopped its quiet movement, and I sucked in my breath. The air was always colder when shunning was mentioned. I didn't personally know anyone who had been shunned, but we'd all heard the stories of names blotted out of family bibles and letters thrown away unopened. Kate looked down, probably thinking about William. He hadn't been shunned because he had never been baptized. Shunning was reserved for adult members of the order who had broken the baptism promise. Instead, William had left freely, of his own accord. But I'm sure that to Kate it felt the same.

"I still can't believe that your parents are letting you go," she said, changing the subject. "Mine won't even let me wear blue jeans."

At that moment, heavy footsteps rumbled up the back stairs. I squinted up in the glare of the setting sun as Daniel approached the porch swing. "Hello girls," he said, taking off his hat. "From the number of buggies parked out front, I'd say that Eliza is having quite a send-off party."

I didn't look at my friends, but I sensed that they were exchanging grinning glances. Kate was the first to get up. "Come on, Annie. Let's go see all those English clothes that everyone's talking about." The porch swing swayed as Kate and Annie slipped back into the house.

"May I sit down?" asked Daniel. Silently, I moved to one side of the swing and felt it rock as Daniel lowered himself to sit beside me. His long legs stretched out in front of him, and his sturdy hands played with the brim of his hat.

A deep silence wrapped around us before he spoke. "Weren't you going to say good-bye to me?"

James had gotten word to Daniel that I was leaving, but I hadn't seen him myself. I knew we should discuss what it meant for us, but it was a conversation I wasn't looking forward to. "I was planning to write to you after I got settled." I forced myself to look directly into his eyes. Daniel's eyes always made me think of summer leaves.

"You should have come to see me," he said, his voice stern.

I tensed. "For permission?"

The swing jolted as Daniel sat forward, his hat tumbling to the floor. I looked away, feeling his irritation. The flowerpots on the windowsill needed watering. I would have to remind Ruthie to take care of them. Turning back to Daniel, I could see ridges in his coppery hair from where his hat had been.

"Not for permission," he said. "To say good-bye properly. After our last conversation I thought I deserved that. On Sunday we were talking about courting. And now you're leaving without even a word to me."

A warm sensation crawled up my neck. I stared down at my lap. "You're right," I said. "I owed you that. I should have come to see you."

"There's something else," he added, his voice gentler. I looked up. "I was worried that you might be running away."

"Running away from what?"

Daniel stooped forward and picked up his hat. He stood, setting the swing to a slow movement, and turned to face me.

"From me."

Just then, the back door opened, spilling a surge of guests onto the porch, and I was swept into a new series of hugs and farewells. I could see Daniel leaning against the porch railing, his arms folded across his chest. But then I lost sight of him as I was carried from one set of arms to another.

The crowd thinned out until Kate and Annie were the last ones to go. We were a tight ring of bonnets and aprons and damp cheeks as we clung together, our arms tangled around each other so that, for a moment, it was hard to tell whose arms were whose.

When we released each other, I wiped at my eyes. Annie ran toward her father's buggy, calling a last good-bye over her shoulder. Kate stayed at my side for another moment, whispering, "Hurry, Eliza. Daniel's leaving."

Following Kate's gaze, I saw that Daniel was walking to his buggy, taking long slow strides. "Wait, Daniel," I called, following him across the grass to where his buggy was parked. He turned, a smile on his face that was tired and hopeful at the same time. "Now you're the one who's leaving without saying good-bye," I said.

He reached quietly into his pocket and handed me a white handkerchief. I turned my back to him and pressed it to my eyes.

It had a lemony smell. "I was going to write to you when you got settled," he said, his voice teasing. I turned to him, grinning shyly, and handed him the handkerchief. He returned it to his pocket.

"Actually, I wasn't going to leave. I was just going to my buggy to get you something."

He reached inside his carriage and pressed a small package into my hands. Gently tearing away the newspaper wrapping, I smiled at the wood carving nestled in my curved fingers.

"I made it," Daniel said, but I already knew that. I recognized the gleaming finish, the soft curves. It was a small nest with a bird rising from it, wings spread and head turned to the side. The bird's feathers were etched in tender lines, and the nest was a complex tangle of woven twigs. I cradled the carving, letting my fingertips roam across the different textures.

"I started to work on it the night of the barn raising, when you told me you wanted to go away."

"I love it." My words were a whispered gasp and Daniel leaned forward to hear them. Those days since the barn raising, when I had been angry with him for bringing Hannah to the party, he was making me this gift. I looked up into his face. "I'm going to take it with me."

Daniel smiled. "Well, I should be going. I'm glad we had a chance to talk."

"So am I."

I waited for him to step away from me, toward his carriage, but instead he stepped closer to me. Before I could speak, he pressed his lips to mine. They felt cool and moist, their touch light and gentle, like the first drop of summer rain. Then just as quickly he stepped back. I touched my lips with the tips of my fingers.

"You'll write to me?" he asked. I nodded, and Daniel climbed into his buggy. As he picked up the reins, he looked down at me. "Enjoy your journey, Eliza," he said. "Then come back to your nest."

10

The next morning, I was the first one up. In the silver quiet of the dawn I looked through the duffel bag that I had packed after the guests left last night. All of my fine new clothes were folded neatly inside, along with a dress, apron, and kapp, which my mother insisted I bring. "So you'll always remember who you are," she had said. A canvas bag held some books, my toothbrush, comb, quilting supplies, and gifts for Rachel's children. Before I closed the bag, I slipped Daniel's wood craving into a side pocket.

I had spent a delicious amount of time deciding what to wear today, finally settling on the blue jeans and the lacy pink shirt. Inside of the new sneakers my feet felt cushioned and snug. I was aware of my bare arms and my uncovered head and the way the jeans clung to my legs.

On the far side of the bed, Ruthie sat up, rubbing her eyes, her hair scattered over her shoulders. She crawled across the bed and leaned her head on my arm, the golden strands tickling my skin.

"I'll miss you so much."

"We'll write each other lots of letters," I said. I stopped as a sudden thought occurred to me. I would be able to read the words of my family and friends, but as long as I was in the fancy world, I wouldn't see their faces or hear any of their voices.

Downstairs in the kitchen, my mother was mixing batter for pancakes. I set my duffel and canvas bag by the front door, where she glanced at them and turned away. James looked me up and down. "You look English," he said.

Ruthie ran her fingers along the fabric of the jeans. "It doesn't feel soft," she said.

"I know. But I hear I'll get used to them." I looked at my mother with a smile.

We sat in our usual places around the kitchen table and joined hands to say grace. After everyone finished chanting the mealtime prayer, my father glanced around the table. One of my hands was nestled in James's large, calloused palm, and the other felt the dampness of Ruthie's small fingers. Finally my father spoke. "And may you watch over our Eliza, who will be far from our sight. Keep her safe and bring her back to us soon."

I blinked away a tear. "Amen," whispered my mother.

The talk over breakfast was about the Fellowship meeting that afternoon and a lumber shipment that was due on Monday. Except for the change in the mealtime prayer, everything was ordinary. I realized that this was how things would be after I was gone. My family would take up their lives without me. The thought was a tiny ache.

While Ruthie cleared the table, my mother and I stood in our positions at the sink. The only sounds were the clinking of dishes and the swish of soapy water. Our movements were smooth and rehearsed, like a dance. When the last dish was settled in the cupboard, my mother turned to me.

"It'll be a long time before we stand this way again," she said.

I couldn't find an answer.

"I've been trying to think of some wise words to give you before you leave."

I listened, trying to memorize the pitch and flow of her voice.

She dried her hands and walked over to the big desk in the corner, where quilting and woodworking orders filled the cubbyholes. I watched as she picked up a black three-ring notebook from the desktop. "Before I left for my rumspringa, my mother told me to keep a record of my life in the English world so I would always have the memory." She ran her fingers over the glossy black cover and looked at me. "Last night I filled my old notebook with fresh paper so you can keep your own record."

I took the worn notebook from her. It felt like a formal moment, so I responded in a formal way. "I'll write in it every day," I said, but I didn't think I meant it.

Just then, the sound of gravel crunching in the driveway

shivered through me. "I guess it's time," my mother said. While I tucked the notebook into the canvas bag, my mother called to my father and James.

I opened the front door as Mrs. Aster walked up the steps. My mother stepped quietly onto the porch.

"I can only guess how hard this must be for you," Mrs. Aster said. When my mother didn't answer, she continued. Her voice sounded careful, as though she were shopping for each word. "I don't know Eliza very well yet, but I know she will add so much to our home."

My mother's words were crisp. "As she has to ours."

"Yes, well," said Mrs. Aster, "my husband and I will care for her like she is a member of our own family."

"I know you will," my mother said, as my father and James bounded up the porch steps. While my father shook hands with Mrs. Aster, James and I carried my bags to the car, and I watched as he settled them in the trunk.

Closing the trunk, James turned to me. His straw hat was tilted back a bit on his head. He had the smooth, clean-shaven face of unmarried Amish men. After marriage, he'd stop shaving and his beard would grow thick and wild, like our father's. I knew that he was courting Helen, and I wondered if I'd learn news of his engagement while I was away.

James glanced at the adults on the porch before turning back to me. He spoke in a fierce whisper. "Try everything, do everything," he said. "This is the only chance you'll get."

I wrapped my arms around his neck. "Thanks for everything," I said.

Mrs. Aster came around to the driver's door and sat down behind the steering wheel. "Take all the time you need," she called.

Ruthie was next. I squeezed her so tightly that our hearts pounded against each other. "Be a big help to Mama," I said. She nodded through a silent stream of tears.

I looked up to see my parents standing side by side on the porch. I stepped over to my mother. "Try their ways," she told me, "but remember ours." I nodded and hugged her.

"Our Eliza, all grown up," my father said. I felt the bristles of his beard against my cheek as we embraced. There was a tightness in my chest that made it hard to take a deep breath. I wanted to say something to him for all he had done to make this happen, but the words were clogged up inside of me. "I love you, Eliza," he said. "Take that with you on your journey."

"I love you, too" I whispered.

My parents seemed to shrink as I headed to the car, taking quick backward glances at the porch. James and Ruthie were there now, too, and I was suddenly glad that I had said good-bye to Margaret at the party. The thought of looking at my entire family congregated together without me was too hard to bear.

At the car I fumbled with the metal handle until the heavy door swung toward me. Mrs. Aster leaned over and helped me fasten the seat belt across my shoulder. "How do I open the window?" I asked.

She pointed to a switch on the door and showed me how to hold it down. The window lowered as though by magic, and I leaned out, waving to my family, blinking the blurriness from my eyes. The porch was a tangle of raised arms, and everyone called to me at once, so I couldn't make out the individual words.

"Are you ready to leave?" Mrs. Aster's voice was gentle. I nodded.

As the car backed down the driveway, I felt the gravel grinding beneath the wheels, and I watched the figures on the porch grow smaller. I leaned back and closed my eyes. I liked the way the top of the seat cradled the back of my head. Taking slow breaths, I settled into the rhythm of the ride.

"I hate good-byes," said Mrs. Aster.

My eyes were still closed. "So do I," I said, thinking for a minute before adding, "But I love hellos."

11

When I opened my eyes, the scenery was rolling past my window. The neighboring farms shot by with a smooth speed I had never experienced before. Fresh summer breezes burst through the open window, flinging my ponytail behind me. I took a breath and tried to put a name to the way I felt at that moment. Full, I thought. I felt positively full.

Just then, my window hummed its way back up, and I looked at it in surprise. "If you don't mind, I'm going to turn on the air-conditioning," Mrs. Aster said.

In a few minutes, I felt a chilling breeze blowing across my bare arms even though the windows remained closed. A quiet settled over the car and an artificial smell enveloped us. Then Mrs. Aster reached forward and pressed a raised circle that made music burst into the car. It was different from the music at the Friday night parties. What came out of those borrowed boxes only pulsed in the background of our gatherings. Nothing sounded distinctive. Now I was hearing a song with words. Confusing phrases flew past me—

something about a dance in a jailhouse and some rocks. But they were cheerful sounds even though I didn't understand them. Mrs. Aster's fingers tapped the steering wheel, and occasionally her voice chimed in with the music. I watched, smiling. I hadn't been gone for very long, but I was already far from home.

When the song ended, replaced by a man reading the news, she turned down the sound on the radio.

"Thank you again for offering me this job, Mrs. Aster," I said.

"I'm so happy it worked out. And I'm going to insist that you call me Rachel."

I nodded, even though I wasn't sure that would be possible.

Then a little laugh escaped her. "I feel a bit strange, though. Like I've gone on vacation and stolen something."

"Well, you're not stealing me," I said. "It's more like you're borrowing me."

"How do you feel about being borrowed?"

I let the question settle into my mind for a moment before I answered. "Ever since I was little I've had this funny feeling. Like I'm in a tiny world and there's this big world all around me that I can't see. Now I'm finally being allowed in."

Rachel took her eyes off the road for a moment and smiled at me. "I hope it lives up to your expectations."

I grinned. "It couldn't possibly."

Soon I stopped feeling amazed at the speed and comfort of the car. There was so much I wanted to know about the life I was about to step into, and Rachel was eager to fill me in. The music was now just a vibrating hum, almost lost by the blowing sound of the air conditioner.

At first I was cautious about asking questions, but Rachel encouraged them, and her world opened up to me as the white lines on the road glided beneath the car, putting home farther away.

I learned that Rachel's husband was named Sam and that he was a kind of doctor who didn't take care of sick people. Instead he talked to people about their problems and tried to make them feel happier. Over lunch at a diner off the highway, Rachel talked about the job she used to have before her children were born. She said she worked in "Human Resources." And now she was back in college, finishing up what she called her master's degree, in anthropology. When I asked what that meant, she just laughed and said, "Something I'll never find a job working in."

Back in the car after lunch, I automatically pulled the seat belt across my chest as though I'd done it my whole life. As the metal buckle clicked into place with a satisfying snap, I found myself smiling.

When we got nearer to Rachel's town, I noticed a change in the scenery. Soon after we got out of Iowa, there was no more buggy traffic. Only cars and trucks were on the road, the absence of horses allowing them to go faster. Billboards lined the highway, each selling a product. Closer to Rachel's house, our surroundings grew greener, but there was a starkness I couldn't figure out. Then, as we turned off the highway into a neighborhood, I realized what was missing. There were no clotheslines. No dresses or pants or shirts fluttered in the breeze. Clothing here dried privately, in a machine, not outside for the world to see.

Rachel's words interrupted my thoughts. "We're almost there. Just another block." The houses, all similar-looking, were placed in a neat row, one next to the other. Most were made of white material that looked too smooth and neat to be wood, with black pavements leading up to garages. Each house had an identical square of grass in front, some cluttered with bikes and children's toys.

Rachel turned onto one of the black stretches of pavement and pressed a button that I hadn't noticed before. With a rumbling noise, the garage door lifted from the ground and disappeared into the ceiling of the garage. Inside, I could see another car that looked like a sleek truck. Long-handled machines and a variety of tools hung from the walls.

Parking the car in the driveway, Rachel switched off the engine and turned to me. "Welcome home," she said.

As we walked around to the back of the car and lifted my bags out of the trunk, the front door burst open and two children scrambled over to us. Rachel wrapped her arms around a boy and a girl, then pointed to me. "Janie, Ben, this is Eliza. She's your new nanny." I bent down until I was face-to-face with the children. They smelled like chewing gum. Ben was a spindly-looking boy, all knees and elbows, almost a full head taller than his sister. His hair, a shock of black curls, was tucked under a backward cap. Janie was softer, with round blue eyes and tumbling black hair. She smiled at me in a politely curious way. Ben stared down at his sneaker, tapping the driveway. "She doesn't look like Missy," he said, his words low and mumbly.

"That's because she's not Missy," Rachel said firmly. "She's Eliza. We've been over this, Ben. Missy graduated from college and she got a new job. She isn't our nanny anymore."

"Does this one know about baseball?" he asked, still looking down.

"This one has a name," said Rachel sternly. She looked at me. "We're working on manners."

"That's okay," I said, but I was thinking that this job might be harder than I thought.

Rachel picked up my duffel, handing me the canvas bag, and we walked through the garage to go inside the house, with Janie and Ben following us.

My first sight of Rachel's home was all black and white—like the country newspaper, or the tile floor of the dry goods store. On the stark whiteness of the wall was a collection of photographs, each picture showing the children sitting in odd, formal postures in front of a white drapery, and surrounded by a shiny black frame. Like all Amish children, I had been taught that photographs steal a person's soul. My friends and I sometimes looked at newspapers and magazines, joking about the people in the pictures walking around without souls. But this was the first time I had seen photographs of people I actually knew. It was arresting, all those frozen moments in time. I couldn't look away.

Just then, Rachel's husband came in and stretched out his hand to me. "Rachel told me all about you, Eliza. Welcome to our family." I shook his smooth, uncalloused hand.

Sam had a smiley kind of face. His eyes were the color of maple bark, and the lines at the corners deepened when he grinned. His hair was the same black as the children's, but with a few flecks of gray. His beard was trimmed and tidy, not like the wild, tangled beards on Amish men, which I always associated with a long marriage.

"Come on, Eliza," Rachel said. "We'll show you the house." The children were galloping around their mother's heels, and I pushed away a feeling that I might not belong here. These people seemed to fit together so well. I wondered if I'd ever feel a part of them.

I followed Rachel and the children through the black-and-white hallway into the kitchen. The light shining down from the ceiling brightened the gleaming white cabinets. Before Janie took my hand and pulled me to the next room, I could make out an assortment of machines on the counter. I was anxious to learn what they did.

My feet moved from white tile to a soft carpet the color of mushrooms. "This is the family room," Rachel said. "It's where we spend most of our time."

The room was shimmering with bold shades of purples and blues and greens and pinks. My mother would say the colors were too loud, but I thought they looked just right. Like a brilliant bowl of fruit. The plump furniture faced a wall that held a big screen and a variety of black boxes with knobs.

Upstairs, Janie's bed was covered with stuffed animals, and the bookshelves were lined with dolls. The walls of Ben's room were decorated with elongated felt triangles, some with the names of cities, and others with words like "Cubs" and "White Sox" and "Yankees." I had a feeling that "Yankees" didn't have the same meaning as the word my friends and I used.

"Here's your room," said Rachel, and the two children scuffled with each other for the honor of opening the door. A bed the size of the one I shared with Ruthie faced the door, covered with a brightly colored quilt. I recognized the log cabin pattern, the first one I'd learned when I started quilting.

Rachel was beside me now. "I bought that from an Amish woman when I was in Lancaster a few years ago," she said. I hadn't expected to travel all the way to the English world to sleep under an Amish quilt, but there was something comforting in the idea.

A dresser stood on the left-hand wall. My father would disapprove of the way the wood had been painted a dusky blue, but I liked it. Beside the bed was a small table made of the same blue wood. The lamp on the table was electric, and I smiled inside at the thought of reading late into the night. Next to the lamp was a clock that had bright red numbers instead of hands. A writing table with drawers and cubbyholes, like a smaller version of the desk at home, sat beneath the window.

"I hope you like it," said Rachel.

"It's the prettiest room I've ever seen," I said. Rachel's husband stepped in and set my duffel and canvas bag near the dresser. "Thank you, Mr. Aster," I said. The children giggled, and I corrected myself. "I'm sorry. It's Dr. Aster, right?" The children giggled again, and I saw Rachel and Sam glance at each other and smile.

"No, it's not that," he said. "Aster is Rachel's name. She didn't change her last name when we got married." Once again I felt the thrill of surprise. "My last name is Morgan, and that's the name the kids have, too. But please call me Sam."

"Let's give Eliza a chance to get settled," said Rachel.

"Wait," I said, remembering the gifts in my bag. "I have something for Ben and Janie." Janie clamored over to me, holding her hands out greedily as I reached into my bag. Ben stood a few feet away, but he looked just as eager. I handed them each their packages and watched as Janie ripped apart the tissue wrapping and stared at its contents.

"It's a doll," I said, surprised that I had to explain. Kate's mother made them in the traditional Amish style and sold them to the gift shops in town. This doll was wearing a purple dress, white apron, and black traveling bonnet.

Janie turned the doll over and over in her hands, and then looked up at me. "Where is she?"

Then I understood. "Amish dolls don't have faces," I explained.

Janie nodded solemnly, then brightened. "Can I draw one on?"

"No, you may not," said Rachel, plucking the doll from Janie's hands. "We'll put this on your shelf with your doll collection. Thank you, Eliza. She's beautiful."

I turned my attention to Ben, who was ripping the paper from his gift. When the wrapping slipped off to reveal a hand-carved wooden train car, he smiled. Then he turned the car upside down and peered at its smooth bottom. "How does it work?"

"Well," I said, "it doesn't actually do anything. It's just . . ." I stopped, disappointed at the children's reactions. Ben and Janie rushed off, leaving Rachel holding both of their gifts. "I guess they didn't understand the presents," I said.

"One day they will. They have a few things to learn."

"So do I," I said.

CHAPTER

 12

It only took me a few minutes to unpack. I folded my new shirts and shorts and settled them neatly in two of the blue drawers. The blouses and the khaki pants hung in the closet, along with my Amish clothes. I looked at the purple dress, white apron, and the crisp white kapp draped over a wire hanger. Quietly, I slid them to the back of the closet and closed the door.

I set Daniel's bird on the bedside table and placed the black notebook from my mother on the writing desk. I put the quilting bag in a corner of the closet. My mother had insisted that I keep my hands busy, but quilting was the last thing on my mind now. I looked around the room with a sense of contentment. For the first time in my life I would have a room all to myself, and the realization made me feel rich.

In the bathroom that I would share with the children, I put away my toothbrush, comb, and hair bands. As I closed the drawer, Rachel called up to me that she was ready to leave for the grocery store, and I hurried downstairs. For this trip we were taking the other car that I had noticed parked in the garage when we arrived. Rachel called it a minivan, but there was nothing mini about it. I noticed that Rachel did not carry a basket over her arm, and I wondered where she would put her groceries.

The store was a short distance away, and Rachel parked in a row of other cars that looked the same as the minivan. As we approached the entrance, a closed set of double doors greeted me. I knew from my visits to town that I was supposed to walk toward them until the doors opened. "Ben used to call these the *magic doors*," said Rachel. "The kids used to love to come with me just to watch the doors open and close."

"And now?" I asked as Rachel reached for the handle of a metal cart with wobbly wheels, instead of a basket, to hold her groceries.

"I guess the excitement wore off," she said with a shrug. I trotted to keep up with her as she walked down the first aisle, tossing a variety of cans and boxes and jars into the bottom of her cart. She didn't look closely at any of the items that she chose, and I wondered how she could decide so casually about her purchases.

At home, my mother and I went almost every day with a carefully written list to the market owned by the Krueger family. After we walked through the four sections, placing into the basket only those items that we don't grow in our garden or preserve in jars or purchase from the Yoders' dairy farm, Mr. Krueger would nod at us from under the brim of his hat and make a neat list of numbers on his yellow pad.

Rachel's pace quickened, and I soon lost track of how many

aisles we had gone down, passing other shoppers with barely a glance. I tried not to gape at the scales, where glowing green numbers revealed the weight instead of a pointing needle, or the rows of iceboxes that kept food in a suspended state somewhere between fresh and spoiled.

Back at the house, Rachel put away the groceries, and I went into the family room to check on Ben and Janie. They were sitting in front of the television set, each holding a small black object and staring at the screen. My eyes raced to keep up with the moving images. Loud bouncy music came from somewhere behind the screen.

"What are you playing?" I asked.

"It's Mario," said Janie, her eyes focused straight ahead.

"But we don't have any extra controls, so you'll have to play later," said Ben.

I watched as they pressed colorful buttons on what they called the "controls." Every now and then one of the children would moan or cheer, and I realized that by pressing these buttons they had power over what was happening on the television screen. On the TV, bright cars carrying odd-looking characters raced around a twisting road, occasionally crashing into an obstacle that appeared out of nowhere. "I'll go see if your mother needs help with the dinner," I said. But the children didn't seem to hear me.

In the kitchen, I watched Rachel moving tentatively. At home, the house would be filled with the sounds and smells of meal preparation by now. "Can I help you with dinner?" I asked.

"That would be great," said Rachel, pointing to the refrigerator. "You can make the salad."

I scanned the refrigerator shelves and pulled open a drawer. I took out two tomatoes and noticed that they were hard and cold, not like the red tomatoes that my mother plucks from a vine in the yard and keeps on the windowsill. I searched for a head of lettuce, but instead I found a clear sealed bag marked with the words "Instant Salad." Pulling open the crinkly bag, I poured its contents into the wooden salad bowl Rachel had left out for me, watching the tiny shreds of lettuce, cabbage, and carrots collide. Some of the lettuce was brown-edged, and the salad had an odd smell, like plastic.

Later, I set the table while Rachel cooked—or, rather, a small oven called a "microwave" did most of the cooking. All through the process of meal preparation, no pots or pans ever appeared on the stove, and no cooking smells seeped through the air. Instead, Rachel kept reaching into the freezer and emptying bags into little white dishes. The contents made clinking noises when they landed in the bowls. Rachel placed the bowls, one after another, into the little oven, pressed some buttons, and waited for three loud beeps, which told her the food had been cooked.

Seated at the table between Ben and Janie, I started to reach my hands out to my sides, as I did at the beginning of every meal. But Sam was already setting food on his plate, and Ben was asking for the corn, so I quickly dropped my hands into my lap, hoping they hadn't noticed. I raced through the prayer in my head before accepting the bowl of corn from Ben, its kernels scraped cleanly off the cob by unseen hands.

Picking my way through the morsels on my plate, I felt bombarded by newness. Ben and Janie were arguing over what television show they would watch after dinner. Then they argued over whose turn it was to pick the show. Sam told them that if they didn't stop arguing, they wouldn't be able to watch any show. The voices swirled around me as though they were coming from a faraway place.

"Do you like the chicken?" Rachel asked. "I know I'm not much of a cook."

I hadn't recognized the white ovals on my plate as chicken. There were no bones, and all the pieces looked alike. I tried not to think of what they had to do to this bird to extract the meat in this smooth, neat shape.

"It's fine," I answered. "I'm just not very hungry."

"It's been a long day for you, hasn't it, Eliza?" It was Sam's voice now, low and soothing. They were all watching me, waiting for me to say something. Ben and Janie stopped eating, and their spirited bickering quieted. Sam and Rachel exchanged glances.

I nodded. "A good day," I said. And Sam smiled.

After dinner, Sam carried his plate to the sink before picking up the newspaper and heading out of the kitchen. The children disappeared into the family room. At home we'd never be able to play until everything was cleaned up. English children have a nice life, I thought.

After the dinner dishes were stacked neatly in the dishwasher, a vibrant humming told me that a machine would now do the work that my mother and I did side by side each night, by the light of a kerosene lantern, our aprons wet with dishwater. Rachel didn't even wear an apron. Maybe nothing messy ever happened in this kitchen.

Rachel sighed. "We're finally done," she said, as though we had been working for hours. "I'm going into my office for a while. You're free to do whatever you want." So I drifted from the edges of one room to another, listening to the distinctive sounds that floated from each space.

In the family room, the children were watching television. I had seen TV before, when I was younger and my mother used to take me to cleaning jobs at the homes of English families. But I could never understand where all that laughter was coming from. Sometimes there were only two people in sight, yet after someone said something unexpected, hundreds of voices chuckled loudly in response.

Janie and Ben lay on the floor, balanced on their elbows, faces tilted up toward the screen. I sat on the couch, excited to see what the children saw in that box.

"Who's that man?" I asked, pointing to a clean-shaven man with a lot of dark hair.

"That's Uncle Jesse," said Janie, without turning from the screen. "He's the brother of the children's mother. She died."

"What did she die of?" I tried not to sound shocked. The children on TV didn't seem to be mourning a dead mother.

Ben shrugged. "I don't know. Maybe a car accident. Maybe cancer."

"And who's that?" I asked.

"That's Joey," said Janie. "He's the friend who lives with them."

"Watch this," said Ben. "This is where Stephanie plays the guitar in a talent show, but she didn't practice, so she's really bad."

"How do you know what's going to happen?" I asked.

"We've seen this one already," said Janie. "It's a rerun."

"Well, if you've already seen it . . ." I began. But my voice dropped off. There was something riveting about what the children were watching. Everyone on the television was so clever—even the youngest girl, who wasn't as old as Janie. I found myself laughing when Stephanie messed up her performance, and I felt a little satisfied when her father talked to her later about the importance of practicing if you want to get good at something. When the show ended, everything was orderly and settled.

The children stayed in their positions on the floor to watch the show that was coming on next, but I wanted to see what Sam and Rachel were doing.

Tiptoeing away from the TV, I slid along the hallway connecting the family room to the living room. Sam looked up and nodded at me before returning his gaze to the newspaper. Music was flowing into the room from an unseen place, as though it seeped in from the walls. He looked so peaceful with his reading and his music. I tried to think if I had ever seen my father without chores to do. I wanted to tell him about the contentment in this room.

In the office, Rachel sat in front of a machine with lettered keys, a larger version of the one she had been using at the inn. "Come on in," she said. "Have you ever seen a computer before?"

I shook my head and stepped beside Rachel's chair, watching as her fingers sent words marching across the screen in neat rows.

"I'm sending an e-mail to my mother," Rachel said. "She lives in Florida."

"What's e-mail?" I asked.

"It's short for *electronic mail*." Rachel's right hand cupped over an oval shape resting on a square pad. "This is called the mouse."

She pressed the mouse and the words on the screen disappeared. "There," she said, a note of satisfaction in her voice. "Now, the next time my mother turns on her computer, this e-mail will be waiting for her." She turned to me. "Do you want to see some other things you can do on the computer?"

"Yes," I said, my voice bursting with interest.

"Well, I can't begin to tell you about the Internet tonight. We'll need more time for that. But I can show you word processing so you can write letters." Soon I was sitting in the armless chair, with Rachel behind me giving instructions. I learned how to make letters, words, and sentences appear on the screen, and I learned how to erase them with the press of a button.

It was great fun. I loved the clicking sound of the keyboard and the sight of the words appearing on the screen. I discovered that the keys weren't placed in alphabetical order, so I had to hunt for each word, letter by letter. After Rachel showed me how to print, I watched a white sheet of paper chug smoothly through a machine next to the computer. When it was spit out onto a tray, I picked up the paper and saw all the words that had been on the screen now printed cleanly on the page.

"Would you like to write a letter to your parents?" Rachel asked.

Shaking my head, I said, "No, thank you. I think I'd rather use pencil and paper."

Rachel opened a drawer and pulled out a yellow pad of lined paper and a box of pencils. "Envelopes and stamps are in this drawer, too. Help yourself."

"Thank you," I said, hugging the pad of paper to my chest.

"As a matter of fact," continued Rachel, "I won't need any help with the children tonight. You can write your letter now."

I waited for Rachel to leave me alone in the office before I set the pad on the desk and prepared to write. The pencil's smooth ridges pressed against the side of my finger in a familiar way, and I tried to decide what to tell my parents about this first day away from home. Then I laid the pencil on top of the pad of paper. I didn't want to share this magic with anyone just yet. I was finally here, and home was far away. For now I wanted to keep it that way.

CHAPTER

13

Red glowing numbers on the small square clock told me that it was 6:30, the time I woke up every morning. At home this was a time when bare feet smacked on the wood floor and the house sang with comfortable morning noises. Now I was alone in a room that rang with silence.

In the closet, an array of choices greeted me, and I pulled on the blue jeans and the T-shirt with blue-and-white stripes. In the bathroom, I brushed my teeth and washed my hands and face. Combing my thick tangle of hair, I searched the mirror for a change in my reflection. It was strange to see myself without the stiff white kapp, but the rest of me was pretty much the same. I had expected a fancier girl to return my stare.

Downstairs, the rooms were dark and quiet except for the occasional humming noises that I had learned were part of electricity. Now I had a new feeling to think about. Idleness. For the first time in my life I had nothing at all to do.

Stepping over to the refrigerator, I pulled open the door and let the cold and light flood over me. I scanned the shelves stocked with food that no one in the family had raised, grown, or prepared. I decided to make the family's breakfast so it would be ready for them when they woke up.

I had to hunt through refrigerator and cupboards, but I finally found the ingredients to make pancakes. While I mixed the batter and prepared the frying pan, I wondered why there were still no sounds from upstairs. I knew that Sam had to go to work and the children would be going somewhere called day camp. I poured the batter to form two circles and listened to the hiss that meant the pan was hot enough. I slid the spatula under the pancakes and flipped them.

When the platter was piled high with steaming pancakes, and the kitchen smelled rich and sweet, there was still no sign of Sam or Rachel or the children. I fumbled with the buttons on the oven until I figured out how to turn it on and set the temperature. Then I set the plate of pancakes in the oven to keep them warm until the family came downstairs. I wanted to make coffee, but I wasn't sure how to work the coffeepot that sat in its own stand. Instead, I emptied the dishwasher, feeling the squeak of the clean dishes as I put them away.

Still, no one in the family was awake. I realized that I would have to learn the peculiar schedule of this place. I helped myself to two of the pancakes and, after whispering the words of the mealtime prayer, ate my breakfast. It was the first time I'd had ever had a meal alone.

After I finished eating, and cleared my dishes, the children came downstairs with noisy thumps, Janie clutching a frayed blue blanket. Ben was dressed in shorts and a shirt bearing the same letters as one of the triangles on his bedroom wall. "What's that smell?" he asked.

"It's pancakes, but I think they're dried out now."

"We have cereal for breakfast," said Ben. "I have Frosted Flakes and Janie has Cap'n Crunch." It sounded like a command.

I opened the pantry door, where I had seen Rachel put away boxes with those words on them. "What about your parents? What do they eat?"

"Daddy doesn't eat breakfast," said Janie, settling herself at the table and spreading the blue blanket across her bare legs.

"And your mom?" I asked, pouring cereal into bowls.

"She stands over the kitchen sink and eats a bagel," said Ben.

I turned off the oven and set a bowl of cereal in front of each child. The milk I poured looked thin and bluish, not like the white, creamy stuff from the Yoder's dairy. When I was done, Ben watched me as though waiting for something.

"Janie needs the cereal box, and I need the sports page."

"Excuse me?"

"Janie likes to look at the cereal box while she eats, and I read the sports page. Missy always had them on the table for us." Then he added, "The newspaper's in the driveway."

These children know what they want, I thought, as I set the cereal box on the table for Janie and stepped out the front door to pick up the newspaper. Back in the kitchen, I rummaged through the sections until I found the sports page. Ben was eyeing me, waiting for the paper, but I held it in my hands for a moment, looking at him.

"Is there something you'd like to say?" I asked.

Ben paused before saying, "Can I please have the sports page?" His voice was a grunt, but it was a start. I handed it to him and stood over the table, waiting.

"Thank you," he said, with a gust of a sigh.

"Oh, Eliza, what smells so good?" Rachel stood in the kitchen doorway wearing a T-shirt that hung almost to her knees. Her hair was fuzzy and uneven-looking, and there were dark smudges under her eyes. My mother always came downstairs looking crisp, wearing her dress, apron, and kapp even in the darkest morning hours.

"Well, it was going to be a pancake breakfast. But I'm afraid I started too early, so it went to waste."

Rachel smiled. "I guess I should have warned you that we're not morning people." Now Rachel was calling to the children. "Finish your cereal. It's almost time for the bus." For the next few minutes the house hummed with activity. Sam came downstairs wearing a jacket and necktie and carrying what looked like a small suitcase. He swigged down a glass of orange juice and hugged each child before heading out the door.

Following Rachel's instructions, I took Janie upstairs to help her get dressed. Her drawers burst with clothes, and it took her a long time until she decided on a shirt with a picture of a smiling mermaid.

In the kitchen, I helped Rachel pack the children's backpacks, each with a bathing suit, towel, lunch box, sunscreen, and water bottle. At the sound of a horn outside, Ben shouted, "Bus!" and both children ran through the kitchen, pulling their backpacks over their shoulders. I watched as they climbed the steps and waved from the windows until the orange bus was out of sight.

Later, I sat at the desk in my room, staring at the first page of my empty journal, wondering how I could find words to describe the magic of this place. *I am a tourist,* I wrote at the top of the page. I had told my mother that I'd write in the journal every day, but now that I was here I wanted to be doing things, not just writing about them. So I closed the journal and set off to begin my work for the day. Before Rachel had left for the library she'd made a list of chores to do around the house, but I knew they wouldn't take all day to complete. I wondered what I'd do during my idle hours.

I picked up the dusting supplies that Rachel had left for me, and headed into Sam and Rachel's room to begin my work. Rachel's dresser was dotted with small framed pictures. Most were of the children, looking more casual than the photographs I had seen when I first arrived: Ben holding a baseball bat, Janie standing in a little pink skirt with her arms raised in a circle over her head. One was a large picture of Rachel and Sam on what must have been their wedding day. Rachel was wearing a sparkling white gown with a flowing veil. She cradled a bunch of long-stemmed pink roses and looked adoringly at Sam, who was dressed all in black. I had read about English weddings, but this was the first picture I had ever seen of a bride and groom.

The children were younger in the pictures than they were now, and I marveled at how a photograph freezes a person in time. I had no idea what I had looked like when I was five, or what my parents had looked like when they got married. For the first time I felt a longing to see my past.

Just then the doorbell rang, and I dropped the dust cloth and hurried downstairs, trying to remember if Rachel had told me to expect any visitors. Through the glass pane I saw what my friends would call a "Yankee boy." I hesitated for a moment before opening the door.

The boy's face had a look of mild surprise when he saw me. "Hey, can you open the garage door so I can get the lawn mower out?"

I hesitated, unsure if I was supposed to let this boy into Sam and Rachel's garage. "It's okay," said the boy. "Rachel's expecting me." Then he added, "I'm Josh Nathan. I live down the block. Are you the babysitter?" His voice sounded like the teenage boys I knew at home, but a bit more twangy, his vowels drawn out.

I stood in the doorway, my fingers tightening until the door-knob pressed a circle into my palm. *Be careful around the English boys,* my father had warned me. *They're not all proper.*

"Nobody else is home right now," I said, and then wondered if that was something I shouldn't have admitted. The boy stayed planted on the front stoop, his hands stuffed into the back pockets of his blue jeans. His hair was dark and spiky, as though it had been chopped with a meat cleaver. A small silver hoop glinted in his left earlobe. He wore a black T-shirt with a picture of a long-haired man in wire-rim glasses, the word "Imagine" etched in a vertical row.

"Well, do you at least have a name?" he asked.

I swallowed. "Eliza Miller."

"A nice old-fashioned name. Are you an old-fashioned girl?"

A smile crept to the corners of my mouth. "I guess you could say that." He seemed nice enough. My fingers relaxed their hold on the doorknob. I wondered who the bespectacled man was on the boy's shirt and what he imagined.

"So, if I can just get into the garage, I'll be out of your way."

In the garage, I found the button and pressed it, startled by the instant rumbling sound as the door crept up on its hinges, filling the space with dusty sunlight. Returning to the cool of the house, I watched from the front window as Josh walked up and down the lawn, making neat rows in the grass. Our mower at home had big blades that turned, and James worked hard to push it, while this machine seemed to be leading Josh across the lawn.

I went back to the dusting, finishing the bedrooms, living room, and family room before the doorbell rang again. Josh was on the front stoop, his T-shirt damp with sweat. "All done," he said. "I put the mower back in the garage."

"Thank you." I turned to leave, but then I heard his voice again.

"So, what's your story?" he asked.

"Excuse me?"

"I mean, where are you from? I've never seen you at school."

"I'm from Iowa," I said. "I'll be living here for the summer to help Mrs. Aster with the children."

"Cool," said Josh. "Then I guess I'll be seeing you."

"Okay," I said, and waited for him to step off the stoop. But he was still there, looking at me in a measured way.

Then he said, "Is it okay if I come in for a pop?"

I stepped back and let him come in, assuming that Rachel wouldn't mind. Josh walked ahead of me to the kitchen, his long legs making easy strides.

"I guess you know the way," I said as he opened the refrigerator and helped himself to a can of pop.

"Yeah, my parents are good friends of Sam and Rachel's. I practically grew up in this house." He sat at the kitchen table and opened the can, slugging down its contents. I sat down in the chair across from him. I couldn't figure out what to do with my hands, so I hid them in my lap. Josh was looking at me, and I thought it might be my turn to speak.

"So," I said, searching for a conversation, "you work mowing lawns?"

"I'm trying to buy a car," he said. "So I'm spending the summer doing everything I can to make some cash. My main job is at the Apple store, but I also mow lawns in the neighborhood."

Somehow, I couldn't picture this boy selling apples.

"So," he asked, "how do you like it here?"

"Well, it's only been one day, but so far I like it."

"And you'll like Sam and Rachel," he said. "For older people, they're actually pretty cool."

There was that word again that he had said before. I'd heard the children say it, too. "Cool?" I asked.

Josh pushed back in his chair so the two front legs rose up in the air and the back legs balanced his weight with a barely perceptible sway.

"Hey, you're *really* not from around here, are you?" he asked.

I shook my head, feeling a blush rising.

"It's hard to explain 'cool.' Cool people are part of the times; they live in the moment." He paused. "But sometimes people spend too much time trying to be cool. Which is *not* cool. Does that make sense?"

I nodded, knowing one fact with absolute certainty. I was not cool. I also knew something else. I liked the way this boy grinned.

"Sam and Rachel still go to rock concerts," Josh said. "In college they were Deadheads. They followed the Dead everywhere." I tried not to look as shocked as I felt. "You know," he added. "The Grateful Dead."

I looked at him, waiting for more of an explanation. The front legs of Josh's chair landed on the floor with a thud, and he looked at me for a long moment before he spoke. "You don't know what I'm talking about, do you?" There was no accusation in his voice, only a faint sense of wonder.

I shook my head. Josh's eyebrows slanted downward. "I don't get it. Iowa's not so far away."

I couldn't help smiling. "I guess I didn't mention that I'm Amish."

'Whoa!" he said, a word that sounded funny to me when there was no horse in front of us. "You mean the people who have no electricity?"

"That's us."

"So no TV? No movies? No cars?"

"They're forbidden," I said, trying not to sound too serious. "But while I'm here, I'm allowed to live as you do."

"Well, we have a lot of work to do," Josh said. He got up from the table and headed toward the living room. I followed him, the casual way he said "we" sending a thrilling ripple across my chest.

"Here," he said, pointing to a spot on the living room rug. I sat down and twisted my legs pretzel style. He reached for a box on a lower shelf that was filled with flat squares. "My iPod needs charging, so we have to do this the old-fashioned way." Then he looked at me and said, "Well, that's fitting, isn't it?"

I nodded, pretending to understand. As I watched Josh rummage through the box, I realized that I was actually alone with a Yankee boy. This was definitely not Good Amish. But I wasn't nervous. I felt like a different person, a cool person.

"So," said Josh, "have you listened to any music at all?"

"I heard a little on the radio in Rachel's car on my way here.

And I've been to a few parties where music played in the background. But I didn't know much about what I was listening to."

"Okay," said Josh. "So we'll start with the basics. There are lots of different kinds of music, but the first thing you should learn about is rock. It started in the fifties, and there are a lot of different bands that play rock music."

"Is he in one of them?" I asked, pointing to the long-haired man on Josh's T-shirt.

Josh nodded with a sad smile. "He was," he said. "This is John Lennon. He was with the Beatles, pretty much the greatest band ever. He was all about world peace."

"Was?"

"Until some crazy guy shot him. It was a long time ago. Before I was born."

So, Josh wore the picture of a man he spoke of with reverence, but who had been dead his whole life. I wanted to know about feeling a passion so strong you needed to wear it for the world to see.

"Anyway," he said, "we'll work up to some newer stuff. But let's start with the classics. The Beatles, the Stones, Dylan." I tried to remember all the words he was saying. Josh went back to the flat squares and pulled one out. "Speaking of classic," he said, holding up a square with a picture of a colorful tongue protruding from a pair of blue lips. "Tell me what you think of this."

He opened up the flat box, pulled out a silvery circle, and placed it in the music machine. A sustained vibration burst into the room, and I kept hearing the same line over and over, the singer complaining about being unable to get satisfaction, the double negative bursting out unapologetically. His voice was loud and hoarse, as though he was frustrated and proud at the same time. Josh was watching me as I listened to the music. "You don't like this, do you?"

"Well, the words don't make sense to me, but there's something so lively about it. I feel like I want to sing along even though I don't understand it."

Josh smiled. "Yep," he said as he pressed a button that stopped the music. "That's rock." He returned to the box of flat squares, sorting through them one at a time, sometimes shaking his head and tossing one back, like a fish that was too small. "Here's one you'll like," he said, holding up a square that read, "Dylan & the Dead." I didn't like the picture of the gruesome-looking skeleton, but Josh was already opening the box, pulling out the silver circle, and placing it in the music machine. That circle had a name that I couldn't think of, something with two letters. Josh interrupted my thoughts.

"Dylan's more than a musician," he explained as he pressed a button. "He's a poet."

I listened to another wave of music flowing from the machine. This time the lyrics about heaven's door rang out with clarity. I grew still as the words floated through the air, repeating again and again until they rose silently to my lips like a familiar greeting. I felt a rustling on the rug and looked up to see Josh gathering himself in the same pretzel shape facing me, his knees almost touching mine.

A warm tickly sensation crept into my knees, as though we were actually touching.

The music continued. The mix of voices, high and low, sounded friendly, like people coming together to share a task. It was exhilarating yet tender. I felt my head nod at intervals, determined by some unseen force. The crooning sounds swirled around me and through me. The sounds weren't coming from one place; they resonated from all over the room. I glanced up to see if Josh felt the same sensation. His eyes were closed and his right hand was curved into a loose fist, as though he were banging a hammer, his hand moving slightly each time I felt my own head nodding. My eyes traveled up from his imaginary hammer back to his face, to find his brown eyes staring at me. There was hopefulness in his expression, and I knew that the way I felt about the song was important to him.

"Did you like it?"

"Jah," I said. "It was such a happy sound."

"Jah?" he asked, a tease in his voice. "Is that the way they talk in Iowa?"

Just then, the front door swung open, and Rachel was framed in the doorway, her book bag over her shoulder. I worried that she wouldn't be happy to find me alone with a Yankee boy. But instead she smiled. "Well hi, Joshua. I was going to call and tell you about Eliza. But I see that you've met her on your own."

"Hi, Rachel," said Josh, his tone smooth and casual. "I hope you don't mind us listening to your CDs." CD, I thought. Those were the two letters.

"Of course not," said Rachel. "I hope you like our taste in music."

"Some of it," I said honestly. Josh and Rachel laughed, and I wondered if I'd said something wrong.

Josh stood up. "I've got to get back to work. I hope you enjoyed your lesson."

"I did," I said. "Thanks."

"Good," he said, walking toward the door. "Well, I'll see you around."

As Josh closed the door behind him, I thought of those words. *I'll see you around.* I hoped they were true.

CHAPTER

14

Over the next three days I slipped into the rhythm of life with this family. I let Ben teach me about baseball, and I taught him to bring in the newspaper in the mornings. I learned which book Janie had to hear right before she fell asleep, and she taught me to leave a cup of water on her nightstand in case she had a dream that made her thirsty. I learned what Sam liked to eat for dinner and when Rachel needed the children to be quiet so she could concentrate on her work. And I figured out how to work the television so I could watch the morning news when I was the only one awake.

And every afternoon when I was alone in the house, I listened to music. I marveled at how each CD produced a different sound, and how the two minutes a song lasted could tell a whole story. I loved the satiny bursts of noise that took charge of my limbs, so doing my chores was what I'd imagined dancing to be. I found myself singing along to songs about love and sadness and hope until my voice mixed with the musicians and I was a part of the music.

On Thursday of that first week, the doorbell rang after the

children left for camp. On the front stoop was Josh, his grin inching up his face. My heart knocked against my rib cage at the sight of him. "I've got some more music for us to listen to," he said. "Can I come in?"

I nodded and stepped aside. He was striding toward the living room the moment I opened the front door, his black backpack slung over one shoulder. By the time I caught up to him, he was bent over his open sack. I liked the idea that he had gathered these CDs for me. So maybe he had been thinking about me over these last three days. I knew that I was thinking about him.

I sat down on the floor, the backpack between us. He pulled out a CD and showed it to me before opening the case and putting the disc in the player. "Aerosmith," he said as music pulsed into the room.

I smiled, remembering another CD that Rachel had played for me. "I like the song 'Dream On.'"

Josh dropped the case with a tiny clattering sound. When he picked it up he smiled at me, looking both surprised and impressed. "You've been doing your homework." I nodded, a quivering feeling in my chest. "What else have you been listening to?"

"I really liked the Beatles." I watched Josh's grin widen.

"Oh, yeah," he said. "I knew you'd like them. Go on."

Pleased at Josh's response, I tried to remember names. "The Doors, The Clash, The Velvet Underground, Madonna, Stevie Wonder." Josh was still nodding, so I kept going, "Johnny Cash,

Jimi Hendrix, Janis Joplin, some kids called the Jacksons. There were five of them."

"All right." Josh's voice was filled with approval, like my teacher when I advanced a round in the spelling bee. With each correct word, the teacher smiled and nodded, and my throat and cheeks warmed, just as they did now.

"I think my favorite was Mr. Armstrong," I said.

Josh's brows rose for a second before he smiled with recognition. "Louis Armstrong?"

"Yes," I said. "His voice is like sandpaper. But it's smooth at the same time."

Now Josh drew out his "Yeah" so that it sounded like a very long word. "That's jazz, Eliza." I wasn't sure if that was good or bad, but Josh's smile took up his whole face. I swallowed back an unfamiliar sensation. It felt like pride.

I wanted this glowing feeling to last forever. "Rachel showed me her favorite CD, and I liked that one, too. Have you ever heard of Billy Joel?"

The smile slipped from Josh's face. "Oh, no." His voice was a groan. "Not Billy Joel."

Incorrect, the teacher had said when I forgot a letter. *Return to your seat.*

My heart pumped heat to my face. "What's wrong with Billy Joel?" I asked, trying to sound as though it didn't matter what he thought.

Josh's face had a sour look, like there wasn't enough sugar in his lemonade. "Let's just say nobody our age listens to him."

"Well, I'm sorry I had an original thought." The anger in my voice surprised me.

Josh flinched a bit, his eyes scanning me. "You're one to talk. Aren't you the people who have to dress alike?"

It was that age-old question about the Amish that my mother had answered a dozen times over apple pie on Stranger Night. I didn't want to talk about how dressing alike keeps us humble and prevents feelings of vanity and pride. So I just said, "Sure, we dress alike, but we're all different."

Josh nodded slowly, as though trying out this new idea. He said one word in response: "Cool." Then he picked up the backpack and continued rummaging through the discs.

"Cool?" I had expected an argument.

Josh set the pack aside. "Yeah," he said. "It's cool to be your own person without having to prove it with your clothes." He paused, seeming to mull over what he'd just said. "And, I guess if you want to listen to Billy Joel, that's okay." He turned to the CD player and inserted a disc. "Let me know what you think of this."

Josh replaced the Aerosmith CD with a new one and pressed the button, sending angry sounds pulsing into the room, sounds that were more like shouting than singing.

He looked at me. "What do you think of rap?"

"Not much."

"I get that. It's not for everyone," he said, turning it off. "And I shouldn't have said that about you guys dressing alike." He paused before adding, "I guess we've had our first fight." I didn't like the sound of that. He seemed so certain that there would be more.

"Wait a minute," he said, reaching into his backpack. "I have a song on my iPod that I think you'll like." He pulled out a black rectangle smaller than a deck of cards.

"What's that?"

"My entire music collection," he said. "There are thousands of songs in here."

I stared at the tiny device cupped in the palm of Josh's hand. It didn't seem possible that it held such riches. His thumb moved around a small circle, and I watched as words flowed down a tiny screen. Then he reached into the pack and pulled out what looked like a thin white wire with two white buttons dangling from the end. Josh fitted the end of the wire into the iPod and handed me one of the small buttons. I took it in my fingers, not knowing what to do with it. It felt hard and spongy at the same time. "We can listen together," said Josh. "We'll each take an earbud." Once again, something new had a name, and it pleased me. I watched as Josh put one of the earbuds into his ear.

As I reached to do the same, the thin wire went taut between us, and Josh scooted closer to me. The bud was in my ear now, and I realized that if we were both going to listen, we would have to be inches apart. I felt the warmth of Josh beside me, and a shiver coursed through me. His nearness was awkward and exciting and just a little bit indecent. But I didn't have too long to think about it because suddenly music was pouring directly into my ear. Words flowed through, sweet and smooth, about a blackbird with broken wings learning how to fly. It was poetry and music together. It made me think of Daniel's gift, and of my dreams to feel free in another place. I listened to the music and the words, and I felt the farness of home and the nearness of Josh. I couldn't move because then the music would stop. And I couldn't stay because I was too close to this boy who I didn't really know. But then I realized that I wanted to know him, so I chose to stay.

The song ended, and Josh took the bud out of his ear, and I took mine out too. We were still sitting in that same way, and with the song over, we didn't need to be this close to each other. I shifted a bit and faced him. "Did you like it?" Josh asked.

"I loved it. I feel like it's still playing inside my head."

Josh smiled. "Hey," he said. "Do they ever let you out of here? Maybe we can go to a movie together."

It was an effort for me to keep my voice calm. "I'd like that."

"Great," said Josh. "How about Saturday night? I can get my dad's car."

"I'll have to check with Mrs. Aster. But I think it should be all right."

"Is there anything special you want to see?" Josh asked.

A small laugh flew out of my lips. "Any movie would be special for me. I've never seen one."

"Shut up!" said Josh, but it didn't sound like he wanted me to be quiet. "So you've never seen *The Wizard of Oz* or *Star Wars* or *ET*?"

I shook my head. Then I remembered something about my mother's rumspringa. "I'd love to see *The Sound of Music*."

"Yeah, if we get into a time machine and go back like fifty years," said Josh, laughter shaking his words.

I looked down, embarrassed without knowing why.

"I'm sorry," said Josh. "*The Sound of Music* was from a long time ago. But we can rent it and watch it on TV if you want."

"Why don't you pick the movie and surprise me."

"Deal," said Josh. "Listen, I've got to go back to work. Call me after you talk to Rachel. She has my number." He said that in such an ordinary way. I hesitated for a minute. "What?" he said.

"I've never used a telephone before."

Josh shook his head back and forth in an exaggerated way. "Really? Are you for real?"

I had to admit that it was fun watching him wonder about me. "Yes, I'm real. And my family doesn't have a telephone."

Joshua laughed as he got to his feet and walked over to the table, picking up the phone from its base.

I paid careful attention as he cradled the phone in his hand, holding it out so I could see the lighted numbers arranged in a rectangle. "Now, everyone has a phone number," he explained. I watched him press a series of buttons, each creating a different beeping tone. When he was done, he reached out his hand and pressed the end of the phone lightly against my ear. I heard ringing sounds, more like a faint buzz than a bell. After three such sounds, I heard Josh's voice, not in the room, where he sat beside me, but from inside the phone itself. "Hi, you've reached the Nathans," he was saying. "We're not home right now. But leave a message after the beep, and we'll return your call." With that, his voice was replaced with a loud beep, and I pulled the phone away from my ear.

"You're supposed to leave me a message," Josh said. "That was voice mail. If the person you're calling isn't there, you leave a message and they call you back. Do you want to try it again?" I nodded, and this time Josh handed me the phone and told me which numbers to press. As I pressed the buttons, he took his cell phone out of his pocket. A moment after I pressed the last number, a musical sound came from the phone in Josh's hand. He signaled me to put the phone to my ear, and he flipped his phone open, silencing the music. "Hello?" he said, his phone pressed against his ear.

Now I heard his voice twice at the same time—in the room, next to me, and through the phone at my ear. I wasn't sure what to do next.

"Just say hello," Josh whispered.

I smiled. "Hello, Josh," I said slowly. Then I realized he was waiting for me to say more. "I'm glad you came over."

"Me too," he said, his voice a little too loud. "I'm going to work now, so call me later." He shut his phone with a snap and reached for the phone I was holding, showing me how to turn it off and put it back in the stand.

"I've gotta fly," he said. "But I'll write down my cell phone number for you, and you can call me whenever you want to talk."

He reached for the pen and paper that Rachel kept by the phone and jotted down a string of numbers. Then he looked at me in a thoughtful way. "I want to see it one day."

"See what?"

"The place where you live. I bet it's real peaceful."

I nodded. "It's definitely peaceful."

After Josh left, I thought that if the pressing of a sequence of numbers could bring the voice of Kate or Annie to my ear, I would be able to tell them my stories instead of writing them out in letters.

Staring down at the numbers that would connect me to Josh, I felt a twinge. Now that I was beginning to understand how to create the magic of this place, I wondered if I'd ever be able to get along without it.

CHAPTER

15

At first, Rachel's face had one of those eyebrow-raised smiles when I told her about my movie plans with Josh. Then she turned serious. "Your father talked to me about dating." We were in the kitchen, where I had become the cook. I realized that I didn't want to hear what my father had told her. I wanted to be here in this moment, not bound to the rules from home. I pressed a spatula into the ground beef until the meat hissed in the frying pan.

"Your father told me that you can go out if you're with people I know," Rachel continued. "So Josh passes that test. And that you should be home by midnight."

"I know," I said. "He told me the same rules."

Rachel looked thoughtful, almost nervous. She cleared her throat, and I waited, the spatula poised over the sizzling meat. "I don't want to go against what you're taught at home."

I looked up. "I'm not sure that the rules at home would work here," I said. I thought about the courting carriages and the barn parties, the boys calling for girls by shining a lantern or flashlight in their window. I turned off the stove and set the spatula on the counter. "Josh is only taking me to a movie. It's not like we're courting."

"Things move a little faster here, Eliza."

"Don't worry," I said. "I can take care of myself. It's not the first time I've been out with a boy. And anyway, Josh and I are going out together as friends. He isn't my. . ." I fumbled for the English word. "Boyfriend." When I thought of that word, a queasiness rushed through me. It was one thing to sit with Josh in Rachel's living room and listen to music. But we were going out to a place I'd never been. I tried not to think of all the mistakes I could make. "But thank you for being concerned about me, Mrs. . . ." I paused and shook my head. "I mean Rachel." It was nice to call Rachel by her first name. Her golden eyes crinkled into a smile.

With this conversation over, there was something else I wanted to ask her. I had spent my whole life hearing that the way I looked on the outside wasn't important. But now I knew that it was. "What do you think I should wear Saturday night?"

Rachel grinned. "It's been a long time since I was on a date," she said. "But after dinner I can help you pick something out."

Later that night, with the children settled in their favorite positions on the couch, laughing at the predicaments of an imaginary family, Rachel and I stood before my open closet door.

In *Seventeen* magazine, the women's clothing looked like artwork. I was realizing that there were clothes for different occasions and for different girls. I thought of Jess and Caroline, and how comfortable they looked in their clothing. My own wardrobe, which had seemed so rich and varied when my mother and I shopped together, now appeared skimpy.

"When I see teenagers out at night, they look pretty casual," Rachel was saying. "I think your jeans and a pretty top would be just right." She reached for the white blouse with the eyelet stitching. I remembered how my mother had insisted that I buy it instead of a more colorful one that I had wanted instead.

"But it's so plain," I told Rachel, just as I had told my mother.

"It looks great with your dark hair. And we can spruce it up," said Rachel. Minutes later, I was standing in Rachel's room, the white shirt tucked crisply into my jeans, while Rachel searched her closet. I had never stood for so long before a reflection of myself. I tried not to stare.

"This is what you need," Rachel said, emerging from the closet with a short jacket made of blue jean material.

I slipped my arms through the sleeves of the jacket. When I saw the way it framed and offset the simple white blouse, I smiled. I could imagine the girls in the magazines wearing this outfit.

"What do you think?" said Rachel.

"I think the people at home wouldn't know me." And it was true. I stared into the mirror. The white of the shirt stood out against my tanned skin, and my legs looked long and slim in the jeans. There wasn't a trace of the girl who, only a week ago, had never gone out of the house without a bonnet, who had never stepped into a pair of trousers, who had never fastened an article of clothing with a button.

The girl who stared back at me from the mirror was anything but plain.

CHAPTER

16

On Saturday afternoon, Josh called to tell me he'd be over at 7:00 to pick me up. He also said that another couple would be joining us. I was happy to hear about the other couple. Now the plans seemed less like a date and more like a group of friends going out.

That night I was too excited for dinner. My entire body felt the anticipation. Rachel seemed to understand when I took my plate to the sink while the rest of the family was still eating.

In the bathtub, I sank into deep warm water, letting my hair fan out around me. I wasn't doing anything wrong, I told myself. Josh and I were going out as friends. And Daniel wasn't my beau, so I wasn't exactly betraying him. Still, the earnest look on Daniel's face as I had unwrapped the wood carving kept slipping into my thoughts.

Later, as I was putting on the jean jacket, Rachel knocked softly on my door. "You look beautiful," she said.

"Thank you." I tried to remember if I'd ever heard those words spoken to me. "Actually, there is one thing I need help with," I said. "At home we always pull our hair back or wear it in braids. But here I see girls with their hair arranged all different ways."

Rachel gave an eager kind of smile, and I found myself staring into a mirror again, this time with Rachel standing behind me. I wondered what my mother would think of all this time I'd been spending gazing at my own image. "You have such pretty hair," Rachel said. "I think it would look nice down." My hair was still damp from the bath. One day I hoped to learn how to use a hair dryer, but for now it would just have to dry on its own, as it always did. I felt the brush pull through the curly layers, and watched in the mirror as Rachel arranged pieces over my shoulders and down my back.

I blinked at my reflection. It felt free to have my hair untethered. "I like it," I said. But what I was thinking in a silent, private part of me was, *I'm pretty.*

When the doorbell rang, the chime went right through me. I grabbed my purse and went downstairs. Sam had already answered the door, and I could see Josh's now-familiar figure beside two other people.

Josh smiled as I stepped toward them. He was wearing jeans and a long-sleeved blue shirt that buttoned down. The first few buttons were open, exposing a white T-shirt underneath. He pointed to the boy and girl beside him, each staring at me curiously.

"This is Greg," he said. Greg's skin was the color of dark caramel, and his fuzzy brown hair was clipped close to his head. His clothes—faded jeans and a shirt the green of a duffel bag—hung on him in a smart way. Until now I had only seen black people from a distance in town. I tried not to stare at him. "Hey," he said, his voice deep and mellow.

"Hey," I answered back, feeling suddenly shy. My hand was engulfed in the firmness of his handshake, and I smiled at his friendliness.

"And this is Valerie," Josh said.

Valerie's hair fell over her shoulders, straight as string, a mix of yellow shades as though someone had painted it unevenly. Her eyelashes were so dark they looked like they had been coated with shoe polish. She wore a black T-shirt with a deep V-neck, tucked into a flouncy red skirt. The skirt settled above her knees, showing off her long lean legs. On her feet were strappy black sandals.

I had worked so hard to put together the outfit I was wearing, and now it looked simple and bulky next to Valerie's sleek clothes.

"So, I hear you're Aimish," said Valerie.

Greg groaned. "Jeez, Val."

"I'm sorry. Was it supposed to be a secret?"

"It's okay, I am Amish," I said, careful to show her the correct pronunciation. "And, no, it's not a secret."

"Well, you don't look it," said Valerie, who seemed unaware of the glances that Greg and Josh were exchanging over her head. "I mean, where's your bonnet and your apron? You look just like the rest of us." I wasn't sure if this was a compliment, but I liked the idea that I fit in.

In the car, Valerie and Greg slid into the backseat, leaving the front seat for me. Valerie leaned forward into the space between

Josh and me. "So, really," she said. "no cell phones, no Facebook?"

I turned, feeling the seat belt shift with my movements. Greg was wincing at Valerie's questions, but he looked as though he, too, wanted to know the answers. "Hey, Val," Josh called into the backseat. "This isn't a reality show." Everyone in the car laughed, so I did too.

"It's all right," I said. I didn't mind the questions or this girl's surprising boldness. Valerie was all on the surface. You didn't have to look too far to know her, and there was something appealing about that.

A few minutes later, we parked in a big lot and joined the messy line gathered outside the building. Josh and Greg reached into their back pockets for their wallets and exchanged money for tickets. When we got inside, Greg turned to Valerie. "You and Eliza can find seats while we get the popcorn." Valerie nodded, accepting the two tickets Greg handed her. Again I followed, still dazed by the number of people and all the steps involved. Valerie led me down a carpeted hallway, past a series of doors, each posting a sign with the title of the movie that was being played behind it. I had thought there would be one theater showing one movie, but instead I found a richness of choices. I wondered how Josh had picked this movie and which other ones he had decided not to see.

Inside the theater, a slanted floor held chairs in perfectly spaced lines. Valerie seemed to know exactly where to go, marching down the sloping aisle toward a row of seats in the middle. I followed her down the row, turning sideways as she did, and watched as she pulled down a seat and flopped into it. I stopped beside her, but Valerie pushed out her hand before I could sit. "Not here," she said. "We have to sit boy-girl-boy-girl."

I moved one seat over and turned to face Valerie while we waited for the boys. "You're looking at my teeth, aren't you?" she asked. She was right: I couldn't help myself. They were so unnaturally white.

She flung her hair back, away from her face, and stretched her lips so each tooth was in full view. "They were getting kind of yellow, so I bleached them."

"I beg your pardon?" I thought that maybe I hadn't heard correctly.

"It's just these strips you put on your teeth to whiten them."

"Well. They look very nice."

Valerie nodded her satisfaction. "I know, right?" Valerie's eyes were on me now. "So, how did this work? On your first day in town, Josh just breezed in?"

"He was mowing the lawn," I said. "He knows the people I work for." Valerie nodded, but she was still staring at me.

"Your eyelashes," she said. "What do you use on them?"

"Excuse me?"

"They're so dark. I'm guessing you don't have mascara where you come from."

I shook my head. I couldn't tell if she was giving me a compliment or criticizing me.

"Lucky you," she said. I still couldn't tell.

At that moment, Josh and Greg returned, Greg sidestepping around my knees to sit in the chair between Valerie and me. Josh sat in the seat at my right, holding an enormous container of popcorn and a paper cup of Coke almost as big.

For a few minutes, Josh and I didn't talk. We reached into the warm bucket of popcorn, our fingers bumping together, and I listened to the chatter around us. The cup of Coke sat in an opening at the end of the armrest we shared.

Then the lights dimmed gradually, the murmuring voices began to quiet, and the large screen at the front of the room glowed white. Colorful images appeared like on the television shows that the children called "cartoons." A large popcorn box, equipped with a face, arms, and legs, waited outside of a cartoon movie theater. Bouncy music played as the box smiled and reached out his hand to a cup of Pepsi. "Is this the movie?" I whispered to Josh.

"It better not be," he said, grinning. "It's just something to make us buy popcorn and turn off our phones."

The picture faded away, and another one replaced it. This time, horses filled the screen, their hooves drumming up dust on the road and flooding the theater with a thunderous rumbling. A man's low voice spoke over the pounding hooves, telling a story about an old Western town. "Is this the movie?"

"No," whispered Josh. "This is a preview. To get you to see the next movie."

I took another sip of Coke and settled back in the chair and watched two more previews. Soon the screen went dark again, and there was an audible sense of settling in the theater. The fidgeting and whispering died down as the screen lit up, and the words

"The Best Bet" appeared. Music played, and the movie began.

What I couldn't get over was how gigantic it was. Everything was spread grandly on the wall before us, hugely magnified. Music surrounded us, lacing through the background, even while the people on the screen were talking. Soon the gigantic people on the screen became part of a plot, like the elements of a novel that I could see right in front of me.

The story focused on one awkward girl who didn't bounce around with the fluid grace of the other girls. Her clothing was baggy, her eyeglasses thick and foggy, and her hair lank. To the girl's surprise, a suntanned boy with a swaggery step asked her out on a date. She was excited and nervous, so the graceful girls took her under their wing, replacing her shapeless clothes with clingy fabrics, styling her limp hair, adorning her face with colors, replacing her foggy glasses with tiny lenses that sat right on top of her eyes.

Each of the characters began to encounter frustrating complications and misunderstandings. It turned out that the suntanned boy had lost a wager, which was why he had asked the shy girl out to begin with. The shy girl, basking in her new popularity, was suddenly looking more like the other girls, so the boy who had taken her out only because he had lost a bet was beginning to feel that maybe he'd won something after all.

But things began to get tangled up. One of the girls told the shy girl about the bet, causing her to burst into heartbroken tears. A friend of the boy vowed to help her make the boy jealous by dating the shy girl himself and flaunting their new relationship in front of his suntanned face. But secretly, this boy had always liked the shy girl. And though he didn't care for all the colors on her face, or the fact that she looked so much like the other girls now, he was hoping that she'd come to see him as more than a friend.

I sat back in the velvety chair, chewing popcorn and sipping Coke, so close to Josh that our arms pressed against each other on the armrest we shared. It was amazing that I actually began to care what happened to the people on the screen. Too soon it was over, and everything was tidier than when it had begun, each character coupled with the person who was most like them. A lively song burst out as the characters faded into blackness, the lyrics of the song neatly fitting the story. Lights filled the theater, and everyone around me started getting up, the velvety seat cushions popping against the seat backs. Murmuring voices surrounded me, and I could feel Josh watching me.

"So?" he said. "What did you think?"

But there were no words to describe the way the sounds had enveloped me, and the story had twisted and turned until I felt like I was inside of it. Now they were all watching me, waiting to hear if I had liked my first movie. I smiled. "I've never had a better time."

Outside, I blinked in the darkness. I realized that I had missed seeing the sun set and the day ebb away, but it was a small price to pay for such magic.

"Where to now?" asked Greg. I didn't know that we would be doing anything else, and I waited to hear what would happen next.

"There's a guitar player at the Bean Scene tonight. Is that okay with you, Eliza?" Josh asked.

I nodded happily. It turned out that the Bean Scene was close to Rachel's house. I recognized the street where she had taken me to show me the library. Inside, the air was thick with the smell of coffee, and the room was filled with small wooden tables and an occasional overstuffed chair that looked like it belonged in someone's living room. In a far corner, a man with a long brown ponytail strummed a guitar.

Valerie signaled to me with a toss of her head. "Come on," she said. "Let's treat." She ordered drinks and brownies for all of us, and I gave her a bill, unsure of how much to contribute. She paid the cashier, handed me some change, and picked up the tray. I followed behind her. For the next few minutes we were all busy getting our coffees just right, with sugar and milk and great clinking stirs, before settling back in the wooden chairs.

The coffee was hot and bitter, but it spread an odd comfort through me, and I curved my fingers gratefully around the heavy mug. I was having a good time, but it was a nervous good time. I felt one minute away from doing or saying the wrong thing.

"So," Valerie said, setting her mug on the table and studying me, "how do you like wearing regular clothes?"

I smiled, thinking that, to me, my Amish clothes were regular. I mentally scanned my new wardrobe, which had once seemed so vast, but was now inadequate. "I feel like I don't have enough."

"Welcome to my world," Valerie said. Then she paused, her

face brightening with an idea. "Do you want to go to the mall with me sometime? I'm always happy for an excuse to shop."

I nodded. "I'd like that." A warm feeling filled me. I wanted clothes like Valerie's, and I wanted her to help me pick them out. "And maybe you can show me the fruit stand where Josh works."

There was a second of silence, just enough time to make me feel uneasy. "Josh doesn't work at a fruit stand," she said.

I could feel Josh and Greg exchanging glances. I cleared my throat, knowing that I was about to make things worse. "I thought he worked at an apple store."

Valerie erupted into snorty laughter. Heat spread across my cheeks.

Josh's voice was gentle. "I work at a computer store," he explained. "The name of the company is Apple."

I took a breath, wondering if it was possible to die from awkwardness. Valerie's laughter dissolved into breathy gulps.

"Come on, Val," said Greg. "How would Eliza know?" I looked up at him gratefully. His brown eyes met mine for a moment, and I could see the kindness there.

Josh was shaking his head. "Sorry, Eliza."

"That's okay," I said, eager to get the attention away from me. "I have to admit that I couldn't picture you selling fruit." Josh smiled at me, and I smiled back.

Then I heard a musical sound—not a song, exactly, but something like chimes with a tune.

Valerie reached into her pocket and pulled out a cell phone. "Hey," she said, putting it to her ear. After a few seconds of silence she said, "We're just hanging out."

Greg and Josh were taking big bites from their brownies, not paying attention to Valerie or her conversation with an invisible party. "Not tonight, I have a curfew. 'Kay, see ya."

Valerie snapped the phone shut and shoved it back into her pocket. "Carly wants to know if we're partying later." The word 'party' sounded ominous when it was used as a verb.

I took another sip of the cooling coffee. The guitar player continued to strum, his music filling the background of the chatter around us. I took the last bite of my brownie, feeling myself relax. I knew that while I was here I would always be on the edge of saying something silly, but I also knew that I could recover. Awkwardness wasn't fatal, after all. Valerie was entertaining us with a lively story of why she had a curfew. Apparently she had sneaked out of the house last weekend, and when she crept back in at a small hour of the morning, her father was sitting in her room waiting for her. Valerie laughed in her snorting way as she told the story, and we all laughed with her, but I had a feeling that it hadn't been very funny when it happened.

"Great," Greg said. "They'll never let me into your house again." Then he added, "Of course, for the record, my parents think it was all Valerie's fault."

There was another burst of laughter, and then Valerie went

silent, glancing at me in a cautious way. "What's wrong?" I asked.

"I don't know," said Valerie. "You must think I'm pretty shady. A good girl like you."

I thought I saw Josh roll his eyes at her, but I couldn't be sure. "Not really," I said, smiling. "I'm guessing you think I'm good because I'm Amish, but we get into trouble just like you do." I paused and added, "We can be shady, too."

Valerie leaned forward. "What kind of trouble?"

"We go to parties and stay out late. Sometimes we go around with people our parents don't want us with." I paused before adding, "There are kids with drug problems."

There was a moment of quiet. "Really?" asked Valerie, urging me on.

"Really," I said, suddenly feeling important. "I know one boy who spent a year in jail for dealing." I always felt a little wistful when I thought about Thomas. He wasn't a bad boy, really. He had just gotten caught up with a wild group.

Everyone was leaning forward now. Valerie's voice burst out of her. "Shut up!"

I smiled and answered in a way I'd heard the children respond. "No, you shut up!"

"Actually," Josh said, through a fresh burst of laughter, "I think we'd all better shut up if we're going to get Valerie home before her curfew."

We pulled up to Valerie's house a few minutes later, and she opened her door. "Well, it was great meeting you, Eliza." She started to get out of the car, then turned back. "What about tomorrow?" she asked.

"Tomorrow?"

"For shopping. I need some summer clothes. Do you want to go to the mall?"

"Is it open on Sunday?" I asked.

"Why wouldn't it be?"

"Yes," I said, my heart pounding in a peculiar way. "I'd love to go with you. Sunday is my day off."

"Great! I'll pick you up at noon."

I watched as Valerie and Greg walked to the front door together, his arm draped over her shoulder. On the porch, Greg pulled Valerie into a tight embrace, their lips clamping together. I turned my head away and found Josh watching me.

"So, shopping with Valerie. Are you sure you're ready for that?"

I smiled. "No, I don't think I am."

"Well, good luck," he said with a grin. Then he paused before saying, "Hey, can we do this again?"

I thought for a minute. Daniel and I had agreed that we weren't courting. He was free to be with other girls. Maybe he was even with Hannah right now.

"Yes, I'd like that."

"So would I," said Josh. He leaned toward me and placed his lips on mine for the briefest moment. It happened too fast. When Greg opened the door and Josh pulled back, I was disappointed that it had ended.

CHAPTER

 17

Preparing for my shopping day with Valerie made me almost as nervous as getting ready to go out with Josh. I looked carefully through my clothes, hoping she'd approve of what I wore. I put on the pink blouse with a pair of white shorts, and then stepped into the sandals. It felt funny going out with all of my toes showing.

I opened up my purse and felt for my new checkbook. Yesterday afternoon, Rachel had taken me to the bank to open an account, and she showed me how to deposit my first week's pay. With her help, I wrote a check to my parents to go toward what I owed them for my clothes, and the rest was mine to do with as I pleased. It seemed like a vast sum of money.

Waiting at the front door, my thoughts strayed to what everyone at home would be doing right now. Services would be over and the Plain people of the district would be gathering together at the home of this week's host, to have lunch and discuss the sermon.

And I was going to the mall.

Valerie pulled up and honked the horn. In the car I felt her watching me as I fastened my seat belt. "So," she said. "Have you ever been to a mall before?" When I shook my head, she said, "Then where did you buy your clothes?"

"At a store near my house," I said. "It's called Walmart."

There was a change in Valerie for just a moment, a little intake of breath, a subtle shift in expression. It was clear Walmart was not a desirable place to shop. I made a mental note.

We didn't talk much for the rest of the drive. Valerie had the radio turned loud, and she drove with one hand hovering over the buttons, ready to change to a new song, often before the one we were listening to was over. Her shirt ended just above the waistband of her shorts, revealing a narrow slice of skin around her middle section, and her long blond hair flew about the open window.

We parked outside the mall, which was bigger than I had imagined. I knew that it was one building that held a lot of stores, but once I stepped inside I realized that it was like a town with a roof over it.

Valerie's pace was fast and determined as we passed stores selling everything from toys to jewelry to shoes. One store sold only undergarments, and another only purses. Valerie walked right by several clothing stores without a glance before pulling me into one where loud music was playing. Inside, the walls were lined with racks of clothing, much fancier than what I had bought with my mother. Valerie stepped over to a rack of skirts and began to flick through them, sliding them past her, one by one, occasionally taking one out and holding it up to view more closely. I wasn't sure what I was supposed to do. At Walmart my mother had showed me what to try on. I stepped closer to the rack of silky-looking shirts and reached forward tentatively. "That's cute," Valerie said. The top was cluttered with flowery designs, and I realized that I didn't know if I liked it or not. Valerie had moved on, and now stood before a rack of blue jeans. "Do you need jeans?" she asked.

I shook my head. "I already have a pair."

Valerie made a snorting sound. "A pair?" she said. "You can't have only one pair of jeans. I have, like, five pairs. And it still isn't enough."

I moved away from the shirts and started looking at the jeans, surprised to see how different they all were. Some had long billowy bottoms; others had pencil-thin legs. The shades varied from deep blue to the color of a December sky. I looked at one of the price tags and was shocked to see that the jeans cost over a hundred dollars. Suddenly my bank account didn't seem so large. I was about to ask if all the clothes were this expensive when I saw that Valerie had already moved to a rack of dresses. A lavender one caught my eye, and I lifted it tentatively. It had embroidery around the neckline and hem, and looked like it would hang just above my knees. The price tag had a line through it with a less expensive number written by hand, a price I could afford.

"That'll look good on you," Valerie said. "You should try it on." I followed her to a row of doors and stepped inside a room that was so small I could barely turn around in it. I took off my clothes, pulled the dress over my head, and looked in the mirror. The fabric was soft, and the dress clung to me in a pleasing way. I opened the fitting room door to show Valerie, who nodded firmly when she saw me. "You have to get it," she said. It didn't sound like I had a choice.

Back in my own clothes, I waited while Valerie stepped in and out of the fitting room, turning this way and that in each new outfit, scrutinizing herself in the mirrors set up to show several different views at once. Sometimes she asked my opinion, but more often she seemed to just be eyeing herself with criticism or approval.

When Valerie was ready, we stood in line at the cashier together. I wrote a check for the dress, figuring out how much money I had left and how little I could still afford to spend. Valerie was just getting started. I trailed after her from store to store, watching her try on shorts and tops and dresses. I was amazed at the way she navigated the mall, walking with confidence and surveying the array of choices each store offered. Every time we left a store and stepped into the main corridor of the mall, I was always a little surprised that there was no sun shining down or wind blowing my hair.

While I waited for Valerie to check out at one store, some small disks of color under the glass counter caught my eye. They looked like they belonged on a painter's palette. I looked up to see Valerie watching me. "That's eye shadow," she said. Then she pointed to her own eyelids, brushed lightly with a pale blue color. "I know a place where they show you how to put makeup on. Do you want to go?"

I looked back down at the colors displayed beneath the glass. The girls in the magazines had painted eyelids, and so did Jess and Caroline. I had never thought about decorating my eyes, but suddenly it seemed necessary, something I couldn't go another day without.

When I looked back up at Valerie, she wore an amused expression. "Come on," she said. "The makeup lesson is free. You just have to pay for what you buy. It'll be fun."

"Okay," I agreed, happy to follow Valerie to yet another store. Inside, I saw aisle after aisle of tubes and containers and tiny packets of color before Valerie led me to a counter, where we perched on high stools. "Are you here for a demonstration?" asked an older woman whose cheeks and eyelids were heavily tinted.

"For her, not me," said Valerie. "And we're starting from scratch here. She's never worn makeup before." I took a deep breath, the thrill of the unknown fluttering inside me.

The woman peered at me the way my grandfather looked at a piece of farm machinery before he bought it. Then she opened and closed drawers and set an array of brushes and tiny pots of color on the counter before me. "All right, then," she said, her voice deep and throaty. "Let's get started."

For the next half hour I felt soft bristles tickle my skin, and listened to the woman explain how to choose colors for my eyelids, lips, and cheeks. She showed me techniques for spreading the color onto my skin so that it looked "natural," as though it was normal to have blue eyelids or plum-colored lips. Sometimes Valerie chimed in, giving her opinion of a shade or pointing to a different color to try.

"What do you think now?" asked the woman, pointing to the mirror. I stared at my reflection and was surprised at the elegant girl who looked back. My cheeks were rose-tinted, as though I had been outdoors on a windy day. My eyelids were brushed from lashes to brow with a light shade of lavender, while a darker tint of purple formed a neat smudge across the crease of my lid. The mascara applied from a thin brush made my lashes look dark and luxurious. I could have stared at that fancy girl all day.

"So?" said Valerie. "Not too Amish, right?"

I forced myself away from my reflection. "Not at all."

Valerie helped me decide what to buy, including a zipper bag to hold it all. The price was higher than I thought it would be, and I realized I wouldn't be able to afford anything else today. But one more glance at my reflection in the mirror confirmed that it was worth it. I turned to Valerie. "Thanks," I said. "I never thought I could look like this."

"Well," said Valerie, "I have to admit that you have a lot to work with."

I looked down, feelings of pride swelling in me. It was wrong to be vain about my looks. But at that moment it felt just right.

"So, I think we've done enough damage for one day," said Valerie, looking at our collection of bags. "Let's get something to drink." Minutes later, we were sitting at a table in a large food area, sipping cold drinks, our shopping bags on an empty chair beside us.

"You didn't buy much," said Valerie.

"I only got my first week's pay yesterday," I said. "And I still owe my parents for the clothes I bought at home."

Valerie seemed to mull that over. "Okay, then. You'll have to come back when you have more to spend." I felt a little slice of disappointment that she hadn't said we would come back together.

"So," she continued, leaning forward, "what's your deal?"

"What do you mean?" I asked.

"What's your plan? Like, how long will you be here?"

"This is a summer job," I said.

"Then what?"

Then I go back to the life I had before, I thought. The life I'd wanted to leave. But I didn't say that. Instead, I said, "I'm not sure."

"I don't get it," said Valerie, stirring her drink with a plastic straw. "So you just pop in for a while and live a totally new life, and then you go back to the old one?"

It did sound kind of silly when she said it like that. I tried to explain. "I met Mrs. Aster, and she was looking for a nanny, and I was looking to get away from home for a while. So it seemed to work out for both of us."

Valerie nodded and leaned back in her chair. "And Josh?" she said. "Where is he in all this?"

"I don't know," I said. "I just met him a week ago."

Valerie looked thoughtful. "Well, this all seems to fit. You come here looking for something new, and that's just what Josh has been doing."

"He has?"

"Oh, yeah. This last year at school, it was like none of us were good enough for him anymore. He didn't go out as much as he used to. He started hanging with a different group every few weeks, acting all aloof." She paused and looked at me. "And then he finds you."

"I don't know Josh very well," I said. "Everything's still pretty new to me here."

"Oh, he'll like that," she said. "He'll want to be the big shot who shows you around. It'll be one more reason why he's not like the rest of us."

I didn't have time to think about what she meant, because just then two girls appeared at our table. They seemed to fall into Valerie's arms, hugging her and talking too quickly for me to make out what they were saying. Valerie interrupted them, pointing to me. "Guys, this is Eliza," she said. "She's Amish."

Heat pumped to my cheeks as the two girls turned to me with open curiosity. Valerie continued the introductions, pointing to a petite girl with dark curls framing a round face. "This is Jill," she said, before turning to a taller girl with pale skin and long hair the color of polished copper. "And this is Carly." I tried not to stare, but Carly had what appeared to be a small needle slicing through the edge of her eyebrow. Looking at it made me feel queasy.

"Really, Amish?" said Jill.

"Yes, really," I said, turning away from Carly's eyebrow. Searching for something light to say, I added, "I can show you my bonnet if you'd like."

They all laughed, and I felt a little better. It was hard to be on display, but there was also something exhilarating about it.

"It's her first time in a mall," said Valerie.

"No way," said Carly. "Did you buy anything?"

"A dress and some makeup," I said, trying to sound casual.

"How was the party last night?" Valerie asked Carly.

"Fun," said Carly. "I'm sorry you couldn't come."

Valerie looked at me as though we were in on a secret. Then she turned back to Carly. "I couldn't come because I was out with Greg. And Eliza and Josh."

Jill's eyes widened at the mention of Josh's name. "Yeah, you heard right," said Valerie. "We got Josh out."

Jill turned to me. "Nice move." I wasn't sure what she meant, but it seemed related to what Valerie had just told me about Josh.

"I know, right?" said Valerie. Then she started lifting out her purchases for Jill and Carly to admire. As I watched them, my thoughts returned to Josh.

Apparently he had a story, and Valerie thought I was a part of it.

CHAPTER

18

I still couldn't figure out what to write in my journal, so I began to list the things I'd done here that I couldn't do at home. Every day I had new items to add, like listening to music through the computer, setting the coffeemaker so the coffee would be brewed when I woke up in the morning, and maneuvering my own set of controls when I played Mario with the children.

Ben had seemed to enjoy teaching me how to play the video game, so I started searching for ways he could show me other things that he knew and I didn't. I thought it might help him get more comfortable about having me around. One day after camp, we leaned together over the kitchen table with the sports page open to the box scores. He pointed to one of the squares of neat, numbered rows and columns. "See this row on the left? These are the players," he said. "And these boxes show how many at bats, hits, runs, and runs-batted-in each player had."

I thought about what he had taught me about the game of baseball and tried to make sense out of the numbers on the page. I pointed to a player's name and followed the line of numbers with my finger. "So, he got up to bat four times, had one hit and scored one run?"

Ben looked up at me, respect in his round eyes. "Yeah, that's right," he said. "It took Missy a lot longer to figure that out."

I felt the thrill of this small victory.

My second week skipped by, and things that had at first seemed magical started to make more sense to me. I forgot to be amazed at how warm the clothes felt when they came out of the dryer, or how the electric lamp let me read in bed late into the night. Ben taught me how to command the television set through the remote control, which would swing me seamlessly from laughter to mystery to romance as I changed the channels. And the ring of the telephone now had the ability to bring the voice of Josh or Valerie right into my ear.

That Saturday night, Josh and I went out alone for the first time. When I answered the door in my new dress, he looked me up and down. "Did you buy that with Valerie?" he asked. I nodded, but he was still staring at me. "Your face looks different." He didn't say it unkindly, but it didn't sound like a compliment, either.

A warm feeling crept up my neck. "Valerie helped me learn how to wear makeup," I said. Josh shook his head. "What?" I asked, feeling a mix of awkwardness and defiance.

"I don't know," he said with a shrug. "You didn't really need any of that. You're pretty without all that stuff on your face."

I felt the rush of his praise, even though I knew it wasn't intended as flattery.

We went to a movie, this time a dark film about teenagers on vacation at a cabin, who start to disappear one by one. There were heart-pounding moments when something unexpected would be on the other side of the door or reflected in a mirror. During one of these moments, Josh slid his arm around my shoulder, and I felt safe in his closeness. When the movie ended, we made our way out of the theater toward the parking lot. Outside, Josh reached for my hand. It was a natural gesture, easy and relaxed, and I let my hand slip inside his, as though familiarity with an English boy was a commonplace occurrence in my life.

The following Sunday, Valerie called to ask me to go with her to a poetry reading. She was taking a summer school class for English credit, and this was something she was required to attend. "So will you come?" she asked. "I really don't want to go alone."

I had no idea what to expect, but I was happy Valerie had asked me. She picked me up after dinner, and we drove to the bookstore where the reading would be. "What's summer school like?" I asked on the way there.

"It's no big deal. Just a Creative Writing class," she said. "My parents said I had to get a job or go to school this summer, so I picked school."

In the bookstore, Valerie led me to the café, where a stool and microphone were set up. We got cups of coffee and sat down at a small table in the back of the room. Valerie took a pink note-book with a flowery cover out of her purse and set it on the table. Looking around, I saw that most of the other tables were occupied by kids our age, ready to take notes, as Valerie was.

I sipped my coffee. I had read some poetry when I was in school, but I didn't know much about it. To me, poetry seemed like urgent stories, cut to their bare bones.

At that moment a woman came to the microphone, welcoming us in an elegant voice. "That's my teacher," whispered Valerie. "She brought these poets here for the reading and she wanted an audience, so she made it a class requirement." At that, Valerie rolled her eyes, but I thought I saw a bit of eagerness in her expression.

The teacher introduced the first poet, a woman with olive skin and shiny black hair. She looked out at the audience and took a breath. Her voice, heavily accented, rang out in the small space. The poem she read told the story of migrant workers from Mexico, bending over snap peas, carrying bushel baskets on their shoulders, squinting in the angry sun. The words flowed like a song, her voice alternating between anguish and tenderness. When she was done, she lowered her head for a moment while applause filled the room. The poem settled inside me in a way I didn't expect. She had read for only a few minutes, but in that short time I was somewhere new—in a world of hard work and the search for belonging. I looked at Valerie, who was scribbling in her notebook. "I liked that," I said. "It took me to another place."

Valerie smiled. "That's what a good poem does."

For the next hour we sipped coffee and listened to poems about lovers and war and children and disappointment and deep desire. Valerie occasionally jotted notes, but mostly she watched and listened. After the last reading, everyone stood and clapped while the poets took the stage for a final bow, and the teacher thanked us for coming.

"Do you have to rush home?" Valerie asked. "I could use some more coffee."

We refilled our mugs and returned to the table, some of the lines of poetry still dancing in my head.

"What did you think?" Valerie asked.

"I loved it. Thanks for bringing me."

"Thanks for coming. My other friends would have thought this was lame, but I had a feeling you'd like it." I was pretty sure that was a compliment.

Valerie closed the notebook and looked at me, a softness in her eyes I hadn't seen before. She cleared her throat. "Um, is it okay if this is just between us? You know, that I like poetry?"

I smiled. "Your secret is safe."

"Thanks," she said, sliding the notebook into her purse. Then she leaned forward. "So, how are things with Josh? I hear you saw your second movie last weekend."

"We had fun," I said, "but the movie gave me nightmares."

"And last night?" she asked.

"Last night I had to babysit, but Josh came over and we watched TV."

"So," said Valerie, "three weekends in a row." Suddenly, I realized that when I was with Valerie, she asked all the questions. I took a breath and prepared to ask one. "What about you and Greg? How long have you been going out?"

"A couple of months," said Valerie, "My parents aren't thrilled, but they'll get over it." I smiled, thinking that Valerie and I would have that in common, courting boys that our parents didn't approve of.

"He seems nice," I said.

"He is, and so far we're pretty good together. And he's not too bad to look at either," she added, grinning. "What about you guys? Where do you think you and Josh are headed?"

I shrugged. "We have a nice time when we're together."

"That's how it starts," she said. Her tone was cheerful, but also a bit ominous.

Sitting at my desk while Ben and Janie were at camp, I looked at a clutter of unanswered letters. I had thought that I'd look forward to mail from home, but now the Friday parties and the quilt circles and the gossip about Sally and Peter sounded as shallow as a puddle. I wrote to my parents with each weekly check, describing my work with Rachel's children and how Ben's manners were improving and how nice the family was to me. But writing to Kate and Annie was a little harder. I wanted to be able to describe to them how the characters in a movie become a part of your life, or how much you miss the strumming of a guitar when the song is over.

Kate and Annie usually dropped a mention of Daniel, but in the four weeks I'd been gone, I had yet to receive a letter from him. When we said good-bye I had promised that I'd write, so I sent him a few letters with descriptions of the music that swelled from black boxes and the voices that traveled from one telephone to another.

Today I sifted through the pile of letters and noticed one in my mother's hand, her carefully looped lettering clear and distinctive. It was a curious letter, short and to the point, with my mother's utter refusal to relate to me in a personal way.

> *Dear Eliza,*
>
> *There is someone I want you to see. Her name is Beth Winters. Her address is 367 Elm Street in the town of Evanston. I don't think it is far away from where you are living, but I don't know how to get there. You will have to find the way. Please don't write to me about this because your letters are not read by me alone.*
>
> *Love,*
>
> *Mother*

She didn't even bother to write that she missed me or that she was curious about my life here. There was just this command that I find some stranger. Knowing my mother, this Beth Winters was probably someone who would convince me to go back home and return to my plain ways. I put the letter at the bottom of the pile and started writing to Kate. I had already written to her about my shopping day with Valerie and the movies I had gone to with Josh.

In this letter I described how every day now held the prospect of Josh stopping over to listen to music or watch a movie on TV with me, and how that possibility charged my days with anticipation. I wrote about how rumpled he looked from his work mowing lawns, and how when we sat close together he smelled like a warm spring morning.

After sealing the envelope, I went downstairs to check the refrigerator and plan for the family's dinner. When the doorbell rang, I rushed over, happy to find Josh on the stoop. "I finished early," he said. "Do you want to get an iced coffee?"

I checked the clock. The children wouldn't be home for another hour, so I fell into step beside Josh on the now-familiar route to town. "Did you get any letters today?" he asked. He had told me that letters delivered by the postman had become a quaint relic—"snail mail" they called it. But there was something wistful in his tone. He seemed envious of the daily arrival of handwritten messages.

"Just two today," I said. "My grandmother and my friend Mary."

"Have you told anyone about me?" Josh asked as he opened the door to the coffee shop.

I raised my eyebrows. "Why would I tell them about you?" I liked the way my voice sounded sly and innocent at the same time. But I didn't tell him that the letter to Kate I had just dropped in the mailbox had described how my time with Josh was beginning to feel like a courtship.

I stirred sugar into my iced coffee and took a long sip. "Listen," said Josh. "I'm not working tomorrow. If I promise to get you home before the kids get back from camp, can I take you out during the day?"

I looked up. "Where?"

"I thought we'd take the train downtown. It's about time you saw the city."

"Yes," I said, already looking forward to it. "As long as it's okay with Rachel."

"Cool," he said, looking pleased. "You know something?" He leaned back in his chair and looked at me as though we had just been introduced. "I wasn't really looking forward to this summer. Working two jobs, mowing lawns, saving money. But it's turning out pretty sweet after all."

I smiled. "Jah," I said. "So is mine."

19

The place they called "downtown" smelled like dirt and metal and old rain. The sounds were sharp bursts and long hums. The sidewalk felt hard and sticky beneath my sneakers. Going into town with my mother was nothing like this. Josh pressed his hand against the small of my back as we walked, and I enjoyed the warmth that settled there.

We turned a corner, and he guided me to a building beneath a set of railroad tracks. I looked up. I had never seen train tracks above the ground before. Bits of gray sky peeked down from between the railroad ties.

"That's the el," Josh said.

I looked at him. "The 'L'?"

"It's short for *elevated*. Do you want to ride it?"

I grinned. "Yes, please."

"Okay," he said. "But first we have to do something. Follow me."

I trotted behind him until we were standing directly underneath the train tracks. People brushed past us, some turning to look, maybe wondering why, in this place, where everyone was going somewhere, these two people were standing perfectly still.

"What are we waiting for?" I asked.

"You'll see," said Josh. "It shouldn't be long now."

I waited, my arms and legs tense. Josh stood behind me, his fingers curved around my elbows. I leaned into him.

Then it started, just a small rumble at first, something approaching from the distance. Then the rumble grew, and a quick breeze shot through my hair, sending it flying around my face. I wanted to leave, felt like I had to leave, fast. Now it wasn't rumbling anymore. It was roaring and dark. I took a step to get away from it, but Josh's hands tightened, holding my arms, keeping me in the spot. "It's all right," he was saying, but the roar carried his words away.

It got louder, a thunderstorm where the thunder doesn't stop. It vibrated around and through me until it was all wrapped up inside me—wind and dark and noise and vibration. And then it was gone. Suddenly gone. My hair settled back on my shoulders, and I could hear the coming and going of voices again. Josh's hands were still on my arms, but his fingers loosened. It had been twenty seconds only, maybe ten. But it was also forever.

Josh was smiling down at me when I turned to face him. I was afraid it would happen again, but more afraid that it wouldn't.

"That was an el train," Josh said. "It went by right over our heads. If you liked it, it happens about every five minutes." His voice had a laugh in it, and I laughed, too. This extraordinary event that took away sound and breath and light—this incredible shaking moment happens every five minutes. It didn't seem possible.

"Can we do it again?" I asked.

He smiled. "Okay, but don't try to get away this time."

I nodded and turned around so my back was against his chest. His body felt warm and solid. I waited for the next train, and this time I wasn't afraid.

When it came, I was ready for it. The rumble, the clanging, the dark, the wind. I was ready when the other city sounds disappeared and all I could hear was the clanging. This time I looked up and saw the dark underside of the train blocking out pieces of the sky. Everything was the same – the wind swirling my hair, the vibrations racing through me, Josh's hands tightening around my arms. And the sudden quiet before the city sounds came back into my ears. It was the same, yet it was different. The feelings weren't as sharp. It wasn't quite as scary, quite as loud, quite as thrilling. I swallowed back a drop of disappointment, and wondered why nothing was ever as good as the first time.

It took me a moment to realize that Josh was talking. I turned to him.

"So, riding the el. This is a big day for an Amish girl."

I laughed. "All I'd have to do now would be to fly on a plane, and there'd be a race to get me shunned." I followed as he led me through a set of heavy doors.

"Great, now I'll have that on my conscience. 'What did you do on your summer vacation?' 'Oh, I got an Amish girl shunned.'"

We laughed while Josh fed dollar bills into a big machine built into the wall. When a ticket came out, he handed it to me and repeated the process. As our laughter trailed off, I felt a warning trickle through me. I followed Josh through the turnstile, trying not to think about what we had just said. The night before I left home I had shuddered at Annie's story about her cousin being shunned. But today it had been a joke that made Josh and me laugh together. As I followed him up a long set of metal stairs leading to a narrow platform, I told myself it was okay to make jokes.

Looking down, I could see the spot on the sidewalk where we had stood a few minutes ago under the roaring el train. An assortment of people waited for the train. Prim-looking businesspeople, students with bulging backpacks, and a mother with a small child in a stroller. My attention went to a man sitting on a nearby bench, strumming a battered guitar. Even though it was a warm day, he looked like he was wearing every piece of clothing he owned: a wool hat, jeans with holes at the knees, a faded denim jacket. In an open guitar case on the ground beside his feet were a spray of coins and a few crumpled dollar bills.

"I know," Josh said, as though in answer to a statement. "He's homeless. It's a big problem."

"Homeless?" It seemed like an impossible word. "Like he doesn't have a home?"

"Right," said Josh, lowering his voice. "Richest country in the world. Then you see people like that. It really makes you think."

"So, if he doesn't have a home," I said, "where does he go at the end of the day? Where does he keep his things?" The man continued to strum an unrecognizable tune, seeming not to notice that we were staring at him.

"He probably doesn't have many things. He just panhandles during the day, and goes to a shelter at night to sleep. Come on," he said, pulling me to another part of the platform. "I hear a train coming."

I continued to look over my shoulder as I let Josh lead me. "So, we're just going to walk away?"

"It's not just him, Eliza. There are thousands of them. I told you, it's a big problem."

Just then I felt a vibration under my feet and heard the rumbling sound of an approaching train. I pulled my eyes away from the man and watched as the el train pulled to a screeching stop. The doors slid open, and I waited as people stepped out. For some, this was where they wanted to be. For others, this was the place they wanted to leave. And for the man playing the guitar, this would be the place he would stay. Collecting stray coins and faded bills.

The crowd waiting on the platform shifted slightly as people exiting the train pushed their way through—a brief mingling of those coming and those leaving. Josh reached for my hand and wrapped his own around it. "Now here's where you have to be careful to stay with me," he said.

The floor inside the el train was made of metal, and the seats were a faded tan color. The train lurched and started to move. Trying to keep my balance, I followed Josh to an empty seat, grateful to have something sturdy beneath me. I looked out the window, but the train had already moved past the station, past the man in his bundles of clothes, with his open guitar case. I felt Josh's eyes on me.

"Don't let it bum you out," he said. "There are agencies that take care of them. They all know where to go for help."

I nodded, but it still didn't feel right. At home we all helped each other. We didn't need agencies to do it for us. When my father hurt his back, the whole district flooded through our doors. Women brought steaming casseroles and carried out baskets of laundry to return clean and folded. Men came in the evening after their own work was done to help with my father's carpentry orders. Daniel was one of those men, I recalled. He finished the bookshelf that my father had started before he got hurt. I remembered how my father, his body still tilted oddly, had run his hand across the wood and nodded his approval of Daniel's work. Daniel had blushed with shy pride.

I realized that Josh was watching me, his expression thoughtful. "Wait a minute," he said. "What do the homeless people do where you're from?"

"There aren't any," I said matter-of-factly. "Everyone in the district has a home."

"But aren't there any problems? What happens if someone's house burns down? Or if they lose their business?"

"The district comes together for them and gets them what they need. If a family loses their home, they stay with another family until the house is rebuilt. If they need money, the elders get up a donation until they're back on their feet." As I was saying this, I realized with a shock that other people might not live that way.

Josh shook his head. "So where you live, it's like a utopia, a perfect world."

"Hardly," I said. "We have our share of troubles."

"But you work them out together," he said. "I live in a place where everyone's an individual unit. You live in a society."

I thought of what Valerie had told me, of how Josh had started to distance himself from his friends. Maybe he really was looking for something new, and I was something new.

"I don't know," I said with a grin. "How long do you think you can go without your cell phone?"

Josh smiled. "Oh, snap!" he said, and I laughed with him even though I didn't know what he meant.

Out the window, scenery sped by. Sometimes the buildings were so close that I could peek inside a window and get a glimpse of someone's life. The next voice I heard was a man's booming instruction: "Next stop Armitage."

When the train stopped, the people who had been waiting at the doors stepped off, and a new flood of people stepped on, their eyes scanning the aisles for empty seats.

"Come on," said Josh. "We'll get off at the next stop."

Once again, I followed him, reaching for the silver poles along the way to keep my balance. After the doors slid open we stepped off the train and made our way across the platform. I looked over my shoulder and saw another cluster of people stepping on before the train charged forward again on the tracks.

I thought about how all day and night the trains kept going back and forth. Dropping off some people, picking up others. It was unsettling, a job that was never completed. "Are you hungry?" Josh asked. I nodded. I was hungry and tired and a little bit sad. But I couldn't tell him that. He wouldn't understand that I felt sad about a man who didn't have a place to keep his guitar, and about a conversation where the worst thing that ever happened in my district was a funny joke, and about how you could get from one place to another and totally miss what was in between.

At a place called Demon Dogs, where the smell of grease hung in the air and the el train rumbled overhead, we stood in line for hot dogs and fries served in a cardboard tray dotted with oil. Then we edged our way to a narrow room and perched on red stools that looked out on the sidewalk.

"How do you like it so far?" Josh asked.

I thought for a minute. "I don't really know. There are too many parts to it to just give one answer."

"Okay, what parts don't you like?"

"I don't like seeing people who have to beg for money. I don't like being pushed along in a crowd."

"All right," Josh said. "Let's start over. What do you like?"

I smiled. "This."

Josh's features turned upward, the look of someone who had just been handed a prize.

"Sweet," he said, in that drawling way he sometimes had. "I like this too."

I dipped a fry in ketchup, and a restful feeling settled around me. I wasn't sure when I had stopped being nervous during my times alone with Josh. He was beginning to feel comfortable, like a new pair of slippers.

"What?" Josh was looking at me, studying me.

"I think I like the city."

"So do I," he said. "I'm more urban than my other friends. The city's a foreign place for them, but I can't wait to live here one day."

"What would you do?"

"I'd go to a lot of Cubs games," he said. "And I'd get into the music scene. I'd go to comedy clubs and the theater. I'd play on a softball league. Some of the bars have trivia contests. I rock at trivia." He grinned. "I just want to be a part of it all."

Me too, I thought. I felt a little envious of Josh. He could look ahead to his future and choose it. He wants to live in the city one day, so he will.

"So, what are you doing a week from Friday?" Josh asked. "Do you have to babysit?"

"I'll check with Rachel. Can we go to a movie?"

"Actually, I was wondering if you want to hear some music. This band I like is playing at an under twenty-one club."

I was excited to hear music that didn't burst from a machine. Already the time until a week from Friday was stretching ahead of me endlessly, with too many days to get through. I had that edgy feeling under my skin, the feeling of anticipation.

"Well?" Josh asked.

I didn't realize that I hadn't answered him yet. "Yes," I said.

"All right," Josh said, looking pleased.

I wondered what I would wear to a club, and I was certain that none of the clothes I had brought with me would be right. I would have to find a way to get more. That thought stunned me for a moment. It was so English.

CHAPTER
🦋 20 🦋

A few days after Josh and I went to the city, the doorbell rang as I was setting the dinner dishes in the dishwasher. I heard footsteps and the low rumble of formal voices; then Janie was by my side pulling on my arm. "Hurry, Eliza, there's a boy to see you. And it's not Josh."

Rachel stood at the doorway, talking to the visitor and watching me approach. Sam was there too, and he stepped aside as I came near, so that I found myself face-to-face with Daniel.

He stood in the hallway, looking so old-fashioned in his suspenders and black buttonless coat, holding his hat in both hands. His smile was big and wide, and a rush of heat flooded through me at the sight of him. He looked like home.

I was vaguely aware of Sam and Rachel stepping away from the door. Rachel said, "You can visit with your friend in the living room." Shooing the children away, she and Sam left me alone with Daniel.

He spoke first. "Can you at least say hello to an old friend?"

"I'm sorry. I'm just so surprised." I stepped forward and reached up my arms, feeling his body envelop mine in a hug.

"How did you get here?" I asked, stepping back.

"My cousin Gary was coming out this way to see a friend, so I took a ride with him. I would have let you know, but it was so last minute that you wouldn't have gotten the letter in time." He looked down at the brim of his hat. "Was it wrong for me to come?"

I tried to shake my head, but it felt like I was shaking my whole body. "Of course not." I reached forward to take his hat, and realized there was no hook to hang it on. I tried not to look foolish holding his hat in my hands. He, too, was looking around. I watched his eyes scan Sam and Rachel's home with a combination of awe and suspicion. I wondered if I had looked the same way when I'd first come here five weeks ago. It was hard to remember that this place had seemed unusual.

I wanted to tell Daniel about these amazing weeks I had spent, and to hear news from home that hadn't yet reached me through the post office.

"How long can you visit?" I asked.

"About two hours. Gary's coming back to get me around nine o'clock."

I handed him his hat. "Wait here," I said. "There's a place we can walk to for coffee. I just have to tell Rachel I'm going out."

Within minutes, I was walking beside Daniel, his hand cupped lightly around my elbow. I glanced up to see him smiling at me. "So how does that English clothing feel?" I looked down at my green blouse, jeans, and sneakers.

"Actually, it took some getting used to. Blue jeans are pretty stiff, it turns out. But it's fun deciding what to wear each day, trying on new things and seeing how I look." I paused for a moment, and then asked, "So, how *do* I look?"

"Just like an English girl," said Daniel.

"I look like an English girl?"

"No, it's just like an English girl to ask a boy how she looks." He waited a moment before adding, "You look nice."

He glanced around as we walked. "The houses all look the same."

I shook my head. "Well, they're not," I said. Then I remembered that I had felt the same way the first time I had seen this street. But eventually each house started to look different. There was the house with the red door, where the neighborhood children always gathered in the evenings, and the house with the colorful flowers that the silver-haired woman tended so lovingly.

"That's what they say about us, you know," I said. "The tourists in town. And the English people who don't know any Amish. They say we look alike because of our clothes. But if they looked more closely, if they knew us, they'd see that we're all different. Just like these houses."

Daniel turned to look at me. His expression was both impressed and amused. "Are you trying to show me that this fancy world is making you wise?"

"It was just an observation." Then I smiled. "Anyway, I was always wise."

Daniel nodded his agreement. "That's why I've been staying around."

I stopped, and Daniel's hand slipped from my arm. "Are you staying around?" I asked. We stood there for a moment on the sidewalk.

"Well, I'm not keeping company with anyone else." He put his hand back on my elbow, and we started walking again.

"You're allowed to keep company," I said. "Remember, we're not courting."

"I know. And when I find someone like you, she can be my girl." His words settled inside me like a spicy meal. If Daniel were with someone else, it would be easier for me to continue to be with Josh, to see where this new relationship might take me.

I hurried to change the subject. "It's nice being so close to town. When I have time off I walk here to go on errands, or to read at the coffee shop. That's where we're going," I said, pointing to the Bean Scene. I knew that Josh was working, so there was no chance that I would run into him while I was there with Daniel. I felt a little twinge at this thought. I wasn't courting either of these boys, so I wasn't betraying them. But I knew there was something untruthful in not wanting them to know about each other.

The shop was quiet. Two men played chess at a table in the

corner, and a woman with fuzzy yellow hair was bent over a note-book at the end of the counter, a stubby pencil making frantic scribbling sounds. Beside her, a student was typing on a laptop. Each one looked up as Daniel and I walked in. Their stares lingered on Daniel, but he seemed not to notice. He looked the place over as I pointed to the menu board and the day's choices.

I walked up to the counter, and felt Daniel hesitate before follow-ing me. "Jasmine tea," I told the clerk, a girl with spiky hair and silver rings on all her fingers, even her thumbs. Daniel was beside me now, holding his hat in one hand and groping for his wallet with the other. "I'll have the same," he said. He flinched a bit at the price before he set his hat on the counter and pulled a bill from his wallet.

I was anxious to get to a table. I had never seen Daniel so fum-bly before, and I wanted to be near the old Daniel again. At home his presence filled up a space. His smile was smooth as cream, his movements easy as a glider. I touched his arm and nodded toward a table, by the wall. He sat down and sighed. I pulled an extra chair up to the table, and he set his hat there, grinning gratefully. He looked as out of place as a surgeon in a cornfield.

"So," he said, "tell me about this fancy world."

I didn't know where to begin. "Well, there's so much to do here. And so many choices."

"What kind of choices?"

"Like when you're done working, you can go to a movie, or hear music, or shop. People find so many different things to do with their time."

"Well," said Daniel, "they seem to have a lot of time to fill."

I nodded. I'd thought of this often. "Every chore is easier here, so work gets done more quickly." Daniel listened intently, his eyes meeting mine in a way that tugged at me.

"And what do you like to do?"

"Oh, I love the movies," I said. The sound seems like it's coming right from the people's lips, even though they're not real people, just moving pictures of people." I pushed aside the thoughts of Josh sitting beside me in the movies. "And they're all different. Some are funny. Some are scary. Sometimes they make you cry."

I took a long drink from my tea and then told him about TV and the shows called *sitcoms* and the reality shows that aren't very realistic. I told him about the appliances in Rachel's kitchen and the video games the children play with. I started to tell him about the music I listen to, but that was too connected to Josh, so instead I asked him to tell me about home.

Daniel leaned back in his chair and told me about who was courting, and who had gotten into trouble, and who had asked about me. "Your friends all miss you."

"I miss them too. How are Annie and Kate?"

"Well, Annie and Marc are finally courting."

I smiled. "She wrote me about that. I'm sure she's keeping him on his toes."

"Jah," Daniel agreed. "But he's up for the challenge. And Kate enjoys her work in town, but she's lonesome for you."

My chest warmed at his words. I looked into my teacup,

watching the leaves swirling on top, breathing in the flowery scent. "It's funny," I said. "I've spent time with other kids our age here, but it's not the same. I feel like I'm a novelty to them. It's not like home, where we know each other so well."

Daniel leaned forward. "I thought it might be like that. It must be hard being in a place where you're different."

I nodded. "Sometimes." I thought to say more, but something about Daniel's posture, his gentle prodding, seemed a little too eager.

His fingers tapped on the table edge. Finally he spoke.

"Come home, Eliza. Come home with me."

Catching my breath, I pushed back my chair. It made a stuttery sound on the wood floor. The clerk with the silver rings looked up for a moment, and then returned to the book she was reading. "Is that what this surprise visit is about?" I asked. "Were you hoping to find me homesick and miserable?" Then I thought of something else. "Did my mother send you here to bring me back home?"

"No," he said firmly. "It's neither of those things."

"What then?"

Daniel pushed his empty mug aside and leaned toward me. "This is my rumspringa, too. All around me, everyone my age is driving in cars, going to parties, watching those movies you tell me about."

"But you can do those things, too."

"I know." Daniel looked down at the table. When he spoke, his voice was so low I had to lean forward to hear him. "But I want to do them with you."

The rush of honesty from Daniel's words wrapped around me like a shawl.

"Oh, Daniel," I said.

"Is that all you can say?"

I tried again. "Please don't make me responsible for your happiness."

He reached for his hat and ran a fingertip along the rim. "Aren't we all, Eliza? Aren't we responsible for the happiness of the people we care about?" I looked down, flooded with shame. "It's the way I feel about you," he added.

My hand crept across the table. My fingers slipped inside of his. "I know you do," I said. "But right now I'm just so anxious to be a part of all this. Can you give me some more time?"

Daniel's smile was a small one. It didn't travel up his face. "I guess I have no choice." He gave my hand a light squeeze before releasing it and setting his hat on his head. "Let's go. Gary will be here soon."

On the way home he didn't reach for my elbow as he had before. We walked in silence. Back at the house we sat beside each other on the bench near the front door, waiting for Gary's car. The breeze carried the scent of honeysuckle, and lightning bugs flickered over the lawn. There was something calming about sitting side by side on a summer night, and I found that I wasn't ready for Gary to drive up. I wanted more of this peaceful time beside Daniel. I asked him the question that had been waiting in my head.

"Why haven't you written to me?"

"I've written you a dozen letters. I just haven't mailed any of them."

"Why not?"

"I read your letters, and each one tells me something I didn't know before. Everything I write seems so silly. You know about the services and the barn raisings. What should I write you about?"

I cleared my throat before I spoke. My words slid out gently. "Write about you. I want to know about you."

"Okay," he said with a smile.

"Do you know the last thing I look at every night?"

He shook his head and waited.

"The carving of the bird in her nest that you made me. I keep it on the nightstand, and every night before I close my eyes I look at it. It keeps home in my thoughts."

Daniel slipped his arm across my shoulder, and I leaned in to him.

"Then keep looking at it, Eliza. Keep me with you while you're here."

A soft horn interrupted us, and we got up slowly. I could feel his breath on my face as I looked up at him. "Do you think you'll be coming back again?"

Daniel shook his head. "There's no place for me to hang my hat here."

I nodded my understanding.

"I'll be waiting for you, Eliza," he said. He picked up my hands and held them in his. "But I don't know how long."

Before I could answer, he stepped off the front stoop and headed for the car. He didn't turn around to wave.

Later that night, after the children were in bed, I sat at my desk thinking of what Daniel had said. I hadn't asked him to wait for me, and his last words sounded a little like a threat. But they were delivered to me in Daniel's soft, earnest way, and I realized that he was only being truthful, a quality I had been lacking lately. I knew then that I didn't want Daniel to wait for me. I wanted him to move along so that I could do the same. But I didn't know how to tell him that.

Thoughts of home rushed back to me. I had been trying not to think about that faraway world, but now Daniel's visit made me realize that I missed my friends. I sifted through all the letters that I had put aside, wanting to see the words, the handwriting. The voices of Annie and Kate and Mary and Sally sang in my ears. Then I saw my mother's letter, the one I had shoved to the bottom of the pile. I opened it up and read it again.

The name Beth Winters gave me no hint of recognition. The words on the page held a warning that this was to be a secret between my mother and me. But my mother was not a secret-keeper; she was up front and no-nonsense. I sat back, blank and wondering.

I went to bed knowing that tomorrow I was going to find Beth Winters.

CHAPTER

 21

The next morning, after the children left for camp, I called Josh on his cell phone, my fingers going right to that particular order of numbers that would bring his voice to my ear. I was always a little nervous calling him. At home, the boys called for the girls, and sometimes I thought that putting Josh's number into the phone was like shining my lantern into a boy's window. But Josh always sounded pleased to hear from me, and his cheerful "Well, hi" coming through the phone gave me a thrill.

"Are you working tonight?" I asked.

"No," he said. "Do you want to go out?"

"I need your help solving a mystery," I said, and explained about my mother's letter.

"I can be there at four," he said. I read him the address, and he said he'd get his mom's car and figure out the directions.

Before Rachel left for the library, I showed her the letter. "Josh is coming over at four," I said. "Do you think you can spare me so I can find out what my mother needs?" Rachel agreed.

I spent the day preparing the family's dinner and getting all of my chores done. When Josh arrived in his mother's car, I climbed in beside him. He had printed up directions from the computer, and I read them, watching for street signs. As my mother had guessed, it wasn't far away, only a twenty-minute drive. When Josh turned onto Elm Street, my eyes scanned the tidy houses. We pulled in front of a modest home with the look of a country cottage. The front door and shutters were a matching shade of green against weathered gray siding. A colorful garden burst in unkempt patches across the small front yard. A white porch swing swayed beside the front door.

"That's it," said Josh, pointing to the house that somehow already looked familiar, like a place I should know.

The doorbell buzzed, and I waited, bursting with a curiosity I had never felt before. My finger itched to touch the doorbell again; my foot tapped to a rhythm that was not part of a song. Then I heard the pounding of hurried footsteps and a woman's voice, almost musical, calling "Com-ing."

The door opened in a burst, and framed in the doorway was a woman about Rachel's age. She wore a long, full skirt made of blue jean material, and a crisp, white collared blouse. Around her waist was a colorful sash that flowed down the length of the skirt. Her brown hair fell past her shoulders in a way that, at first glance, made her look like a teenager. But up close I could see tiny lines at the corners of her eyes. Gray eyes. Almost silver.

"May I help you?" she asked. Her voice sounded familiar. Like home.

I opened my lips, but couldn't find any words. Josh took over, firm and friendly. "I hope we're not bothering you," he said. "We're looking for Beth Winters."

The woman nodded. "I'm Elizabeth Winters. Everyone calls me Beth." When she turned her gaze to me, she looked startled for a moment. Her eyes clung to my face. Then she took a step back, pointing vaguely toward the inside of her house. "Would you like to come in?"

Josh and I stepped into her foyer. The colors were muted and settled, like an October afternoon. I felt Josh's nudge and found my voice.

"My mother wanted me to find you," I said. The woman looked to be as jittery as I felt.

"And who is your mother?" she asked, a tiny lilt in her voice. The sound settled like a tickle in my throat. I took a long breath before answering.

"My mother is Rebecca. Rebecca Miller."

Beth Winters gasped, a tiny sound. Then, for a second, her body started to sag. Josh jumped forward and reached out to steady her, but she shook her head. "I'm all right," she said quickly, her words choked and breathy. She regained her posture, then turned to face me fully, her eyes wide. "You're too young to be Margaret," she said. "Which one of Becky's children are you?"

"I'm Eliza," I said, waiting for it all to make sense. No one ever called my mother Becky. I was only distantly aware of Josh standing beside me.

"So she named you for me after all," Beth Winters said. The woman's eyes welled with tears, and she reached out her hand to touch my cheek. Her fingers were cool and dry against my skin.

"Who are you?" I asked.

The woman smiled. "I'm your Aunt Beth," she burst out in a hoarse whisper as twin tears rolled down her cheeks. "Your mother was . . . is my sister."

The next minutes were a jumble. She stumbled toward me until we were gripped together in a trembling hug, our tears mingling, gulping sounds that were my own cries, Beth's hand stroking the back of my hair. Josh had stepped back quietly, but he was part of it, too. Finally, Beth and I released each other, our hands grasping each other's elbows.

"I didn't know." It was all I could think to say. Beth motioned us to the couch. She perched on a chair.

Josh looked at me. "Do you understand this?"

I nodded. There was only one explanation, and it was something that I didn't want to say.

"Go ahead," said Beth.

The words didn't want to come. Finally I said them. "She was shunned." Beth nodded and made it true.

"No way," said Josh.

I turned back to meet his eyes. I couldn't think how to respond. "Way," I said.

Shunned. It was the worst thing that could happen. And here it was before me, in the face of a woman with my mother's silver eyes.

This woman had once worn a kapp and sat in a quilt circle and sung in a one-room schoolhouse. Then something happened that made her have to leave. Forever.

"I suppose you want to hear about it," Beth said. I nodded. "Okay," she said. "But first tell me how you came to be here, dressed like an English girl?" She looked at Josh. "And who is this young man?" Josh looked at me expectantly, as though he, too, wanted the answers to these questions. "So," said Beth, "can I make you dinner while we spill our secrets?"

In the kitchen, Josh and I sat at a wooden table that looked like it belonged in a farmhouse. As Beth moved around, tossing salad ingredients into a wooden bowl and setting pasta to boil in an iron pot, she kept a steady gaze on me.

"I figure that you're sixteen now," she said. "And this is your rum-springa." I nodded. "And this is a boy you met here in the big fancy world." I grinned at Josh. He smiled back and reached into his pocket, turning off his cell phone. The gesture filled me with gratitude. "Okay, where are you staying? And, more important, how did you get your parents to let you leave home?" While Beth chopped vegetables and added them in handfuls to a simmering pot of sauce, I told her about my dream of leaving the Plain world, and of meeting Rachel at Stranger Night. My voice quavered as the whole mix of emotions came rushing back to me—the letting go and stepping away and reaching for something new.

I looked up and saw that Beth and Josh were watching me intently, waiting for the next part. "Josh can tell the rest," I said.

"Well," he began, "I was mowing Rachel's lawn and I came in for a drink, and here was this girl from another place. And I mean *really* from another place." Beth giggled, the laughter of a young girl being tickled. "She'd never heard of the Beatles. She'd never seen a movie, never talked on a phone. It was like, I don't know, like when a blind person gets her sight. She wanted to see everything." He paused and looked at me. "And I got to see it all with her."

I fiddled with a thread that had come loose from the bottom of my shirt. It was strange listening to the way Josh described me. Maybe being called a blind person should have made me angry. But I liked how he sounded so pleased to be a part of my story.

"Well, this all sounds familiar," Beth was saying. She had a dreamy expression on her face.

I was aching to hear about Beth. "Your turn," I said. Beth wiped her hands on a dish towel and placed a lid on the pot of sauce before sitting down at the table, across from me.

"Well," she began, "I was the baby of the family. I watched Miriam grow up the way she was expected to. Then there was your mom. She was more rebellious. She hated cooking, couldn't ever finish a quilt. Our mother would grumble about how we were ever going to marry her off."

This didn't sound right. I had grown up watching my mother's careful work in the kitchen and with her quilts. There was nothing but competence in her hands.

Beth continued. "When Becky was a little older than you are

now, we had financial troubles." I knew what was coming—my mother, homesick and miserable, working at the tailor shop and sending money home to help her family.

"Our parents planned to send Miriam," said Beth, "but your mother begged to go. That was fine with Miriam. She was already courting Ike. So off your mother went, with hardly a backward glance. I was heartsick seeing her leave."

I shook my head. "No, you have it wrong. They forced my mom to go."

"Not at all," said Beth. "Your mom couldn't get out the door fast enough. I was thirteen and I missed her so much. One weekend I got to take the train and stay with her in the city. It was like being in a dream. She showed me television and took me to the movies."

"Did you see *The Sound of Music*?" I asked.

"Yes, as a matter of fact, we watched it on video."

Josh let out a laugh that sounded more like a groan. "You and that movie. I've got to rent it for you one day."

"Afterward," Beth continued, "it was like coming back from the fair. Everything at home was so common." I pushed back a worry that it would be the same for me one day.

Beth shoved her chair away from the table and went back to her cooking. A few minutes later, over dinner, I found myself waiting to see if Aunt Beth would bow her head and pause over the mealtime prayer. But she was already stabbing her fork into the lettuce.

She continued with her story. "It was hard to be back home. Miriam was planning for her marriage. I was in my last year at the one-room school. Then your mom came home earlier than we'd expected because my father had been able to clear up our debt. I was so excited to have her home, but she had no time for me. All she cared about was her baptism. I tried to talk to her about her time away, but she brushed me off."

That sounded more like the mother I knew—practical, organized, never one to linger over details. But I wondered how she'd returned so easily to the life she'd run away from.

"Before I had time to enjoy having Becky back home, she was planning her wedding, and I was alone again. So I finished school and got a job in a quilt shop in town."

"Selling quilts?"

"Worse," said Beth. "I sat every day in the middle of the store on a little stool and stitched together squares while the tourists gawked at me. I was miserable. When I turned sixteen, all I wanted was to get out."

"What did you do?"

"I was not Good Amish," said Beth, shaking her head. "I hung out with the wildest of the Amish groups. I got drunk on the weekends. I stayed out all night."

Josh let out a whistle. "You Amish. Who would have believed it?"

Beth laughed. "Miriam and your mom were both married with children by then. I spent time with your mother, and helped her with Margaret and James." She paused and reached across the table to touch my hand. "Oh, Eliza. I'll need to hear about everyone. There are others, too, right?"

"Jah," I said. "One more. My sister Ruthie is eleven. James and my father work together in the furniture shop. Margaret got married last year. She and Jacob have a farm about a mile away. Beth pressed a napkin to her eyes. "Are you all right?" I asked.

She nodded. "After all these years it's still hard for me to believe that my sister has children I don't know."

"How long has it been?" Josh asked.

"Becky was pregnant with this one here when I left," she said, nodding toward me. "She told me this was going to be the baby named for me. But then things got a little complicated."

She got up and started to clear the table, and the story stopped while we all set about tidying the kitchen. Later, sitting in the living room, the dishwasher buzzing, Beth told us about getting a job at the library, where she read about other worlds and thought about her possibilities. But in the end she agreed to be baptized, making the promise to the church.

"Then," she continued, "one day I was working at the desk and I saw a man bent over his books. He had a rumpled look about him that I liked. At closing time he was still there, and somehow we ended up going out for coffee, and that was the beginning."

"You fell in love with an Englisher?" I asked.

"I did indeed."

A silence slipped into the room. I had been waiting to hear those very words, but still they sounded strange. Love between an Amish girl and an English boy was the stuff of hushed stories after services and behind barns. But they were always distant tales of unseen people.

"Soon John took to learning my schedule, and waiting for me when my shift was over. He was in graduate school, working on his PhD in history. He wanted to know everything about the Plain life. And I wanted to know everything about him and this place that was forbidden to me."

"Did you tell your parents about him?" I asked.

"Eventually. You've never heard such yelling. But that wasn't as bad as the silence. The silence told me there were no words that could make this right. I would have to choose."

"Was it hard?"

"The hardest thing I ever did. First I told John I couldn't see him anymore. But no Amish boy came near to making me feel the way he did. Eventually, I knew that I wanted the life I would have with John, even though it meant giving up my other life."

"How did you do it?" I asked.

"I went to the person who I thought would understand. Your mother."

"What did she say?"

"She said that I wouldn't be her sister anymore."

A tear slid down my cheek and splashed on my pink shirt.

"Then she said that she couldn't name her baby after someone who wasn't Amish."

"I'm sorry," I whispered. Josh's arm slipped around me, and

I leaned my head on his shoulder. Then I remembered one of the first things Beth had said to me when we met. *She named you for me after all.*

"I understand now," I said suddenly, sitting up. "My mother once told me that they wanted my grandfather to approve of my name, and that they had to come up with a few before he finally agreed. Maybe they were trying to get as close to Elizabeth as they could."

Beth was smiling. "Half a name is better than none."

Outside, the daylight was seeping away, leaving a blue-black sky. Beth turned on a lamp, casting the living room in an artificial white glow. At home, my mother would be lighting the kerosene lamp now, blowing on it, coaxing the yellow flame.

I looked at Beth. "What was it like? Being shunned."

For a moment, Beth stared at something that wasn't in the room. But when she spoke, her voice came out smooth as pudding.

"It wasn't all at once," she began. "First, my parents spoke to the bishop, and I was excommunicated until the elders could meet about my case. Life was the same for me, but I couldn't go to services. Then the bishop came to the house and told my parents I was 'under the bann.' That's when things started to change."

"How did they change?" asked Josh. But I knew. I'd heard stories about people under the bann.

"I couldn't sit at the table with members of the church, so at mealtime my parents would pull up a small table and I would sit there. Then one day my mother was serving soup, and I held my bowl up to her. She told me I had to put the bowl down on the table, and she would fill it there. Now that I was shunned, she wasn't allowed to take a dish from my hand or serve food into a dish I was holding."

Josh shook his head. "That's so harsh." I listened in silence.

"Yes," Beth agreed. "But I was already baptized, so I'd gone back on my promise to follow the church's rules. If I had asked for forgiveness, the bann would have been lifted and I would have been welcomed back. You see, in a way, it was my choice."

"How long did you stay at home after the bann?" I asked.

"Just a few weeks," said Beth. "Miriam and Ike wouldn't see me. No great loss, but at the time it hurt. Then one day I went to visit my best friend, Emily. Her mother answered the door and told me she was sorry, but I couldn't come in. I stepped off the porch and looked up to Emily's window and saw her looking down at me. I could tell she was crying."

Beth busied herself moving things around the coffee table—a jar of white stones, a book on women authors, a candle. I waited for her to continue.

"That's when I realized that by staying among them after I had been shunned, I was putting my family and friends at risk. They could be excommunicated if they didn't follow all the rules of shunning. Then I knew that I couldn't be a part of both worlds."

"What did you do?" I asked.

"I packed my things and John picked me up to take me to his parents' house. He came in to meet my mother and father, but they refused to talk to him. On his way out the door, he turned around and said, 'I'm sorry that you didn't get to know me. I think you would have liked me.'" Beth smiled. "Do you see why I love him?"

Josh was grinning. "He sounds pretty cool."

Beth nodded. "Then he said, 'And don't ever worry about Elizabeth. I'll always love her.'" Beth was still smiling, but her eyes looked sad.

"What did Grandma and Grandpa say to you?"

"My father didn't say anything. My mother just said four words: 'Elizabeth, are you certain?' When I said yes, she looked down at the floor, and I slipped out. Before John and I left town we drove to your parents' house so I could say good-bye to your mother. John waited in the car." Beth's voice sounded fragile, like someone who was getting over the flu. "I told Becky I was leaving, and she said, 'It's probably for the best.' Then I said that I'd write to her, and I asked if she'd write me back. And she said no."

I let out the breath I'd been holding. Beth went on. "I started to leave, and when I looked back at Becky, her head was bent and her shoulders were shaking. Then she said, 'I won't write you back, but send me letters anyway.'"

I closed my eyes. It was what we were all warned about, and it had happened to my family. I didn't want to hear another word, and I wanted to know everything. "What happened next?" I asked.

"I wanted to run to her, but I was afraid that I wouldn't be able to leave if I did. When I was just out the door, I called out, 'I love you,' and she said, 'And I you.' Those were the last words my sister said to me."

"Did you cry?" I asked.

"Only for about a year," Beth said with a laugh. "I lived in Chicago with John's parents while he finished his dissertation, and I did a high school equivalency program. After John and I got married, he got a position at Northwestern and we moved to Evanston."

"Do you work now?" I asked.

Beth nodded. "I work for a pediatrician, managing the office." She paused before adding, "We have a nice life. We have lots of friends, and I have a niece and nephew I'm very close with." Then she looked at me. "And now I have you."

"Right," I answered. "Now you have me."

At that moment I heard the metallic clink of a key in the door, and I glanced at Beth. "Well, it looks like you're about to meet your uncle John," she said, jumping up and reaching the front door just as it opened. "John," she burst out, before he was even inside the house, "you'll never believe who's here."

John stepped in and looked over at Josh and me with a question on his face. We stood up from our places on the couch as he walked into the room. He wore khaki pants and a plaid button-down shirt. His brown hair was flecked with gray, and his eyes had downward creases at the corners, which made him look both tired and kind.

Beth took John's hand and pulled him toward me. "This is Eliza," she said. "She's Becky's girl. She came and found me."

John's face burst into a smile, turning up the lines around his eyes. "Oh, my," he said. "I don't know what to say. This is wonderful!" He reached out his hand to shake mine, and then seemed to think better of it. "Well, I'm not going to shake hands with my niece," he said, holding his arms out and pulling me into a sturdy hug. I didn't have time to be shy about this instant familiarity. Somehow it felt right to be hugging this man who had promised my grandparents that he would always love their daughter.

"And this is Joshua," Beth said, as Josh and Uncle John shook hands. "He's Eliza's . . . well, what do you call each other?"

I turned to Josh. He was looking down, fiddling with his cell phone. "We're good friends," I said quickly. When I looked at Josh, he seemed relieved. I swallowed back a disappointed feeling before turning to Beth. "When can I see you again?"

"Every day?" she said with a giggle. She wrote a row of numbers on a piece of paper, along with the words *Aunt Beth and Uncle John* and tore the sheet from the pad. Handing it to me, she said, "I assume you've uncovered the mysteries of the telephone."

I smiled and reached for the pad and wrote down Rachel's phone number. There was something magical about those two pieces of paper that would connect me with my newfound aunt. I folded the sheet with Beth's number on it and slid it into the pocket of my jeans. Feeling the crinkle of paper was reassuring.

I walked slowly to the front door, reluctant for the night to end. Uncle John, his face lit up with a smile that was already familiar to me, gave me another hug, and then shook Josh's hand. "You're family now," he told me. I swallowed and nodded.

Beth kissed Josh's cheek, and then turned to me. "Thank you for finding me," she said in a choked whisper. I stepped inside of Aunt Beth's hug, flooded with warmth. When we stepped back from each other, she suddenly reached for my hands, holding them in her own. "One more thing." She pronounced each word slowly. "My parents. Are they . . . ?" Her words trailed off.

Understanding, I squeezed Beth's hands. "They're well," I said, and saw relief flood her face. "They live with Aunt Miriam and Uncle Ike. Grandpa still works the farm, and Grandma helps Aunt Miriam with the children."

Beth closed her eyes for a moment. "Thank you, God," she whispered. She released my hands and leaned against John, who had quietly appeared at her side.

Josh and I stepped together onto Aunt Beth's porch in the quiet summer darkness. In the car, Josh turned to me. "So, we're good friends?" he asked, a teasing grin on his face.

I nodded, something stirring inside me. Josh leaned toward me, and our lips found each other. In that moment, I didn't need a word for what we were. I didn't need words for anything.

CHAPTER

22

That night I couldn't sleep. There were still so many questions, and the more I relived the evening, the more it was a puzzle. How could it be that no one in the family had ever slipped and told a childhood story that included a third sister? I searched my memory, but I couldn't remember a clue about a girl who took back a promise and as punishment was told that she didn't exist anymore.

Then I remembered something I had heard the night I pressed my ear against the wall and listened to my parents argue back and forth. At one point my mother had said in a fierce voice, "Don't forget what happened to my sister." I had assumed that she was referring to Aunt Miriam. Now I realized that she must have been talking about Aunt Beth, and I tried to remember what my father had said in response to those words.

Then it came to me. In a voice that was stiff as a plank of wood, my father had said, "I *am* thinking about your sister, and I'm hoping that history doesn't repeat itself."

Everything changed after I met Aunt Beth. Now when the phone rang at Rachel's house, I snatched it up if the Caller ID revealed Beth's number. Josh showed me how to get to her house by train, where to get off, and how to walk the four blocks from the station to the gray house with the green shutters.

Later that week, Beth and I worked together on a letter home that would secretly send information to my mother.

Dear Family,

I miss you all, and think of you often. I am enjoying my work here, and have made some nice friends. I have a new friend named Betty, who is so much fun to be with. She has a bubbly laugh, and she loves to tell stories about her family. I can listen to her all day long. As a matter of fact, she is sitting beside me as I write these words. We're getting to be as close as sisters.

My mother hadn't wanted me to write about Aunt Beth, but I thought this message would be clear to her and no one else.

When I was with Beth I was like a starving person. I couldn't get enough of her lilting voice. I loved the stories of her funny mishaps as she adjusted to living among the English—like all the things she'd blown up in the microwave, and the times she would search for matches when the sun went down, forgetting that she could turn on a light.

Aunt Beth, too, seemed to drink *me* in. She wanted to know everything about home. Sipping a cup of tea on her porch swing, I said, "The last time you were with my mother, you said that you would write to her. Did you?"

"I did for a while," she said. "Then I got a letter from your father, asking me to stop because the letters upset her. The last letter I had sent was around the time that John and I moved to this house. A couple of years ago, John mentioned the idea of moving, and I told him that we could never leave because Becky wouldn't know where to find me."

"Do you miss them?" I asked.

"Every blessed day. Especially your mother. When I was little, whenever Miriam was mean to me, or I got in trouble for being fidgety at services, I'd crawl into Becky's bed and she'd put her arm around me and smooth out my hair. And she'd always tell me the same thing. 'It's okay, Elizabeth. Your sister is here.' And I'd always feel better."

We were quiet for a few minutes. The porch swing swayed gently, and the tea was beginning to cool. I bent down and placed the mug on the floor. "Aunt Beth," I began, enjoying the smile that spread across her face at the words, "what do you call yourself?"

"What do you mean?"

"Well, I wondered what you are if you're not Amish."

Beth paused for a moment before speaking. "I used to be Amish." That seemed to say everything.

CHAPTER

 23

Things were changing with Josh and me. He continued to find ways to sneak over when Rachel was out and the children were at camp. But our time together was more urgent now than it used to be. We talked on the phone at odd intervals throughout the day, sometimes just to say "Hey," or "What's going on?" I always called his cell phone just before I went to bed, to hear his voice as the last sound of the day.

There was an odd restlessness when we were together. We reached to touch each other for no reason except that we wanted it, our lips pressing together softly, then insistently. I positively itched to be near him. It was almost frantic. I knew I could only go so long without feeling his skin against mine, without smelling the muskiness around his neck when he pulled me close.

I found that I didn't wake up easily at the crack of dawn anymore, but I shook off the sleepiness every morning and continued to be the first one up, with hot breakfast ready for the family when they came downstairs. I wanted to show Rachel that my relationship with Josh wouldn't interfere with my work, so my dinners became more elaborate, and the house shone under my cleaning rag.

After camp, I was the children's playmate, taking them to the park or the library, swallowing back yawns during Candy Land, doing art projects on the kitchen table. One day we went out hunting for butterflies, but they always flew away as soon as the children approached. Janie loved listening to stories, leaning against me as she sucked her thumb. Ben stopped talking about Missy. He was curious about my life at home, and peppered me with questions about what it was like living in "olden times."

Josh, too, wanted to know about my other life, and he seemed to glorify the Plain world. He liked to comment on the failings of his society in comparison to the simple way we lived.

On the Friday that Josh and I would be going to the under twenty-one club, Rachel stood beside me as I finished wiping down the counter. "Can we talk?" she asked. I looked at my watch. Josh would be picking me up in an hour. Rachel pulled out a kitchen chair and sat down. I sat across from her, trying not to look impatient.

Her voice was soft and even. "Eliza, in these past couple of weeks, you and Joshua seem to be spending a lot of time together."

I tried to appear casual. "I guess we have," I said, as though just realizing it myself.

"I'm not sure if you know this, but your parents gave me strict instructions about you."

"What kind of instructions?" I asked, feeling uneasy.

"For one thing, they said you weren't ever to be alone with a boy. I've been lenient about you and Joshua because I know him so well. And you were usually with other friends when the two of you went out. But lately things seem a little more serious."

"We're just friends," I said, trying to keep my voice light.

"That's what I thought," said Rachel. "But I just wanted to be sure."

"And if it makes you feel better, we can be sure to always have other kids with us when we go out. Tonight we're going to a club, so we definitely won't be alone there. Okay?" I asked, getting up from the table. "Is there anything else?"

"Yes," said Rachel quietly. "Please don't put me in a difficult position. Please don't make me have to send you home."

I took in a breath. "I promise not to let that happen."

Rachel nodded, but her face had a pinched look, like she wasn't convinced.

I hurried to my room, shut the door, and reached for the phone.

"Hey," Josh answered, in the drawly voice that usually made me feel tingly.

"Listen," I said. "Rachel gave me *the talk*."

"Oh no, *the talk*," said Josh. Then he paused. "What's *the talk*?"

"It's not funny. I guess my parents spoke with Rachel before I came here and said that I'm not allowed to be alone with boys."

Josh's voice was still teasing. "Well, you're not alone with boys," he said. "Just one boy."

"This is serious," I said. "Rachel can send me back home."

There was a pause on the other end of the phone, and I could picture Josh suddenly sitting up, the mocking expression slipping from his face. "What should we do?" he asked, his voice more solemn. "Maybe we shouldn't see so much of each other."

I knew that Josh was right, but I couldn't bear to think about it. "We just have to be sure that Rachel doesn't think we're too serious."

"Okay," said Josh. "Whatever it takes. I'm not letting you go back without a fight."

I smiled. I liked the way that sounded. "All right," I said, and hung up.

I hurried to get ready, feeling a new kind of nervousness. We would have to start being more careful. In the bathroom, I brushed my teeth and washed my face. I opened the top drawer and took out the makeup that Valerie had helped me pick out at the mall. The skinny mascara brush looked like it was covered in black paint, but I liked the way my lashes looked darker and shinier after I used it. I brushed a bit of eye shadow on my lids and some blush on my cheeks. I combed my hair and pulled it back into a ponytail. Satisfied, I started downstairs. The sound of a conversation stopped me. I could hear Rachel's voice, sterner than usual.

"I mean it, Joshua. I have to be able to trust you."

"It's cool, Rachel," he said. "You don't have anything to worry about. Eliza and I are friends. Didn't you say yourself that you wanted me to take care of her this summer? Well, that's what I'm doing."

"Joshua, if anything happens with this girl . . ."

"Nothing's going to happen. We're going to movies and concerts. We're not drinking. We're not doing anything that you didn't do at this age."

"Well, that's the problem," said Rachel. "Eliza's from a different culture and we have to respect that. And she's going home at the end of the summer. Don't make it hard—for either of you—when it's time for her to leave."

I started down the stairs, making enough noise to let Rachel and Josh know I was there. They looked up at me, Rachel's face firm, Josh's uncertain.

"Do you have the concert shirt for me?" I asked. My voice sounded artificially bright.

Josh tossed me a green T-shirt with the words FORT MINOR emblazoned across the chest in bold black print. "Thanks, I'll be right back," I called. I went back to my room, trying not to think about the conversation I'd overheard. I pulled off my top and slipped on the concert shirt. It hung past my hips, and it had Josh's earthy smell. I didn't ever want to take it off.

I headed down the stairs and called out to Rachel, "I'll be home before midnight," then hurried out the door.

"So," I said when I was in the car, the seat belt fastened at my waist. "You agreed to 'take care of me' this summer?" My voice held mock irritation. Really, I was pleased.

"Yeah," Josh said with a grin. "I didn't know what I was getting myself into when I signed on for that."

We laughed and then fell silent. "So you heard us," he said.

"Jah. I mean yeah."

"Rachel said something that I haven't been letting myself think about," he said. "You're leaving after the summer. You're going back there." He said "there" as though it were the name of the place. *There.*

I waited a moment before speaking. "That was the arrangement," I said. "I'm supposed to go back home in September. That's about six weeks away." I felt a pang, realizing that my time here was half over.

"Is this negotiable?" Josh asked. "Can you get more time?"

"I don't know. It was so hard for me to convince them to even let me come for this long."

I looked at Josh. He was staring at the road ahead, but I could tell that he was listening intently. "And if they had any idea about— you know, *us*—my mother would be on the next train here, hauling me back home."

Josh nodded and continued to stare ahead. "Then they can't ever know."

"Right," I agreed. "And Rachel can't know either."

Josh turned to look at me. Our eyes met. His face was full and open, without a hint of teasing. "I won't do anything to get you in trouble," he said. "I promise."

The prickly excitement of the past two weeks was giving way to another feeling. A taut complicity. We were in this perilous place together. The feelings of danger were as exhilarating as the feelings of attraction.

We pulled into a parking lot and got out of the car. From the outside the building looked like an ordinary storefront. But as we got closer, noise seemed to be pulsing from it. At the door, a burly-looking man stopped us. "Ten dollar cover charge," he said. "Are you carrying any bottles or cans?"

Josh shook his head and handed him a twenty-dollar bill. The man stamped our hands with a red mark. I stepped in the door and was immediately enveloped in noise and vibration and the press of bodies. People, mostly our age but a few who looked to be in their twenties, were stacked throughout the small space. The room was dark and warm, and the throb of music was so loud that when Josh turned to tell me something, I could see his lips moving but couldn't hear a sound. I held tightly to his hand as we wove our way through the crowd to a spot near the wall. Josh bought us each a Coke, and I savored the cold sweetness.

On the stage, the band was playing a song I recognized from Josh's iPod. Live, the song had a wildness to it. Now that I was adjusting to the darkness, I could see that people were perched on a scattering of stools, chairs, and mismatched couches. But many were standing, holding their hands high over their heads to clap in an exaggerated way to the rhythm. Josh put his arm around my shoulders, and I felt his warmth and the muscular lines of his body. His lips were close to my ear, tickling me with heat. "Later we'll move closer to the stage so we can dance."

I sucked in my breath at the word. Amish teens whispered about dancing, and it was often a secret part of rumspringa parties, when no adults were around. But I had never danced before, and I was afraid of looking foolish. I'd worked so hard to fit in here, but if I tried to dance it would be obvious that I wasn't really a part of this place.

Someone got up from a seat next to us, and I climbed onto the stool, with Josh standing beside me. I leaned against him and felt his breath against my hair. We listened to one song after another, each ending with the usual round of cheers and requests. Then the atmosphere changed. The next song started with a noticeable shift in tempo and volume. It was a song I knew, a plaintive tune about a man and woman who feel they don't know each other anymore. Josh nudged me. "This is it." He took my hand and started leading me to the small dance floor in front of the stage. After a few steps I pulled back.

He stepped beside me. "I thought we were going to dance." I waited, unsure of the words to explain. "Oh," he said, disappointment clouding his words. "Is this something you aren't supposed to do?"

"Well, yes, but that's not the problem," I said. "It's just that . . ." I paused, embarrassed. "I don't know how."

"It's okay," he said. "All you have to do is follow me."

I hesitated and glanced at the dance floor. The other couples gathered there didn't appear to be dancing as I had imagined dancing to be. Instead they each looked like they were in an embrace, swaying slowly to the music.

Josh's voice was gentle now. "Come on. I think you'll like it."

Taking a breath, I let Josh lead me to the crowded floor. The other couples adjusted in subtle ways to make room for us.

Josh's words were a whisper. "Put your hands here." He guided my hands up to his shoulders. "And mine go here." I felt his hands, firm and warm, on each side of my waist.

"That's it," he said. "Now you just let your body follow mine and move with the music." But I found that we were already doing that. Even as he spoke, his body was swaying from side to side, and my body was following his, as if connected.

The music swam around us, and Josh's hands moved from my waist to the small of my back, his body encircling mine until the space between us began to dissolve. Then, somehow, the music was inside us, directing our movements. My hands had been on his shoulders, where he had placed them, but as our bodies drifted closer, my arms wrapped around his upper back, and my head rested on his shoulder. It happened so naturally, just another step in the dance. Our bodies pressed together, and I could feel the muscles in his upper arms and his thighs. My skin buzzed with the nearness. It was like melting, surrendering. The room faded away, and it was only the two of us now. I was certain that no one had ever felt this way before.

Then the music ended, replaced by a humming stillness. The other couples returned, or maybe they hadn't gone away at all, but I could barely make out their forms. I was still inside of Josh's embrace, the one they called a dance, and I could no more step away than I could fly to the sun. And then he said the words that I didn't realize I had been waiting for. They were a rush of heat against my ear.

"Don't go back there, Eliza."

My lips parted, and when I spoke, it was to give him what seemed like the only possible answer: "I won't."

24

We stayed there as the music shifted to a louder, more insistent rhythm. The other couples released each other, dancing beside their partners rather than connected to them. But our bodies were as close as when the slow song had played.

I looked up at Josh with a mixture of shyness and defiance. Part of me wanted to take back those words. And part of me wanted to climb on top of a table and proclaim them to this roomful of strangers. "I won't," I had said. Out of context it had no meaning. But in the moment it meant everything I feared and longed for.

Josh's fingertip traced the shape of my cheek. Then he slid his finger down to my chin and raised my face so we were looking at each other fully. Our lips pressed together, our tongues gentle, then probing. His hands slid into the back pockets of my jeans and pulled our hips together. There was a warmth between my legs that made me feel weak and quivery. The song ended. Another song started. Still we stood there in our own private dance. I wasn't sure how many songs started and ended before Josh whispered, "Let's go." I didn't know if he meant back to where we had been sitting or back to Rachel's house. But it didn't matter. I just wanted to go with him.

It turned out he wanted to be in the car. He opened the back door with a sweep, and we climbed in, the quiet settling around us. "What are we doing?" I whispered. Josh didn't answer. He lay across the backseat and pulled me down on top of him. It was so inviting, stretching out across his body, my head on his chest. He reached under my shirt, and I felt his fingertips on my skin and over my bra. I needed to stop and think, but it felt so fine.

I had to consider what we'd said to each other, what it meant. I had to figure out what my boundaries were in this new closeness. But I didn't want to think. I wanted to stay here forever. I felt myself drifting, giving in. Then I was suddenly alert.

"What time is it?" I whispered.

Josh's body tensed for a second. He slid his hand out from under my shirt. "Way to spoil a moment."

"I know. But I have to be back by midnight."

Josh looked at his watch. "We have a few minutes," he said. "Do you want to talk?"

"No," I said. "Let's not talk anymore tonight."

"Okay," he said. "Can we do other things?"

I shook my head against his chest. "Not tonight."

We stayed in the backseat, every part of me touching a part of him. At home, if Josh and I were courting, we'd be allowed to "bundle." We'd have permission to close the door to my room and stretch out on my bed, fully clothed, wrapped in each other's arms. I wondered if English teenagers had a custom like that.

I felt Josh shift his weight to check his watch again. "We'd better go," he said, and we began the task of unwinding ourselves from each other. In the front seat, I busied myself with the seat belt, feeling suddenly awkward. We had jumped to a new place, and like the ride on the el, I didn't know how we'd gotten there. There were things to discuss, but now I just wanted to be back at Rachel's house, where life was ordinary, where I could think about those words I had said and figure out what they meant.

CHAPTER

25

When I woke up the next morning, I felt thick with sleep. I drifted back, remembering that it was Saturday and I didn't have responsibilities with the children until later in the afternoon. Somewhere in the distance I could hear Janie arguing with Rachel, her voice shrill and insistent about some injustice that had been done to her. Beeps sailed up from the video game Ben was playing. Sleep tugged at me, pulling me down. There were things I was supposed to do. It had been days since I'd sent a letter home, and I'd promised Janie a trip to the library. I was going to call Aunt Beth to talk to her. About what? Then I remembered. I had promised Josh something last night, and I was worried about it. Aunt Beth would help me.

The phone rang, slicing through my last remnants of sleep. I looked at the clock. The red numbers glared at me: eleven thirty. I bolted up in bed, my heart hammering. I had never slept so late before.

I hurriedly stepped into the jeans I had left on the chair the night before. Pulling on a T-shirt, I padded to the bathroom to wash up. There were dark smudges under my eyes from the mascara, and I scrubbed them with a soapy washcloth, closing my eyes against the sting. My hair was a mass of tangles, and my face was pale and puffy-looking. The dark romance of the night before felt different with this disheveled reflection facing me.

I yanked my hair into an untidy ponytail and went downstairs. Rachel looked up from the newspaper spread on the kitchen table when I entered the room.

"Did you like the club?"

"Yes," I said, shaking cereal into a bowl. "The music was wonderful. And loud!" I brought the cereal and a mug of juice over to the table, and sat across from Rachel.

She moved the newspaper aside and leaned forward. "Eliza, I'm sorry about last night. I don't want you to think I don't trust you."

"I understand why you're worried," I said. "Josh and I talked about it, and we don't want anything to happen that would get in the way of our friendship." Rachel looked relieved.

After my late breakfast I was happy to have the list of tasks Rachel gave me. These last couple of weeks with Josh had been fun, but it was a dangerous fun. It brought me to places that I wasn't ready for.

Later in the afternoon, while Ben was out with Sam at a ball game, I gathered the scant gardening tools and took Janie to the yard. I felt better now than I had in the morning. My head was clear, and I was being useful.

While I helped Janie fill the watering can, I thought about Josh and the jumble that our relationship was becoming. Our friendship had been a comfortable place, but maybe it was inviting because it held the possibility of romance. And now the romantic feelings were pulling at me, tempting me. Then there was the warning from Rachel that a serious relationship could send me home.

So maybe friendship with Josh was the answer. But I wondered if it was possible to go back in time. Once I'd felt the allure of a courtship, would I be able to settle for friendship? I didn't know the answers, but I knew that Josh and I needed to talk. When he called, I'd tell him how I was feeling and see if he had the same concerns.

I practiced in my head what I would say. But as it turned out, I didn't have to say anything because Josh didn't call.

On Sunday afternoon I helped Beth make dinner and listened to her story about the first time she used a cash machine. "I put in the card John gave me, and I just thought that money would come spewing out. There was a man behind me who said, 'It wants your PIN number.' Then I got all distracted thinking about how a machine could 'want' something. Pretty soon a line formed behind me, and a manager was walking toward me to see what the trouble was. And I just started pushing these random buttons to try to get my card back so I could go home. Oh, I just felt ridiculous."

I thought about the way Beth laughed at her own predicaments, and I tried to think if there was anyone else in the family like that. Aunt Miriam was positively dour most of the time. And my mother enjoyed a good story, but always seemed too busy to tell them. "No one in the family tells stories the way you do," I said. "No one in the family is funny."

"Your mom was," said Beth. "Before she went away, that is. In school she'd imitate the teacher or pretend to fall asleep during boring lessons. I'd bury my face in my apron to hide my laughter."

Here was yet another story about my mother that I couldn't reconcile. "Why do you think she stopped being funny?" I asked.

"I've wondered about that myself," said Beth. "Things started changing when she came home. First there was her baptism, then the celery got planted and she and your dad were 'published.' I think life just got more serious for your mom."

I smiled as I thought about Amish wedding feasts and how rumors would fly around the district when celery appeared in the garden of a family with a marriageable daughter. Then, during Sunday services, the deacon would announce or "publish" the intent of the couple to marry, making it official. It was nice to talk about these customs. I wondered if Beth felt the same way.

"I was happy that Amos picked Becky," Beth was saying. "He was always nice to us girls, and he had a kindly way about him. Before she went away, he used to come by most nights and shine the lantern in her window to call her out for courting. When she came back home, the first thing she did was send me to Amos to let him know she'd be waiting for the lantern." Beth sighed. "And I remember one day I saw your mom smiling at your dad while he was holding Margaret in his arms. I thought she looked positively grateful to have him."

I was flooded with warmth, thinking of how my parents loved each other. I chopped vegetables for the salad while Aunt Beth mashed potatoes in a big blue bowl. "Where's your young man tonight?" she asked.

I concentrated on the tomato I was slicing. "I don't know."

"Uh-oh," said Beth. "I don't like the sound of that. Do you want to talk about it?"

I told her about Rachel's warning and about dancing with Josh and bundling in the car afterward.

"That's all right," said Beth. "You're allowed to do those things during rumspringa."

"Well, while we were dancing, we said some things to each other that seemed right at the time. But now I'm all mixed up about it."

"What did you say?" Beth prodded gently.

"He told me not to go back home, and I said 'I won't.'"

"Did you mean it?"

"I don't know. At the time I felt like I meant it. Then later I thought about what I'd said. It's the same as saying 'I won't be Amish.'"

"Yes it is," Beth said.

"The next day I felt awful about it, and I decided that when he called I would have a talk with him, about maybe not being so serious in our relationship right now."

"Did you?"

Tears gathered in my eyes. "Well, that's the thing. He didn't call."

Beth's sigh was like a gust of wind. "Oh, Eliza," she said. "Boys may act full of bravado, but they're pretty insecure at this age. He must be as nervous about what you said to each other as you are."

I nodded. "So why didn't he call?"

"I don't know. Maybe he's waiting for you to call him. I'm sure the last thing he wants to do now is have Rachel answer the phone when he's calling you."

That did make sense. Before everything got tangled up with the promises and the closeness, we had sworn that Rachel couldn't know about our feelings.

In the next room, Uncle John groaned and turned off the TV. "Is it over?" Beth called.

John appeared in the kitchen, shaking his head. "Down by one run in the bottom of the ninth. First and third. Nobody out. The Cubs can't score one lousy run."

"Well, you've both had some disappointments," said Aunt Beth in a hearty voice. "So I think we should eat."

I sat at the table with my aunt and uncle, who I hadn't known existed two weeks ago, and who now welcomed me to their table as family. It had been a confusing weekend, but this was something that felt just right.

CHAPTER

❧ 26 ❧

The next morning I got up at 6:30, feeling more like myself than I had over the weekend. Anxious to get back to my usual routine, I washed and dressed and went downstairs. I packed the children's lunches in brown paper bags and put up a pot of coffee for Sam and Rachel. Janie came down first, her hair rumpled, clutching a threadbare stuffed rabbit named Sophie.

"What are we making for breakfast?" she chirped.

"French toast," I said. Janie pulled a chair over to the counter and stood on it, ready to help. Ben came down a few minutes later as I was helping Janie add a drop of vanilla to the egg batter. "Good morning, Ben," I said. He set the table for breakfast before going out to the driveway to bring in the newspaper. Back at the table he scanned the box scores from yesterday's games. "The Cubs lost again," he said, looking up from the page.

"I know," I said with a smile. I watched as Janie dipped a slice of white bread in the batter and turned it to coat the other side.

Then I dropped it, sizzling, into the pan. "Bottom of the ninth, no outs, men at first and third, and they can't score."

Ben stared at me, his mouth open. I laughed. "I was at my Uncle John's house last night. He told me."

I ate breakfast with the children, and then sent them upstairs to brush their teeth and get dressed in the clothes I had laid out for them the night before. I cleaned up the kitchen and assembled the children's backpacks. When they came back downstairs, Rachel was with them. "French toast?" she asked.

I nodded. "There are two slices for you in the refrigerator. You just have to put them in the toaster oven when you're ready to eat."

I knew that Sam would be downstairs in a few minutes, his tie knotted against the crisp collar of his shirt. He would smile at me, take two deep swigs from a mug of black coffee, and head out the door, briefcase in hand, after hugging each child and kissing Rachel on the side of her lips. Rachel and I would help the children put on their sunscreen and bug spray, then send them outside at the rumbling sound of the bright yellow bus.

Then Rachel would eat the French toast dry, standing at the counter, scanning the front page of the newspaper before gathering her materials and heading off to the library.

There was a predictability to this morning routine that gave me comfort. I realized I had become a part of it.

Alone in the house, I sat at the desk to write a letter to Daniel, but it felt awkward when just days ago I had danced with another boy and bundled in his car. I had received a couple of short letters from him since his visit, mostly descriptions of the work he was doing in his father's store and stories of the friends he saw on his trips into town. Each letter ended with the words, "Missing you, Daniel."

I still thought about him at odd moments during the day, wondering how he would react to the saying on a T-shirt or the number of piercings in someone's ear. But it had been soon after his visit that things with Josh had started to heat up, and now I felt a pang of guilt every time Daniel came into my mind. But then I would remind myself of the last words he'd spoken during his visit. I had never asked Daniel to wait for me, and I shouldn't have to be accountable to him. With that thought, my guilty twinges were replaced by defiant ones, and that was a more comfortable way to feel.

I pushed the letter to Daniel aside, knowing that I would have to contend with Josh and all that was unspoken between us over these past two days. Shaking away a nervous feeling, I picked up the phone and called him.

"Hey," he said. "I'm glad you called. Can I come over in an hour? Is it safe?"

"Yes," I said. "Rachel's gone and the kids are at camp. I'll see you soon."

When he came up the walk, I opened the front door and saw his familiar grin. It lit me a little, though I didn't want it to.

"Hey." He stepped in and leaned forward to kiss me. I pulled back for just a second, but then accepted the kiss.

"This is weird," he said, following me into the kitchen.

"Weird how?"

He opened the refrigerator and took out a can of Coke. "Do you want to sit outside?" he asked. I nodded and opened the sliding door to the small patio. We sat side by side on a big cushiony chair. Josh opened the can and took a deep drink.

"What do you mean, weird?" I asked again.

"I don't know. Friday. Just when we decide that we have to be more careful and act like you're my 'summer pal,' we go and have a pretty intense night."

I cleared my throat. "You know, we said some things while we were dancing." I felt my voice rising a bit. "And we probably shouldn't have said them." I expected Josh to agree with me, but instead he just waited for me to continue. "You asked me not to go back home. I shouldn't have agreed."

"Okay," said Josh.

"Just okay?" I said, feeling a nameless anger stirring in me. "Do you realize what you were asking me?"

"Yeah, I was telling you how much I enjoy being with you. Does that make me a bad person?"

"You were asking me to leave my family. You were asking me not to be Amish."

"Hey, don't freak out on me," he said. "I said what I thought was nice, what I was feeling. I wasn't planning to have you shunned."

It was unsettling hearing that word from him. "Well, that's what it feels like," I said. But I had to admit that it hadn't felt that way at the time. The words had sounded sweet and loving. I had been happy to hear them. The anger had come later, and it wasn't anger at Josh, but at myself for being so reckless. I lowered my voice, regretting the confrontation. "I'm not 'freaking out,'" I said. "But maybe Rachel's right. Maybe we are going a little too fast." I waited for Josh to say something, but he didn't. "Maybe we shouldn't just pretend to be summer pals. I'm thinking that I want to go back to when we didn't say things like that to each other."

Josh set the empty can on the patio and leaned back in the chair. He was wearing shorts, and I liked the sight of the dark hairs on his legs. I looked away.

"Well," said Josh, "I didn't see this coming. I just thought if we were more careful around other people, and no one suspected anything, that we could keep going. That we could still be together."

"So that's why you didn't call me all weekend?"

"Is *that* what this is about?" Josh said.

"Not really. But it was a little surprising that we could have a night like we did and then not talk all weekend."

"You were pretty clear that Rachel couldn't find out about us," he said. "And it's not like you have a cell phone. I'd have to call you on the family's line, where anyone could pick up."

I nodded. "That's what my aunt said."

"Good old Aunt Beth," said Josh. "At least someone's on my side. So, what do you want now? Do you want to be a couple, and just play it cool so no one finds out? Or do you want to go back to the 'friend zone'?"

"I don't know," I said. And that was honestly how I felt.

"Well, *buddy*, I've got to get back to work. Let me know when you decide." Josh got up and walked across the patio, sliding his iPod out of his pocket and tucking the earbuds into his ears. I winced at his words and the tone of his voice. Even though I knew I had set this all in motion, it hurt to see how easily he could get up and walk away from me.

As he crossed the lawn on his way to the front of the house, his body swayed a little to the song playing inside his head. For an instant I wanted to hear that song, too, so our bodies could sway the same way. I didn't like the sarcasm in Josh's voice, but I also didn't like the sight of him leaving. I followed him. "Wait a minute," I said. He turned around, and I stepped closer to him, gently lifting the buds out of his ears. "I really had a good time Friday night."

"So did I."

"I don't want to be your buddy," I said.

He grinned and pulled me to him. I dropped the little white wires and linked my fingers through his belt loops. "We'll be careful," he said. "And no more talk about you not going home—or going home, for that matter. Let's just live in the moment."

"In the moment," I agreed.

CHAPTER

❧ 27 ❧

The new plan with Josh seemed to work. I found that I enjoyed being in the moment. It was much less worrisome. We agreed that Josh would never call the house, and when it was safe for him to come over for a visit, I'd call him on his cell phone. Sometimes we met at the Bean Scene or at Josh's house if his parents were out. One night of the weekend, whichever night Sam and Rachel didn't need me to babysit, we would go out with Valerie and Greg or another couple. I would also bring Josh to my now-regular Sunday night dinners at Beth and John's house.

Since we were living in the moment, we decided that kissing, and maybe more, was acceptable. I told Josh about bundling, and he adopted the term for his own use. But whenever he said, "Do we have time for a little bundling?" it was in a sly, flirtatious way.

Sometimes he'd want to do more than bundle, and eventually I'd have to be the one to pull away. One night he asked, "Are you ever going to be ready?"

I tried to be funny. "You're with an Amish girl," I said. "What do you think?"

"Right?" he said. "Or maybe I should say, 'What was I thinking when I decided to go out with an Amish girl?'" He smiled and shook his head at his joke, and I knew that the moment was over. I settled against him, enjoying the feeling of skin against skin, and wondered how long a Yankee boy would be happy with the small intimacies we had together.

It wasn't easy for me to stop, either. I was finding myself more and more drawn to him. But thoughts of consequences invaded the pleasure. I had been raised with rules about what was decent, and those lessons were still inside me. More important, I didn't want to be sent home.

By the beginning of August I found myself thinking about the approaching end of my time here and I couldn't bear the thought of leaving. The list in my journal was bursting off the page. Every time I thought there would be nothing new to add, something would happen. Valerie and I would get manicures. Or I would keep score for Uncle John while we watched a Cubs-Mets game on TV. Or I would take the children to the library to see a magician perform.

Then there was Aunt Beth. Every time I was with her I felt like I was unwrapping a new gift.

And there was no way I could think about going home without grieving over leaving Josh.

I realized that my life here was bursting off the page, and I wasn't ready to leave it behind. I talked with Aunt Beth, who agreed that I might check out the possibility of extending my time away from home.

One day, when Rachel and I were elbow to elbow in the kitchen making dinner, I brought it up. "You know, I hate to think about this, but the summer's almost over."

"I've been thinking about it, too," said Rachel.

"How are you doing on your thesis?"

"I'm making progress," said Rachel. "But I'm not as far along as I'd hoped to be. Do you think there's a possibility that your parents would let you stay a little longer?"

I smiled. "That's what I was hoping you'd say."

In my next letter home, I wrote, *Mrs. Aster talked with me today. She still has work to do on her thesis, and she's hoping I might be able to stay on a little longer. I know that the agreement was for me to return home at the end of the summer, but I'd like to be able to stay here through autumn, if I may.* I read the note over, then added: *I'm enjoying my work and I believe I'm very useful here. I don't want my absence from home to be a burden to you, and I'm sure that you miss my help when the inn guests come for dinner. But if you can spare me a while longer, it will be good for this family, and for me.*

I slipped the letter into an envelope and wrote my family's address on it. Putting on the stamp, I thought for a minute about giving a little prayer for the letter to bring me the answer I wanted. Then I realized that I had all but abandoned my prayers since I came here, and I thought with a twinge that God probably had more important prayers to answer than this one.

Every day I waited for the mail to be delivered. A week went by and no letter came from home. I tried another letter, filling it with news of the work I'd been doing and the interesting things the children said. Then in the PS, I wrote, *Have you had a chance to consider letting me stay here a little longer? Mrs. Aster needs more time to work on her thesis, and I would like to help her. Please let me know.*

A few days later a letter arrived from my mother.

Dear Eliza,

I am wondering how you would feel about receiving a visit from your mother. I am thinking of coming for a few days to see you and perhaps take in the city a bit. I would come by train, and hope that you will be able to meet me there. I look forward to spending some time with you.

All my love,

Mother

PS I hope to have the opportunity to meet your friend Betty as well!

CHAPTER

28

I didn't know what to make of my mother's letter. There was no mention of my request for more time, and I worried that she might intend to personally bring me home at the end of her visit.

But she did want to see Aunt Beth. Right away, I called Beth and asked if she could stop by on her way home from work. She arrived at Rachel's door just as I was putting a casserole in the oven for the family's dinner. I took Beth's hand and pulled her upstairs. She hadn't seen my room before, and I watched her smiling approval of my space in Rachel's home. Then I handed her the letter, waiting for the moment of recognition.

Her face changed. She made a sound like she was out of breath, and she put her hand over her mouth. Her eyes were wide.

"I know!" I said, although she hadn't said anything. She lowered her hand and reached it out toward me. I rushed to hug her, feeling her body tremble against mine.

There followed a flurry of letters back and forth between my mother and me, selecting dates, confirming the time of arrival at the train station, arranging for her to stay at Rachel's house (though Beth was already preparing her guest room). Her arrival was a week away. She would be staying for six days, the longest she had ever been away from home as a married woman.

All the while I was filled with worry. I worried about how the meeting would go between the two sisters. And I was concerned with what her plan was for me. I also had to reconcile my feelings about this woman who had shunned her own sister.

One afternoon, with the children off to camp and my household tasks completed for the day, I sat on my bed with my journal open on my lap and flipped through the pages, reading snatches of my rumspringa life. *Buttons everywhere,* I had written in one of my first days. *Beeps and buttons.*

I smiled and turned to another page. *ANNIE WAS RIGHT,* I had written in big letters. *Yankee boys are cute! Josh draws out his grin in a slow way, until his face becomes a smiling one by inches.*

On the night of Daniel's visit, I wrote:

Daniel appeared at my door
I was
happy to see him
sad to see him leave
a little mad at him during the visit
relieved that we made up
nothing is new.

One day, after Valerie and I returned from the mall, I wrote, *Valerie envies my eyelashes. What an odd thing. And why does that make me feel so satisfied?*

One Sunday, after returning from Beth and John's house, I wrote, *Oh, Uncle John, you didn't cause the Cubs' losing streak. No, you're not a jinx.*

I closed the journal and hugged it to my chest. I hadn't kept a meticulous record, as I'd promised my mother, but I enjoyed these little glimpses into my English life. I thought about what it might be like to read it later, when I was grown and remembering this place and this time. I tried to imagine what this future Eliza would look like as she read the journal. Would she be sitting in a kitchen lit by kerosene lamps, her kapp snug on her head, her apron cinched around her waist? Or would she be in a kitchen surrounded by beeping machines, wearing trousers and a blouse with buttons?

I turned to the end of the journal to see how many blank pages remained, and a puffiness inside the back cover caught my attention. It crinkled against my fingertips. My fingers roamed the inside the back cover until I felt the opening of a pocket that I hadn't known was there. I reached in and pulled out a sheaf of folded pages, yellowed and creased. Opening the pages, I saw my mother's familiar looped lettering in blue ballpoint ink. My heartbeat quickened and I began to read.

I am only one week here and it feels like I've always lived in this world. Now I flip on the light switch without a thought and turn the knob on the radio to listen to music. How will I be able to leave the ease of this life? How will I ever go back to hanging wash on a line and drying the dishes one by one with a damp towel?

I swallowed back a gasp. This was my mother's rumspringa journal. She must not have remembered that these pages were there.

I read her writing like I was thirsty, gulping it, inhaling it. The early pages detailed the wonders of television, movies, the dishwasher, the dryer, the garbage disposal. Others were musings. In one entry she wrote, *I thought I would miss the Sunday services and the quilt circles. But they have been replaced with other activities. Discussions around the dinner table about things that happened in the news. Trips into town to museums and movies. Shopping excursions to find a shirt in just the right shade of blue to match a new pair of pants. I want to miss the gentle affairs of home, but they seem far away and unimportant. Here I am, and there's a chance I will stay put.*

I turned to another entry, with the lyrics of every song on James Taylor's *Sweet Baby James* album. It was hardly possible to think that my mother had listened to pop music. How could those songs not have stayed a part of her when she returned home? How could she have left them so completely behind?

Another entry read: *The chores here take up so much less time. Laundry at home occupies an entire backbreaking day. Here, the clothes don't have the same smell of the wind and sun, but they are clean in an hour or two. Is it sinful to cherish these bonus hours that are tacked on to each day? If so, then I am a sinner and I don't plan to repent.*

Some entries were about Debbie, the tailor's daughter, who

taught her how to use the CD player and what stores in the mall had the cool clothes.

About halfway through the pages, a name caught my eye. *I know that Beth is lonesome for me, and I admit that I don't think about her as much as I should. This is such a selfish time, this rumspringa. I am consumed only with my own wishes. I am not Good Amish while I'm here. Actually, while I'm here, I'm not Amish at all.*

Drenched in my mother's words, I read on. There were only a few pages left, and the entries were shorter and farther apart. I realized that I was searching for something. And then I found it.

Matthew came over tonight. We went down to the basement to talk and et cetera. His hair is such a golden color I can't stop looking at it.

Matthew. My mother had had an English beau and his name was Matthew. My heart was throbbing now. I turned the page eagerly and scanned ahead.

Matthew's name was mentioned a few times, but with scant details. I stopped reading for a moment, unsure if I should go on. Should I be reading about a romance my mother once had with a boy whose name, over all these years she has never mentioned? I wondered if I should set the pages aside, but then I thought about this gift from my mother. She could have given me any book of pages for journal writing, but she had purposely handed me this one. I inched toward a new realization. My mother wanted me to know about this. These tucked-away pages were a message from my mother to me. I went back to her words, to the story my mother had never told me.

Now some entries were only one or two sentences long. *We fit together perfectly. We are supposed to be together.* Others alluded to the complexities of their relationship. *We talked for hours and still said nothing new. We argue even though we are both in agreement.* On the second to last page the writing was faint, as though she wasn't sure about committing the words to paper. *I shouldn't have let things get so far. I don't know if there is a way out of this.*

My chest tightened and I closed my eyes. My mother had been in trouble. I turned to the last page. *I leave tomorrow on the 8 a.m. train. Debbie cried when I told her I was going. She said, "I thought we were friends." I told her lies. I said that my family needed me. That I'd write to her. That I'd see her again. All lies. Matthew said he was sorry. He offered me money. I waited to see if that was all he would offer. It was.*

Then, at the bottom of the last page was one sentence:

I hope that Amos is a forgiving man.

I caught my breath. I felt dizzy, the air around me too thin to take in a full breath. I didn't want to think about what this meant.

But I knew. It all made sense now, my mother's rush home, her transformation into a dutiful Amish woman, her hasty marriage to a man she might not have loved at the time.

My hands shook as I folded the pages and pushed them back into the hidden pocket. I closed the notebook and felt the wild need to hide it. The camp bus was rumbling up the street, and I went downstairs. Taking in breaths of the too-thin air, I pasted a smile on my face as the children tumbled off the bus, backpacks slipping from their narrow shoulders.

Janie greeted me with a hug, as she always did, and I squeezed her tightly. Walking the children into the house, I listened to their jumbled chatter about the day's adventures. I made them a snack and put their damp towels and swimsuits into the washing machine, setting their backpacks aside until I would repack them in the morning. My movements felt outside of myself. My body was here, carrying out my commands, but my mind was somewhere else. It was in a place over twenty years ago, when a girl named Becky tiptoed too close to the edge.

CHAPTER

 **29**

I waited on the platform at Union Station for my mother's train, my body feeling odd and jumpy. That morning, Rachel had driven me to Beth's house to drop off my suitcase, and then took me to the train station with a reminder of how to get downtown. Since then I'd been pacing, thinking about my mother's visit and what it would mean.

Finally I saw the light of the approaching train, and waited as the doors opened and people poured onto the platform. My mother stepped slowly off the train, a small brown suitcase in one hand, her basket over her other arm. I waved and watched her expression change from caution to happy recognition when she saw me. Despite the August heat, she wore her black traveling bonnet with the wide brim, and a black cape over her dress and apron. I noticed the quick glances she got from the other passengers rushing from the platform to the station. Dodging around the swarms of people going in the other direction, I walked toward my mother. She set down her suitcase and basket and opened her arms, letting me slip into her embrace.

"Oh, Eliza, look at you," she said when I stepped back. "You look just like them!"

I was wearing a sundress that Valerie had helped me pick out, in vivid shades of violet and yellow. "Okay," I said. "I'll take that as a compliment." Then I added, "If it's all right with you, I thought we'd get some lunch before we . . ." My voice trailed off. I was about to say, *Before we go to Aunt Beth's house.*

Minutes later we were facing each other in a booth in a restaurant I had spotted earlier. My mother took off her cape to reveal a lime-colored dress. I thought I noticed some new lines around her eyes, but her face looked peaceful, if a bit shy. After seeing the waitress's stare, I realized that I hadn't considered what my mother would wear during her visit, or how much she would stand out in her traditional attire.

We ordered chicken salad and iced tea, and handed the menus back to the waitress. I sprinkled a packet of sugar into my glass. When I looked up, my mother was watching me. I took a sip and returned her gaze. The last time we were together, she was reluctantly sending me off. Since then I had acquired a new aunt and a journal filled with my mother's secrets. I waited for her to start the conversation.

"Well," she said with a sigh, "I guess it's time for one of us to mention her."

I nodded, eyes fixed on her face. "I have an aunt named Beth."

She looked down. "Thank you for finding her."

I felt an unexpected rush of irritation. "She wasn't so hard to find. You had the address. All I had to do was show up at her door."

I waited for my mother to say something. She stirred her tea while silence crept in and settled between us, like a third person at the table. Then I understood. Her eyes were filling with tears. "It's all right," I said, trying to keep the anger from my voice. "I know how things were." But even as I said the words, I knew that I would never understand how a woman could shut her sister out of her life.

My mother shook her head, and the tears stood in her eyes. When she spoke, there was a shakiness in her voice I had never heard before. "It didn't have to be that way. I know that now. I've seen other people under the bann. We have our restrictions, but they're still among us. Why did we let Beth leave us?"

In that moment, I saw her differently. Suddenly she wasn't the mother who had tried to keep me at home, or the sister who had turned away from Beth. She was a woman who had gulped down sadness over the years and who had fought those feelings with strictness and rules. "Aunt Beth isn't angry," I said softly. "She just misses everyone, especially you. She's so grateful that you sent me to find her."

My mother shook her head, and the tears finally flowed. "Then she's a merciful woman," she said in a choked voice. "I wasn't a good sister to her."

I didn't know what to say to that.

The waitress set down our plates. My mother pushed hers

aside and set her elbows on the table, covering her face with her hands. They were the competent hands I always thought of when my mother came to mind, slender fingers reddened from work, the nails cut square and blunt. I waited a moment before I spoke.

"Does anyone from home know that you'll be seeing Aunt Beth?"

"Your father does," she said, fumbling in her basket for a handkerchief and dabbing at her eyes. "I'm tired of keeping secrets."

I let out a great breath. It felt good to know that my father was a part of this. "What did he say?" I asked.

She smiled. "He said, 'Give my sister-in-law my good wishes.'"

A tear slipped down my cheek, and I wiped it with the back of my hand.

My mother lowered her head. Too late, I realized that she was saying grace. I swallowed the bite of tomato I had just taken and bent my head. The old prayer raced through my mind. When I looked up, my mother was smiling at me. She dipped her fork into the chicken salad. "Tell me about Beth."

"When she laughs, it fills the whole room," I said. "And she looks you right in the eyes when she talks to you. Like you're the only person she's thinking about at that moment."

"She was always like that," my mother said. "Even in her wild teenager days, when no one knew what to do with her."

"She feels bad about those times," I said. "She knew she gave Grandma and Grandpa fits." I paused before adding, "Do they know?"

My mother shook her head. "Not yet. But I think I'm going to tell them when I get back home. They never speak of Beth, but she wears on them. I know they think about her."

I set my hands on the edge of the table, steadying myself for what I was about to say.

"Mom," I started.

She set down her fork and looked at me fully, waiting. "Go ahead."

"I read your journal."

"So you know."

"Yes." I tried to think of what to say next, but no words seemed to fit. "Yes, I know."

"Well, I did say that I was tired of keeping secrets."

"I didn't tell Aunt Beth. I thought it should come from you."

She nodded. "It's my story, and I'll tell it when we're all together." Then she asked, "Will I be staying with . . . your friend Betty?" We both laughed, and it was a laughter that flowed right through my limbs. I could feel it in my fingernails and knees and the soles of my feet.

"Yes," I said. "My friend Betty has a room for both of us."

Before we left the restaurant, I had one more question to ask my mother. "Are you here to take me home?"

My mother shook her head. "We told Mrs. Aster that you would be working for her through the summer. We won't be going back on our agreement."

I was relieved. She hadn't said anything about my wish to stay longer, but at least I knew I wouldn't be going home before the end of the summer. That was all I could hope for right now.

After lunch, my mother paid the bill and I guided her back to the train station, smiling boldly at the people who stared at us. On the train we sat with the suitcase squeezed in at our feet, the basket on my mother's lap. We talked about home, and I found myself hungry for details about the family and my friends. Ruthie was becoming a competent helper on Stranger Nights, and I was surprised to feel a little envious that she had taken my place at our mother's side.

"And how is Daniel?" I asked, uncertain of the answer I wanted to hear.

"He's fine," she said, eyeing me. "He seems to be staying to himself, mostly. He asks about you whenever he comes by the shop."

The recorded voice announced that Evanston was the next stop. Struggling to haul the suitcase into the aisle, I inched my way to the doors with my mother behind me. We stood together, holding the handrail for balance as the train came to a stop and the doors swept open.

When we reached Beth's house, I pointed. My mother looked to be taking it all in. Then she smiled at me. "I'm ready."

Inside, I led her upstairs to the guest room we would share, with two twin beds covered by quilts Beth had made. A smile filled my mother's face. "My sister still quilts?"

"Yes," I said, feeling a curious pride. "It's her passion."

She set her suitcase on one of the beds and opened it. On top lay a crisp white kapp. She took off her black bonnet and set the kapp on her head, adjusting it with practiced fingers. I watched, familiarity flooding me.

I sat on the other bed while my mother unpacked the small suitcase, hanging up the dresses and cape, setting her nightgowns and undergarments in a dresser drawer, and placing toiletries and robe in the bathroom. I noticed the spareness of my mother's life. The items she'd brought for a six-day trip took up such a tiny bit of space. The night before, I had spent hours scanning my drawers and closet, deciding what to bring, thinking about what to wear each day. The suitcase I had borrowed from Rachel was bulging.

When my mother finished unpacking, I showed her around the house. "I remember thinking that I'd never be able to live without these machines," she said, glancing around Beth's kitchen. Then she paused and looked at me. "But I've managed just fine."

I nodded, understanding. We went into the living room to wait for Beth, sitting side by side on the couch, each turned slightly to face the other. My mother's eyes occasionally went to the front door. "Tell me about this man Beth married," she said.

"He's very smart, a university professor. But he doesn't show off his smartness. You'll meet him later. He's teaching a night class, so it'll be just us three girls at dinner." My mother looked relieved to hear that.

Just then, I heard a car pull into the driveway. My mother sat forward on the couch, her fingers absently straightening her kapp.

The car door slammed, and I heard hurrying footsteps on the front walk and a key jangling in the lock. The front door flung open, banging into the high table in the entryway. My mother stood up and walked slowly around the coffee table as Beth stepped through the door. Her face was wildly alert.

For a long, silent moment they both stood frozen, facing each other across the room. Then my mother lifted both arms in front of her, reaching out, her fingers stretching toward Beth. Beth's face contorted with what looked like a smile and a cry, and she ran to my mother, her arms reaching forward, her braid swaying against her back, until they tumbled into each other's arms.

I inched closer, wanting to be near, but wanting them to have their moment together. A howling sound, rich and low, came from the center of the embrace. Then each sister reached an arm out to me, and I stepped into the fierceness of the hug. I wasn't sure how long we stood together, arms interlocked, wet cheeks pressed together. I took a step back and felt my lips turn up at the corners. "Mom," I said, "I'd like you to meet my friend Betty."

My mother and aunt fell back into each other's arms, their shoulders shaking with laughter. There was a lightness in my chest and limbs. It was the way I had felt when Josh first played the Beatles for me. Watching my mother and aunt in each other's arms, I knew that everything would be all right. The bann and the harsh words were part of another time.

They sat down on the couch, still holding hands, still gazing at each other. I perched on the chair, my elbows pressed against my rib cage as though to keep my emotions from dancing out of my body.

"Where do we start?" asked Beth.

My mother was quiet for a moment. "Let's start with now."

CHAPTER

30

They started with now. Over dinner at the big kitchen table, and later in the living room sipping steaming cups of tea, Beth and my mother talked about their lives. I listened closely, even to the stories I already knew.

During a pause in the conversation, Beth leaned forward. "Tell me about Emily," she said. Her voice had an urgent quality, and I recalled the story of Beth looking up at her friend's window after she was turned away from the house.

"Oh, jah, I forgot what good friends you were," said my mother. "Emmy married Adam, and they have four children. But, you know, I always thought that he wasn't her first choice for a husband. I had a feeling she was more interested in Joseph."

"She was," said Beth. "It's funny. Emmy shunned me for choosing my own husband. But in the end maybe she wished that she had done the same." Her hands trembled around her cup of tea, and she looked at my mother. "What was it like when I left?"

"Awful," said my mother, without a hesitation. "We all went

over to Mom and Dad's house that night—Amos and me, Ike and Miriam, the children. We wanted to be together. Then, just as we were about to say grace, Mom looked at your empty chair and started crying. Dad got up from the table, lifted the chair over his head, and marched out of the room with it."

"That's Dad for you," said Beth. "Did he say anything?"

I hugged myself, waiting, and glanced at Beth, whose fingers were fiddling with the end of her braid.

"He said, 'Everyone knows that we've had a terrible loss tonight. We have one less member in our family now.'" My mother's voice slipped to a whisper. "Then he said, 'We all need to remember that Elizabeth chose to leave. We didn't send her away.'"

"Was that all?" asked Beth. She sounded disappointed.

"There was one more thing," my mother added. She sent the words out slowly, as though it was a struggle to let them leave her lips. "He said that no one was to mention your name again. That we were never to speak of you."

Beth nodded. "I guess I'm not surprised."

My mother put her hand on Beth's arm. "I've had so many regrets since that day, Beth. When you came to say good-bye to me, why didn't I beg you to stay?"

"Because you couldn't," said Beth. "You were following the rules."

"I didn't always follow the rules," my mother said. She turned to me then. I nodded and looked down, surprised that she seemed to be asking for my permission to speak.

"What's going on?" asked Beth.

"I need to tell you something," my mother said. "Eliza knows some of it. But I was wrong to keep it a secret for so long. It may explain some things about me."

"What is it, Becky?"

"Well," she began, "you know that I came home ahead of schedule from my rumspringa. But it wasn't because Dad had cleared up the debt."

"Oh, no," said Beth. "I always wondered if something happened there."

"Something did." My mother closed her eyes for a moment, as if to see it all in her mind before she spoke. I wrapped my arms around my knees.

"I loved it there. For a time, I thought it was a world I could live in."

"So what happened?" asked Beth. "Why did you rush home?"

"I met a boy. His name was Matthew, and of course I thought I loved him. He was interested in politics, and we read the newspaper together and talked about current events. In the fall he was going to leave for college. We talked about my coming to visit him at the university, and I actually thought I would be able to do that."

My mother told the story plainly in a voice that didn't shake with emotion or drift off dreamily. "We talked about how we might stay together," she continued. "But it seemed impossible. He had four years of college ahead of him, and I was supposed to go back home when the debt was settled. So I decided that I wouldn't be baptized, that I would stay with him."

The room was quiet. I was sure I could hear all of our heart-beats. Finally Beth spoke. "What happened, Becky?"

My mother looked at Beth, and then at me. "I got pregnant."

I closed my eyes and felt the sick, dizzy sensations I'd had when I read the journal. Beth gasped. "Oh, Becky."

"I know. I was one of those girls who seemed so good, but really I wasn't."

I shook my head. "No, Mom. This isn't about good and bad. It's about a mistake."

My mother turned to me. When she spoke, her words were measured and serious. But they were also kind. "Eliza, there is something you need to know before I say anything more." I waited. "What I did with that boy was a mistake. But you must never think that Margaret was a mistake."

My mind filled with commotion. All through this week, think-ing about my mother's journal and waiting to have my fears con-firmed, I hadn't thought about Margaret. I hadn't taken that step. Now I knew that my older sister, the Good Amish girl who had refused rumspringa, was born because of a coupling between an English boy and a rebellious Amish teenager planning to leave the Order. It didn't seem possible.

"I had this notion that I would go to the university with him.

I would take care of the baby and he would study. It was foolish, I know."

"What did Matthew say?" I asked.

"He said everything you're thinking now. Where would we live? How could he finish school with a baby to support?" She paused, and we waited in silence. "But he wasn't unkind. He was scared. He looked like a child about to get a spanking. It wasn't the way I wanted him to take the news."

"So that was it?" Beth asked. "Did he just walk away?"

"Not exactly. He apologized and cried. We both cried. Then he asked for my address at home so he could send me money each month to take care of the baby. And I understood that he wanted me to leave, and I knew that I'd never see him again."

"Then what did you do?" asked Beth.

"I was up all night long," my mother said. "Making my plans. Crying into a big towel so I wouldn't wake anyone. In the morning I went into town and bought a train ticket and sent my parents a telegram saying that I would be home the next day, that the tailor didn't need me anymore. Then I told the tailor and his wife that my family needed me back home. Everything about me was a lie."

I crept from my chair and sat on the couch beside my mother. She put her arm around me. "I'm sorry, Mom," I whispered.

"It's okay," she said, her voice soothing. "Everything's fine now. I admit that for a while I thought I was in an impossible mess. But it all worked out."

"How?" I asked.

My mother smiled and turned to Beth. "Well, you didn't know it at the time, but you helped me. Right after I got home, I told you to go find Amos and tell him I'd be watching for his lantern. Sure enough, I'd barely gotten to my room that night when I saw his lantern glowing in the yard. I slipped out of the house and said a prayer that Amos would still love me and still want to marry me. We went off to a little spot by the pond. Oh, he was so happy to see me." Her voice trailed off.

"What did you do?" Beth asked.

My mother's voice was firm. "I stopped lying," she said. "I told him everything. If we were going to start a life together, I wanted it to be an honest one."

"How did he take the news?" Beth asked softly.

"He was very quiet at first. When he didn't say anything, I asked him what he was thinking." Her voice choked at the next words, and she stopped talking. We leaned closer to her. She took a breath and started again. "He said, 'Before I ask you to marry me, I have to be sure that this baby will have no other father but me.'"

"And how did you answer him?" whispered Beth.

"I said that the baby would be so lucky to have him for a father."

A tear ran down my cheek. I saw Beth reaching for a tissue. Only my mother's eyes were dry. Her face was suddenly peaceful, just as it was when she said grace before meals. I realized this offering of her story was like a prayer.

"I can't believe this all went on and I had no idea about it," said Beth. She sounded out of breath, like she had walked a long way.

"Well, things got very busy in our house. We didn't waste any time because we didn't want tongues wagging about how soon the baby arrived after the wedding. The day after I got home we told our parents we wanted to marry, and right away Mom planted the celery and Dad went to speak to the bishop about publishing us. I was baptized the next week."

"Did people wonder about how soon Margaret was born?" I asked.

"We did tell one more lie," my mother said, with a wisp of a smile. "We told our friends that Amos had visited me while I was away, and what a good time we'd had together. So we hoped that if anyone was counting the months from our wedding to Margaret's birth and coming up with less than nine, they would just assume the baby got started during Amos's visit."

"Did you ever hear from Matthew again?" I asked.

"For a while he sent a check every month. I opened the first envelope and saw that there was no note, just a check made out to me. I tore it up and returned the next letters unopened. After a few months they stopped coming."

The room filled with silence. We were still together on the couch, my head on my mother's shoulder, Beth holding her hand as though seventeen years hadn't come between them. During the quiet, the front door opened and John stepped inside. His smile was a cautious one.

"John," said Beth, getting up from the couch and walking to greet him. "She's here, John. My sister is here."

Beth took her husband by the hand and led him to the couch. My mother stood up. I hoped that John wouldn't greet her with a big lumbering hug, as he had when he'd met me. I worried that she would find it too familiar. To my relief, I saw John stand formally before my mother and reach a hand out to her. "Thank you for coming here," he said, his smile widening as my mother returned his handshake. "I hope you know what an important day this is for Beth. And for me."

"I'm happy to meet you, John." My mother took her hand out of John's grip, and his smile slipped for an instant. Then she reached her arms around his shoulders and pulled him into an embrace.

"Now, this feels strange," came my mother's voice from the twin bed beside me.

I turned on my side to face my mother in the darkened room. I thought about all that must feel strange to her right now. Being in the home of the sister she hadn't seen or talked about for seventeen years. Lying in a bed without her husband beside her for the first time in her marriage.

"What feels strange?" I asked.

"Sleeping under a quilt in August."

I laughed. "Right? All summer I've been thinking about what a fine invention air-conditioning is." In the silence after my mother's laughter I said, "Can I ask you something, Mom?" She turned to face me. "Did you want me to find the journal?"

"Yes," she answered. "I wanted you to know that this world

is exciting. But it can also be dangerous. And, honestly, I wasn't comfortable about having the conversation, so I hoped the journal would do it for me."

Suddenly I thought of something. "Does Margaret know?"

"She does. We told her when she came of age. Your father was a bit reluctant, but I thought she should know before she started to make her adult decisions."

"How did she take it?"

"Quietly," my mother said.

I waited for her to say more, but I understood that this was my sister's story, and that our mother would want to respect Margaret's privacy. I tried to remember my sister in the days before her baptism and marriage. Margaret had always been a dutiful girl, and now I realized that her calm obedience wasn't because these were solemn occasions. She might have been working out the new understandings about her life. I remembered what she said to me when I was complaining about our mother at the barn raising. "You think Mother's against you, but really she's not." Then she had said, "Trust me," as though she knew more than I did. And it was true.

"Margaret was always such Good Amish," I said.

"That was partly my doing, I'm afraid," said my mother. "In those early years I was always aware of Margaret's beginnings. I guess I was harder on her than I was on the rest of you. I was determined that she be a good Amish girl so there would never be a question of where she belonged."

There was something else I wanted to know. "Why did you

agree to let me go away after what happened to you? And to Aunt Beth?"

My mother propped herself on her elbow to face me. "Your father wanted to send you *because* of all that happened," she said. "He told me he'd always wondered how things might have been if my parents had let Beth go away. He thought that if they had let her see that other world, she might have chosen ours."

"And you?" I asked. "Was that your reason, too?"

"No," she said. "My reason was in the atlas."

I sat up in bed and watched her, waiting to understand. "I looked in the atlas after Mrs. Aster told me where she lived, and I saw how close her town was to Evanston. I wanted you to find my sister."

CHAPTER

31

My mother's visit sped by. Aunt Beth had arranged to take the days off from work, and then set about filling them with plans. We went to the art museum and the historical society and the botanical gardens. We spent one night outside among a patchwork of picnic blankets, illuminated by citronella candles, and listened to the symphony.

Sometimes Uncle John was with us, but most evenings he slipped into his study after dinner. It was the end of summer session, and he was busy grading final exams and getting lesson plans ready for the fall. But I also suspected that he was giving us our time together. I tried to call Josh each day, sometimes just to hear how delighted he was at the sound of my voice.

I was most excited about the musical play my aunt had told me about, and when that night arrived, I entered the theater with a giddiness I hadn't felt since the lights had dimmed at my first movie. But unlike in the movies, the people were real, and they stood a mere few feet away from us. It was over too soon, and when the actors assembled on the square stage to bow to the audience, I felt a little sad to say good-bye to them.

As we filed out of the theater, slowed by the crowd, a little girl who had been walking beside us stopped and pointed at my mother. "Were you in the play?" she asked.

"I'm sorry," said the girl's mother, tugging at the child's pointed finger. Heads turned toward us, and we were enveloped in stares.

Smiling at the girl, my mother said, "No, I wasn't in the play. This is how I dress."

The mother pulled the girl away, and the crowd resumed their movements toward the exit. I could hear murmurs around us. "Must be Amish," a man whispered loudly.

Beth turned around, her eyes searching for the source of the whisper, a look of irritation on her face. We reached the door and stepped out into the cool evening, walking to the car in silence.

In the car, Beth sighed. "All that gawking."

"Let it go, Beth." My mother's voice was quiet, but there was a tightness around her words. "When we choose to be different, we have to expect a little attention."

Back at Beth's house, we went into the kitchen for tea, as had become our custom during these days together. We sat quietly, a plate of cookies on the table, our cups of tea warm and fragrant.

"It still bothers you, the way people look at us," my mother said to Beth. It was a statement, but also a question.

Beth nodded. "It does. I hated it, Becky. I hated that life."

"So, John didn't really take you away."

"No," said Beth. "I probably would have left eventually. He just made it easier."

"You know, I always felt responsible," my mother said. "I always wondered if there was something I could have said or done that would have made things different for you."

When Beth spoke, she exhaled the words, making them sound weighty. "There was."

My mother's voice was quiet and formal when she asked, "What should I have done?"

Beth looked up from her cup of tea, her eyes searching my mother's. "You should have been on my side when I went under the bann. I needed you to be on my side."

My mother shook her head in a sad way. "That's why I told you my story. I wanted you to understand that when you were facing the bann, I wasn't in a position to support you. Being Good Amish was the only way I knew to put my life back together."

Beth got up from the table and carried her cup to the sink. I glanced at my mother, but she was looking down, studying her cooling tea. Finally Beth spoke, her back to my mother and me. "I just realized something," she said. "You were welcomed home for telling a lie. I was driven away for telling the truth. I guess the Amish are funny that way. It doesn't matter if you're being honest or not, as long as you say what they want to hear."

My mother pushed her chair away from the table and stood up.

"I've been punishing myself for the last twenty years," she said, her voice sliced with anger. "I don't need you punishing me, too."

Beth turned around to face my mother. "I don't judge you for what happened, Becky. I think you were very brave. It was just hard to lose my sister."

"It was hard for me, too," said my mother. "You broke my heart when you stopped writing."

I caught my breath and looked at Aunt Beth. Her eyes were wide, but she didn't speak. I turned to my mother. "Dad wrote to Aunt Beth and said that her letters were upsetting you. He asked her to stop writing, so she did." I looked at Beth, her eyes filling with tears, then at my mother, frozen in her spot, her hand covering her mouth. "Aunt Beth thought you knew about Dad's letter," I went on. "She thought you wanted him to write it for you."

She sank back into her chair, her shoulders slumped forward. "No," she said. "When the letters stopped coming, I thought you were done with me."

Beth came back to the table and slipped quietly into the chair beside my mother. "Never, Becky," she said. "I'll never be done with you. I always hoped you would come and find me."

My mother looked up and met Beth's eyes. "And finally I did."

They sat looking at each other for a moment, small smiles on their faces, before Beth got up and reached forward to pick up the teacups. My mother placed her hand on Beth's wrist. "Wait," she said. Beth set the cups down and pulled her chair around so it faced my mother. "There's something else you need to understand." My mother swallowed and took a raggedy breath. "I wanted it for you, Beth," she whispered. "Do you know what I'm saying?"

Beth leaned forward, her knees touching my mother's. "You wanted me to leave?"

"Staying at home was the right choice for me, but I knew it wouldn't be right for you," my mother said, her voice breaking. "I knew you needed to leave to be happy, so I was willing to shun you just to be sure you got this life."

"Oh, Becky." Beth reached forward, wrapping her arms around my mother. They were both crying now. I swallowed hard and pushed back my chair. I stepped toward the kitchen door, my eyes still on my mother and Aunt Beth, holding each other, breathing deep, jagged sobs. "Oh, Becky," Beth said again, as I slipped out of the kitchen.

I tiptoed upstairs, my heart pounding, a worry nestled in my chest. Had my mother accepted a life she didn't want? When I went back downstairs a few minutes later, my mother and aunt were sitting together on the living room couch. Their eyes were red-rimmed, but their expressions were peaceful. I settled on the couch beside my mother. She was silent for a moment before she turned to me. "Do you understand about the trouble a girl can get into?"

"Of course I do," I said.

She shook her head. "So did I. But it happened to me anyway." Her voice grew gentle when she added, "I know about your young man, Eliza. And I think that he's the reason you asked for more time here."

That was the first time my mother mentioned my wish to stay longer. Aunt Beth must have told her about Josh. I wanted to be angry, but instead I felt relief. I wanted my mother to know. "He's only part of the reason," I said, trying to sound casual. "I'm enjoying all the things I can't do at home. I also love my work with Rachel's family. And now that I've found Aunt Beth, I can't bear the thought of leaving her."

"I know," said my mother. "But you'll be leaving a lot more if you stay here."

I closed my eyes. I wanted to ask her how she felt about the choice she had made, but the words felt tangled up. I opened my eyes to see that my mother and Beth were both looking at me. "You shunned Aunt Beth."

"I was taught that there is only one way to live," she said. "And anyone who doesn't accept that has to leave. It was the only way I could think of to help her."

"I wish we hadn't lost those years," said Beth, her voice like flowing water. "But now I know that my sister wasn't rejecting me. She was allowing me to have the life I wanted." Her eyes met my mother's. "She did it because she loved me." My mother nodded and made it true.

I turned to my mother. "Do you regret your choice?" I asked. "Do you wish you had this life?"

"I have to admit that at first it was hard. Sometimes I'd catch myself humming a James Taylor song while I hung the clothes on the line, and I'd think about Debbie's big collection of CDs." She paused. "But gradually I realized that what I missed were just things. We can do without things easier than we can do without people. What was waiting for me at home was more important than what I left behind."

"And Dad?" I asked, my voice almost a whisper.

My mother's eyes locked with mine. "Your father is my hero."

Relief trickled through me. My mother's story was told, and mine was still in the making. There was so much work ahead.

CHAPTER

❦ 32 ❦

On Friday night, Beth and John had a dinner party. They invited Sam and Rachel and the children, and I was eager for my mother to get to know this family that had welcomed me so warmly into the fancy world. Also coming were John's parents, his sister and her family, two women from Beth's Tuesday night quilting group, and a professor who worked with John. On the day before the party, we added one more guest: Josh.

Beth had approached me while my mother was out in the garden, and asked how I would feel about including Josh in the dinner party. I was surprised at the question. During my calls to Josh we spoke in urgent whispers and assumed that we wouldn't see each other until my mother went back home. Now I looked up at Beth. "I don't know," I said. "How do you think my mom would feel about having him here?"

Beth smiled. "It was your mother who asked me to invite Joshua. She wants to meet him."

I took in a shaky breath and reached for Beth's phone. Josh picked up after the first ring.

"Hey," he said. "I miss you."

"I miss you too," I said. "I was wondering if you'd like to come to dinner at Aunt Beth's house tomorrow night."

"Tomorrow?" he asked. "I thought your mom wasn't leaving until Sunday."

"She's not. She'll be at the dinner, and she wants to meet you."

All Josh said in response was "Whoa."

"Dinner's at six," I went on. "Rachel's family will be there, and Uncle John's family, and a few other people, too. Do you want to come?"

"Count me in," he said.

Helping Beth and my mother get ready for the dinner, I felt the way I did on Stranger Nights: excited in a nervous way. My hands fumbled with the simplest of tasks, and I felt out of breath, as though I had just run up a flight of stairs. Beth and my mother worked easily together, and I wondered if they felt nostalgic for a time when they used to help their mother in the kitchen of their childhood.

My mother smoothed her blue dress and starched white apron. Her kapp sat serenely atop her head, and her bun was perfectly arranged. I had told Josh what my mother's clothes would be like, but I worried that he might stare at her in surprise, as so many people here did. I was wearing the lavender dress I had bought on that first shopping day with Valerie.

Now, waiting for the guests to arrive, my mother looked me up and down with an approving smile. "Every day I'm eager to see what you'll be wearing," she said. "And you never disappoint me." At that moment I felt a rush of affection for my mother, and I leaned over to kiss her cheek. She looked surprised for a moment, and then reached her arm around me and pulled me close. I breathed in the scent of her, that lemony smell I had almost forgotten. Our moment was interrupted by the tumult of Ben and Janie bursting through the front door. They ran to me, flinging their arms around my waist.

"Well, look at the two of you," I exclaimed, planting a kiss on the top of each head. "I think you miss me!"

Leaning over the children, who still clung to my waist, Rachel gave me a hug. "We all miss you," she said. Then she turned to my mother, who had been standing quietly at my side, and reached for her hand. "Mrs. Miller, it's so nice to see you again."

My mother shook Rachel's hand. "Please," she said, "call me Rebecca." Rachel smiled.

"And this is my husband, Sam," Rachel continued. Sam shook my mother's hand and turned to me, his eyes crinkling at the corners.

"It's good to see you, Eliza," he said. "We miss your cooking." He winked at me, and Rachel made a grunting sound before leading him away to meet John and Beth. As my mother went to stand near Beth and greet her guests, I sat on the couch, with a child on each side, turning my head from one to the other as their high-pitched voices competed to fill me in on their days without me. Ben's gaze roamed to the other side of the room and settled on my mother. I followed his stare.

"Is that how you look when you're at home?" he asked.

"Yes and no," I said. "I do wear clothes like my mom is wearing now, but I never look as neat as my mom. My apron usually has stains from whatever I've been cooking, and my kapp is always slipping off my head."

Ben shrugged his shoulders. "Maybe you're not supposed to dress that way," he said matter-of-factly.

"Maybe I'm not," I whispered.

The front door opened and closed as each new guest arrived. When I heard Josh's voice, I jumped up from the couch, my heart rattling. By the time I reached the door, he had stepped inside and was being greeted with a hug from Beth and a handshake from John. His eyes met mine, and I could tell he was as nervous as I was. He carried himself like someone wearing an over-starched shirt. I reached for his arm and gently led him to where my mother was standing, talking to Rachel. "Mom," I said, with a breathlessness in my voice that I couldn't control, "this is Josh."

I watched as my mother and Josh faced each other. He reached his hand out and said, "It's nice to meet you, Mrs. Miller." She shook his hand, a trace of a smile on her face.

"And I'm happy to meet you as well," she said. Her voice sounded cordial, the way it did when she greeted dinner guests on Stranger Night. But she didn't turn away, as she did with the visitors at home. Instead, her eyes traveled from Josh's choppy dark hair to his blue button-down shirt, to his khaki pants and sneakers. They moved back up to his left earlobe, where a small silver hoop sparkled. I was so accustomed to Josh's earring that I didn't notice it anymore, but in the early days it had always startled me.

The doorbell rang again, and my mother said, "I suppose I should let Beth introduce me around. But I hope we'll have the chance to get acquainted later in the evening."

Josh nodded. I had never seen him look so shy. When my mother went off to meet Beth's quilting friends, I slipped my arm around his waist and leaned in to him. His solid warmth settled around me, and I realized how much I had missed him these past few days.

The next hour was a clutter of introductions and half-finished conversations before moving to a new guest or a new task. I had met John's family at one of our Sunday night dinners, and they greeted me warmly when they arrived. Beth welcomed them affectionately, and I realized that she had spent almost as much of her life with her in-laws as she had with her own parents.

John's sister Barbara reached out to grasp my mother's hands as though they were old friends. "I feel like I know you already," she said. "Beth has told me so much about you."

My mother smiled. "And she's also told me about you." She paused, and I could tell that she was searching for the right words. "Beth has needed a sister," she said. "Thank you." Barbara looked pleased.

Finally it was time to sit down at the table. My head hurt from keeping up with all the introductions and from worrying about my mother and Josh. I was relieved to settle into a chair and watch the other guests file in. My mother appeared, still talking to Barbara, and I waved her to the chair at my right.

I turned to her and said, "I forgot to warn you about Josh's earring."

She smiled. "Don't worry. Josh isn't the first boy I've seen with an earring. I'm not as sheltered as you think."

We were laughing when Josh came into the room and sat in the chair to my left. "Are you laughing at me?" he asked.

"Sort of," I said. "I was wondering what my mom thought of your earring, but it turns out she's cooler than I thought."

"Yes," my mother agreed. "I'm often accused of being 'cool.'"

Josh grinned and placed his hand on my back, stroking it gently. Despite the laughter and Josh's light touch, I felt tension on both sides—Josh on my left and my mother on my right. I was afraid it would be a long meal.

All the guests were now gathered around the table. I reached for my fork when the tinging sound of a spoon hitting a glass stopped me. I turned to the head of the table to see Beth looking out at her guests. "Thank you all for coming," she began. "As you know, I've given up most of my Amish ways. But now I feel the need to bring back one tradition."

She looked at my mother and me in a meaningful way and then reached for John's hand at her right and Barbara's at her left.

I turned to Josh and placed one of my hands in his and the other in my mother's. Around the large dining room table and the small children's table, everyone reached for the hands of the people sitting beside them, and then looked expectantly at Beth. She took a deep breath and closed her eyes for a moment, as though trying to remember something. Then came the words that used to rise to my lips at the start of each meal. "We thank you, our heavenly Father, for the gifts which we are about to receive. May we be truly grateful for the bounty you have bestowed."

I was about to say "Amen" when I realized that Beth wasn't finished. "In the past weeks," she continued, "I've received two great gifts. The first gift was my niece Eliza. One day she appeared at my door, and suddenly I . . . " She stopped, her voice choked. "Suddenly I didn't feel like someone who had been shunned." She cleared her throat and went on. "Then this niece brought my precious sister back to me." I listened, my throat tight, my hands gripped on one side by my mother and on the other side by my beau. I looked at Aunt Beth, whose expression teetered between laughter and tears. "When we say grace," she went on, "we ask to be grateful. Well, tonight I don't have to ask for that feeling. I'm filled with it."

There was a silent moment before my mother spoke. "Amen."

"Amen," I whispered, and a murmur traveled around the table. The tension began to slip away.

After finishing my salad, I got up to help with the serving. I worried about leaving Josh alone with my mother, but I also wanted them to have a conversation without me. I brought the salad plates into the kitchen and accepted the platter of lasagna and the spatula that Barbara handed me. I started at the head of the table, then made my way to the children, who each pointed to what they thought was the biggest piece. I was back home now at Stranger Night, tiptoeing around the table, listening to snatches of conversation. I served John's parents, and heard them telling the professor about how John had been fascinated by the Colonial era, even as a little boy. I set lasagna pieces on Sam's and Rachel's plates, and listened as Rachel told the quilting ladies about how she had met me.

Then I found myself standing beside Josh, who was turned toward my mother. Their voices came to me, open and easy. Breathing in a feeling of comfort, I served each of them a piece of lasagna and put a piece on my own plate as well. My mother was asking him about school. "A junior," Josh was saying. "As a matter of fact, school starts in two weeks."

"Junior year," my mother said. "Isn't that the year when you have to take your college entrance tests?"

"Yeah, the ACTs and SATs," Josh answered. "That's all everyone's talking about now. I'm not looking forward to it."

I brought the empty platter back to the kitchen and returned to my seat.

"What did I miss?" I asked.

"Let's see," said my mother. "Josh's brother is at the University of Illinois, but Josh is hoping to go to Northwestern because they have a better journalism program. He's going to be sports editor of the school paper this year, and he loves the Cubs, but he's not as obsessed with them as Uncle John is." She turned to Josh. "Did I leave anything out?"

"Not really." He paused before adding, "Except that I'm really happy you let your daughter come here."

My neck warmed, and I was filled again with that breathless, nervous feeling. I turned to my mother, who set her fork down and looked past me at Josh.

"Well," she said.

I waited to hear what else she would say. The silence grew. Josh was staring at his plate. I wondered if he regretted what he had said.

"Well," my mother said again. "I'm glad." Josh smiled, and I breathed in my relief. Then she continued. "I'm glad you're having a nice summer."

Side by side in the kitchen, I scraped the dinner plates and Josh stacked them in the dishwasher. We had asked for this task, looking for a few minutes alone.

"'I'm glad you're having a nice summer,'" said Josh, in a voice higher than his own.

"Well, you set yourself up for that one," I said.

Josh shook his head. "Right?"

I looked to be sure no one was about to walk through the kitchen door before pulling Josh toward me for a kiss on the mouth.

"What was that for?" he asked.

"It was for being a good boyfriend. I thought that was a nice thing to say."

I started the dishwasher and left the remaining dishes soaking in the sink. Josh and I returned to the living room in time to say good-bye to the guests. Then we sat on the couch and watched as all of John's family surrounded my mother, each giving her a hug. At first she looked a bit startled, but after Barbara's boisterous embrace, she appeared to enjoy being passed from one person to another. Each whispered a few words in her ear, and she nodded and smiled in return. Watching this open affection, I thought again of the people at home who had sent Beth away. And I felt a warm gratitude to these people who had become Beth's family when her own had let her leave them.

When the door closed behind them, the house was suddenly quiet. "You have a wonderful family, John," my mother said, in the voice she used with old friends. "Beth is very lucky."

"So am I," said John, slipping an arm around my aunt.

John and Beth looked at each other and then at me. Josh and I were sitting near each other, but not touching. "Well," said Beth, "John and I are going to finish the cleanup so you can visit for a while." Her voice sounded overly bright, as though she had rehearsed the words.

My mother nodded and perched in the chair facing us. I waited, feeling that something was about to happen.

"So, Joshua," she began. Josh nodded and sat straighter. "I've had the chance to talk with Rachel tonight, and she had a lot of fine things to say about you and your family." She paused. "My sister also speaks of you with high regard."

Josh looked at me and then at my mother. "Thank you."

We waited. I sensed that my mother had more to say.

"I've been thinking about what you said before, Josh," she went on. "About how you were happy I let Eliza come here."

Josh cringed. "I'm sorry. Maybe that wasn't the right thing to say."

"It's okay," she said. "When you're a parent, you want two things for your children. You want them to be happy, and you want them to be near you. But sometimes you can't have both of those things at once." She took a breath before continuing. "I can see that Eliza is happy. And I think I have to accept that, at least for now, she won't be near me."

My heartbeat quickened. I looked at my mother, and she returned my gaze. "Before I left home, your father agreed to allow you to stay here through November if I approved." I waited, holding my breath. "And I approve."

I let out my breath. I could feel Josh watching me. "Thank you," I whispered.

I looked down. I didn't trust myself to look at my mother or Josh. I didn't want my mother to know that my heart was singing. She turned back to Josh. "I trust Eliza," she continued. "And I'm told that I should trust you as well. What I'm trying to say is, I give you permission to court . . . I mean, to date my daughter."

Josh and I looked at each other, and then turned back to my mother. Our expressions were the same—eyes wide, mouths slightly open.

My mother smiled before turning more serious. She spoke to me. "The same rules will apply to your courtship that would have applied at home. You won't stay out past midnight. And you'll behave in a way that your father and I would approve of. Is this something you can both live with?"

We nodded in unison. My mother's smile touched her lips, but didn't spread to her eyes. "Well, I think I'll go help my sister clean up."

When she left the room, Josh let out a great breath. He turned to me and reached for my hand. "I didn't see that coming."

I shook my head. "I know, right?" My head was exploding with this new information.

Josh put his arm around me and kissed the top of my head. I settled against him, feeling the warm closeness. Then I felt his lips against my ear, the heat of his whisper. "It's official," he said. "You're my girlfriend."

I shifted so I could whisper into his ear. "And you're my beau."

If this were a movie, a song would be playing now.

CHAPTER

33

On Sunday morning, I heard my mother moving around the room. I sat up in bed. "You can sleep a little longer," she whispered. "It's early."

I shook my head. "I'm up."

Gray light leaked between the blinds, leaving pale stripes on the walls. My mother was wearing the green dress she'd had on when she stepped off the train six days ago. Her suitcase stood near the door, her basket, black cape, and traveling bonnet on top of it. "The time went so fast," I said.

"Good times always do."

I went to the bathroom to wash and dress. When I returned, my mother was sitting on the edge of the bed. "Come here," she said, patting the place beside her. "I want to say something to you before we go downstairs." I sat beside her as she reached for the hairbrush on the bedside table and began to brush my hair. I remembered how my childhood had been filled with mornings like this, quiet ashy dawns with my mother beside me, pulling a brush through the tangles of my long hair. "So, now you've seen both sides. You've seen your aunt's life and you've seen mine. One day you'll make your own choice."

I sat still, enjoying the tickle as my mother worked the brush through my hair and smoothed it with her sturdy hands. This was the first time she had ever discussed the possibility that I might not return to Amish life.

"What are you saying?" I asked softly.

"I'm saying that I don't want another member of my family under the bann."

"So if I decide to stay here . . ."

The brush fell away from my hair with an abruptness that startled me. My mother shook her head urgently. "Let's not talk about that now," she said. "I can't bear to think of it."

"Okay," I said. Then I added gently, "But you were the one who brought it up."

"I know. But there are some things on my mind." I waited. She went back to brushing my hair. "Lately I've been thinking about Kate's brother. His mother's heart is broken. I've wondered how things might have been different for that family if they had agreed with William's decision not to be baptized. Maybe they'd still be in contact now."

I listened quietly.

"So I want you to know," she continued, "that I don't want to live the life that Kate's mother is living. Do you understand?"

"I do," I said softly.

"And whatever choice you make," she said, "don't make it for a boy. Don't stay here for Joshua, and don't come home for Daniel. Make the choice for yourself."

I looked at my mother. She stopped brushing my hair and waited for me to answer. "I understand."

"All right, then," she said, her voice sounding more like the brisk, no-nonsense mother I had left behind, and less like the unexpected friend I had found in the last six days. "Now, let's go downstairs and face those good-byes that we've all been dreading."

In the kitchen, Beth was standing at the sink, staring out the window, her fingers wrapped around a mug of coffee. When she turned to us, I saw that her eyes were red and swollen. "Well," she said, with forced cheer in her voice, "what would you like for breakfast?"

"Whatever's easy," said my mother, pouring herself a cup of coffee.

While Beth whisked the scrambled egg batter, I set the table and my mother made toast. Minutes later we gathered around Beth's kitchen table. I scooped a bit of egg onto my fork, but when I tried to swallow, my throat ached with the effort. I glanced at my mother and aunt, who seemed to be having the same trouble.

My mother set down her fork. "Is there any way we can have an easy good-bye?"

Beth shook her head, a tear rolling down her cheek. "Not a chance."

"I didn't think so," said my mother, with a sad laugh.

I got up and carried the plates and coffee cups to the sink, listening to the quiet comfort of the sisters at the table together. When I turned back, I saw my mother and Aunt Beth, their hands stretched across the table, their fingers interlocked. Watching them, I realized that one day I'd be saying good-bye to one of them.

Forcing myself to look away, I saw John standing in the kitchen doorway.

"Is it time already?" asked Beth. John glanced at the clock and nodded. My mother and Beth released each other's hands and stood up from the table, their movements slow and fluid.

"I'll put your things in the car, Becky," said John. "And I'll wait for you outside."

I followed my mother and aunt through the living room to the front door. My mother was walking with exaggerated straightness. At the front door she turned and reached for me. I stepped into her arms. She pulled me close and whispered into my ear, "Remember what we talked about." I nodded. My throat felt clogged. "And take care of your Aunt Beth. This is going to be a hard day for her."

I stepped back, my hands gripping my mother's arms. "This was . . ." I fumbled, groping for the right words. I tried again. "This was an important time for me."

"For me too," my mother said.

I stepped aside and let Beth take my place in my mother's arms. She was crying now, and my mother stroked her hair. My mother's face was pale, and her lips twitched. "Watch your mailbox for letters, Beth. They'll be coming."

"The bann." Beth choked out the words. "You can be punished."

"I've been punished all these years without you," my mother said. "There's nothing worse they can do to me. It can't be Good Amish to give up someone you love." She reached for the door and opened it, then turned back to look at Beth, whose face was twisted with emotion.

"It's okay, Elizabeth," my mother said. "Your sister is here."

My mother was right about one thing. It was going to be a hard day for Aunt Beth. After my mother left, Beth looked like a child lost at the fair. I helped her clean the kitchen and then followed her to the guest room to strip the sheets off the beds. She stood in the middle of the room with the bundle of bedding in her arms.

"Do you want me to put them in the washing machine for you?" I asked gently.

Beth shook her head and sat down on one of the beds, letting the sheets drop from her arms, onto the floor. I sat beside her and put my arm around her shoulders. "Everything's good now. You and my mom are together again."

Beth laid her head on my shoulder. "Yes," she said. "Together but apart. I guess it's better than the way it was before."

"Much better," I said. But I thought about Beth's words. *Together but apart.* That's how it was for me too. I'd have letters, and maybe other visits, but I was apart from my family and friends. It was something I hadn't let myself think about during the excitement of coming here.

Beth turned to me, her face drawn, as though she had just finished a long day of work. "I think I need to lie down for a while," she said. "Is it okay if I take you back to Rachel's a little later?"

I followed Beth to her room, feeling protective and grown-up. Beth crawled into bed, and I pulled the quilt over her.

"I just need a few minutes," she murmured as I turned off the light and closed the door.

While my aunt rested, I started a load of wash and remade the beds with clean linens. Then I cleaned the guest bathroom and hung up fresh towels. I was anxious to get back to Rachel's house, to call Josh, to see the children. But the sadness in Beth's eyes was tugging at me. It was a relief when Uncle John returned from the train station.

"Aunt Beth is lying down," I told him. "I think she wants to be alone for a while."

John nodded. "I've been dreading this day," he said. "It was so hard when she said good-bye to her sister the first time."

"How was my mom?"

"She barely said a word in the car. And she wouldn't let me walk her into the station." He paused and looked at me, a question in his eyes. "And how are you?"

I wasn't sure how to answer. I would miss my mother, but there were other things on my mind now. I had promised Josh I would call him as soon as I got back. This was going to be a new beginning for us. The truth was, I couldn't wait to see him, but I worried that saying it would sound like I was happy my mother had left.

"I'm okay," I said.

"All right, then," said Uncle John. "Let's get you back to Rachel's house."

I ran upstairs to get my suitcase.

My room at Rachel's was comforting and familiar after the days away. I sat on the bed thinking about the time I had spent with my aunt and mother, hearing their revelations, seeing their faces etched with emotion.

All through the week they had treated me like an adult, and I had been proud to be trusted with their secrets. But now I was tired of being an adult. I was ready to be sixteen again.

I picked up the phone and called Josh.

CHAPTER

34

Josh and I were "official." That's what he called it. Back home, my friends would say that we'd gone from "keeping company" to "courting." Whatever we called it, one thing was true: for the first time, Josh and I could present ourselves as a couple.

There were two weeks left of summer, and we spent them in delicious closeness. Each evening, when my chores were done, I called Josh and he was over in minutes to take me out for coffee or to a movie or to someone's basement where other couples had gathered. When we were alone, we were starved for each other, and though we'd stepped beyond bundling, I knew that there was one limit that was absolute. One evening, after watching a movie, wound around each other on his basement couch, I told him what I'd learned about my mother's rumspringa. It had been her secret, but I had an important reason for letting Josh know about it. "Whoa," he said. "That's intense."

"It is," I said. "And I think my mother wanted me to know so that nothing like that would ever happen to me."

"Okay," he said, his voice a low hum. "Then it never will." I felt relieved. Now Josh was sharing the burden of keeping our limits. It wouldn't only be up to me.

The last days of summer galloped by as only summer days can. I felt a new exhilaration when September neared, because this was the time I would have been returning home. Instead, I was still here and we were still together. And we didn't have to hide our togetherness.

When Josh's class schedule arrived in the mail, he called one friend after the other to find out who would be in class with him. I felt a little left out, but I kept busy. Camp ended for the children, and I occupied them during the day while Rachel worked at the library or in her little office. School would be starting for the children, too, with Ben in fourth grade and Janie in first. I was the only one not making a fresh start in the fall. So I clung to those last summer nights, with the warmth of Josh's arm draped comfortably over my shoulders, and the air rich and sweet.

On the last day of summer vacation, Rachel took the children to their school for an orientation program. I waited excitedly for Josh, and when he greeted me at the door, he handed me a blue cap with the red letter C above the brim. Uncle John had told me endless stories about the Cubs, and I had watched so many games with him on Sundays that I was beginning to understand his proud and painful possessiveness of the team. But I had never been to a game. Now Josh and I would be sitting in the bleachers of Wrigley Field.

The whole afternoon I sat elbow to elbow with the other fans, feeling the sun's warmth pressing into my back and shoulders. I ate peanuts and threw the shells on the ground, where they crunched beneath my sneakers. In front of me was the field, so green and precise, with white lines and bases forming a perfect diamond.

I had never seen so many people together in one space. It was a place where strangers were all in partnership for the same cause. When the Cubs scored runs, we cheered and slapped each other's outstretched hands; and when a Cub player struck out, we all groaned in unison. What happened down there with the nine ball players on the green grass was the most important thing in the world. And when the Cubs right fielder caught a fly ball in the ninth inning to win the game, I stood up and shrieked my excitement with everyone else.

Riding home on the el, I smiled while Josh replayed the game to me, as though I hadn't just seen it myself. I was tired and sunburned, and happy that the Cubs had won. But I was also a little sad. This was another thing to put on my list, something else that I had wanted to do and had looked forward to with anticipation. Now it was over, like my first movie and play and concert. If I came to Wrigley Field again, I would already know about the emerald grass and the smell of peanuts and the cracking sound the ball makes when it hits the bat. I had been to only one baseball game, but already I could imagine it feeling ordinary.

I turned to face Josh. He was talking about a play in the fourth inning when he was sure the umpire had incorrectly called a Cub player out at second.

"But they won in the end, so that doesn't really matter, does it?" I asked.

"I know. I just like to analyze it. It's the sportswriter in me."

I smiled. The boys at home talked about their future jobs, too. Most would end up doing the same work as their fathers. When the girls discussed their futures, they talked about their husbands and children.

I shook away the thoughts of home that were taking me out of my present. I didn't want to be back there, where the options were narrow and predictable. I wanted to be here, in the swaying el car, next to a boy who planned to earn his living by writing about sports.

"Can we rent a movie tonight?" I asked.

"Not tonight. I have to be at school early tomorrow." I felt the hot rush of disappointment. "But I'll call you after school." I nodded, not wanting him to see that it mattered to me.

Now that school had started for Josh, I no longer waited for the phone in the middle of the day in the hopes that we could snatch some time together before the children got home. He left for school in the early morning and came home after he was done with his work for the newspaper. His lawn-mowing business ended, and his hours at the computer store were scaled back. Our schedules were suddenly at odds with each other. During the day while I was alone, with time weighing on me, Josh was at school. By the time he got home, I was helping the children with their homework and getting dinner ready for the family. In the evening, when my work was finished, Josh was studying.

My life slipped into a five and two pattern: five days of work, two days with Josh. I spent my Fridays racing through my tasks, checking the clock, waiting for the weekend to begin. Most Friday nights I babysat while Sam and Rachel went out, and Josh was allowed to come over to spend the evening with me. After the children went to bed, we'd order pizza and watch a movie together, stretching out on the couch, our limbs intertwined. Saturdays and Sundays were my days off, and I usually spent them with Josh, as long as he didn't have too much homework. On Saturday nights, Josh and I went out to a movie or party or a concert. At Sunday night dinners with Aunt Beth and Uncle John, I felt an unaccustomed sensation, a dismal feeling that the week loomed ahead.

I'd often think about Josh and the mysterious place where he spent his days. High school. The only thing I knew about it was what I saw on television and read about in books. Students sat at desks listening to teachers until a bell rang, and they slung their backpacks over their shoulders and moved into another classroom to listen to another teacher talk. Between classes they gathered in large areas, like the cafeteria or gymnasium, where they talked and flirted with each other. Josh and his friends told me that school wasn't like what I saw on TV; that the days were long and dull. But I wanted to find out for myself.

One warm September Friday night, while I basked in the airy feeling of the weekend, Josh tried to explain it to me. Sam and

Rachel had gotten home early, so we had walked to town for ice cream, and sat on a bench, the breeze catching the ends of my hair. "There are all these random rules," Josh said. "Like we can't use our cell phones or leave the room without a pass. And then each teacher gives homework assignments like theirs is the only class we have, so even when we're out of school, our time isn't our own."

I listened and tried to share his dismay with the rules and the work, but the whole idea of school felt like privilege. Suddenly I had an idea. "Can you take me there?" I asked. "Can I see your school?"

Josh slid his arm around my shoulders, and I leaned into him. It was an easy movement, as natural as blinking. "Sure," he said. "As a matter of fact, Homecoming's next month. I was going to find a clever way to ask you to the dance, but I guess this will have to do. Will you go with me?"

I nodded happily. I wasn't sure what "Homecoming" meant, but dancing was involved and I'd get to see the school. And Josh wanted to take me. It was something else I could step into and try on. I smiled and nestled against him. The smell of his skin was achingly familiar, and the weekend stretched ahead of us, long and enticing.

CHAPTER

35

It turned out that Homecoming was a pretty big deal. I found that out when Valerie and Jill showed up at Rachel's door the next day, their faces shimmering with excitement.

"We heard you're coming to Homecoming with us," said Valerie.

"We're going together?"

Jill nodded, her dark curls bouncing. "There are twelve of us in the group—six couples. I'm going with Steve." I quietly readjusted my image of the dance to accommodate this new information.

"So," said Valerie, "do you have a dress?"

I thought about the dresses in my closet, then realized that Valerie must mean a differnt type of dress. I shook my head.

"Okay, we'll shop together. I need one too," said Valerie. "And I'll help you order Josh's boutonniere. Pictures are going to be at my house."

"Pictures?"

"Yeah, we go to someone's house before the dance, and the

parents take pictures of us all dressed up. It's kind of lame, but the parents like it." Valerie stopped. "Oh," she added. "Can the people you work for come in place of your parents?"

"I guess so." This was sounding complicated.

Within an hour we were at the mall, starting with lunch in the fast-food area.

Valerie punched her fork into her lettuce. "I hate salads."

"Then why did you order one?" I asked, looking around at all of the other choices she could have had.

"I want to lose weight before the dance."

I looked at Valerie. She was a slender girl. I couldn't imagine that she wanted to take up even less space than she already did.

Jill turned to me, her face full and open. "So, what are the boys like where you're from?"

"Yeah," said Valerie. "Are there any hotties?"

Valerie and Jill were both leaning forward now, their elbows resting on the table. I thought of Daniel and wondered if these girls would think he was a "hottie." But I wouldn't tell them about a boy whose voice was as tender as a ball of cotton. So I just said, "Yes, there are. And my friends at home all want to know what the Yankee boys are like."

Valerie raised her eyebrows. "Do they know about Josh?"

I thought about Annie and Kate reading my letters, perhaps disapproving of me in a thrilled, breathy way. I smiled. "They know."

"Josh is one of the good ones," said Valerie. "When we went out, he was a perfect gentleman. Our breakup was mutual."

Heat prickled around my ears. I looked down at the table and busied myself gathering the crumpled remains of my lunch. Josh had never told me that he and Valerie had been a couple. When I looked up, I thought I saw an exchange between her and Jill, the quick meeting of their eyes. "Anyway," Valerie said, her voice a bit too loud, "we'd better start shopping. It always takes longer than we think to find the right dress."

I followed them through the mall, shaking off thoughts of Josh holding Valerie's hand, pulling her toward him for a kiss. Or more. I took some deep breaths, willing myself back to the moment.

I trotted to catch up with the girls, who were taking long, sure strides along a path that would have been called a sidewalk if we were outside, but that didn't have a name in a place where there was no outside. Valerie looked over her shoulder at me and pointed at a store with a big red star in the window. "Come on, we're starting at Macy's."

Within a few minutes, I didn't have time to think about my boyfriend and his secret ex-girlfriend. My world shrank into the narrow realm of fashion. Did I want short or long? What color? What fabric? What style?

I followed Valerie and Jill along the seemingly endless racks of dresses. They flicked through the plastic hangers, periodically pulling out a dress and holding it up for scrutiny. I reached out tentatively for a dress the color of a cherry blossom. The fabric felt silky between my fingertips. Smiling, I draped the dress over my arm and walked forward briskly.

Minutes later, my arms were heavy from the weight of the dresses I had chosen. Valerie and Jill were also embracing armloads of colorful fabric. Together we made our way to a large fitting room and hung the dresses on wall hooks. Immediately, Jill and Valerie pulled down their jeans and stepped out, leaving them in denim pools on the floor. I looked away as they took off their shirts and stood before each other unself-consciously, wearing only bras and panties. Even after all the days I had spent with Valerie at the mall, I was still getting used to the lack of modesty here.

I stepped out of my jeans and pulled off my shirt, then reached for the pink dress and slipped it over my head. Its soft folds slid over me, clinging to my waist and hips. I stared at my reflection. The dress made me look curvy, and the neckline crept down low. The skirt stopped a few inches above my knees. "I like it," said Valerie. I turned away from the mirror. Valerie was wearing a short black dress with a similarly plunging neckline. Jill was pulling a red dress over her head.

I soon found myself slipping out of dresses as comfortably as if I were in my room at home, whirling around, eager to see what the girls thought and to share my opinions of their dresses. It was luxurious to step in and out of these fancy clothes, to feel the sensations of the different materials against my skin. Soon I forgot about being humble and plain. I forgot that the important thing was how people treated each other, not how they looked on the outside. In this miniature place filled with extravagant clothing, I felt like one of the fancy people I had been warned about all my life.

I stared at myself in the mirror, wearing the last of the dresses I had brought into the room. It was the blue of a dusky sky, and it fitted itself to me as though someone had sewn it around my form. The skirt fell to my calves and billowed around my legs when I moved. At once, Valerie and Jill were on either side of me, and I saw their satisfied reflections in the mirror. "This is it," said Valerie. "You found it."

"You think?" I asked, but already I was imagining myself wearing the dress, dancing with Josh the way we had at the club, when our bodies had melded together. I pictured how he would smile in that surprised way when he first saw me, and how proud he would be to introduce me to all the people in the group. Then I remembered that I hadn't thought to look at the price. The small white tag fluttered down the side of the dress, and I reached around to look at it. One hundred and fifty dollars. I sucked in my breath. Valerie was stepping back into the black dress she had first tried on, and Jill was glancing around to see how the gray dress she was wearing looked in the back. They both turned to look at me.

Valerie glanced at the price with a nod. "That's how much most of these dresses cost." I looked back at my reflection, noticing that my eyes were just a little bit bluer when I wore this dress. And the fabric hung in a way that made my waist look small, a quality that I had recently learned was sought after.

I thought quickly about how much money I had. My debt to my parents was paid, and there was enough in my checking account to pay for this dress. "Do you think I'll ever wear it again?"

Valerie glanced at Jill and shrugged. "We usually wear a different dress to each dance." So this would be an entirely frivolous purchase. For a few hours on one night I would be pretty in a way that I had never been before and might not ever be again. And the cost of this vanity would be a hundred and fifty dollars.

"I'll take it," I said, my voice filled with the bravado of impulse. My words were met by excited shrieks from Valerie and Jill, and I basked in their attention, pushing aside my teachings about humility and frugality. I stepped out of the dress slowly, reluctant to bring an end to the richness of these feelings.

Back in my jeans and shirt, I perched on the one chair in the room, my arms wrapped around the blue dress, and watched as Valerie and Jill made their decisions. Jill chose the red dress, and Valerie decided on a black-and-white print. Minutes later, after I wrote a check, and the other two girls plunked down their charge cards, we stood together holding identical shopping bags emblazoned with red stars. It was then that Valerie asked the question that I hadn't considered. "What about shoes?"

I glanced down at my sneakered feet and thought about the sandals and the sturdy black shoes in my closet. I looked at Valerie and shook my head. In the shoe department, I watched as Jill and Valerie held up one shoe after another for me to consider, each with overly high and slender heels, and signaled a salesman with our choices.

The salesman emerged from an unseen room, balancing four rectangular boxes in his arms. I sat down and reached for one of the boxes before I realized that the man, seated on a low stool before me, was already opening it and reaching for my foot. He deftly slid the sneaker and sock off of my right foot and slipped the black shoe on, adjusting the buckle at my ankle. I blushed that a strange man was helping me on and off with my shoes, but a quick glance around the room showed me that everyone was being assisted in the same way. When both of my feet were settled in the shoes, the salesman pushed back the stool he was sitting on and urged me to stand up. My ankles wobbled, and I staggered until he reached for my elbow to steady me. I took a few shaky steps, wondering how I would walk, let alone dance in these shoes. Valerie and Jill offered me words of encouragement each time I stepped around in a different pair of shoes.

"We all feel the same way in heels," said Jill. "You should practice walking on them at home before the dance."

"And bring a pair of white socks in your purse," added Valerie. "We all dance in our socks."

I finally decided on the pair that felt the least uncomfortable, and watched as the salesman placed them back into the box. Again the checkbook came out, and again I signed my name to an amount of money that seemed obscene.

Now, carrying two shopping bags and trying not to think about the amount of money missing from my checkbook, I let the girls lead me to the panty hose department to buy sheer stockings. "Are we done yet?" I asked, setting the checkbook back in my bag for what I hoped was the last time.

"What about jewelry?" asked Jill. And in minutes we were standing at the jewelry counter, staring at necklaces and earrings. "I'm guessing your ears aren't pierced," said Jill. I shook my head.

Valerie spoke up. "They do it for free here; it only takes a minute."

Jill pointed to the silver earrings that shimmered from her earlobes. "I got mine pierced when I was eight years old." Valerie leaned forward and pulled back her long hair to reveal three silver earrings marching up the side of her ear.

I shuddered at the thought of a needle slicing through my earlobe. But that wasn't the issue. Making a permanent wound in the body in order to hang decorations could never be accepted among the Amish. And I realized that these girls, waiting eagerly for my response, would probably know this.

Valerie leaned closer. "It only hurts for a second. We'll be with you."

"No," I said. "Thanks for the offer, though."

"Here are some clip-ons," said Jill, pointing to a small rack on the counter.

But Valerie wasn't finished. "Is it because you're not allowed?"

"That's right. I can wear jewelry while I'm here, but I can't do anything permanent." I hoped that my voice sounded final, because that's the way I was feeling.

"You know," said Valerie, her tone like a mischievous child, "you can get your ears pierced and wear earrings while you're here. Then when you go home you'll just take them out."

"Val," said Jill. "Let it go."

Valerie reached up to her earlobe and lifted out an earring. "See?" she said. "You can't even see the hole. No one would ever know."

I looked at Valerie and said simply, "I would know."

Jill quickly reached for a pair of dangly earrings with light blue stones and held them up to me. "These would be good with the dress. And, look, they're clip-ons." She unhooked the earrings from the cardboard that displayed them, and snapped them gently to my earlobes. I loved the way they glinted in the light, looking like tiny bits of indigo.

I was grateful that they had stopped talking about ear piercing, but something felt familiar about all this attention. Then I remembered. It was the first movie I saw, the one where the popular girls fixed up the unattractive girl so she could go out with the handsome boy.

I looked in the mirror at the reflections of Valerie and Jill smiling beside me. They seemed to be having fun dressing me up, making me like one of them. I wondered why this would bother me. After all, I had dreamed about fitting in here. But one thing kept leading to something else, as though there was no end to this task. Getting ready for the dance made me think about the el trains, going back and forth all day and night, never done with their work.

"I'll take these," I said, pointing to the earrings with the blue stones, and to a simple silver necklace. Jill and Valerie murmured their approval and nodded to the saleswoman. I pulled out my checkbook once again, and watched as the woman set the earrings and necklace on a pad of cotton inside a small white box.

"Will this be all?" she asked.

"I hope so," I said. And I meant it.

Walking through the parking lot to Valerie's car, I looked at my assortment of packages and imagined Kate and Annie reaching for each item, gasping at the jewelry, fingering the material of the dress, and shaking their heads in wonder at the shoes and panty hose. In the backseat of the car, I listened to Valerie and Jill chatting about the other friends who would be going with us to the dance—Chelsea and Michael and Ashley and Oscar and Carly and Alex. I had met a few of Josh's friends over these past weeks, but still there were more names to learn. There would be more curious faces, more questions about how I could get through life without a hair dryer and an iPod.

Valerie pulled the car into Rachel's driveway and turned around to me. "Can we come in for a while?" she asked. Upstairs in my room, Valerie reached into the closet for a hanger and carefully hung up the new dress. It looked like it didn't belong in there among the blue jeans and the other casual clothing I had bought to be a part of this world. "What's this?" Valerie asked, still facing the closet. She reached for the Amish clothing my mother had made me bring. I had almost forgotten about the purple dress, the kapp, and the apron, pushed to the back of the closet on the day I arrived.

Jill walked over to where Valerie was standing. Both girls stared at the dress as though it had walked into the room under its own power. "Wow," said Jill. "So this is what you wear at home."

"Yes," I said. "It's what all the girls wear."

Valerie turned to me, still clutching the hanger. "Can I borrow this?"

I looked at her quizzically. "What for?"

"I'd like to show it to my little sister. I hope you don't mind, but I've told her about you, and I think she'd love to see these clothes."

I nodded, shrugging off that old feeling of being on display. But Valerie looked so satisfied when I agreed that I felt all right about the request.

"What's this?" Jill asked. I glanced over to see her by the nightstand, Daniel's wood carving in her upturned palm.

"Oh, that's something my friend made for me before I came here," I said, forcing my voice to sound casual.

"Someone made this?" Jill asked. "By hand?"

"Yeah," I said. "It's pretty common for Amish boys to do woodworking."

"So, who's the guy who made this?" Valerie asked, her voice playful. "And is he cute?"

I looked from one girl to the other—Valerie holding my Amish dress, and Jill clutching the wood carving of the bird leaving the nest. The two remnants of my other life were on exhibit in the hands of these English girls. "My friend Daniel made it," I said, keeping my voice bland and final.

Jill set the carving back in its place, and Valerie draped the dress across her arm. "Well," said Valerie, "I have a ton of homework waiting for me. Thanks for letting me borrow your outfit. I'll take good care of it."

Standing at the window, I watched the girls walk out to Valerie's car. I had to admit I felt a bit uneasy at the sight of my purple dress fluttering in the breeze.

CHAPTER

36

On the next Saturday afternoon, a week after the shopping day and with the dance still two weeks away, I sat at the kitchen table huddled over my checkbook, staring at the amounts of money that had gone out of my account, and the smaller-than-expected amount I had left.

Rachel sat down beside me. "Has this been an expensive time?"

I nodded, closing the checkbook and putting it back in my bag. Then I remembered something. "I forgot to tell you that I won't be coming home the night of the dance. The girls are all sleeping over at Valerie's house."

Rachel seemed to be mulling that over. "Well, it's not exactly in keeping with our promise to your parents that you'd be home by midnight."

"I know," I said quickly. "But at home I sleep at friends' houses all the time, and my parents don't mind."

Rachel still seemed doubtful. "I guess it's okay," she said. "I trust you to keep a good head on your shoulders." I wasn't sure why Rachel seemed concerned about the sleepover, but I was relieved that she wouldn't keep me from going.

Just then the doorbell rang, and I jumped up to get it. Josh was waiting on the stoop. He smiled when he saw me, waving a DVD. "Okay," he said, walking in and heading toward the family room, "I think you've gone long enough without seeing *The Wizard of Oz*."

I sat on the couch and waited while Josh put the DVD in the slot and turned on the TV. Within minutes I was in another place, caught up in the life of the girl and her dog who had blown away from their gray Kansas farm to a world with color and music and magical adventures. Curled next to Josh, I laughed at the exploits of the fearful lion and the brainless scarecrow and the tin man who didn't have a heart. I cringed at the evil of the green-faced witch, and was filled with disappointment when the wizard turned out to be a phony. Rachel joined us, humming along with the songs and occasionally saying a line along with a character. When Sam and the children came back from their outing, Ben and Janie climbed onto the couch with us, their high voices joining in with the singing. Sam perched on the end of the couch and added his voice to what now had become a sing-along. Apparently, I was the only one who didn't know the movie by heart.

At the end, when Dorothy was back in her drab clothes on her gray farm, Josh and Sam and Rachel and the children all chanted together, 'Oh, Auntie Em, there's no place like home.'"

Everyone clapped and cheered, and I joined in, buoyed by the sense that everyone here shared this movie, that it was a part of their lives. "How do you all know this so well?" I asked.

"Before DVDs it used to be on TV once a year," said Rachel. "It was always a celebration, that day. My cousins would come over and we'd order pizza and watch it together."

"Now we can watch it anytime we want," said Josh. "It's the one movie everybody's seen."

It was one of those moments when I could have felt like an outsider. I chose not to. "Well, you've finally met someone who'd never seen *The Wizard of Oz*."

"Yeah," said Josh. "Now you're one of us."

I smiled, but there was one thought I couldn't get out of my mind. Why did Dorothy want to leave Oz and go back to Kansas?

That night, Josh and I went out to dinner at a place that he called a "sports bar." Television sets were perched high on the walls around the restaurant, each turned to a different sporting event. Josh's eyes kept darting around from the baseball game on one TV to the football game on another. I felt like I had to work hard for his attention.

I tapped on the table. "Remember me?"

"Sorry," he said, slowly lowering his eyes from one of the TV screens and facing me. "It's the play-offs."

The waiter brought our cheeseburgers and fries, and refilled our Cokes. When he left, I looked back at Josh, only to see that he was glancing down at his cell phone cradled in the palm of his hand, his thumb moving back and forth over the buttons.

"What?" I asked.

"The party's moving to Greg's house tonight. I just got a text from him."

He poured ketchup on his cheeseburger, and I waited. He looked up. "You'll get to meet a few people from our Homecoming group at the party tonight."

"Good," I said, happy that we were having a conversation. "Tell me about them."

But Josh's eyes were downturned again. He smiled at his cell phone.

"What?" I asked again.

"Nothing. Just something funny Oscar texted me."

"So, who's going to be there tonight?"

"Ashley, Chelsea, Michael, Oscar. They're excited to meet you."

His eyes slid down to the table, where he had set his cell phone beside his plate. He reached for it and tapped a few more keys with his thumb.

I cleared my throat. "I didn't know that you and Valerie used to be a couple."

He looked up from his phone, a blank expression on his face. "That was random. Yeah, we went out for a few months sophomore year. Why?"

I shrugged. "I don't know. It's just that you never mentioned it to me."

He tapped a few more buttons on his phone and looked back at me. "I didn't think it was important." He paused. "Have you ever had a boyfriend before me?"

I hesitated. "Sort of."

"Daniel?" he asked. "The guy who made you that wood carving on your nightstand?"

I looked at him, startled. "How did you . . . ?"

"Valerie told me. By the way, in case you haven't already figured it out, she's not good at keeping secrets."

"Well, it wasn't a secret," I said. "I just didn't want you to get the wrong idea. Daniel and I weren't exactly courting."

"It's no big deal," said Josh. "I didn't expect that I was your first boyfriend. I know you had a life before you came here. And I had one too."

"Fair enough," I said, feeling a little foolish. I took another bite of my cheeseburger and looked back at Josh. He was staring down at his cell phone.

"How many people are actually out to dinner with us?" I asked, anger rising in my voice.

Josh's eyes returned to mine. "I'm sorry." He slid his phone into his pocket. "So, what do you want to talk about?" he asked.

I couldn't help myself. "Why did you and Valerie break up?"

Josh groaned. "Really? This is what you want to talk about?"

I nodded.

"Okay," he said. "I'll admit something. This is the longest relationship I've ever been in. Before I met you, I would be with someone for maybe a few weeks. Then I'd find something wrong with her."

"What kinds of things were wrong?" I asked, trying to hide my eagerness.

"Mostly, I had this feeling that the girls were all interchangeable. I know they weren't, really, but that's how it seemed. I guess I was always looking for something distinctive in the girl I was with, something that set her apart. And I never found it." He paused and looked at me, his grin inching upward. "Until now."

I looked down, feeling self-conscious and pleased.

"Your turn," he said. "I came clean, now you have to."

He was right. If I wanted to know about his other relationships, it was only fair that he know about mine. I took a breath. "There was really only one boy. Daniel. We hadn't gotten to courting yet, but if I had stayed at home, we'd probably be together by now."

"What's he like?"

"He's what we call 'Good Amish.' He follows the rules, doesn't feel rebellious, like I did." I thought for a moment. "He's the one you'd go to if you needed help. He'd always be there for you."

"Do you miss him?"

"Sometimes. We know each other pretty well, so I always felt easy around him."

"But you didn't feel 'easy' around me?"

"Not in the beginning," I said. "I was always worried about

saying the wrong thing. Like when I thought you worked at a fruit stand. Or when I told you I liked Billy Joel. Or when I asked you to take me to *The Sound of Music*." We both laughed.

Josh smiled. "Well, I'm glad you're comfortable now." I nodded. Then he asked, "Does Daniel know about us?"

I swallowed and shook my head. I was beginning to think this conversation was a bad idea.

Josh tapped his spoon on the table. "Maybe you should tell him, so he has the freedom to see someone else." I fiddled with the wrapper of my straw, trying to find an answer. Josh leaned forward. "So what's your plan here? Are you going to leave that poor guy on the hook?" Then he sat back and dropped the spoon on the table. It made a clattery sound. "Or am I on the hook until you go back to him?"

"No one's 'on the hook,'" I said quickly, shaking my head at the odd expression. "You're my boyfriend. I'll send Daniel a letter and tell him about us. He deserves to know."

CHAPTER

37

Josh was right. It wasn't fair of me to keep our relationship a secret from Daniel.

I had sent Daniel a few short letters since his visit, but I'd never told him anything about being with another boy. That night I forced myself to do it.

> *Dear Daniel,*
>
> *You have always been honest with me, and I want to give you the same respect. I want you to know that I have been in a relationship with a boy here. I don't know where this courtship will lead, but I feel it is only fair that you know about it. I think of you often, and I appreciate our friendship. I hope you are well and that you are enjoying this time of freedom.*
>
> *With warm thoughts,*
>
> *Eliza*

A few days later I received a letter from Daniel.

Dear Eliza,
Thank you for your honesty.
      Daniel

On Friday night, I didn't have to babysit, and we went to the school football game. The evenings were getting chilly, and I realized that I hadn't brought any warm clothing with me when I left home. Josh gave me one of his sweatshirts with the word "Giants," the name of the school team, across the chest.

Sitting on the metal bleachers, I felt the camaraderie that had surged around me at the Cubs game. But this was closer to home. Everyone here knew players on the field and cheerleaders in their short skirts and members of the marching band with their rousing spirit.

I didn't understand the game at all. It looked like groups of well-padded boys huddling together before ramming their bodies into well-padded boys in different-colored uniforms. But I loved the cheers and the fight songs and the sense of being in a community. And sitting in the stands, dressed in school colors, I was like everyone else. Just one of the crowd.

After the game, we went out with Greg and Valerie to celebrate the victory. At the table, Josh fiddled with his phone. He had been taking pictures with it during the game, and he was looking through them to see if he could use any in his newspaper story.

"Can I see?" I asked. He leaned over and showed me the small flat surface of his cell phone. Etched under the glass was a miniature frozen scene from the football game, a player running with the ball cradled in his curved arm, while a player from the other team chased him. Josh pressed a button and the picture changed, showing the players together in the close circle they call a huddle.

"So phones are also cameras," I said.

"Oh, yeah," said Greg, pulling his phone out. "My whole life is in here." I've got my photos, playlists, e-mails." He held his phone in front of him. "Smile, Eliza," he said. Instinctively, I put a hand in front of my face. For all that I had experienced in this fancy world, I had never had my picture taken. My soul had yet to be stolen.

"Typical girl," said Greg, with a laugh. "They never want their pictures taken."

"Wait till next weekend," Valerie said, playfully elbowing me. "There'll be so many cameras on you, you won't know where to look."

I caught my breath. We had talked about getting our pictures taken before the dance, but I hadn't considered what it meant for me. Now I thought about the impending stealing of my soul. Smiling, I realized that I'd have something new to add to the list in my journal.

That Sunday, Josh and I sat at the dinner table with Beth and John. Josh was in an animated discussion with John about Northwestern.

"So, do you have any connections with the admissions office?" Josh asked. "I think I'm going to need all the help I can get."

John shook his head. "Sorry, Josh. I'm afraid you're on your own. But when the time comes, I'll be happy to look over your entrance essay and give you some pointers."

"Thanks. It's still a year before I'll be applying, but everyone talks about it like our whole future hinges on where we go." He shook his head. "I try not to think of it that way. I just want to be in a good journalism program."

"You're pretty young to know what you want to major in," said John.

Josh leaned forward, and I readied myself for stories of his love for journalism. I enjoyed hearing how, as a little boy, he wrote sports headlines and drew pictures to go along with them, and how he'd turn the sound down on the television to give the commentary on the baseball games, talking into an imaginary microphone. "I don't know exactly where I'll end up," he continued, "but I know I want to work in an area I'm passionate about. I'm not going to spend my life chasing the dollar."

John nodded, and I could see he was pleased. I got up to help Aunt Beth clear the table. I always felt uncomfortable when Josh talked about the future. The only thing I knew about mine was that I'd be here through November. After that, things got murky.

"What are you thinking?" asked Aunt Beth, filling the teapot. I set the plates down in the sink and turned to her.

"I wish I could talk about my future."

"Do you think about it?"

I laughed. "Only all the time."

Beth's voice was cautious. "Sixteen is young to know what you want to do."

"I know, but I've been thinking since my mother's visit that from now on this will be my decision. I needed my parents' permission to come here, and then to stay past the summer. But I know now that if I decide to stay, they'll respect my wishes. It'll be hard for them, but I think they're ready to take that step."

Beth looked hopeful. "Do you think you will? Decide to stay?"

I thought for a minute before I met Beth's gaze. "I imagine it."

She smiled. "And what's it like in your imagination?"

"Well, I have a cell phone and playlists and my own computer. I drive a car." I paused. "I guess I imagine living like you. And like Rachel."

"And what do you imagine when you think about going home?"

I was quiet. I realized that I'd never thought about that possibility. My imagination never took me home.

CHAPTER

❦ 38 ❦

When the day of the dance finally arrived, I didn't know if I was excited or relieved. I packed a small bag with pajamas, toothbrush, and a change of clothes, and gave it to Josh, along with a sleeping bag I had borrowed from Rachel, to bring over to Valerie's house for the girls' sleepover.

Then I spent the better part of two hours washing and primping, staring endlessly at my changing reflection in the mirror. Rachel helped me draw a thin black line on my upper and lower eyelids, close to my lashes. I added eye shadow and blush, and then coated my lashes with mascara until they looked thick and inky. I still hadn't gotten the hang of using the hair dryer, so Rachel did it for me. When she was finished, my hair fell over my shoulders, smooth and shiny with a hint of curl.

Putting on the panty hose was a little tricky. Rachel had told me to inch the stockings up, one leg at a time, and to be careful not to poke my fingernail through the hose. When the stockings were finally on, they encased my legs in a way that felt smooth but a little itchy. I stepped into the blue dress and again felt the thrill I'd had in the fitting room when I first tried it on. I clipped on the blue earrings and fastened the silver necklace. A small black purse I borrowed from Rachel was ready with lipstick and a pair of white socks. Last, I stepped into the black heels. I had dutifully practiced wearing them, and was starting to get used to the feeling of walking so high off the ground.

By the time the doorbell rang at 6:00, I didn't feel that a speck of me was Amish. When I met Josh at the front door, his eyes widened and a smile slid up his face. "You look beautiful," he said. His voice was soft and warm and held a little hint of wonder.

"Thank, you," I said, filled with a sudden shyness. "You don't look so bad yourself." In fact, Josh looked very handsome in his gray suit and burgundy tie. His hair looked like he had worked hard to get the right amount of spikiness in it. He reached for my hand and pulled me forward in a tender way. Then he brushed my lips with a kiss and whispered in my ear, "I can't wait to show you off."

We handed each other identical clear boxes. Rachel helped pin the white boutonniere to Josh's lapel, and I slipped the corsage of pink roses over my wrist.

"You both look gorgeous!" she said, her voice bouncy and energetic. If the whole dance could be like this moment, with each of us looking elegant and feeling happy to be together, then it would be a perfect night.

"Listen," Rachel said. "I know we're about to go for pictures, but do you mind if I take a couple before we leave?"

While Rachel went off to get her camera, I swallowed back a sense of unease. This would be the first time that a frozen image of me would exist to mark a time in my life.

For the next few minutes she posed us together, holding the camera down around her chin and peering into it before a clicking sound and a flashing light meant the picture had been taken. I held very still, not wanting to seem nervous, trying to brush aside the stories I had grown up with about graven images and stolen souls. Suddenly Rachel stopped and said, "Oh, Eliza, what am I doing? I'm so sorry."

"It's okay. I guess there's a first time for everything, right?" Josh was looking at me with surprise. "Just another thing that the Amish don't do!" I said.

"Really?" he asked. "So I've been around for your first phone call, your first movie, and now your first picture? You are some girlfriend."

He reached out for Rachel's camera. "Here," he said. "Take a look at the first picture ever taken of you." He held the camera up to me. On the small screen I saw myself in my new blue dress, standing next to Josh, our hands clasped together, a smile on my face that was a little anxious but mostly happy. I looked up at him. "Thanks."

I was glad for that first picture-taking experience because a few minutes later we were at Valerie's house with a sea of teenagers and parents and cameras. I recognized some faces from the recent party, but everyone looked different now, and I couldn't readily attach the names.

Rachel had followed us there with Josh's parents, and the three of them stood together at the edge of the room. I had met Josh's parents a couple of times before. They were smiley people, and I could see why they were good friends of Sam and Rachel's. They greeted me warmly, and Josh's mom reached out to give me a hug.

For the next half hour there was a scramble to get every possible combination of poses. Then the adults herded us over to the big curved staircase, and we all staggered ourselves up the steps for a last group picture, the parents looking up at us from the floor below, their cameras flashing.

It was finally time to go. We spilled out of the house amid good-byes and hugs and last instructions from the parents about safety. Josh had his father's car—he had still not managed to gather enough money to buy his own—and Valerie and Greg climbed into the backseat. It was a short ride to the high school, and a cheerful sentiment of expectation flowed around us.

After leaving the car in the crowded lot, we filed through the open door and lined up with the other couples, all admiring each other in our dressy clothes. Everyone was stepping up to a long table, behind which sat three adults who looked sharply out of place. As the students approached the table, they presented the adults with a ticket and showed a little card with their picture on it. Josh had two tickets in his hand, along with his picture card, and he held them forward when he got to the table. "Hey, Mr. Rozey," he said, as the man behind the table took his tickets and nodded at his card.

"Hello, Joshua," he said. Then he looked at me. "ID, please?"

"She's my date," Josh said. "She doesn't go to school here, so I registered her when I bought the tickets."

The man nodded. "Then I'll just need to see an ID from your school or a driver's license."

I looked at Josh. He was shaking his head, concern on his face. Around us, I could hear some murmurs. Greg and Valerie glanced behind them when they saw we weren't following. "We'll meet you in there," Josh called to them. "Save us seats." Then he turned back to the teacher. "Mr. Rozey, can we talk over there for a minute?"

The teacher pushed back his chair, and we stepped over to the side. My chest was warm with discomfort.

"I thought everyone understood the rules, Joshua. Guests from other schools have to show their ID. It's for security."

"This is my girlfriend, Eliza," Josh said. " I registered her, but she doesn't have any ID because she doesn't drive, and she doesn't go to school."

The teacher looked at me, startled. "How old are you?"

"Sixteen," I said.

"Are you homeschooled?"

I shook my head. "No, sir. I work as a nanny for a family in the area." I felt heat rising to my cheeks from all the scrutiny.

Josh reached his arm around me and curved his hand around

my hip. "I guess I should tell you that Eliza is Amish. Can we find a way to make this work?" Mr. Rozey's eyebrows lifted. "I know," Josh said with a smile. "She doesn't look Amish, right? But there's no way I could make this up."

"Well, that doesn't mean she can't follow the rules. Doesn't she have any kind of ID?"

"Mr. Rozey, today before the dance was the first time Eliza's ever had her picture taken. Can't you make an exception?"

The teacher stepped back to the table and leaned over to talk to a woman. They were both glancing at me, as were the other students waiting to check in. It might have been my imagination, but Josh seemed to be enjoying all the attention. "Don't worry," he said. "That's my French teacher. She's chill."

The woman teacher came over to us. "Hi, Madame Harvey," Josh said. "Can you give us a break here?"

She smiled at me. "We just need the name and phone number of the people you work for," she said. I wrote Rachel's information on the paper she handed me.

"Okay," she said. "You can go right in."

I breathed my relief and Josh squeezed my hand. "Sorry about that," he said.

Inside the gymnasium I was catapulted into a different world. Billowing sheets of black paper covered all the walls, and the round tables throughout the room were draped with black tablecloths. The lights were dim, and all of the dark decorations added to the sense of gloom. The noise was piercing. It reminded me of the club we had gone to, but in addition to the loud music was the chatter of hundreds of voices. It took me a moment to get my bearings and make sense of the place. Along one wall, I was startled to see a long box that resembled a coffin. I looked away quickly. Hanging all around the room were mesh bags filled with what looked to be cloves of garlic. Josh was leaning toward me, trying to tell me something. I could feel his warm breath in my ear. "I forgot to tell you," he said. "It's a vampire theme."

Now it all made sense. At home, some of my friends secretly passed around books about a girl who is in love with a vampire. Annie and Kate would want to hear about this.

Greg was waving to us from the other side of the room, and we wove our way through the thick sea of people to get to him. He looked particularly handsome in his black suit and colorful tie. Valerie patted the chair next to her, and I plopped into it gratefully. She pointed to the floor, where her black high-heeled shoes were thrown, and then to her stocking feet. I took off my shoes, replacing them with the white socks from my purse. Jill and Steve waved to me from the other end of the table.

Greg leaned over to us. "Did Rozey give you a hard time?"

"Yeah," said Josh. "I had to play the Amish card." Everyone laughed, and I joined in. "Do you want to dance?" Josh said into my ear. I looked out at the crowded dance floor. The couples weren't dancing slowly, holding each other, the way we had at the club. They seemed like one big group, moving in a way that was vaguely keyed in to the music. I looked back to Josh uncertainly. "Come on," he said. "You'll get the hang of it."

I took his hand and let him lead me. When we stepped onto the dance floor we became part of a swarm of people, bodies close together. Here I discovered that dancing meant moving in small ways in some sort of rhythm, swaying from one foot to the other, swinging the arms just far enough not to bump a nearby dancer. I relaxed a little. It wasn't hard to look like the rest of them. Then the song changed and everyone reacted with whooping sounds and slow clapping with their hands high in the air. They looked like they knew the song and wanted to be a part of it, and I wanted that too. So I raised my hands high and clapped with them.

We stayed on the dance floor through the changing songs and tempos, and friends danced their way over to say hi to Josh and introduce themselves to me. We kept dancing through the introductions. I smiled my greetings, and tried to attach names to faces so that if I saw them again I would know what to call them.

One girl with cascading yellow hair looked me up and down. "I didn't think you'd be allowed to dress like this."

I didn't know how to answer, and then Josh stepped in. "I think she looks beautiful. Is that what you meant to say?"

The girl danced away and Josh whispered, "Sorry about her. I should have warned you about the mean girls."

Before I had time to think about that, the tempo of the music slowed, and the chaotic mayhem on the dance floor shifted as everyone coupled up, and the large crowd became a set of pairs. I slipped easily into Josh's arms and reached my hands around his shoulders in the now-comfortable way. His hands pressed into my lower back, tugging me closer to him. My head rested against his chest. I drank in the closeness and wanted it to be forever. But it wasn't. In a few minutes the music was loud and fast again, and the pairs melded back into one big crowd. Josh nudged me away from the dance floor, and we moved to the other side of the room, where food was being served.

We filled our plates with pasta and salad, and grabbed blissfully icy bottles of water and went back to the table. Occasionally, other people came over, and the girls would jump up and hug each other as though they hadn't been together in a long time, even though they all were at school yesterday. There was much complimenting of dresses, and then the inevitable introductions to me. The girls were mostly friendly, but I sensed a curiosity as well. It was clear that everyone knew about Josh's Amish girlfriend and wanted to get a closer look.

At one point, Josh was nearby talking to Steve when a leggy girl with billows of black hair, and skin that looked like it had been overly bronzed by the sun, sat down in his seat. "I'm Courtney," she said. I started to introduce myself, and she interrupted. "I know all about you. We all do." I looked past her and saw that two other girls were standing a bit behind her. They were wispy girls with long hair that fell in perfect waves, and a lot of makeup. They didn't introduce themselves to me. I guessed they were Courtney's audience.

I set down my fork. I wasn't sure where this was headed, but she seemed to have come over to make a point. "So," she said, flicking her hair back with a shake of her head, "you guys are the ones who shun people, right?"

I flinched, feeling more shocked than angry. "That happens sometimes, but not very often." The girls behind Courtney were still watching us.

"Well," she said, "that's basically what your boyfriend did to all of us. So it seems fitting that you found each other."

Just then, I felt a hand on my shoulder, gentle and warm. "What the hell, Courtney," said Josh, standing behind me. "If you've got issues with me, tell them to me. Eliza doesn't even know who you are."

Courtney shrugged. "Now she does," she said, before flouncing off, followed by the two girls.

Josh sat down in the seat she had just left. He was shaking his head, speechless.

"What made her so mad at you?" I asked. My voice sounded wobbly.

"Remember when I told you about the girls I used to date? Well, she was one of them." He smiled. "My taste has definitely improved."

I knew I should have been warmed by these words, and by Josh's protectiveness of me. But there was something unsettling about this contact with Courtney. It was a reminder that maybe what Valerie had said was true. Maybe I was just that bit of difference he was looking for. I sipped from my water bottle and looked around the room, wondering if any more of Josh's old girlfriends were waiting to have words with me.

After dinner, Josh took me to a corner of the gym where a little area had been set up for pictures. A curtain hung in the background, and couples posed in front of it. Some put on vampire capes that the photographer provided. Each picture came instantly out of the camera, and each was placed in a shiny black frame.

When it was our turn, we stood in front of the curtain and Josh put his arm around me. "Look at the camera," said the photographer. But at that moment we were looking at each other, turned inward just enough to face each other fully. Josh's smile reached up to the corners of his brown eyes. I knew that no matter who his other girlfriends had been before me, this smile was mine alone. A light flashed and then another. "Next!" the photographer called out, and we moved slowly to the side, still smiling, both of us knowing that it was a private, personal smile.

While the photographer posed the next couple, a woman handed each of us a picture inside a frame. I stared at the couple in the picture, staring at each other. It was my graven image, my stolen soul, and it was beautiful. I couldn't turn my eyes away from it.

Outside, I breathed in the cool fall air and let the quiet seep into my skin. When the dance had started and everything was brilliant and lively and new, I hadn't wanted it to end. Then, when the lights came on and a group of students set to work taking down the decorations, I was ready to move on to the next events, the party at Valerie's house, the girls' sleepover.

This was a getting to be a familiar sensation. I was always anxious for the next new thing. I briefly wondered how I would feel once I'd experienced everything and there was nothing new to look forward to, but I brushed the thought away.

Back at Valerie's house, we all headed to the basement, which was more like a downstairs living room—so unlike the dingy cellars at home. Here, comfortable furniture faced a big TV screen, and music fell into the background of our conversations.

I looked around at the group that had gathered and realized that we all looked far less fine than we had when the night began. The girls had taken off their high shoes and were walking around barefoot or in white socks. Some of them had pulled their hair back into ponytails, and their faces showed makeup smudges. The boys had taken off their sport coats and ties, and their once-crisp shirts were webbed with wrinkles. I went into the bathroom and slipped off my pantyhose and unclipped my earrings. My hair was a bit disheveled, and some specks of mascara dotted the area around my eyes. I wasn't as smooth and glossy-looking as I had been when Josh rang the bell a few hours ago, but I still enjoyed the fancy reflection that stared back at me.

I rummaged through the pile of overnight bags in the corner of the room, and slipped the panty hose and earrings into my bag.

Jill and Steve were also searching through the bags. Oscar came to join them. There seemed to be a lot more overnight bags than six girls would need.

I settled next to Josh on the couch. "The girls brought a lot of bags," I said.

"It's not just girls. We're all sleeping over."

I pulled away from him, surprised, and took a big breath to calm the mix of feelings settling over me. I remembered Rachel's concern when I had mentioned the sleepover, and now I wondered if this was what she had suspected.

"It's okay, isn't it?" Josh asked. "This way we're not out after curfew, and no one's driving."

"Do the parents know?"

"Yeah, there was some negotiating about it, but all the parents agreed eventually," he said. "Valerie's parents are upstairs, but they promised us our privacy."

I turned this information over in my head, trying to remember how it had been presented to me. I was pretty sure that Josh had said, "The girls are sleeping at Valerie's after the dance."

I was caught in two places now. I knew I should call Rachel and have her pick me up so I would be following the rules I had agreed to. But I wanted this place, the big downstairs living room filled with boys and girls I hoped would be my friends.

I decided to worry about it all later. Tomorrow I would tell Rachel that I didn't know the boys were staying over, and when I found out it was too late to call her. That was almost true. And all of the other parents had agreed, so maybe this was a common occurrence here. When I felt the light tickle of Josh's fingers roaming through my hair, I knew that I was supposed to be right here with him.

Then Jill came toward us with a large clear bottle in her hands. Oscar followed with a similar-looking bottle. At a tall table in the corner, bottles were being deposited one by one as they were pulled out of the overnight bags. So, I thought, my lies would be growing. Still, I wanted to stay. My brother's words came back to me. *Try everything, do everything. This is the only chance you'll get.*

"Who's tending?" asked Valerie. Oscar raised his hand as though he were in school, and sprinted to Valerie's side. She was busy gathering things from a box and setting them on top of the table. A tall stack of plastic cups and a long spoon. Bottles of orange juice, cranberry juice, and Coke. From an unseen place around the corner, Greg appeared with a big bag of ice.

"The bar's open," announced Valerie. Everyone assembled around the table, calling out their requests to Oscar. Josh turned to me. "What do you think?" he asked. "One drink?"

I was feeling mightily tempted, and I did not want to be on the outside of this occasion. "Okay," I said. "One drink." Josh smiled, and I knew I had made the right choice.

He got up from the couch and joined the group around the table, where Oscar arranged the blue plastic cups in a row, dropping ice cubes into each. In the next few minutes I watched from the couch as Oscar poured from one of the large bottles, added some juice or Coke, stirred the contents with the long spoon, and handed the cup to someone's outstretched hands. When it was Josh's turn he said, "Two vodkas and cranberry juice." Oscar nodded and mixed the drinks.

Back beside me on the couch, Josh handed me the blue cup and I looked inside. The red drink, with ice cubes swimming along the top, looked sweet and appealing. All around us couples settled on couches and chairs and big cushions on the floor, holding blue cups and grinning at the contents. Greg slapped a deck of cards on the coffee table and said, "Who's first?" I wasn't sure what cards had to do with these drinks we were holding, so I waited to see what would happen next.

"I think we should let the bartender start," said Valerie. "He's been working hard."

Oscar smiled and reached for a card, turning it over on the table so that everyone could see what he picked. "Four!" shouted Valerie. Oscar raised his cup to his lips and everyone around me counted aloud. "One, two, three, four!" During the counting, Oscar drank greedily, his Adam's apple moving up and down with his swallows. At "four" he lowered his cup in a way that looked a bit reluctant.

There were a few cheers before Ashley reached forward and picked a card. She looked disappointed that she had drawn a two. "One, two!" everyone shouted, as Ashley took a short drink and brought the cup down. Next was Josh's turn. He reached forward and showed everyone his card, a seven. He raised his glass and drank while we all counted to seven.

"Are you ready?" he asked me. I nodded and reached for the top card. When I flipped the card onto the table and saw the number ten, there were excited murmurs in the group. I knew now that I would be drinking for longer than anyone else had, and I felt a jumble of excitement and nervousness as I raised the cup to my lips. As everyone counted to ten, I took big swallows of the red liquid. It tasted like a mix of sweet and tart and something else I couldn't name. Something pungent and sharp that stayed in my throat after the chanting around me reached ten and I took the last swallow. I drew a shaky breath. "Are you okay?" asked Josh. I smiled in response.

I joined in the counting now as Jill pulled a three and Steve a nine, watching excitedly, waiting until it would be my turn again and all eyes would be back on me and I could taste that sweet sourness again. When it was Carly's turn, she pulled an ace, and everyone shouted at once, "One or eleven?"

"Eleven!" Carly cried out, and there was a burst of cheering before the counting started.

When it was finally my turn again, my card was a queen. I looked around, uncertain of what number went with the card. I felt a wave of excitement around me as Greg explained, "For face cards you get to pick your own number, anything between one and eleven." I looked at all the expectant faces and I knew what they were waiting for.

"Eleven!" I shouted, and the resulting cheers made me feel rich inside. I raised the cup and began to gulp the red liquid as everyone counted. The drink tasted a bit less harsh than on my first turn. The counting seemed slower this time, and the ice swam against my upper lip as I raised the cup higher and tried to breathe and swallow at the same time. When the counting ended, I lowered my glass and turned to Josh with a grin. "Take it easy," he said. "You need to pace yourself." His voice had a smile in it, but also a little note of concern. I peered into my cup and saw that it was almost empty. I shrugged and looked up to see who would be drinking next. I was anxious for it to be my turn again, to feel the attention of these new friends, to taste that sweet fluid on my tongue. I reveled in a new sensation of easiness, of settling in. I was one of them now, receiving the same attention as everyone else. There was a looseness in my limbs that felt like liquid running through me. The cushions on the couch were swallowing me, and I was drenched in a sense of deep comfort.

The turns were coming faster now, the counting louder. I held up my empty cup, as I had seen others do. "Are you sure?" asked Josh. His words sounded slushy.

"Yes," I said. But it came out more like "Yesh." A cold, full cup found its way back to my hand. Michael turned up an ace, and I shouted with everyone else, "One or eleven?" and cheered when he yelled, "Eleven!" My turn again. An eight. The last drop slid down my throat. Another full drink found its way into my hand.

More turns, more counting. It was getting hard to keep track of whose turn it was. Some people were lying down now, sitting up only when it was time for them to reach for a card. My turn again.

A five. Too short of a turn. I took bigger gulps to make the most of it. A softness surrounded me, a gentleness. I wanted more of this feeling, so I took another sip even though it wasn't my turn. No one noticed, so I took another. The ice bumped against my teeth. I held up my cup, but no one took it, so I got up to mix the drink myself. The room was tilting, and I felt myself swaying with it. Josh was next to me, his arm tight around my waist. "I'm cutting you off," he said, taking the cup from my hand. His voice was gentle and he guided me back to the couch in a tender way. I felt myself tumbling into him, and even after he was lying on the couch and I was stretched out on top of him, my head on his chest, it still felt like I was falling.

"Whose turn is it?" I asked.

I felt Josh's shrug against my cheek. "I don't think we're playing anymore," he said. "I think everyone's just drinking without the game."

I was disappointed. "But I love counting," I said. It was a funny thing to say, and I laughed. Josh laughed too, and that made me laugh more. Then I couldn't stop laughing, and I had to gulp to get air. I liked being funny.

Then I noticed that no one else was laughing or talking. Some couples had gone off to the far reaches of the room, and were curled up together. My blue dress felt damp and it was bunching up in places. Josh's hands roamed over my back, and somehow his fingertips were on my skin without the dress between us. I wanted to shift around to straighten out the dress, but his hands felt warm and his touch was light. I knew I should feel immodest, but it was dark in the room and no one was there except for us. Or maybe they were there but I couldn't see them, and it didn't matter anyhow. The red drink in the blue cup had made everything soft and cottony. I was drifting now, and the couch we were on rocked ever so slightly. I thought of Rachel warning me to keep my head on my shoulders, and I wanted to laugh again because I knew that wherever my head had gone, it wasn't on my shoulders.

When I closed my eyes, I was spinning the way I had with Margaret and James when we were little, turning in circles and feeling the sun on our faces.

I couldn't imagine a better feeling.

CHAPTER

39

I couldn't imagine a worse feeling. The room was circling around me and I wasn't spinning in the spring sun. My body was pressed against Josh's. My legs were cold and bare, and whatever I was wearing was hiked up in a way that I was sure was improper. Small sounds invaded the silence. Loud breathing, whispering. Who else was here? From far away another sound. Someone retching. I swallowed back a sudden nausea and opened my eyes.

The room came jarringly into view, the windowless living room below Valerie's house where we had all come in our finery. It didn't seem like it could be the same night. Josh and I were still on the couch, where we had plummeted together into a dizzying sleep. He was still asleep, his breathing raspy, his breath sour. I was stretched out on top of him. I carefully disentangled myself, straightened my dress, and sat forward at the edge of the couch. Josh didn't move. I sat for a while, breathing deeply and letting my eyes adjust to the darkness. A sickly feeling had settled in my chest.

The table was littered with the blue cups that had been the

source of delicious laughter a few hours ago. Around the room, couples were sprawled out together the way Josh and I had been, some on furniture, others on the floor. I went to the table that earlier had been used as a bar and poured some Coke into a blue cup. It tasted warm and sweet.

My head was pounding. I wanted to be back in my room at Rachel's house, in a clean nightgown and a soft bed. I wanted to shower away the dirty feeling and drink gallons of warm Coke.

From across the room I heard the toilet flush and the bathroom door open. I looked over to see Oscar, his face pale, his steps unsteady. I tiptoed across the room, stepping around the sleeping bodies, and slipped into the bathroom. Before I fully realized what I was doing, I knelt before the toilet, my arms encircling the seat. A long flow of pink vomit gushed into the toilet, and I took in a ragged breath. The tile pressed into my bare knees. I flushed the toilet and then vomited again, this time my stomach seizing and my breaths gulping. At the sink I rinsed my mouth and splashed water on my face. Someone was knocking on the door. I opened it and Carly rushed past me and leaned over the toilet. Closing the door behind me, I tried to think of what to do next.

I went back to the couch and sat beside Josh, who was still stretched out in the same position I had left him in. I reached for his left hand to see his watch. It was a little before four o'clock. I leaned forward and whispered, "I want to go home." He stirred but didn't wake up. I shook his shoulder and leaned closer. "Josh, I want to go home."

He opened his eyes, looking at me in a foggy way, and I watched him wake up. His usual grin started to slide up his face. "What's up?" he asked, but it sounded more like "Tsup."

I said it again, more firmly now. "I want to go home."

He looked confused. "Back to the Amish?" he asked. It would have been funny if I hadn't felt so miserable.

"No," I said. "Back to Rachel's house. I don't feel well."

Josh's eyes slid closed again. "Okay," he said. "In a little while."

I went back to the corner of the room and searched through the piles of belongings to find my overnight bag. I unzipped it and reached for my sneakers. Inside the bag my pajamas were neatly folded, awaiting a different kind of night. A night where girls sat around and replayed the events of the evening and watched movies about boys and girls who discover that they love each other, even though all the girls sitting together in their pajamas knew it already. I longed for the comfort of that night.

I stepped into my sneakers, feeling the rubbery sensation against my bare feet, grabbed the sleeping bag and overnight bag and returned to the couch. Now I shook Josh impatiently. "Please take me home," I said when Josh's eyes slid open.

"Now?" he asked. He sat up slowly, shaking his head. "But we were all going to have breakfast in the morning."

My stomach turned at the thought. I shook my head. "I need to leave now," I said, and finally he seemed to understand. Too slowly, he got up and searched around the bags for his belongings and shoes. In the morning there would be a great mess to clean up, and everyone would wonder where Josh and I had gone, but I didn't care about any of that. Finally, we were making our way up the stairs, through Valerie's quiet house, and out the front door.

I gulped in the coolness of the early-morning air. It was still dark outside, but the sky was losing its blackness. Josh turned to me.

"So what happened? Did you get sick?" I nodded, embarrassed. "Okay," he said, his voice gentler. "Let's get you home."

We threw our bags into the back of the car, and I climbed in the front seat. Josh took a long look at me before he turned the key. "Let me know if you need me to pull over," he said. "Remember, this is my dad's car." He reached over me and pressed a switch on the armrest. The window came down with a humming sound, and I leaned toward the fresh air. He was still looking at me, and I felt suddenly unattractive with my messy hair and makeup smudges and wrinkled dress. "I'm sorry," he said. "I should have taken better care of you."

I swallowed back a tightness in my throat, feeling shaky all of a sudden, as fragile as a piece of glass. I leaned back against the headrest and closed my eyes. As the car started moving, I thought about the photographs that froze me in time as a pretty girl going to a dance. The girl in the picture was nothing like the girl sitting in the car right now.

"Keep your eyes open," Josh said. "It's worse when they're closed."

I obeyed, wondering how he knew so much about it. The

motion of the car made the nausea worse, and I leaned my head closer to the open window. "We're almost there," Josh said. "Can you keep it together?"

"Just get me home," I said, hoping I would make it to Rachel's house before getting sick again.

"It's another two blocks," he said. I was glad that he was driving so fast. It would get me there sooner, and this would all be over, this sickness and ugliness that had come over me.

"Tell me if you need to stop," he said, his voice urgent. He was looking at me, and I thought he should be looking at the street in front of the car. That sick feeling was sweeping through me, and I couldn't stop thinking about the sweet-and-sour taste of that red drink.

"We're here, Liza, hang on," he said. I felt the car turn sharply with a screeching sound, and then there was a crash and a jolt, but all I wanted was to get out of the car. Josh was shouting something, but I couldn't hear him. I flung open the car door and I was outside on the lawn, the grass cool and rough against my knees and the palms of my hands. This time I didn't throw up, but my stomach lurched like it wanted to. I lay down in the grass, and it felt so good to be out of that basement and out of that car. Now Josh was leaning over me, saying something about how I had to get up and how he was in trouble. Then the front door opened and Sam and Rachel were there. Sam was wearing a bathrobe and Rachel had a jacket over her pajamas, and I laughed because it was funny that they were outside in their pajamas in the middle of the night. But then I knew that it wasn't funny at all, and it felt like nothing was ever going to be funny again, but still I was laughing.

I sat up and tried to feel alert, swallowing back the last of my laughter, because it felt like something important was happening. Rachel was talking to Josh, who was standing over me, but looking toward the car in the driveway. "Is she all right?" Rachel asked.

"She's okay," he said. "She had a drink at the party and she's not feeling well. That's why I took her home."

"She doesn't look okay," Rachel said, in the voice that she used when the children were on her very last nerve. "Really, Josh. How did you let this happen?"

"I'm sorry," Josh was saying. He and Rachel and Sam were standing over me in the grass. "How bad is it?" Josh asked. At first I thought he was talking about me, but then I realized he was talking to Sam about something that happened to the car.

"It's not great," said Sam.

I looked up from my place in the grass, and Rachel looked down at me. "I'll get her inside." She sounded weary, like she was at the end of a long day. "Josh, Sam's going to drive you home, and then walk back. We'll talk tomorrow."

I felt Josh and Rachel on either side of me, lifting me to my feet. I was reluctant to leave the coolness of the grass, but they seemed to know what they were doing. "I'm sorry, Rachel," Josh said. He sounded like a little boy in trouble, and it made me feel bad for him even though I knew that he wasn't the only one who had done something wrong. For a second I felt Josh's hand nestle into mine, and then he was gone and Rachel was leading me into the house and up the stairs, her arm across my back. In my room, she opened and closed the dresser drawers until she found a nightgown and set it next to me on the bed. "Do you need help changing?" she asked.

It seemed like a silly question, but all at once I knew that I did need help. So she unzipped my dress and lifted it over my head and then pulled on the nightgown and helped me find the armholes. It was embarrassing to be undressed and dressed like I was a little girl, but I couldn't seem to figure out how to make everything work myself, so I had to let Rachel do it for me.

Rachel told me she'd be right back, and when she returned she put a big bowl on my nightstand. "This is in case you need to throw up again," she said. I nodded, hoping I wouldn't need it. Then she put two white pills on the nightstand. "You're going to have a headache tomorrow," she said. I took some gulps of water from the glass she handed me, and then climbed into bed. Rachel pulled the covers up to my chin. I nodded my thanks, feeling a heaviness pulling at me.

Rachel rested her hand on my shoulder for just a minute before whispering, "Sleep it off."

And I did.

CHAPTER

40

It was a cluttered sleep. Sometimes I felt like I was actually awake and repeating the events of the night. I was on the dance floor and in Valerie's basement and on Rachel's lawn, but this time I knew what would happen in the end, so I tried to make things turn out differently. A couple of times I woke up and took a few sips of water before dropping back into sleep. As the room got lighter I could hear Ben's and Janie's voices, and then Rachel telling them to be quiet because I wasn't feeling well. I was grateful to her but also uneasy, and I knew, even in my sleep, that there were things to take care of when I woke up.

Finally, I pulled myself out of bed, dreading the day in front of me. My head throbbed and a bitter taste filled mouth. White pills in hand, I made my way to the bathroom, my head pounding with each step. I swallowed the pills, gulping the water greedily. Then I washed my face, scrubbing at the remains of the makeup, and brushed my teeth three times until the acrid taste left my mouth. I stepped into the shower and stood gratefully in the hot steam, soaping every inch of myself as if I could wash away all that had happened. Back in my room, I pulled on my blue jeans and a sweat-shirt, my wet ponytail dampening the hood. My new blue dress was draped over the chair, and I lifted it tentatively. It was a mass of wrinkles and stains. I thought about how much money I had paid for it, and how excitedly I had slipped it on the night before. Then I heard a light tap on my door, and opened it to see Rachel standing in the hallway.

"How are you feeling?" she asked. I tried to remember if I had seen her last night. Then it came rushing back: Rachel leading me from the front lawn to my room, helping me change. Shame filled me.

"I've been better," I said. Then, in a small voice, I added, "I guess I didn't keep my head on my shoulders."

Rachel nodded, wearing a serious expression. "Sam's out with the kids," she said. "Can we talk?" I stepped back into the room and sat on the edge of the bed. She sat beside me.

"We have some things to figure out about last night," she said. "I've been on the phone with Josh's parents."

"I'm sorry, Rachel. I didn't mean for this to happen. I didn't know there was going to be drinking at the party. But, still, I should have said no."

Rachel sighed. "Your parents trusted me, and I let them down. We both let them down."

My chest tightened. I hadn't thought about my parents. I looked at Rachel. "Can we please not tell them about this? They'd be so disappointed in me." I didn't say what I was really afraid of, that they would make me come home.

"I need to think," said Rachel, her voice cautious. "I don't see how I can keep this from them."

"Can we check with Aunt Beth," I pleaded, "and see what she says?"

"Maybe, but first we have to deal with everything else."

"Everything else?" I asked.

"The car," Rachel said. She sounded impatient. "Josh's parents are pretty angry. They're bringing it in tomorrow to see how much it'll cost to fix."

"What happened to the car?" I asked.

Rachel looked at me with surprise. "When Josh pulled into the driveway, he crashed the car into our garage door. You don't remember?"

Then it flooded back. Josh driving too fast, a banging noise, the feeling of being jerked. "Oh, no," I said. It came out like a moan. "Oh, we really messed up." Rachel was quiet. She didn't disagree. "Did we damage the garage door?"

"There's a dent," she said. "Sam had to do some work to get it to open. I'm going to call someone tomorrow to find out what it'll take to fix it."

Then I knew what I needed to do. "I'd like to pay for the garage door. You can take it out of my wages."

Rachel put her hand on my shoulder. "We'll talk more later," she said. "The important thing is that neither of you were hurt." I nodded, feeling awful. "Come on," she said. "Let's get some food into you."

In the kitchen, I watched Rachel slice a bagel and set it in the toaster oven, and tried to piece everything together in my mind. Josh had crashed his father's car because I had made him drive me home when he was tired and probably still a little drunk. He was distracted because I was sick, so he wasn't paying attention to his driving. And I was sick because I had been drinking. Everything that had gone wrong last night pointed back to me. It was all my fault.

Rachel set a plate on the table with a toasted bagel spread lightly with butter. She also brought me a glass of orange juice and a mug of steaming coffee. Nothing looked appealing to me except for the juice, which I drank with mighty gulps. Rachel sat on the chair beside me. "I know you probably don't feel like eating, but it's important to get something into your stomach."

I took a small bite of the bagel and chewed it slowly. I turned to Rachel. "When you were taking the pictures of us before the dance, I was so happy. I can't believe that a night that started out so nice could end this way."

"I know," Rachel said. There was kindness in her tone, and I was grateful for it. "There are some lessons that we have to learn the hard way."

I spent most of the day in my room, dozing into restless naps, listlessly turning the pages of a book, drinking big glasses of water. I wrote a long letter to Kate describing what happened at the dance. It felt a little better to pour the words onto the page.

Josh called late in the afternoon, and I grabbed the phone, anxious to hear his voice. "Are you feeling better?" he asked.

"A little." I took a breath. "I shouldn't have made you take me home last night."

Josh didn't answer right away, and I could picture him shaking his head, his face unsmiling. "There were a lot of 'shouldn't haves' last night."

I closed my eyes, waiting for him to say something that would make me feel better. When he didn't, I asked, "Can you come to dinner at Aunt Beth's tonight?"

"No," he said. "I'm not going to be allowed out for a while." Then he added, "Tomorrow we'll find out about all the damages, so I'll see you when I come over to talk to Rachel."

I hung up feeling worse. The reaches of my blame felt endless. When it was time to go to Aunt Beth's house for my regular Sunday dinner, Rachel said she would drive me. Beth greeted me at the door with an excited expression on her face, which changed to a question when she saw that Rachel was with me.

"Hi, Beth," Rachel said, after my aunt ushered us inside. "I'd like to talk with you for a few minutes before your dinner, if that's okay."

Beth turned to me. "Your uncle is in the den watching baseball. I'm sure he'd love some company."

Uncle John got up from the couch and greeted me with his usual hug. I sat in an armchair and tried to pick up the threads of the baseball game. I felt Uncle John looking at me. "Is everything okay, kiddo?"

I shook my head. "Not really. I wasn't very Amish last night."

Uncle John gave a tiny laugh before saying, "That's all right. Some of my best friends aren't Amish." He turned off the television and said, "Do you want to talk about it?"

Something about his calm voice made me want to tell him what happened after the dance. He winced when I got to the part about Josh crashing the car. "It could have been a lot worse," he said. "I think you and Josh were lucky."

"I know," I said. "But I don't feel very lucky right now."

"Well," he said, "you haven't had too much experience. I guess you weren't prepared for how those nights can turn out."

Just then, I heard the front door close, and I knew that Rachel had gone. I followed John into the kitchen. Beth was standing at the stove, and she turned around when we came in. "It sounds like you had a rough night," she said, wiping her hands on a dish towel and walking toward me.

I nodded, blinking back tears. We all sat down at the table, and I waited to hear what Beth would say. When she spoke, her voice was breathy, like she was talking and sighing at the same time. "I don't know what we should do about your parents. I'm in a tough situation now."

I looked down. "I don't want them to know about this."

"You know," said Beth quietly, "I really fought to get your mom to let you stay here. And to let you go out with Josh. I'm beginning to wonder if I might have been wrong."

I shook my head, tears slipping down my cheeks. "I'm sorry, Aunt Beth. I wish I could start over and do it better."

Her hand stroked my back. "I know." She was quiet for a while. I sensed that she and John were glancing at each other over my head, having a conversation without words, like my parents do. Finally Beth spoke. "It may not be the right thing, but I'll feel better if we don't worry your parents about what happened." I looked up at her. She was watching me closely. "And I have a feeling that you won't ever find yourself in that situation again."

"Never," I said.

"Okay, then. They don't have to know."

I wiped my tears with the back of my hand. "Thank you," I whispered.

A few minutes later we were eating dinner, the food filling me in a comforting way. Beth turned to me and said, "So tell us about the dance."

I looked at her, confused. "You've already heard about it."

Beth shook her head. "No, I've only heard about what happened *after* the dance. I'm thinking there are also some good parts of this story. Can we hear them?"

I shrugged. "Do you want to?"

"Of course we want to," said Uncle John. "We want you to be able look back on the whole night—not just how it ended."

I smiled and let the memories of the dance fill my head. I took a breath and started to tell my aunt and uncle about the night. They leaned in eagerly, and I told them all the good parts.

CHAPTER

41

The doorbell rang after dinner Monday night, and Rachel looked at me. "That's Josh."

I got up, feeling the same nervous shyness as when he picked me up for our first date, but this time with none of the excitement. I opened the door and he met my eyes with a cautious half-smile.

"Are you feeling better?" he asked. I nodded and stepped toward him. He reached his arms around me, but the hug felt loose and awkward.

We went into the living room, where Rachel was waiting. I sat on the couch beside Josh. "I screwed up," he said. "I'm really sorry."

"I know you are," Rachel said. "But I have to be honest and tell you that this feels a little personal because I trusted you."

"Yeah," Josh said, looking at Rachel and then at me. "I lost a lot of trust over the weekend."

"How bad is the car?" she asked.

"It's in the shop now." He looked down. "The money I earned over the summer will take care of fixing it."

My heart sank at his words. He'd been working so hard to get enough money together to buy his own car, and now he'd be starting all over.

"I also have a check for the garage door," he said, reaching into his pocket.

I turned to Josh. "Rachel and I already talked about that. I'm going to pay for it out of my wages." I glanced at Rachel, and she gave me the smallest of nods. Josh looked at me as though he was about to object, but I shook my head before he could talk. "It's only fair," I said. "I made you take me home. If we'd stayed at the party like you wanted, none of this would have happened."

Josh looked like he was trying to smile. "Thanks, Liza." Then he turned to Rachel. "You've always been like a second mom to me," he said. "Now both of my moms are pissed at me."

Rachel took a long breath. "There's something my father told me once after I'd gotten into some trouble. He said, 'We all make mistakes. But it's what you do after the mistake that shows the kind of person you are.'"

Josh looked at her and nodded, a mix of sadness and relief on his face. Standing up he said, "I've got to head out now. I'm going to the mall to see if the Apple store will give me more hours." Rachel stood and put her arms around him. He returned her hug.

"We've all had a night we wish we could get back," she said.

I walked Josh to the front door, slipping my hand tentatively into his. He gave it a light squeeze before he let go. He turned to me and said, "We're going to be all right." After he left, I realized that he had said it as a question.

The next day, Rachel arranged to have the garage door fixed, and we agreed that she would deduct money from each of my paychecks until the cost of the repair was covered. Josh called to tell me that he was able to get more hours at the Apple store, but some of them would be over the weekends. "It doesn't really matter, though," he added, "because I'm grounded for the next two weeks except for work and school." Hanging up the phone, I could already feel the loneliness of the two weeks that lay ahead.

Later that afternoon, I went into the Bean Scene. The children were at a reading in the library, and I had a half hour before I had to pick them up. When I walked in, I saw Valerie at a corner table with Jill and Carly. They had books and papers spread around them, but it didn't seem like they were studying. Valerie looked up and saw me. I thought I noticed the girls exchanging glances before she waved me over to the table.

"So," said Carly, "we were hangover sisters Saturday night."

"I'm afraid we were," I said. "Are you feeling better?"

"Yeah," said Carly. "Sunday was a little rocky. How about you?"

"I'm fine," I said, looking down. I felt a pang every time I thought about Saturday night.

"I guess it was your first time drinking," said Valerie.

"And my last."

"That's what we all say," said Jill, with a giggle. "But we don't seem to learn from our mistakes."

They all laughed, and I tried to join in. When the laughter died down, Valerie turned to me. "So, anyway, do you mind if I ask you something?" I waited. "Like, what were you thinking?"

"Excuse me?"

"Why did you make Josh drive you home? The whole reason we planned the sleepover was so no one would be on the road. And now we're all in trouble."

"You are?" I asked, shame filling me.

"Yeah," Valerie continued. "After what happened with you and Josh, all the parents know we were drinking. I'm back on curfew. Oscar's grounded. Alex can't drive for a month."

Heat pumped to my face. "I'm sorry, but I was sick."

"You were hungover," said Valerie. "We all were. And nobody else went home."

I felt like I was sliding into a hole.

"Chill out, Val," said Carly. "This isn't Eliza's fault. She didn't know we'd be drinking." I looked gratefully at Carly. "And she didn't even know that everyone was going to be at the sleepover. Remember, we told her it was just going to be the girls."

I straightened in my chair, recalling my confusion when I learned that the boys would also be sleeping over. I looked at Valerie, who was staring angrily at Carly.

"Nice going, Carly," said Jill. "That was supposed to be a secret." Carly shrugged.

I turned to Valerie. "So everyone knew but me?"

"Yeah," said Valerie. "If you want to know, your boyfriend was the reason no one told you about the sleepover. Josh told me to say it would just be the girls."

"And why was that?" I asked, my heart pounding.

Valerie shrugged. "Why do you think? He was afraid that if you knew about it, you wouldn't stay overnight. You know, because of the Amish thing."

They were all looking at me, waiting for my response, but too many feelings were clattering through me. And Valerie was looking a little too pleased that she had been able to tell me this information about Josh.

I reached to select the right words. "Well," I said slowly, "Josh was right about something." I waited a moment, watching Valerie's face. "He told me never to trust you with a secret. I guess he should have taken his own advice."

Valerie's eyebrows lowered. She opened her mouth as if to say something, then closed it again. Carly burst into laughter. "Oh, burn!" she said when her laughter died down. I wasn't sure what that meant, but Carly was smiling at me in a satisfied way, and I felt that I had won a tiny victory. I looked at my watch. "I have to go pick up the kids," I said. Then I turned to Valerie. "I'm sorry I wasn't there to help clean up in the morning. It must have been a big mess."

"Yes, it was," she said. "And it still is."

The next day I got a letter from Kate. *I'm so sorry about the troubles you had after the dance,* she wrote. *If you were home I'd be giving you a bag of starter batter and we would bake friendship bread to help you feel better.* I smiled, remembering the Sunday afternoons I had spent mixing ingredients with my sister and later sharing the batter with our girlfriends.

Everyone who shared in the batch of batter baked their friendship bread at the same time. So while I bent over my stove, I would know that three of my friends were all doing the same in their own kitchens. Here, friends didn't need anything like that to feel connected. All they had to do was sign on to the computer or pick up a cell phone. I looked down at Kate's letter and read on, imagining the cinnamon smells of the bread we would be baking together if I were at home right now.

CHAPTER

42

During the next week, my daily talks with Josh were more somber. I listened to his stories of working extra hours and staying up later to finish his homework. But now my feelings of responsibility were mixed with anger that Josh had lied to me about the sleepover party. I hadn't yet told him I knew about the lie, because it was a discussion I didn't want to have on the phone.

As I expected, the weekends were lonely. I agreed to babysit both weekend nights while Josh was grounded, and in exchange, Rachel reduced my debt. After the children were in bed on one of those nights, boredom felt like it had climbed inside my body. I watched television for a while, but the shows seemed to have the same tired stories. A boy found himself with two dates for a dance. A woman lost a ring she had borrowed from a friend. A baby was born in an elevator. I turned off the TV and went to my room, looking for something else to fill my time.

I noticed the quilting bag that I had tossed into the closet on the day I arrived. Suddenly, the thought of the close, exacting work of quilting appealed to me. I turned the bag over on my bed, watching the colored fabrics fall into a hushed pile. At home, I had cut the shapes for the Pinwheel Block pattern, and I reached for the plastic bag where I had gathered the triangles and rectangles that would come together into the quilt square. I had chosen two shades of blue, the colors of morning and midnight skies, to provide a soft effect in the center. I liked when colors that are near each other on the color wheel sat beside each other on a quilt. To contrast with the blues, I had chosen burgundy and pink fabrics to bring definition and harmony to the square.

I laid out the pieces as they would be in the quilt square, the dark and light blue triangles alternating in the center, the burgundy around them, and the pink at the corners. I'd always enjoyed this part of quilting, arranging the pieces like a jigsaw puzzle until they reflected the pattern I had chosen, and provided the color balance I was looking for. Satisfied with the way the square looked laid out on my bed, I lifted up two blue triangles from the center of the square and stitched them together so that the alternating colors shimmered.

I continued stitching the shapes together until the quilt block was finished, a twelve-inch square with colors radiating out from blue to burgundy to pink. There was order and balance in the quilt block, with the shapes fitting together and the colors bringing just the right amount of complement and contrast.

I reached for the pattern book, flipping the pages to find the next design I wanted to stitch. The Grecian Square was interesting, and I had always been partial to the Checkerboard Basket. I searched through the cut swatches, organizing them by color and shape. I'd have to cut more shapes tomorrow, I realized. Maybe Janie would like to help me. I'd started helping my mother with her quilting projects when I was Janie's age.

When Josh called, I settled the phone between my shoulder and ear to keep my hands free. "What're you doing?" Josh asked.

"I'm quilting," I said.

I could hear the grin in his voice when he said, "No way!"

"Next time we're together I'll show it to you," I said, rummaging through the fabric to see how many primary colors I had.

"How about next Saturday? My two weeks will be up by then."

"Good news!" I said, reaching for some pink squares. They would look nice in the Tulip Nine patch. I'd need some light green for the leaves. Josh was saying something, but I didn't hear him. I was sure I had packed some green fabric. I rummaged to the bottom of the bag until I found it.

"Hello?" Josh said.

"I'm here," I said, setting aside the pink and green fabric to work on later. "So, next weekend, right?" I tried not to sound distracted, but Tulip Nine is a complicated square.

"Yeah," said Josh. "And, Eliza?" I waited. His voice sounded hopeful. "I owe you a nice weekend." I set aside the material so I could listen fully. "I guess we'll have some things to talk about when we're together."

"I guess we will."

I hung up the phone and started searching for some fabric that would make a good background. The evening hummed along, and I couldn't remember what it felt like to be bored.

I spent the week quilting, and felt invigorated by the work I'd completed. I had forgotten the satisfaction of finishing a square, of sitting back and looking at the pleasing array of colors and the straight tiny stitches, of placing the squares side by side and imagining what the quilt would look like when it was finished.

I brought my quilting to Aunt Beth's house on Sunday, and we stitched together after dinner, talking animatedly about color values and pattern arrangements as our needles rose and fell. In the late afternoons, when Janie's homework was done, I helped her measure and trace the shapes, and cut them carefully so the edges were neat and straight.

Quilting was always waiting for me when Ben and Janie were at school and my list of chores was checked off, or at night after the children went to bed. By the time the weekend came around, I had finished the twelve squares I needed for the quilt top. Aunt Beth took me to the quilting store on Saturday to buy the batting that would provide the soft cushion between the quilt squares and the backing. My date with Josh would be later that night, and I was surprised to realize how quickly our time apart had gone by.

It had to be a cheap date, Josh had explained; just coffee and dessert at the Bean Scene. I wore blue jeans and a pink sweater, and I let my hair hang loose over my shoulders. When I answered the door, he was waiting there with a smile that was a little bit shy. His hug was warm and tight, the way it used to be, and I felt the heat deep inside me. I was still angry, but it was a thinned-out anger, not quite as sharp as it had been two weeks ago.

We walked to the Bean Scene holding hands, the October night cool and fragrant around us. Josh talked about his extra shifts at work and how it wasn't so bad after all because he was learning so much about the new products. We got to the coffee shop and settled into a corner table, each with a steaming cup of tea and a cookie. He talked about history class and how he was sure Mr. Rozey gave more homework than the other history teacher. He talked about the French teacher he just calls "Madame" and how he wants to spend a semester in Paris when he's in college. He stopped and looked at me as though for the first time. "I'm sorry," he said. "I've been doing all the talking."

"That's okay," I said. "I like hearing about your school." But it wasn't okay. He was talking about a future I couldn't have. He said it all so casually, like it was nothing to go to high school and then head on to the university and then hop on a plane and study in Paris. And where would I be during all of this? I took a long sip of tea. I'd been so eager to see him again, but this wasn't what I was expecting.

"Look," he said. "I have to explain some things about the dance."

"I already know."

"Valerie?" he asked. I nodded. "I was wrong not to tell you

about the party. I just really wanted to be with you. And I was afraid if you knew that everyone was sleeping over, you wouldn't be allowed to stay. So I thought that if you didn't know . . ." His voice trailed off. "It sounds pretty lame now that I'm trying to explain it, right?"

I nodded my agreement. "It does sound pretty lame."

"So, anyway," he went on, "I'm really sorry for everything. I shouldn't have lied to you about the party. And I should never have let you get drunk and sick." He reached for my hand, and I let him take it. "I promise to be a better boyfriend from now on."

I felt his hand, warm and firm around mine. "Thanks," I said. Then I remembered my talk with Aunt Beth and Uncle John. "And there were some good parts of the night, you know. I want to remember getting all dressed up and dancing with you."

He smiled. "So do I."

"And I don't want to be mad at you," I said. He leaned back in his chair, looking grateful. I smiled. "But is it all right for me to be mad at Valerie?"

He picked up his cup and clicked it against mine. "That's a deal."

We chewed on our cookies and sipped tea in a comfortable silence for a few minutes. A guitarist was in the corner strumming gentle tunes. Quiet conversations hummed through the place, and I felt peaceful again. Josh broke the silence. "So tell me about what you've been up to."

I couldn't think of what to say. The colors sang in my quilt squares and I was all caught up on my letters home. But I didn't think Josh would be interested in any of that. So instead I asked him questions about his friends and his job at the Apple store. And the evening went along just fine.

But not really.

The next weekend we met Greg and Valerie for ice cream. I hadn't seen her since the afternoon at the Bean Scene, and I felt a wave of nervousness when we slid into the booth while the boys were placing our order. Valerie was fidgety, tugging on her hair.

"So," she said, as though continuing a conversation, "I guess I owe you an apology."

I looked back at her, surprised, and waited for her to continue.

"I shouldn't have made you feel like you got us all into trouble after Homecoming." She ran her hand through her hair, shaking it with her fingers.

I waited for her to say more, but she didn't. "Thanks," I said.

"So, are we okay?"

I thought about "okay." It was not bad and not good. A teacher wrote "OK" on your homework if you completed it, but she wrote "Good" or "Excellent" if you had done it well. "Yes," I said. "We're okay."

"Good," she said, smiling.

And I thought, not good, Valerie. Just okay.

CHAPTER
43

Halloween was ringing through Rachel's house, and it was all the children talked about. Janie was dressing as Madeline in a costume Rachel had ordered from a catalog. Ben was going to be a baseball player.

In the days before the holiday, I helped the children scoop the slimy insides out of their pumpkins and carve them into jack-o'-lanterns. Janie used marker on hers to draw brows and lashes around the carved-out eyes. Ben just wanted his to look creepy, and he thought that the more eyes it had, the better. We baked the pumpkin seeds in shallow pans, though no one wanted to eat them. Janie helped me decorate the front window with dark streamers and cutouts of pumpkins and witches' hats, while Ben sat by us complaining that it wasn't scary enough.

On Halloween morning the children were up early, excited to go to school in their costumes. They stood in front of Rachel's camera, Janie in a blue dress and yellow hat, and Ben in his Little

League uniform and Cubs hat. After school they burst off the bus, ready to go trick-or-treating.

"And we're not going to the Robbinses' house," said Ben, as Rachel gathered their bags and flashlights.

Rachel smiled at me. "Dr. Robbins is a dentist," she explained. "Instead of candy he gives out toothbrushes." I felt the airy sense of held-in laughter as I watched them leave the house.

I tried to imagine how I would describe this event to my parents. It all seemed harmless enough. The begging for candy would be hard to explain, but maybe if they realized that the entire community participates, it would seem more like trading than begging.

When the doorbell rang a few minutes later, I opened it excitedly. On the doorstep were two boys dressed as dinosaurs.

"Trick or treat!" they cried in unison.

"Well, don't you look scary," I said as I plunked a tiny Milky Way bar into each extended bag. But by the time my words were half out, the children had dashed from the stoop, their tails flailing behind them. It continued like this for the next hour. I opened the door to a variety of dark creatures and colorful characters, all with bags extended, all anxious to catch their loot and trot off to the next house. After I gave candy to a small pirate, I closed the door only to have the bell ring again. Josh was standing on the stoop, his backpack slung over his shoulder. "Trick or treat," he said.

He stepped inside, and I put down the candy bowl as he pulled me into an embrace, his lips and tongue searching for mine. I smiled against his kiss. "They'll be coming home any time," I said.

He stepped back and looked at me in that hungry way that made me feel a little bit pretty and a little bit mischievous. The doorbell rang again, and I dropped a piece of candy into the bags of two girls dressed as fairies. After I closed the door, I turned to Josh. "I wasn't expecting you so early. Rachel's still with the kids, and she and Sam won't be going out until later."

"That's okay," he said. "I brought some homework, and I thought I'd keep you company during the trick-or-treating."

A warm contentment filled me as I answered the door to a doctor and a ninja and a cowboy. An evening with Josh awaited me after the children were in bed, and I was looking forward to it. The holiday was getting boring, with all the outstretched bags and ungracious retreats. The next time the doorbell rang, I considered not answering, but Rachel had told me that older children sometimes vandalize houses where they don't get treats.

While I opened the door, I absently reached for the half-empty bowl of candy. Then, facing the two figures on the doorstep, I froze. The smaller girl was dressed as a princess, a shiny crown atop her blond head. The taller girl had a different costume. The first thing I noticed was the kapp, the one I hadn't worn since I'd left home. My eyes traveled down the familiar purple dress and the starchy white apron, then up to Valerie's face.

"Trick or treat," said the little girl.

"This is my sister Michelle," said Valerie, her grin spreading up her face. "How do we look?"

I stared in silence at the image before me. There on the doorstep

I saw myself and my mother and sisters and friends, and all the Plain people who filled my other world.

"Well, you said I could borrow it, didn't you?" said Valerie, shifting her weight. "And don't worry. I'll clean it before I give it back."

Still I couldn't speak. I stepped back from the door and felt the smoothness of the bowl against my palms before it slipped from my fingers in an explosive crash. Michelle looked startled at the sound, and Valerie reached for her hand. Ignoring the fragments of glass on the floor, and the scattering of candy at my feet, I looked at Valerie, the reflection of myself, and saw what she saw. Someone in a costume, someone to be mocked.

"Liza?" came Josh's voice from the kitchen. "Is everything all right?" I couldn't answer.

Bending down, I began to pick up the shards of glass, almost enjoying the roughness of the jagged edges against my skin. In front of me, Valerie and her sister stood quietly on the stoop. Josh was beside me now. I sensed him looking down at me and then out at the scene before him. I heard his intake of breath before he spoke. "Valerie, seriously?"

"Eliza knew about this," said Valerie. "She said I could borrow her dress to show my sister. Right, Eliza?"

"Yes," I said in a small voice. "To show your sister." I could feel something stinging the palm of my hand, and saw a red drop fall on the floor. I was thinking that I needed to clean up this mess and that I needed to get fresh candy and that the children would be back soon for their dinner. I looked up and saw that the smile had slipped from Valerie's lips. The kapp was slightly askew, her hair hanging past her shoulders in limp strands. She didn't have it right, I was thinking. Her hair should be tied back or braided. She couldn't even mock me right. Valerie tugged her sister's hand and they hurried off the stoop.

Josh slammed the door and turned to me, the expression on his face inching from anger to concern. He stooped beside me and reached for my hand. "Come on," he said. "We have to take care of this." He led me to the kitchen and held my hand under the faucet. The cut stung under the water, but it wasn't a bad feeling. It wasn't like seeing the fake Amish girl who was sometimes my friend looking at me with blank amusement. "It doesn't look too deep." He pressed a piece of paper towel against the cut. "Here," he said, his voice tender. He guided me to a chair and placed my other hand where his had been. "Hold this with pressure while I clean up the mess."

He opened a fresh bag of candy and brought a broom and dustpan to the front door. Listening to the clinking sounds of the broken glass, interrupted by the doorbell ushering in more trick-or-treaters, I thought about what a silly holiday this was.

A few minutes later, Josh was back, the dustpan brimming with glass pieces and miniature candy bars. He emptied it all into the garbage with a clattering sound and then returned to my side. "Looks better," he said. We went upstairs, and Josh helped me wash the cut and apply first-aid cream. Then he carefully covered the wound with a bandage. "All better?" he asked. I nodded, swallowing back a trembling feeling. He paused before adding, "Listen, I don't know what Valerie was thinking. I'm sorry this happened."

I looked at Josh, and he met my gaze. "So am I."

He reached for me. I felt the reassurance of his arms wrapped around me, my head against his shoulder.

Back downstairs, I went to work making the children's dinner—macaroni and cheese from a box, the noodles shaped like one of their cartoon characters. The cheese was nothing more than a packet of powder, but it was their favorite meal and I wanted everything to be easy. When Ben and Janie tumbled into the house, with Rachel following wearily behind them, I served them dinner.

Sam came home and smiled as he listened to their descriptions of Halloween. Later, with the children bathed and busy sorting their candy, I found Josh at the kitchen table with Rachel and Sam. They all looked up when I came in the room.

"I'm so sorry about what happened with Josh's friend," said Rachel.

Josh interrupted her. "My former friend."

His face was firm and unsmiling. A feeling of satisfaction crept over me.

Sam cleared his throat. "I don't know Valerie, but I think she's either completely clueless or just very self-involved."

Josh laughed. "I guess you do know Valerie. And she's both." We joined in Josh's laughter, and I felt myself beginning to relax.

Rachel and Sam left for their evening out, and I put the children to bed. When I came down to the family room, Josh was waiting, a smile wide across his face. "Here," he said. "I brought you a surprise."

I looked at the DVD in his outstretched hand. On the cover was a picture of a woman in a black dress and striped apron, her arms outstretched, beautiful mountain scenery in the background. The words sprang out at me: *The Sound of Music.* I threw my arms around Josh's neck, and he kissed the top of my head. "Now don't tell Greg about this. I'll never hear the end of it."

We settled on the couch and started to watch. I was quickly pulled into the story of the nun who didn't fit in with the others and was sent away to care for a widower's seven children.

It was a wonderful movie, and Josh and I watched it bundled together like we were melting into each other. When it ended we stayed together on the couch, neither one of us wanting to reach for the remote, the picture now only a bluish glow. "What are you thinking?" Josh whispered, his hand rubbing my back in soft, slow circles.

My voice was a murmur. "I've been wanting to see this movie since I was a little girl and my mother told me about it."

"And?"

I paused, trying to figure out exactly what I was feeling. "And now I've seen it."

I waited, thinking that there must be more to say about this moment. But there wasn't. That was all I could think of. *Now I've seen it.*

A few days later, as I was getting Janie into bed, Rachel called up the stairs to me. "Someone's here for you." I stepped out of Janie's room and looked down the stairs to see Valerie standing in the hallway by the front door, the hook of a metal hanger looped over her fingers. Beneath the transparent plastic, I could see my dress, apron, and kapp.

I went downstairs, and Valerie stepped forward, extending the hanger to me. "I had it dry-cleaned." Her voice sounded squeaky, her words measured. I felt the soft stickiness of the plastic as I took the hanger from Valerie's outstretched hand.

The chemical smell wafting from the dress was clean but not fresh. I thought of wash days at home, when my mother and I cranked the wet clothes through the wringer and hung each item in a row on the clothesline.

At the sound of a cough, I looked up, surprised to see that Valerie was still standing there. "Was there something else you wanted?"

"Yeah, I thought you'd like to know that everyone's mad at me. Again. And you did tell me I could borrow your dress, didn't you? And I did take good care of it, didn't I?"

I cleared my throat. "I guess I didn't like being turned into a joke."

Valerie nodded. "Well, to be honest, I'm tired of worrying about what you like and don't like. You know, things haven't been too wonderful for me since you got here. I didn't just get in trouble after Homecoming. I got in trouble for corrupting an AH-mish girl." She flicked her hair behind her shoulders with a toss of her head. "And Josh. It's ancient history, so I shouldn't really care, but when we were together he always looked bored. Or he rolled his eyes like I wasn't *worldly* enough for him. Then you come along, and he's totally fascinated by you. Go figure that out."

"So you decided to embarrass me?" I asked, my voice gaining strength.

"Not exactly. I just wanted to take my sister out for Halloween, and I needed a . . ." Her voice trailed off.

"A costume?"

Valerie paused and squinted at me, as though trying to see me more clearly. "Well, isn't that what you're doing here? Aren't you dressing like us?"

I sucked in a breath, but I didn't have an answer for her.

"I thought I was being pretty nice to you, taking you shopping, introducing you to my friends. Then you go and say that I can't be trusted. Well, I just want you to know that you aren't the only one who's been insulted."

This was a lot for me to take in. Valerie had been hurtful, and I would never forget that. But in her own way she had been hurt, too.

"I'm sorry," I said. "When I came here, I thought we could be friends."

Valerie didn't answer. Her eyes looked far away, her features flat. Her thumbs hooked through the belt loops of her jeans, and her sneakered foot tapped the floor. She wasn't going to return the apology. She was waiting for me to release her.

"Thank you for cleaning the dress," I said.

She nodded and turned to leave. As I watched her go, I thought about the words she usually used when she said good-bye. "See you around," or "Later" or just "See ya." I was glad she didn't say any of these words, because they wouldn't be true. I wouldn't be seeing Valerie around.

I carried the dress up to my room and pulled off the clear wrapping, letting it drift to the floor. It was so carefully pressed, it almost looked artificial. I pulled off my blue jeans and sweat-shirt, leaving them in a colorful pile on the floor beside the plastic wrap. As I stepped into the dress, my skin tingled with familiarity. I tied the apron around my waist and set the kapp on my head with the bonnet strings hanging over my shoulders. In the mirror I saw myself the way I used to be, the way I'd looked every day before I'd come here. I had fought against this image, but now it was hard to remember why.

Opening the door to the closet, I stared at the English clothes I had been so proud to acquire, hanging in a neat row. I reached to touch the second pair of blue jeans that Valerie had insisted I needed, the fabric stiff against my fingertips. I had thought these clothes would liberate me, but maybe Valerie was right. Maybe they were my way of wearing a costume.

I changed back into the jeans and sweatshirt and put the Amish clothes on a hanger. For a minute I stood holding the hanger, look-ing at the familiar shape of the dress, the clean whiteness of the kapp and apron. Then I hung it in the front of the closet, beside my other clothes.

CHAPTER

44

The quilt was coming along. I was working on the decorative stitching that would attach the connected quilt squares to the fabric backing, with the fluffy batting material in between. It's a satisfying time in the quilting process, but not quite as exciting as choosing the pattern and colors for each square, fitting it all together piece by piece, imagining what it will be when all the pieces are in place. The wondering was over for this quilt. I knew what it would look like finished.

Pulling the thread through the layers, I thought about sitting in the quilt circle with my friends in Margaret's living room, our knees bumping comfortably beneath the taut fabric. We had worked carefully, timing our movements so our needles all pulled up at the same time, and pushed back into the fabric at the same time. The watchful sequencing of these movements was natural to us. And our conversations flowed throughout that synchronized work, keeping us connected, reminding us of our history and what we shared. Now I realized that I had enjoyed piecing together the swatches and squares of this quilt, but I missed the comfort of my friends as I began the final steps of the process.

I looked at the clock. There were still two hours before the children would be home, but I didn't feel like stitching anymore. I set the quilt aside and went into Rachel's office. Boredom was twitching at me again. It was becoming a common feeling.

Sitting down at the computer table, I marveled at the comfortable feeling of the mouse under my fingertips. When I'd learned to operate the computer I'd been afraid that I would make some massive mistake that would shut it down forever. But soon the computer became another device, like the garbage disposal—scary at first, then a natural part of my day.

Josh had taught me about Google searches, and I found I could sit for hours typing in a topic and then reading about it in quick gulps before searching for another topic. It was an unquenchable cycle—the curiosity, the tidbits of knowledge, the search for more.

After Josh and I watched *The Sound of Music,* Rachel told me that the movie was based on the life of a real family. Now I wanted to learn more about the real governess and children who had sung their way from one world to another.

I slid the mouse on the pad and saw that there was some text on the screen. Realizing that Rachel had forgotten to close down after her last writing session, I started to point the little blinking line to the command Rachel had taught me that would save the work. Then the word *Amish* caught my eye. I started to read. *During rumspringa, Amish teenagers, who have been sheltered from popular culture* and trends, can respond irresponsibly when they encounter the freedoms and potential dangers of American teenage life, such as those associated with drinking and sex.

My heart rattled inside of me. I pressed the down arrow to let new words roll onto the screen. *It is a vulnerable time for these indoctrinated youth, inexperienced amid their newfound freedom.* I kept reading, recognizing in these words my awkwardness in navigating this new world, my lapse of judgment on Homecoming, my struggles to fit in with English teens.

Heat crawled up my chest and arms. This is what Rachel was doing with all of her trips to the library and all of her hours in front of the computer. She was reporting on me. I had felt so welcome here, like someone who belonged in the household. Now I knew the truth. I was being studied. Rachel didn't want a babysitter; she wanted a science experiment. I was her little Amish girl transplanted to the fancy world to see if I'd grow. While I stumbled my way around this new place, Rachel had been tapping out my quaintness onto her keyboard and storing my mistakes in tiny folders inside the computer.

Puzzle pieces were latching together in my head. The wealth of Rachel's knowledge about the Amish, her haste at hiding her books when I came to her room at the inn, her vagueness the few times I'd asked about her studies. I slid the chair back from the computer table and stepped away. It was hard to take in a deep breath. Everything was a lie in this place. I had to get out.

I ran up the stairs to the room I had called mine, seeing again the Amish quilt I had found so comforting on my first day here. I ripped wildly at the buttons on my blouse, thinking how much easier it is to unlatch a snap. I wanted to be out of these English clothes that I had paid for with my own money but that didn't really belong to me.

Leaving the shirt and blue jeans in a heap on the floor, I reached for my Amish clothes, hanging where I had left them last week. In minutes I was wearing the dress, the apron, and the kapp, and I didn't have to look in the mirror to see my reflection. I knew that I looked like myself.

I reached into the back of the closet and pulled out the duffel bag and set it on my bed. Flinging the hangers across the closet rod, one by one, I watched my English clothes sail past me. The jeans, the khaki pants, the button-down blouses, the wrinkled blue dress that I had never laundered after the dance. I didn't want any of it. I flung open the dresser drawers and rummaged through shirts and sweaters and sweatshirts, pulling out only one thing—the band shirt Josh had given to me for our first concert. I put the shirt in the duffel bag along with pajamas and underwear and socks. Then I went to the desk and lifted out the journal, with my mother's pages stuck inside the hidden compartment, and all of the letters I'd received, folded and bundled together with a rubber band, and I packed them carefully into the duffel. I added the picture from the dance, and Daniel's wood carving. Looking around at the open drawers, the disarray in the room, I felt no need to tidy up. I stepped into my old work shoes, leaving behind the sneakers and the sandals and the silly high heels. I also left behind the necklace and earrings I had bought for the dance. In the bathroom, I gathered my toothbrush and comb and shampoo, leaving the makeup in the drawer.

I carried the duffel bag downstairs, adding the canvas bag with the unfinished quilt to my scant belongings. I was ready to leave, but I realized that I couldn't go anywhere. Rachel wasn't home yet, and the children couldn't come back to an empty house. I would have to wait until Rachel returned, which meant facing her with my discovery. I dropped my bag by the front door and paced nervously. I picked up the phone and called Josh, hanging up when I heard his voice mail message. Then I called Aunt Beth, and when her scripted voice mail came on, I said, "I need to come over. If you're not home I'll come in through the garage door. If it's okay, I'll be staying the night."

I hung up and looked at the clock. The children would be home in a half hour. Then I heard Rachel's key in the front door, and I looked up, alert and ready. The door closed, and there was a quiet moment before Rachel called in a cautious voice, "Eliza?"

I stepped out of the family room and walked toward the front door, my heart throbbing. Rachel was standing at the front door, staring at my duffel bag. She turned to look at me, and I could hear her take a tiny gulp of a breath when she saw me in my Amish clothes.

"What's happening, Eliza? Is everything all right?"

"I'm leaving," I said. "I was just waiting for you to get home for Ben and Janie."

"I thought you were staying through November. Did something happen?"

"Yes. I saw what you've been writing."

Rachel clapped her hand to her chest. "Oh, no," she said. "Please, it isn't what you're thinking." Her voice had a choky sound I had never heard in her before.

I shook my head and walked to the front door, passing inches away from where she was standing, her face twisted with emotions that I didn't want to know about. Picking up my duffel bag, I looked at her for a moment. Rachel's eyes were pleading with me. I turned away. "Tell the children I'm sorry I didn't get to say good-bye."

Rachel's hand was on my arm now. "Please, Eliza. Let me explain."

I looked at her and thought of how I had met her at Stranger Night, and how excited I was when I got permission to come home with her. "No," I said. "You'll have to find another Amish girl to study."

Then I was outside, heading away from this house. I walked awkwardly to the train station, the duffel bag bumping against my leg, thinking about the day I ran from services. I didn't want to be someone who was always running. I wanted to stay put, to be happy where I was. Waiting for the train, I felt the stares and heard the murmured whispers, and I knew that I was different again.

Aunt Beth was waiting for me at the door, worry etched in the mild lines on her forehead. She took my bag and pulled me inside, grabbing me into one of her hugs. My tears spilled onto the front of her blouse. She led me to the couch, and we sat down facing each other. "Rachel called me," she said. "She's very upset."

I couldn't answer. My breath was coming in hiccups. "Okay," said Beth, her voice low and smooth. She put her arm around me, and I lowered my head onto her shoulder. "I'll talk, you listen." I nodded, trying to breathe normally. "Rachel made a mistake. She should have told you what she was writing about. But this is the research she's been doing for years. It isn't about you."

"Then why didn't she tell me?" I asked, my voice stuttery.

"That was her mistake," said Beth. "From what I could understand, she just didn't know how to bring it up. She didn't want you to have the wrong idea, and then too much time went by and she thought it was too late to explain it."

It made sense in a jumbled way, but I was too upset to let myself understand. I leaned against Aunt Beth's shoulder until I was able to stop crying.

"I've never seen you in your Amish clothes," Beth said. "How do they feel?"

I looked up at her. "Good," I said. "They feel good."

"So," she said quietly, "what's your plan?"

I lifted my head from her shoulder and turned toward her. "I'm going home." It was the first time I'd realized that it was my plan.

Beth nodded slowly. "Okay, but I think you should stay here for a little while until you're sure. I don't want you to run away in anger."

When I'd sat on the porch swing with Daniel the night before I'd left, he had asked if I was running away from him, but I wasn't.

"I don't want to run away from something," I said. "I want to run *to* something."

Aunt Beth's voice was as delicate as a dandelion spore. "Is that what going home will be? Is home where you want to run to?"

"I don't know."

"Then maybe you should wait until you know."

I nodded, and relief flooded Beth's face. I realized how sad she would be if I left.

Upstairs in the guest room, I went into the bathroom to wash my face. An Amish girl looked back at me from the mirror and surprised me for a moment. I stared at her until I knew her. We nodded to one other.

At dinner that night, John and Beth and I talked about Rachel, and why she had kept this secret from me.

"You know," Beth was saying, "I thought Rachel was different. But maybe she's like all those other tourists who come into town to stare at us."

John shook his head. "I don't know, Beth. I think she felt awkward talking about her research because she was afraid you and Eliza would take it the wrong way."

"Is there a right way to take it?" Beth asked.

John's voice was gentle. "It's academic research. She started working on it long before she met any of us."

I spoke up. "But that doesn't make it right."

"No it doesn't," said Beth. "And you'll need to think about whether or not you can forgive her."

"You know," said John, "I think one of the most important

things we learn when we grow up is that sometimes we have to let other people make mistakes."

Beth glanced at John with a small smile. "And those same people will let us make mistakes."

At that moment, the front doorbell rang, and John got up to answer. I heard Sam's voice, quiet and measured. "Go ahead," said Beth. "I'll clean up."

Sam smiled cautiously when he saw me. "Is it okay if I come in and talk to you?" he asked. I led him to a chair in the living room and sat facing him on the couch.

"Rachel's a mess," he said. "She never meant to hurt you."

"But she did," I said.

Sam nodded. "When you first came to us, Rachel and I had a little argument about this. I thought she should tell you about her research. She was afraid it would make you uncomfortable knowing she was studying the Amish. And at that time we thought you'd only be staying for the summer. A few weeks ago we talked about it again, and she said I was right, that she should have told you."

Sam looked at me, his face serious. "Eliza, when you and Josh made some bad choices the night of the dance, Rachel forgave you. She tried to understand your side of the story." He paused for a moment, and I let his words slip inside me. "Do you think you can do the same for her?"

I finally spoke. "I want to," I said. "But I'm not ready yet."

Sam took a big breath and let it out. "Rachel called her professor after you left. She told him she isn't going to finish her thesis."

I didn't answer because I didn't know what to say. He stood up. "Well, I have to get back home. Things are pretty chaotic over there." I stood to walk him to the door. Sam put his hand on my shoulder. "Eliza, I hope you don't leave. But if you do, please come back and see the kids. We told them you're spending some time with your aunt, but they'll need to say good-bye to you."

I swallowed. I hadn't thought about how Ben and Janie would feel. "Don't worry," I said. "I would never leave without saying good-bye." Sam seemed reassured.

Later, Beth brought the phone to me in the guest room. "It's Josh," she said.

"What are you doing at your aunt's house?" he asked. "It's not Sunday."

I told him the story. "That explains something," he said. "One day I was waiting for you to come downstairs and I saw Rachel put a book in her bag. I could swear it was something about the Amish. And when I asked her, she just mumbled that it was overdue from the library."

"Everyone has secrets," I said.

Josh was quiet, and I waited. When he spoke, his voice was low, almost mournful.

"You're going to leave, aren't you?"

"I don't know," I said. It was an honest answer.

CHAPTER

45

The next morning, I woke up sluggish from a night of half-sleep. I went downstairs in time to see Aunt Beth before she left for work.

"Have you decided what you'll do today?" she asked.

"No," I said. "I still have a lot to think about."

Beth checked her watch and then sat at the table beside me. "Let me tell you something my mother used to say to me when I was angry. She used to say, 'Elizabeth, let your anger be like March snow.'" I waited for this to make sense. "When there's a blizzard in January, you know that the snow is going to stay around for the rest of the winter. But when there's a blizzard in March, it's not cold enough for the snow to last too long. March snow seems fierce when it first comes down, but then it melts away." She got up and reached for her purse. "I have to get to work," she said. "And you have to figure out if your anger is going to be January snow or March snow." She kissed me on my forehead like a mother checking for a temperature. "Let me know what you decide."

After Beth left, I thought about what I should do. I had made a commitment to Rachel and her family. And if I were to leave early, I would need to explain it to the children and help them understand.

I sifted through the clothes in my duffel bag, regretting that I hadn't packed a pair of pants to wear today. I stepped back into my Amish clothes and repacked my bag. Downstairs, I left a note for Aunt Beth:

Thank you for letting me stay last night. I'll call you later. Eliza.
PS It was March snow.

I walked back up to Rachel's house and stood on the stoop for a moment. The key was in my bag, but I felt that today I should approach as a guest. Rachel opened the door, and I watched as her expression went from surprise to hopefulness. I stepped inside and set down my duffel bag. "I shouldn't have left yesterday without letting you explain."

Rachel looked nervous and uncertain as she ushered me inside. We sat at the kitchen table, where we'd had so many talks. Janie's cereal box and Ben's sports page were on the table.

"I'm so sorry, Eliza. I've been working on this thesis for years. It's about coming-of-age in the Amish community. That's why I was in your town. I was doing field research and getting oral histories. What you read was from that research. It wasn't about you."

She got up and poured herself a cup of coffee and took a long sip before sitting down again. I listened quietly. "It was a dilemma for me," she said, "having you here, given the kind of work I was doing."

"It wouldn't have been a dilemma if you had told me."

"I know that now," she said. "And I would do it all differently if I could." She curved her fingers over the top of her coffee cup. It was a gesture that had become familiar to me.

"Once I made the mistake of not telling you about it, I didn't know how to fix it." She set the mug on the table. "But I want to fix it now."

I shook my head and looked down. "Everything's different now," I said. "Every time I remember one of our conversations, I wonder what you were trying to learn from it."

Rachel shut her eyes and pressed her fingertips over them. "I've made a mess of everything," she said. Then she took her hands away from her eyes and looked at me fully. "I understand if you need to leave early. But can you give the kids some time to get used to the idea?"

I nodded and got up. Rachel stayed at the table, staring into her coffee cup. "Do you have my chore list ready?" I asked her. She shook her head.

I went upstairs and found my room the way I'd left it, with drawers and the closet door open and yesterday's clothes on the floor. I changed back into English clothes, unpacked my duffel, and straightened up the room. The day drifted by with an unnatural quiet, and I kept myself busy with laundry and housework. In the afternoon, when I came into the living room to dust, I found Rachel there reading the newspaper. She looked up when she saw me. I felt self-conscious around her now, but there was something I still wanted to understand. I sat down and put the dust cloth aside.

"Why are you writing about the Amish?"

She put down her newspaper. "I was always interested in the Amish and how they've been able to keep to their ways even while everything around them changes," she said. "And I was interested in studying a culture that was different from my own." She looked at me in a knowing way. "I think you can relate to that."

I looked down. It was true that my curiosity about the English wasn't so different from Rachel's interest in us. We were both a bit hungry for a life we didn't have.

"The difference between us," Rachel continued, "is that you can come here and, after a bit of adjusting, fit right in. If I came to live in your district, I'd be way out of my league. I don't think I could last a week."

I tried to imagine Rachel with no cell phone or computer or car, hanging clothes on the line and washing dishes by lantern light. She may have been curious about my world, but she belonged in hers. "A week might be a stretch for you," I said. I watched relief rise in Rachel's face that we were able to share a smile together.

"I know you had the right intentions," I said. "I don't want to be mad at you."

"Thank you, Eliza," she said, her voice wobbly with emotion. "You know, you've become an important person to me—to all of us. And I was devastated to think I had hurt you."

Then I remembered something Sam had told me. "I don't want you to stop your research. You should finish your thesis."

"Thank you," she said. In a quieter voice, she asked, "Will you be staying?"

"I made a commitment to work for you until the end of November. After that, I'm not sure."

Rachel nodded, and a look of calm came over her face. I thought about how she had said I fit in here, and I felt oddly heartened. I realized that it was true.

Josh came over that night, and we went out for coffee. He tapped his spoon on the table in his fidgety way.

"I'm glad you're back," he said. "I was worried that you were going to leave."

"All along, my parents have been expecting me to come back home," I said.

"I know," said Josh. "I've been trying not to think about it."

"Me too," I said. "But in a way it's been on my mind ever since you went back to school. Things have been different for me."

"They don't have to be," he said, his voice low and urgent. "I've been thinking that you can go to school, like your aunt did. You've always told me how you didn't want to leave school."

"I know," I said. "But I think it was my one-room school I was missing. At your school you're doing science experiments, and I don't even know the name of the math class you're taking."

"Calculus. And you're smart enough to learn it. I would help you," he said. His voice was sincere, and I believed him. I could learn anything I wanted. But I shook my head.

"The thing is, I don't want to learn calculus. I just wanted to know that I had the option."

"So you would just leave?"

"That's what I'm trying to figure out," I said. "This was only supposed to be for the summer, remember?"

"But there's nothing for you back there."

I sat up straight. "Excuse me?"

Josh shook his head. "That's not what I meant. It's just that you're always talking about the things you don't have back home."

I tried to keep my voice even. "We may not have computers or telephones or television, but we have books and conversations. And we talk to each other in person, not through e-mails and texts."

Josh sat back and looked at me. When he spoke, his words were slow and deliberate. "So, if everything was so perfect there, why were you so anxious to leave?"

I pushed my cup of coffee to the side. "Lately, I've been wondering."

We were quiet on the walk home. When we got to Rachel's house we stopped and turned to each other. "I'm sorry," Josh said, pressing both of my hands between his. "I shouldn't have said there was nothing for you there. You know I don't believe that."

"I know," I said, enjoying the feeling of my hands sandwiched inside of his. "And for a while, I *did* think I wanted to leave home. But really, I just wanted to see this world."

"And now?" he asked.

"And now I've seen it."

Back in my room, I pulled out the journal and flipped through the scribbled details of my life here. My list of new experiences was getting scanter. I had added the football game and the Homecoming dance and drinking alcohol and Halloween. Now, at the end of each day, it was getting hard to find new things to include.

Josh's words had made me angry, but I understood. He had watched me take in this place as though it was a big present that I kept unwrapping, and he couldn't see why I might want to leave it. Realizing that this latest anger at Josh was March snow, I thought that when I got home I'd tell Kate about this expression that Aunt Beth had taught me. *When I get home.* I gulped in a breath at how naturally the thought had come to me.

I closed the journal and thought about my mother's visit, and how she had told me not to make a decision for a boy. She had also said that we could do without things easier than we could do without people. And she was right. When I thought of what I would miss if I left here, I didn't think about television or movies or the computer. I thought of Aunt Beth and Uncle John. Of Rachel and her family. Of Josh.

I went to sleep washed in melancholy, knowing that either choice I made would lead to good-byes.

46

For the next two weeks I tried to follow Josh's advice from earlier in the summer, and I lived in the moment. He and I stopped talking about the possibility that I might leave, but when we bundled at the end of the night, our bodies connecting to each other, there was a distance inside that kept us just a little bit separate.

At the end of the two weeks, a thin letter came from my father.

Dear Eliza,

You have not written again to ask that your time be extended, so I assume that Mrs. Aster has completed her work and can let you return home. Please write back to tell us your plans.

All my love,

Dad

I brought the letter with me to Aunt Beth's house that Sunday. She glanced at it and looked at me. "So, you've decided?"

"I still have some things to think about," I said. She turned the fire down on the pot of stew, and we sat together at her kitchen table. "What do you think it'll be like for me at home?"

"You'll be happy to be with your friends again," she said. "I think you'll settle right into those Friday night parties. And it'll be nice to be with your family." I smiled thinking about sitting at the table, reaching for James and Ruthie before saying grace. "Of course you'll miss some things. Movies, phones, Josh." She paused before adding, "Me."

"Will I still be able to stay in touch with you even though you're under the bann?"

Aunt Beth nodded. "It'll be a while before you decide to be baptized. And your mother didn't get any sanctions from the district when she came to see me. So I think I'll be able to be your aunt even if you join the Order."

I breathed in my relief. "There's something else I'm wondering about," I said. "I'm not sure what my plan would be if I go back home."

"What was your plan before you came here?"

I grinned. "My plan was to come here." Suddenly I felt an odd freedom. My list was finished. Nothing else was lingering, waiting to be experienced. "Now I need to think about what happens next."

"Amish women do stay pretty close to home, but some of them venture out a bit," Beth said. "Teaching is always an option. And some Amish get permission to go to school or training programs. I think your parents would be open to that."

"Now I think they would," I agreed.

"And there are other jobs besides teaching and quilting," Beth went on. "I loved my work in the library. And two of my friends were working when I left home. Holly was a veterinary assistant and Regina was studying to be a midwife. I think there are more possibilities at home than you realize."

I had always pictured that my adult life would be like my mother's, but now I was thinking maybe it didn't have to be.

"And, remember, all of your friends at home will be in the same situation," said Beth. "They're all in that time before they're baptized, wondering what's ahead." I smiled. It was comforting to think that my friends and I would be facing the questions about our future together. We would share our ideas during quilt circles and Friday night parties. We would sit together at services and think about each other when we baked friendship bread.

Beth's voice was low now, and I realized it was hard for her to talk about my leaving. "And everything you've learned in your time here, it doesn't go away. It'll all be part of you." I closed my eyes and thought about these words. Then I looked at Beth.

"Here's a question," I said. "What would I do with all my English clothes?"

"I was thinking that we can leave them here at my house. One day I may need you to come for a long visit and you might want to wear them." She paused for a moment, looking at me carefully. I waited, sensing there was something Beth was trying to tell me. "John's been wanting us to start a family, but I haven't felt ready. I didn't know if I could be a good mother after all that happened between my family and me. But having you in my life made me feel what having a child could be like, and I know now that I do want it." She paused, her voice breaking. "And if that happens, I'm going to need your help around here."

Warmth filled my throat and chest. I reached across the table for my aunt's hand. "It's the right thing," I said, and she nodded.

After dinner, Beth and I curled up on opposite ends of the couch, our quilts spread over our laps and across the space between us, our needles rising and falling in unison. When Beth spoke, her voice was a murmur. "So, when would you leave?"

"Next weekend," I said.

"Uncle John and I have been talking," she began. "I'm going to ask my boss for some time off so I can drive you home. And maybe I'll stay a little while."

I gasped. "Can you? Are you allowed?"

"I've been thinking about that ever since your mom came here. I know there'll be restrictions, since I'll be there under the bann. I won't be able to sit at the table or go to services. Some people won't see me, but others may take a chance." She stitched quietly for a moment, her face tight with emotion. Then she set her needle down and looked at me. "I want to see my parents. I want to meet your sisters and brother. And I'm hoping to be able to talk to Emmy. I think she'll see me now; it's been so long."

My eyes clung to Aunt Beth's across the couch and the expanse of our quilts. I couldn't think of what to say. I was going to bring my aunt home.

We decided to leave on Saturday. I would finish my week of work and give the children time to understand that I would be going. When I got home from Beth's house I went into Rachel's office. She looked up from the computer screen, and I sat down in the chair facing the desk. "I got a letter from my father," I said. "He wants to know when I'll be coming home."

Rachel nodded and bit her lip. "What did you tell him?"

"I haven't answered him yet, but I'm going to write tomorrow and tell him to expect me on Saturday."

"I knew this was coming," said Rachel. "But it still feels like a jolt."

I told her about my evening with Beth and about her plan to come with me. A smile crept up Rachel's face. "I hope she has a nice homecoming."

I told the children the next day after school. Janie's lips quivered, and tears collected in her eyes. Ben's face twisted for a moment, but he gathered himself together. I pulled Janie into my lap and looked at Ben. "I'll miss you both."

"Will you visit us?" he asked.

"Yes, I will. And I'll write you letters. Will you write me back?"

"I'll e-mail you," he said.

I shook my head. "We don't have a computer."

"Can we talk on the phone?"

I shook my head again. "No phone and no computer. Remember, I live in the 'olden times.' It'll have to be snail mail."

Janie looked up at me, tears spilling down her cheeks. "I'll write you every day," she said solemnly.

A few minutes later they were back in front of the television, control panels in their small hands, maneuvering the images on the screen to avoid scary obstacles that popped out of nowhere. This is how I would remember them, their thumbs moving frantically, their eyes glued to the screen.

I called Josh and asked if he could come over after dinner. There was a moment of quiet on the phone before he said, "I'll see you at eight."

At a corner table in the Bean Scene, Josh looked at me and waited. I couldn't think of what to say. Finally he said it for me. "When are you leaving?"

"Saturday," I said. "My aunt is going to drive me home."

"And there's nothing I can say to change this?"

"Nothing," I said. "It's what I want to do."

He nodded. His brown eyes were cloudy and his face had a pinched look. "Can I just ask you one question? Are you going back to him? To Daniel?"

"No." The word came out forcefully. "No," I said again, quietly. "This isn't a decision about a boy. It's a decision about me."

He looked reassured. "So, how should we spend your last few days?" he asked.

"Just like this," I said.

Josh came over every evening that week. We went to the Bean Scene or watched movies, our arms and legs tangled around each other. We talked about all of our times together, recalling the day we met and how he'd played music for me. We laughed about all the things I didn't know about then, and the way I fumbled with each new device before I learned how to use it. We talked about going to the city and the Cubs game and the under twenty-one club. We even found a way to laugh about Valerie's party.

One day after school, Carly and Jill came over to say good-bye. I smiled at memories of how Jill helped me shop for the dance, and how Carly stood up to Valerie on my behalf. Each girl hugged me and promised to write me letters, but they probably wouldn't. They would buy dresses for the next dance and take their college tests, and I would be a small memory of someone they once knew. That is what they would be for me as well, and it was all right.

Later that same night, the doorbell rang and Greg was on the stoop, his smile wide and friendly. He visited with me in the living room, and we laughed together about how excited I had been to see my first movie, and about how Mr. Rozey almost wouldn't let me into the dance. "Hey," he said. "My man Josh is going to be one hurting dude when you leave."

My throat felt tight. "It'll be hard for me too."

Greg laughed, a mischievous look in his eye. "I might have to go to his house and watch *The Sound of Music* with him to make him feel better."

I smiled. "You weren't supposed to know about that."

"I know about a lot of things," he said with a grin. At the door, Greg gave me a hug. "Take care of yourself in Amish country." He stepped outside and then turned back. "Oh, and I'll say good-bye for Valerie too. In case she doesn't get around to it." Our eyes met, and he nodded to me in what I thought was a knowing way.

Josh and I agreed to have our own good-bye on Friday night. He was going to work early on Saturday, and I was happy to have one less good-bye on the day I left. That night Josh took me out to dinner to a restaurant with no television sets on the walls. He turned off his cell phone, and I was the only one with him at the table. All week we had talked about the time we'd spent together. Now we talked about the time ahead. "Do you think I can ever visit you?" he asked.

"I don't know. There wouldn't be much for you there."

"You'd be there," he said.

I was filled with a fragile feeling, like I was going to laugh or cry or both, and I had no control over it. But I didn't feel like I was going to break, so I knew I would be okay.

Rachel's house was quiet when we got home. We went into the family room and sat close together on the couch. "I have a present for you," he said, reaching into his jacket pocket. He pulled a shiny silver disc out of a white envelope. I waited, not understanding. On the disc he had written the names of songs in black marker. "I burned this for you," he said, proudly. "It's all the songs we listened to together." He pointed to titles one by one. "See? This is the Dylan song you liked, 'Knocking on Heaven's Door.' And here's the song we danced to at the club. Here's the slow dance from Homecoming. Here's 'Blackbird,' the first song we listened to on my iPod." He smiled proudly. "I even put on a Billy Joel song. That just about killed me."

He looked at me, waiting for my response. I wasn't sure what to say. It was the most thoughtful gift anyone had ever given me. It was also the silliest. "Thank you," I said, waiting for him to understand.

Then his face changed. "I'm an idiot," he said, slapping his forehead with the palm of his hand. "You don't even have a way of listening to this. What was I thinking?"

I smiled and took the disc from his hand. "It's okay," I said. "There'll be parties at home. Someone will have a CD player. Or I can take it with me to the library and listen." I looked at the disc and heard parts of each song in my head as I read the titles. "I love that you did this for me."

We said good-bye to each other on the front stoop, our arms wrapped around each other, our teeth chattering in the November cold. Josh whispered something in my ear, the heat from his breath tickling me. "I'll never forget you." I nodded against his chest, my throat too filled to speak.

The next morning, I was up early. I put on the purple dress, the white apron, the kapp. My English clothes were packed in boxes at the front door, waiting to be stored at Aunt Beth's house. My duffel was repacked with the same items I had carried to Aunt Beth's house in anger a few weeks ago. The room was clean and empty.

I went downstairs and set my duffel by the front door near the boxes. In the kitchen I made coffee and began to mix the batter for pancakes. A knock at the front door startled me. It was too early for Aunt Beth to be here. I ran to answer the door and found Josh standing on the stoop.

"I wanted to see you one more time." He stepped inside, and I felt his eyes on me, looking me up and down. "I've never seen you in your Amish clothes," he said. "You look so . . ."

I waited to see what he would say. Out-of-date, old-fashioned, quaint.

"Pretty," he said. "You look so pretty."

I stepped into his arms one last time. We had talked of visiting and of writing to each other, and maybe it would happen. But more likely we'd both just recall this moment, a boy in blue jeans embracing a girl in a dress and bonnet. I held the picture in my mind so I could commit it to memory. This is what I wanted to think about when I remembered our time together.

Back in the house, I cooked the pancakes and ate a quick breakfast, leaving the rest for the family. Rachel came downstairs followed by the children. "Sam's taking them out today," she said. "I thought it would be easier for them to say good-bye to you if they had an outing to look forward to."

Ben and Janie climbed into their seats at the table, and I served them breakfast. Rachel sipped her coffee and nibbled on a pancake at the sink. These images would also be in my memory. Ben looked at my clothes. "You look just like your mom did when she came to visit," he said.

Janie's face was more curious. Then she lit with an idea. "You look just like the doll you gave me, only with a face!" Rachel and I exchanged a smile.

A few minutes later, Sam came downstairs and walked over to me with a shy look on his face. "Thank you for everything, Eliza. It's been wonderful having you in the family." I felt the bristles of his closely trimmed beard as he hugged me. "Come on, guys," he called to the children. "We have some adventures to get to today."

The children bounded up from the table and ran to me. I felt two pairs of arms wrap around my waist, and I looked down to see their round upturned faces, etched with the kind of temporary sadness that comes over children until they move on to their next emotion. I kissed each of them and inhaled their salty scents one more time.

"I promise to write to both of you," I said in a choked voice.

I watched as Sam led the children out the front door. They turned around to wave to me before running to the car.

I turned to Rachel. Tears were brimming in her eyes. "I don't know what I'll do around here without you."

I swallowed back a tightness in my throat. "You'll do fine."

She shook her head. "I've loved having you in my life."

I searched for the right words to tell her. Finally I found them. "You changed things for me," I said. "I needed this, and you made it happen."

Rachel pulled me to her. I felt her hand cupped at the back of my head and my tears against her sweater. We stood like that for a few seconds or a few minutes. It was hard to tell. But neither of us wanted to let go. Finally we did, and we stepped back and laughed at our wet faces and red eyes. "You'll be coming back to visit your aunt?" Rachel asked.

"I plan to. I'll let you know."

"I'll be checking my mailbox every day, waiting for letters."

"And me as well." Then I thought of something. "When you finish your thesis, I'd like to read it."

Rachel smiled and nodded. "I'd be honored."

Just then the front door opened and John and Beth stepped in. We greeted them, and Aunt Beth went back out to her car carrying my duffel. As Uncle John prepared to pick up one of my boxes, he turned to me, speaking softly. "I want to thank you for finding Beth."

I smiled. "And I hope to hear some good news soon. I'm ready for a new cousin."

John pulled me into the bear hug that I'd come to expect from him ever since the day I'd surprised him in his living room. "This isn't good-bye," he said.

Finally I was in Beth's car, the hugs and farewells behind me. I turned to my aunt, who had taught me that there wasn't only one way to live. Even in her rebellion she held some love for the life she had left behind. It would be that way for me, living in one place and carrying another place in my heart. She had told me that there were other choices than the ones I knew about, and I was determined to find them. She reached for my hand and squeezed it before turning the key and backing the car out of the driveway.

I looked out the windshield and watched the white lines on the road disappear beneath the car as it moved forward. Rachel's street led to a highway that, in a few hours, would lead me back home, to the place I had been so eager to leave a few months ago. Soon the sight of buggies and clotheslines would be tenderly familiar. I settled back in my seat, enjoying the ride.

My life was ahead of me. And it was filled with possibility.

ACKNOWLEDGMENTS

My greatest lesson during this journey has been that no book has one author. My dear friends, Barbara Kline and Debbie Stone, were with me at the Amish dinner table when this story found me. Then, during yearly trips, they listened to the scant pages I had written since our last gathering and always wanted more. My writing teachers—Randall Albers, John Schultz, Betty Shiflett, and Ron Suppa—gave me the tools and confidence to go forward, and the members of my Monday night writing group were gentle midwives at this novel's birth. Later, the Ragdale Foundation provided a setting conducive to reflection and productivity. There, I met Sheri Holman, who became my mentor, adviser, and friend.

Many thanks to Jan Caron, Wendy Herst, and Jackie Gross, who read an early manuscript and saw the possibilities through the flaws. Thanks also to Jason Anthony, whose interest and guidance helped me fix the flaws, and Barbara Chandler, who helped me write the quilting scenes. I appreciate the nine girls who inspired me to write about the love between an aunt and niece, and my many students who helped me recall what it was like to be a teenager. And to Debbie Batko and all the women in my life, thank you for making it easy to write about friendship. I'm also thankful to Steve and Gary for reading a book about a girl; Fern Schumer and Travis Ross for setting aside their writing to help me with mine; and Marsha Hoover for reading boring stuff and helping me understand it. And I deeply appreciate my wonderful boss, Helen Marlborough, who supported this book even when it meant shouldering my work on top of her own.

I'm grateful forever to my agent, Holly Root, who changed my life one August morning when she called to say, "I loved your book." My thanks, also, to Dina Sherman, who gave the book an early vote of confidence from someone who knows the heart of the girl in the library. Thanks also to Laura Schreiber for her insightful editorial assistance, and the staff at Disney-Hyperion, who gave this book their attention and expertise. And I will always be indebted to my editor, Abby Ranger, for seeking this project and for pushing me to know more about the story and its characters. Thank you, Abby, for wanting this book, and for insisting that it could be better.

To my son, Kevin, love and thanks for being the first boy reader, for giving me the information I needed to write the party scene, and for not telling me how you got the information. To my daughter, Maggie, my cherished reading partner and first editor, thank you for uttering the words that rang in my head through all the years of writing: "Oh, Mom, I feel like I'm reading a real book!" Finally, to my husband, Ken, I'm grateful for everything you've done over the years to make sure this book got finished. Thank you for accepting my marriage proposal in that Omaha bar. Since then I've felt lucky every day.